Between Scenes

Susan Schussler

Cover photo licensed through Shutterstock.

ISBN: 0989033368

ISBN 13: 9780989033367
Rocky Shore Media LLC
St. Paul, Minnesota

To Katya
for loaning my character your name.
May you someday find your fame.

Build on your truth. Don't let others tell you who you are. The real you is worth fighting for.

Chapter 1

Katya

My phone buzzes and I swipe left, ignoring him for the millionth time. I wouldn't talk to him if he were the last man on earth. With my silenced phone in hand, I step around the corner from the elevator and freeze as I spot them.

Oh, hell. When is this going to end?

"There she is," a shrilly voice yells from down the hallway in front of my hotel room.

The pack of paparazzi rushes toward me like I'm the last item for sale on the eighty-percent-off table. My heart races as I jerk back into the elevator and frantically tap my keycard against the access pad. I'm going up rather than down into the media circus I escaped minutes ago. How did they find me? How did they get on this secure floor? One of them must have bought a room.

I shake my head to push back the tears budding in my eyes. This is so unfair. Jake's the one who deserves their questions. Why are they chasing me? I don't even know what to tell them. The door closes, and as the floor lifts my stomach lurches. I take in a quick breath, trying to calm my brain and my stomach.

When the elevator door opens on the twenty-third floor, I step off and peer out of the alcove. I hope the hallway is clear. Immediately, the muscular backside of a guy returning from the pool catches my eye. He carries a towel, swim goggles, and an oversized bottle of water. His hair is wet, probably from doing laps. He looks like an Olympic swimmer, lean and well-built. This could be impossibly good luck, or it could be a disaster. The shirtless man could hide me and help me sneak out of here. Or, he could be a really hot serial killer. I'm terrible at reading people. I don't know why I try. But I know one thing for sure: I'm out of options.

As I near his room, I spot the plastic keycard on the floor just outside the door. He must have dropped it when he entered the room. I pick it up to return as an offering, hoping to soften him up. But when I raise my hand to knock, the elevator dings and I change my mind. Paparazzi. I can hear them laughing at my expense. I press the card against the keypad and the light turns green. I'm going in.

The door clicks closed behind me as I press my ear against it, listening for the vultures to pass. I can't catch my breath. Am I hyperventilating? I listen to them walk by, talking about how I will never escape because they're working as a team to find me. I can't believe Jake did this to me. I hear them pass a second time and I turn to assess my situation.

Decorated in a modern style with charcoal drapes and white walls, the luxurious suite fills me with the calm of déjà vu, somehow welcoming me. It's identical to mine downstairs. Large windows flank a massive TV screen. At least the drapes are closed. Finally feeling halfway safe, I draw in a deep breath, and the aroma from the fresh calla lilies arranged on the table near the door fills my lungs.

I scan the suite for the guy I followed in, realizing I'm going to need to explain myself. That's when my eyes lock with the brightest sapphire-blue eyes I've ever seen. Shirtless pool boy cocks his head at me without blinking. He doesn't look irritated I'm in his hotel room. He looks bored, as if girls slip into his room all the time.

"If you're looking for Tom, he probably won't be back tonight," he says, glancing around, before picking up the TV remote.

"I'm not looking for Tom." I twist the ring on my finger, not sure how to spin this conversation into a plea for help.

"If my brother sent you for me, tell him I'm not interested in his castoffs.

You are clearly not my type." His face is stone-cold sober. He means every word he says.

What is his problem?

"Really? I thought I was every guy's type." I've never had a guy tell me I wasn't his type. Who does he think he is? I don't see any supermodels in his room. Sure he's hot, but he doesn't have to put me down. I don't deserve this after the day I've had. What did I do to *him*? He spreads out on the couch, propping his feet on the table in front of him as I approach, my jaw dropped in disbelief.

"Oh, God . . . did he pay for you? He doesn't know when to stop, does he? Just go. Tell him I had a great time. You rocked my world. Wahoo. Tell him whatever you like. You'll still get paid." He runs his fingers through his wavy, dark hair. "I can get girls on my own. I don't need him to buy me hookers."

"I am not a hooker!" I can't believe he thinks I'm a hooker. He doesn't recognize me. With all the press lately, I didn't think there was anyone left in the world who doesn't know who I am.

"Call girl. Whatever. I didn't mean to insult you. It's just not my thing. I don't pay for sex." His nose scrunches before he turns away from me and flicks on the TV.

"I am not a call girl, either."

"Sorry, I just assumed. As I said, Tom's not going to be back today. I might not see him until Sunday. I can let him know you stopped by if you give me your name." He points to the hotel notepad and pen on the desk.

"What kind of guy buys his brother hookers?"

"He thinks he's doing me a favor. You know what he's like," he says, meeting my eyes again and sitting forward. "But I'm not like him. I've never had an STD, and I plan to keep it that way."

"Tom has an STD?"

"Forget I said that. I just mean, with all the girls he sleeps with, he could get one. I like to know where a girl's been before we swap fluids. You know what I'm sayin'?"

Did he just say that?

"I know what you mean," I say. "Honestly, I don't even know your brother, and I've never swapped fluids with him."

"Wait a minute. You don't know my brother? Who gave you a key to our suite? You need to leave." His voice elevates as he stands and steps back away from me.

"I'm not going to hurt you," I say as my eyes glide over his toned form. I can't help myself. He's so damn cute. "I found your keycard on the floor in the hall. I planned to knock on the door and return it, but then the paparazzi found me and I made the snap decision to escape them by coming in. I was going to ask if I could hide out for a couple of hours until they give up looking for me. That's all."

"Who are you?" he asks, knitting his eyebrows as if he doesn't believe me.

I hold out my hand. "I'm Kat. Katya Avery."

His hand wraps around mine. "Micah Fallston," he says.

"No. No. No!" I shake my head as I pull my hand back. I can't believe it. "Why? What are the odds I would end up in Tom Fallston's hotel room?" FML! Tom is Jake's best friend, and if he were here right now, he'd call Jake and tell him exactly where to find me. I cover my face with my hands as I plop onto the couch, trying to gain control of my emotions. Tears well in my eyes, and I can feel the weight of Micah's gaze on me. I'm not going to cry. I can't . . . I'm strong. I'll figure a way out of this. I look up and meet his stare, and he's smiling down at me. He's got an incredibly sexy smile, and that makes it worse.

"It's not that I hate your brother . . . okay, yeah, it is. I can't stand your brother. He's so arrogant, as if he's better than everyone. Can I still stay here? I'll get slaughtered by the paparazzi if they find me coming out of Tom Fallston's suite."

He laughs and sits back down on the couch. "I don't like my brother either. You can stay if you tell me why the paparazzi are after you. I mean, I've never heard of you before, so you're not that famous. You must have done something crazy. What did you do?"

"I didn't do anything."

"The door is right there." He points to the exit.

Damn, he plays hardball. For a second I wonder if the paparazzi have given up yet. I check my watch. Nope, it's only been fifteen minutes. When Jake and I first started dating, the paparazzi waited in the bushes for days outside my condo to snap a picture of us kissing. Scandals make them even hungrier. They'll be looking for me all night. "Please, you have to promise to hide me from your brother too. I don't want him to know I'm here either," I say.

"I'll do what I can." He sucks his lip into his mouth and squints as if he's trying to figure me out.

I lean back and take in a deep breath. I shouldn't hesitate. If he wanted, Micah could Google me and find out every detail of my last twenty-four hours. The entire world knows. I swallow hard.

"Okay, to make a long story short, my boyfriend—" I stop to correct myself. "My ex-boyfriend got caught on camera cheating, and now the paparazzi are stalking me."

He turns toward me, placing his arm across the back of the couch. "Who's your ex?"

"Jake Gorboni," I say and immediately regret telling him.

"You're dating Jake Gorboni?" He laughs, shaking his head like it's the funniest news he's ever heard. "That tells me a lot about you."

What does that mean?

"We broke up. And what does it tell you about me?"

"You're shallow. You date guys based on their looks, money, and influence, no matter how much of a douche they are. And there is no one douchier than Gorboni."

"You don't know me." *What a jerk.* "Maybe I'm just a romantic. Naïve." I tilt my head, shrugging one shoulder.

He rolls his eyes as if I'm making an excuse. "I know Gorboni." He raises his brows questioningly.

"I was attracted to him, yeah. He's got a great body, but so do a lot of people in Hollywood. He's not always a douche. One on one he's sweet. It's just in public he puts on a show."

"You don't have to defend him. Please don't defend him. Does his cheating surprise you?"

"I don't know. I just wish it weren't so public." I try to smile as if it doesn't bother me, but I am sure it looks more like a grimace.

"What lewd act did Jake get caught doing?"

"They filmed him making out with a redhead, her hand on his crotch, his up her skirt. It's not a fake. He has a thing for redheads, and he's wearing a shirt I picked out for him a week ago. It could have been a setup, but it's not a fake. We've been going out for seven months, and I've seen girls use every trick in the book to get him to notice them, but up until now it's never worked."

"You've dated for seven months. In Hollywood that makes you his common-law wife. I'm surprised you're not carrying his love child."

I glare at him. "It's not funny." Why does this guy think so little of me?

"Oh, damn. You're pregnant with his kid, aren't you?"

I smack his leg with my fist. "No. Do you always assume the worst of people?"

"Only when they're hiding from the press in my hotel room." He tries to hide a smile, but can't.

He's driving me crazy. The paparazzi can't be this annoying.

Katya

What now? My phone goes off again. It's gone off three times in the last five minutes. I'm ready to answer it and rip Jake limb from limb with my words when I realize the call is from Mom. *What do I tell her?* She likes Jake.

"It's my mom. She'll keep calling until I pick up." I nervously spin the wide silver ring on my index finger as I answer the call. "Hey, Mom."

"Oh, thank God. Honey, I was getting worried about you. Jake said he's been calling you all morning and can't get ahold of you. Are you all right? I thought you and Jake were staying downtown because of that premiere tomorrow. Why is he calling me looking for you?"

"It's a long story." I'm not going to drag her into my problems. She has enough to worry about on her own.

"Tell me where you are. Jake's really worried."

Screw him. He shouldn't have involved my mom. "I'm fine, Mom. Don't worry about me. I'm staying with a friend." I look up to meet Micah's eyes, and his eyebrows raise as if he questions my words.

"Did you and Jake have a fight?"

"Yep. And I need some time to figure things out. I don't want him to find me, so I'm not telling you where I'm staying." She'd think she was doing the right thing and tell him.

"I'm sure it's just a misunderstanding. Give Jake a chance to explain. He sounded upset."

He's a fricking movie star. He can make people believe anything he wants them to believe. That's why he makes the big bucks.

"Mom, I have to go. I'll call you soon. Love you." I end the call and toss my phone on the coffee table in front of me as I collapse back on the sofa.

"Sounds like you could use a drink," says Micah as he walks to the mini fridge. He pulls out a bottle of alcohol and fills two shot glasses, then reaches back in the fridge and takes out a container filled with lime wedges.

"All I have are tequila shots. It's Tom's drink of choice, not mine."

Great idea. "Hit me," I say.

"I'm not into that either. No hookers or whips, sorry."

This guy is funny. "I just meant give me a drink."

"I know," he says, winking at me.

He carries the shots, a salt shaker, and the open container of limes to the coffee table in front of me. I lick the back of my hand, and he hands me the salt shaker. When a sufficient amount of salt sticks on my skin, I toss the shaker back to Micah, and he does the same.

"On the count of three," Micah says as he hands me a lime wedge. "One, two, three."

We simultaneously lick the salt, then guzzle the shot and suck the wedge, slamming the shot glasses down on the table in front of the couch at the same time. The tequila burns my throat and then warms me from head to toe.

"That works," I say before bringing my hand to my mouth to taste the grains of salt I missed the first time. "Tell me something about you, Micah."

"Like what?" he asks.

"I've never met you, and I hang out with Tom all the time. You're not part of his usual all-female entourage, or I would have run into you. What do you do?"

He doesn't meet my eyes when he speaks. Instead, he fiddles with the edge of his swim trunks. "You're going to laugh."

"So? You're nice enough to let me hide here." He is incredibly adorable. I don't think I have ever met a guy who wasn't all about promoting himself.

"I'm a student."

I almost laugh at his short answer. "Okay. What are you going to school for?" He is not like his brother at all. Tom would have taken my asking as an open invitation to talk about himself for an hour.

"You're going to think it's stupid," he says matter-of-factly.

"No, I won't. Just tell me."

"I go to clown school. It's a bachelor of arts in clown performance."

"You do not."

"I do." He looks at me as if I'm making fun of him. "Did you know clowns date back to the ancient Greeks and Romans? Look it up. I learned it in clown school."

"I didn't know clown school was even a thing." I try hard not to laugh, but one slips from my lips, and I can't keep the smile off my face.

"Are you making fun of me? I'm not going to be one of those funny clowns. I'm going to be the serious kind. There is nothing funny about my clown face, so don't laugh at me."

"Are you going to be a mime?" I cover my mouth with my hand as my eyes tear up because I'm trying so hard not to break out in giggles.

"God, no. Mimes have to go to school for six years. I am not that dedicated," he says straight-faced, and then he breaks out laughing. "You are so gullible. No wonder you dated Gorboni."

"If you're going to tease me like this, I need another shot." I nudge his shoulder with mine and do my best to glare at him without breaking a smile.

He starts setting up another round of shots with the biggest smile on his face.

"Don't mess with me. What are you actually studying in school?" I ask.

"Graphic design and visual marketing."

"So like, advertising? Or what does a graphic design degree get you?"

"Freelance advertising if I have to. But what I want to do is write graphic novels and comic books. Maybe write my own cartoon series." He rubs his thumb against the bridge of his nose, looking down, and then slowly raises his eyes to meet mine. He seems more apprehensive than he did when he was in clown school.

"You're kidding. I love comic books."

"Do you though?" He watches me intently. "You're just saying that to get even. How about every time we take a shot, each of us has to answer a question, truthfully, no more lies?" He gets up and grabs the tequila bottle, setting it on the table in front of us.

"Okay. I wasn't the one lying about clown school, and I do love comic books." I take out my phone and pull up the picture of Hailey and me wearing our cat heads. "See? This is a picture of a friend and me at Comic Fest last year."

"Oh, the classic Kitten Bastet and Mr. Cuddles. How do I know it's you? Your face is covered by a giant cat head and as far as I can tell your skin isn't blue."

I could flip to a picture of Hailey and me getting ready, but I'd rather show him my stomach. It's not fair he gets to flaunt his hard pecs, and I can't even show off the abs I worked so hard to get. I stand up and lift up my shirt. "See? Same belly button piercing. The blue is just body paint."

"Let me see that." He clicks off the TV and scoots to the edge of his seat, giving my phone his full attention. He zooms in on my belly button. Then with his other hand, he reaches out grasps my hip and pulls me in for a closer look. His thumb swipes across my navel, flicking the ring, and it sends unexpected tingles to my toes. Micah pulls his lower lip into his mouth, sucking on it as he sits back on the couch.

Jake laughed at me when I told him I was going to Comic Fest, and he would have never been able to identify my costume.

"It could be a good body double," Micah says when I pull my tank down.

"It's me. I've been reading *Kitten Bastet* comics since I was fifteen. I love her."

"I never would have taken you for a nerd-girl."

"She's the only one I care about, but I'm open to other comics as long as the female character isn't a damsel in distress." I sit back down, taking the salt shaker from him and loading my hand with salt. Do I admit I played the violin in my high school orchestra?

He licks the inside of his wrist, and before he can take the salt shaker back, I grab his hand, smoothing my fingers across his palm to upright his wrist. Then I sprinkle the salt as his eyes meet mine. I've never seen eyes that blue before. They're like island water on a sunny day. He slowly retracts his hand, then hands me a lime wedge without saying a word. I think I shocked him.

"On the count of three," I say, and he nods.

We pick up our shots, and he says, "Three."

We run the ritual and slam the glasses on the table. Warmth spreads through my limbs, remaining there, and it's not just the alcohol. But a knock on the door shocks me like a glass of ice water in the face. It's either Jake or the paparazzi. I feel panicked again. Should I hide? My eyes meet Micah's, and he appears calm.

"It's about time," says Micah. "I ordered food before coming up from the pool. Hope you like pizza."

"Everybody likes pizza." I don't usually get to eat it, but I deserve to indulge today.

"Good, because it took an hour and a half to get this from room service." Micah takes the box from the delivery guy and then hands it to me behind the door before signing the charge slip.

I set the food near the tequila on the table. A whiff of the sweet peppers, tomatoes, and fresh-baked crust makes my stomach growl. I sit on the couch and inch up the corner of the box. "It smells amazing," I say.

"Dig in." Micah smiles. He gets it. He seems to know exactly how to make me feel better—alcohol and carbs.

We devour our first slices quickly. It's veggie and cheese, and amazingly good. I eat way too much as we chat about pizza toppings for thirty minutes.

"Do you want the last piece?" he asks.

"No. Go ahead. You worked out at the pool. You deserve it."

"The hotel pool is incredible. I never get to swim for my workouts." He picks up the last wedge. "The pool has fifty-meter lanes. I had to take advantage. I used to swim the breaststroke in high school. But I rarely see a pool these days."

"You look like a swimmer," I say, dramatically ogling his abs.

He smiles. I hope that didn't come off creepy.

"How did a comic book girl hook up with Jake Gorgeous Body Gorboni?" he asks.

"I hate that people call him that. If you ask me his muscles are a bit overdeveloped, but he eats it up."

"I'm sure he does," he says, rolling his eyes. "How did you two meet? Be honest."

"I work with a good friend of Jake's on *Impassioned*."

"You're on *Impassioned*? That show's lit," he says, his eyes avoiding me, and I'm not sure why.

"You've seen it?"

"No, but I've heard of it. My roommate watches it. I prefer drawing to watching TV. I don't watch much."

"The guy who plays my character's boyfriend introduced me to Jake."

"Liam Nordstrom? He's the only one I know on that show."

"Yes. Liam's girlfriend was worried there was more going on between Liam and me than our professional relationship, and Liam wanted me to get to know her to ease her worries." Why did I tell him that?

"Was there something going on between you and her boyfriend?"

"No." I turn to him with narrowed eyes. "Anyway, they had me over, and Jake was there. Jake was charming. He asked me out, and we've been going out since." I reach for the salt shaker and turn it around in my hand several times before asking, "What's your favorite comic book character?"

His eyes brighten when he starts to speak. "Johanna Redemption is my absolute favorite. She's obscure. Really rare to find the originals in print. Have you ever heard of her?"

I shake my head, and he says, "It's a post-apocalyptic vampire world.

She's a vamp who protects the innocent. Wanna see her?"

"Sure."

He stands and I expect him to take out his phone, but instead, he pulls his swim trunks down until they are just barely covering the critical parts. Inked in the crease of his glorious, sculpted V poses a beautiful five-inch-tall warrior with long dark hair and humongous tits, sketched in black. I'd seen the top of the tat sticking out of his swim trunks. It's even more intriguing now that I see it in its full form.

"So you're a breast guy," I say, and he smiles. I like that he's a breast man, because my breasts are one of my main attractions. They're probably the reason he didn't call hotel security. I have this strange desire to trace the lines of his tattoo with my finger. I imagine the skin is soft. But just as I get up the nerve and start to move my hand, his shorts snap back into place.

"She's a badass. I think you'd like her."

"I bet she'd never run from the paparazzi."

"She'd slaughter them, but only in the dark when she could hide her identity." He fills the shot glasses again, and we prep our wrists with salt.

I'm drinking this shot a little slower. I slam the glass down a couple of seconds after Micah, then rub my hand across my face.

Micah touches my shoulder as he stands. "We should slow down, or you'll be spending the night." He walks over to the refrigerator and pulls out two bottles of water. "Not that I would complain, but I'm sure you have better things to do."

"Would it be okay if I stayed?" I look over to meet his gorgeous blue eyes. "I can't go back to my hotel room. The paparazzi were camped out in front of it on a secure floor. The hotel staff must have tipped them off. They probably booked a room on my floor to get access. I'm sure they're at my condo too. I'm not very good at giving them the slip when I'm by myself." I'm pretty sure it's just an excuse at this point. I want to get to know Micah better. He's funny and sweet, and not at all like Jake. "Could I sleep on the couch? I don't know where else to go."

He hands me one of the waters, still holding my gaze. "Yeah. You can stay." He sits next to me. "You're not a native?"

"Of Los Angeles? No. Born and raised in the Midwest. Suburban Chicago. I moved here when I got the role on *Impassioned*, a year ago."

"Do you like it here?"

"I love my job. Everyone I work with is incredible. And I feel a bit guilty because I have this great first job and never really paid my dues to get it. I mean, I auditioned and did some bit parts in *CSI*, but I never had to do tampon commercials or anything like that." He doesn't cringe at the word "tampon," and I think that alone gives him maturity points.

"My brother used to model," says Micah. "He started when he was five or six. I remember being stuck at his shoots for hours with just a pad of paper and some crayons. Eventually, he worked his way into acting, but that didn't change anything for me. I was still stuck tagging along with him and Mom. Tom's life didn't explode until he got the role in the *Pure Magic* series."

"Maybe being stuck at your brother's photo shoots made you the drawer you are today."

"How do you know I like to draw?" He stretches his hand across the back of the sofa and examines my face.

"Graphic design, comic books . . . duh. And you told me you'd rather draw than watch TV. Do you have any drawings you can show me?"

He pulls out his phone and starts thumbing through it. As he shows me a few of his drawings, he moves closer to me, wrapping his arm around my shoulder. His touch makes my heart race. Okay, he's not as big, muscle-wise, as Jake, but he's toned in all the right places. His abs, pecs, and arms are as good as his movie star brother's. And his ass? It's way better than Jake's. He's so sweet and genuine too. Definitely not as conceited as Jake. "You drew these?"

He nods, a grin forming on his angular face.

"They're incredible." I click back through the files he's shown me. "Wow." He is an amazing artist. "These look like pictures. The detail and shading are unreal."

He smiles, and it reaches his eyes. "Thanks."

His phone pings with a text and I hand it back to him. My first thought is that it's his girlfriend, because irony-wise this guy has got to have a girlfriend. I know his relationship status should be the last thought in my head, but I can't fight the idea.

He sits back against the couch, removing his arm from my shoulder as he reads the text. I miss his arm around me. I recognize that I'm just looking for validation after Jake's cheating, someone to tell me I'm desirable, but I am getting more attracted to this guy by the minute. And the tequila doesn't help either. I down the bottle of water in my hand.

"Tom's not coming back tonight. At least we won't have to worry about him crashing our party."

I kick off my sandals and curl my legs up next to me. I may as well get comfortable. If Tom's not coming back, I am not leaving. I'm safe here.

"Do you want to watch a movie?"

"As long as the female lead isn't a redhead," I say.

He flicks through the movies available on the TV, and we settle on an old nineties one. It's pretty tame on the explicitness scale so far, fading to black whenever a scene gets too hot, which I see as a win for me. Watching steamy sex scenes with Micah could do me in. I don't want to use him as a pawn in my and Jake's fight. He doesn't deserve that.

The best part about the movie is that I don't personally know any of the actors and they're not friends of Jake's. I swear Jake is better connected than Google. It's not just actors either. He always seems to know what I'm doing, even when we aren't together. He learns the names of the regular paparazzi we see all the time and they do favors for him. Then there are his fans. Jake's fans wouldn't hesitate to tweet my whereabouts if he admitted on social media that he was looking for me. He'll never suspect me to hide right under his nose, in the same hotel where we're supposed to be staying together.

I settle back to watch the movie because I have a whole evening to waste and I need something to distract me from worrying about what is being said about me in the press. Thirty minutes into the film, I realize this is a psychological thriller. The main character's home all alone and she just invited the guy who is probably the rapist–serial killer in her front door. "What an idiot! Who would invite a guy she barely knows into her house like that?"

"I let you in," Micah says, leaning toward me and poking me in the side.

I laugh as my eyes rake over his ripped abs. "You should put on a shirt. I could be a serial killer."

He stands up, pauses the movie, and retreats to the bedroom without a word. That's when I realize he hasn't mentioned my looks. He hasn't told me I'm beautiful. His eyes haven't raked over my body like mine just did to him. Maybe I'm not his type. Maybe he prefers redheads, like Jake. I feel as if we're making a connection though, and I hope it's not one-sided.

Katya

When Micah emerges from the bedroom minutes later, he's wearing athletic shorts and a tight-fitting athletic T-shirt stretched across his chest. I can still see every sinuous muscle of his abs.

"Is that better?" His smile says he likes that I've been ogling him, and I feel relieved.

I cock my head, acting as if I'm studying him. "No, I was wrong. Take it off."

"Serial killer." His bright blue eyes meet mine before he plops next to me on the couch and pours two shots. "I think we need a break from the movie. You get the first question." He passes me the salt, waiting for me to load my wrist before handing me a shot.

When I'm done, I watch him load his and then he meets my eyes again. "One. Two. Three."

We run the ritual and slam the glasses down.

It's my turn, and my brain isn't in a creative mood, so I ask the lame question everyone always asks. "If you had a superpower what would it be?"

He gets up and grabs two more waters from the fridge, tossing one to me. I catch it and crack the cap open.

"It's funny that you ask, because I actually have a superpower." He smiles, his tongue churning in his mouth as if he can't wait to tell me what it is, but he doesn't continue.

"Okay. What's your superpower?" I gulp the water, expecting him to say X-ray vision or the ability to fly on an airplane. What I don't expect is his response.

"The ability to give multiple orgasms."

Water shoots from my nose, and I start coughing. *Sweet mother of kittens.* He surprised me. My cough turns into a laugh, and I can't stop it.

Micah sits and leans back on the couch undeterred by my laughter. "It's true. I've been told it's my superpower."

"I believe you." I giggle. *Oh my God.* "I thought that was a myth, only found in movies and romance novels."

"Not a myth. I'll show you sometime," he says, and then launches into his next question. "Tell me something Jake doesn't know about you."

I'm still thinking about multiple orgasms. Do I tell him I fake it with Jake more times than I make it, just to keep on the orgasm theme? I can't say that out loud. I think for a long minute. *Keep it neutral. Non-sexual.*

"I have every *Kitten Bastet* comic ever made except volume twenty-six—which I am pretty sure is a myth. And I always buy two of the new releases. One for me and one for my brother."

"How old is your brother?"

"He'll be eighteen this summer, but he's not a normal eighteen. Ever since the accident, he's been kind of obsessed with comics. Of course, *Kitten Bastet* is his favorite. I don't know if it's because he saw me in costume or what." I talk a bit more about my brother until my mood starts to crash. The guilt weighs heavily on my mind and my mood can't help but plummet. I think Micah senses the change in me and pours two more shots, gearing up for our next set of questions.

I take the opportunity to run to the restroom. My fight-or-flight response with the paparazzi had shut off my need until now. I expect to see wet towels on the floor and other typical male housekeeping deficits, but Micah is surprisingly neat. Just a razor and a few bottles of product litter the counter. When I look in the mirror, I almost scare myself. *Here I am talking about multiple orgasms with Micah and I look like this?* All my makeup is gone, except for black smudges in the corners of my eyes. No wonder the paparazzi were chasing me. I look awful—the perfect tabloid cover shot.

My dark hair falls messily around my face, not even pretending to be pulled back in the hair tie it was initially placed in this morning. I splash my face with water, rubbing at the corners of my eyes with a clean white washcloth. I need to get the makeup from my purse, but that would be too obvious since my purse is on the table next to the couch.

Screw it.

Micah looks up from his phone, meeting my eyes as I reach for my bag.

"I didn't realize how awful I look. I need some makeup," I say, grabbing it off the table.

Before I reach the bathroom, he says, "You don't need makeup. You look beautiful."

He thinks I'm beautiful without makeup. Jake always reminds me to fix mine. He says I'm too basic without it. I reapply it and then run my brush through my hair, pulling it back up into the tie.

When I return, we down the shots without a word. Micah looks at me with a somber face and asks, "Have you ever cheated on anyone? A boyfriend? A fiancé? A best friend?"

"How do you cheat on a best friend?" His question confuses me. "You mean have a second best friend behind her back?"

"Sleep with her boyfriend," he answers with raised eyebrows.

"No. I've never slept with any of my friends' boyfriends. I'd never do that. I'm actually very loyal to those I care about. And I fall in love really quickly. If I were a superhero that would be my fatal flaw. Once I'm in love, I'm in love. I don't like to rock the boat. Every relationship has ups and downs, and maybe I'm stupid but I don't jump ship until I know the boat will no longer float."

"What you're saying is that you won't cheat once you fall?"

"Yeah. I'm loyal until the guy disillusions me, breaks the spell as Jake did. Why do you ask?"

He pulls his phone from his pocket as he answers. "The tabloids say you're sleeping with Liam Nordstrom and that's why Jake strayed."

"Of course they do. Jake can't do anything wrong. He's Mr. All-American. His fans don't want to believe he's a cheater. They want to believe the breakup is my fault. Liam and I are just friends. There was a time I thought I was in love with him, but we've never slept together." I don't know why I'm opening up to him, but it feels safe. I don't think he will betray me. And after what Jake did I don't feel as if I can trust anyone. Besides, he's Tom's brother, he has to understand Hollywood better than the average Joe.

"You thought you were in love with Liam?"

"Like I said, I fall in love easily. We work together. He's my character's love interest on our show—it's completely understandable, method acting and all. But once I saw him with Megan, I knew I'd never have a chance. It changed me. I'm not in love with him anymore."

"So you fall out of love easily too?"

"I guess . . . I never looked at it that way. Have you ever been in love?"

"Is that your shot question?"

"Sure."

"Once," he admits. "I thought she was the one. We'd even talked about marriage. Until she cheated."

"It's just like Jake." I watch him as a thousand expressions flit across his face. I can't help but wonder what's going on behind his eyes. Maybe he doesn't believe me. "I didn't cheat on Jake. Did the internet say anything else? I've avoided looking . . . mostly because my phone's about to die." I show him my phone, and the blinking red light indicates it needs to be plugged in.

"Nothing worth reading." He shoves his phone back into his pocket. "I've got a charger that should work with that phone." He goes back into the bedroom and returns with a charging cord.

"Is it bad?" I ask. *I know it's bad.*

"Just a couple of pictures of you holding hands with Liam Nordstrom as you walk into your condo and a few of you riding on the back of his motorcycle." He plugs the phone in near the bar.

"Those are recycled. They're almost a year old." I pause. "I never slept with Liam." I regret the word vomit the second it spews from my mouth. I already told him that and now it sounds like I'm making excuses, denying it too much.

His eyebrows raise. "Let's not worry about the tabloids. We've got a serial killer to watch."

I sit back on the couch, nodding in agreement, and he leans back, spreading his arms across the couch's spine. He's much closer to me than he was before, and I can feel the warmth of his arm inches behind my head as the movie resumes. I'm not sure what to think about his new position. I don't mind the move. There is something about Micah Fallston that comforts me. He's real, not caught up in the perils of Hollywood like his brother or Jake. He teases me but seems to instinctively know my limits. Jake doesn't know when to stop teasing me and always seems to push me to the verge of tears. I am so done with that man. I try to push Jake from my mind and concentrate on the movie, but I can't seem to get back into the plot. I can tell that Micah isn't really paying attention to it either. He keeps glancing at me and I really want to know what he's thinking.

I reach over him to get the remote, burying my nose against his shoulder as I stretch to retrieve it. Micah smells incredible—like masculine musk and sunshine mixed with baby powder—light and enticing. Jake always smells overpowering, like he's trying to dominate the world with his scent. Jake's scent burns my nostrils and seeps into my clothes. My sheets. My pillow. I can't escape it. Micah wraps an arm around me to help right me after I've claimed my prize, and his touch feels incredible.

When I'm positioned back on the couch, I click off the TV and say, "Thanks for the hand. I'm done with the movie. Do you mind if we just talk?"

He smiles, settling back in his seat. "It wasn't worth our time, was it?"

"No. It was bad."

As he sits forward to pour two more shots, I glance at my phone, wondering how many calls I've missed. Have my friends seen the video? My mom? I'm still looking for a way to forget all my problems, and just because the movie didn't work doesn't mean the tequila won't.

We down our shots and I ask, "Do you live in Los Angeles or are you just here for your brother's movie premiere?"

"I go to school in Austin. I'm working for my brother for the summer as his driver slash personal security. Tom had a bad experience over the holidays with the service he was using, and he wants at least one person he can trust who's not for sale."

"What happened?"

"One day, a bunch of girls got into Tom's car, and he didn't want them there, so he ordered them out. They refused, saying they wouldn't leave unless they got their money back. They'd paid one of his security guys from the service to let them in. Tom wants me to monitor that kind of stuff."

"So he trusts you?"

"I guess." He runs his hand through his dark wavy hair, as his lips twist with a question. "You've dated Gorboni for seven months, right?"

I nod.

"Why? I mean, was it the exposure for your career? His biceps? He's not a good person; why would you stay with him so long?"

His question blows me away. Everyone loves Jake, why doesn't he? "Truthfully?"

"That's why we're here."

"It was a novelty at first." I try to clear the alcohol swirling in my head and give Micah an honest answer. "I was an actress with a three-year contract. I had a following, and I wasn't worried about my next meal or anything. But when I started dating Jake, the world opened up to me. A world I couldn't even fathom. Private jets. Designer clothes. Celebrity privilege. It was beyond what I dreamed. When the novelty wore off, it was too late. I'd already fallen for him. I fall and stay loyal. That's what I do. I can't deny being with him has helped my career. But . . . I think I could have gotten this far on my own eventually. I haven't had any big movie offers yet."

"Then why stay with him? I've seen his junk. It's average."

I laugh. He's seen Jake's junk? I tuck my chin back and stare at him in disbelief, my eyebrows raised.

"You wouldn't believe the crap I've seen," he says.

I would. That's the problem. "Honestly?" I hesitate because I know what I'm going to tell him sounds insane. "I think it's because Jake doesn't make grand gestures. He doesn't believe in them. He says if a girl is looking for expensive gifts, then she doesn't really want him. Most guys in his income bracket buy their girlfriends new cars or diamond necklaces. You know what Jake got me for Christmas? A new pillow for my bed. It's a great pillow, but I know it cost less than a hundred dollars."

"You don't like gifts?"

"I like gifts, but, I'd rather a guy take me out to dinner and spend time with me than ignore me and buy me expensive presents."

"You're so weird."

"It's my daddy issue, if you must know." Why is he so easy to talk to? "After my parents got divorced, my father was never around except when it was convenient for him, and he never paid his share of child support. My mom scraped and saved to put food on the table and clothes on our backs, while my dad lived carefree, and banked offshore." I shift in my seat, wondering if I'm saying too much.

"Then every few years he'd make a grand gesture, buying my brother or me an expensive gift as if it would make up for the second-hand clothes or the years of not seeing him. When he bought me a car for my eighteenth birthday, I didn't accept it, just on principle. I'd rather feel the love every day. Jake and I check in with each other every day when we're apart, and he never buys me expensive gifts. The opposite of my dad."

"You're very different than my first impression of you."

"Yeah. You thought I was a hooker."

He looks down at his lap as if embarrassed and then lifts his impossibly long lashes to meet my eyes. "It's nothing against you. It's my brother. He does shit like that. He drives me crazy."

"All right. I won't hold it against you." I smile. "You don't think I'm an idiot for hating grand gestures?"

"Not at all. Any eighteen-year-old who passes on a new car to follow her principles has to have a superhero's heart. It's right out of a comic book."

I want to kiss him for that comment. Most people wouldn't understand. They'd think I was stupid. And after all that's happened, I realize they'd be right. But I am not sharing the rest of the story with this guy. Or any guy, for that matter.

"Let's do another shot. I have more questions," he says.

He pours two more. I don't know what inspires me, but I snag his hand, licking the soft flesh near his wrist before shaking salt over the moistened skin. He watches me intensely but doesn't pull his hand away.

"Sorry. I forgot about your issues with swapping fluids."

His breathing picks up and, still, he stays silent, watching me.

"I can lick the salt off if you're worried about my germs. I figure the salt and tequila would kill anything."

"Can I kiss you?"

My usual response to that question is, *if you have to ask, the answer's no.* I like a man who takes charge. But Micah is different from the guys I usually kiss. He's confident but way less cocky. He doesn't act as if he has something to prove or he's doing me a favor by kissing me. It fits his character to ask, and I want him to kiss me.

I nod, and his hand grasps my chin, pulling my lips up to meet his. His kiss is gentle and sweet, just as I would expect from what I know of him. I open to him, and his tongue pushes inside, stirring the magical fairies deep within me. *Oh . . . baby kittens.* He's an excellent kisser. My breath catches. I want more. I push deeper, sliding my hands into his hair. It's so soft. We're not close enough. I nip his tongue softly with my back teeth, and he growls, a deep and husky sound. And that's all it takes for me to ovulate. He is clearly mating material.

He breaks the kiss and rests his forehead against mine. "We better stop," he whispers.

Definitely not the usual guy I kiss. As the fog clears my head, I remember our interrupted task.

"Next question," I say, picking up a tequila shot, but I don't have any salt. I set the glass back on the table and load my wrist with salt. My brain's a bit fuzzy. Micah licks the salt remaining on his wrist and reloads again. When we've slammed our drinks, I ask, "What's your biggest pet peeve?"

"People who push stuff on me they know I don't want."

I hope he doesn't mean the kiss. It sure felt as if he wanted it as much as I did. Wasn't he the one who asked if he could kiss me?

"Not the kiss. I wanted that." He amends. "I just think . . . if we keep moving in that direction…it wouldn't be the right thing to do. You haven't even officially broken up with your boyfriend."

"As far as I'm concerned I have. He's the one who ended it by cheating. I am so done with him. I'm just…I don't know what I'm doing. It just felt good. And when you've had a day like I have, you deserve a distraction." I need to stop talking. "What do you mean about people pushing stuff on you?"

"Like Tom. He thinks that just because he wants a different woman every night, I should too. He pushes that lifestyle on me even when he knows it's not what I want. I'm not really looking forward to spending the summer with him because I know that's what he's going to do. He's just like my parents in that way."

I break out in giggles. "Sorry. It must be the alcohol. Your parents push illicit one-night-stands on you?" I start laughing again. I can't help it.

He starts laughing too. "No. Religion. Apparently, theirs is the best. The one and only true way to salvation. They've written Tom off as unsalvageable, but there's still hope for me. And they take every opportunity they can to guide me to the truth while judging me every step of the way."

"That's my dad." I turn to face him. "So he cheats on my mom multiple times, gets another woman pregnant, divorces Mom 'because he wants to do the right thing,' and then doesn't marry the woman carrying his child. Instead, he finds another woman to get pregnant and then marries her. The guy doesn't know how to use a condom. He and his new wife join a church, and suddenly they're perfect. They have no past, no responsibility to anyone but God. He can ignore all the wrong he does because he is one of the chosen few. He puts on this show that he's the most righteous man on the planet, but he doesn't do anything to atone for his past."

Micah watches me with a slight smile, no lust on his face, just fascination.

"I'm ranting, but that one hit an artery." I hold out my index finger to make a point. "My father is such an ass. He's too busy judging everyone around him to look in the mirror."

Micah pours two more shots and holds one up for me. "To putting up with hypocrites and their judgment."

"Exactly. Bring on the judginess," I say, taking the glass. We both down the shots without lime or salt and he wraps his arm around me.

"What's your biggest fear?" Micah asks, tugging me closer.

"That my brother will never return to his old self. That the doctors are right and he's never going to recover. I worry that my mom's going to lose their house because of all the medical bills. My dream is to pay it off so Cam can concentrate on recovering."

"Wow," he says, shaking his head. "You are amazingly complex."

I like the way he's looking at me, as if he can see more than my looks. He sees beyond my body.

"How much money do you need?"

"More than I make on my cable show, but nothing a couple of blockbuster movie contracts couldn't finance."

"Then what you need is a movie contract."

"But it's probably not going to happen now that Jake and I have broken up. Hollywood only wants the top players, and without Jake's influence, I'll fall between the cracks. *Plop.* Right in the middle of the ocean where no one can find me."

"You can swim. I believe in you." He reaches out and touches my nose.

"I think my nose is numb." I tap it several times with my finger. Yep, definitely losing feeling.

"It's a cute nose," he says, touching it again with his finger and smiling.

His touch makes my stomach flutter. He tucks a loose tendril of hair behind my ear.

"I'm not cute. I'm sexy."

"It's a very sexy nose." His smile grows as he stares into my eyes.

"I thought you were a breast guy."

"I figured you'd slap my hand if I touched your tits. Are they real?"

"Yes, they're real. Why do guys always ask that?" I turn toward him to give him a better look and to see him better. The tequila's blurred my vision around the edges. I can't see beyond the tunnel directly in front of me. "I can spot a pair of fakes a mile away."

"I don't believe they're real. They're too . . . amazing."

That's really so sweet. I can tell the alcohol is affecting him too. He's stopped blinking. It's like he hasn't blinked in five minutes. We've been drinking all afternoon and the alcohol is starting to accumulate.

I puff out my chest because his scrutinizing gaze tells me he definitely can see that the right one is just a tiny bit bigger than the left.

"Absolutely perfect," he lies. "They can't be real."

This is the most fun I've had with a guy in a long time. I know he's just playing me, but I indulge him. Most guys would just help themselves. "Give me your hands," I say. Taking them, I place them on my girls. "Satisfied?"

He cups my breasts, pushing up as he squeezes. "Not yet." He meets my eyes, his thumbs strumming over my nipples. His touch zings right to my core, perking my entire body. *Holy catnip.* A small moan involuntarily hums from my throat. His touch feels absurdly good.

Before my brain can figure out what I'm doing, I tug my loose top over my head and peel off my tank. Within a nanosecond, Micah's fingers nudge under the lace of my bra. His touch purrs through me. *Sweet baby kittens. I want to sleep with him.* I reach back, unclasping my bra, and his hands slide the straps down my arms, pulling it off completely. When he tosses my lace garment onto the table in front of us, one strap rings the tequila bottle like a carnival game, and I start to laugh. I can't help it. But then his mouth lands on one of my freed breasts and the laugh morphs into a whimper. I turn my brain off and go with it.

Micah

I hear a loud clunk in the suite and manage to pry open my eyes seconds before the door to my room explodes inward.

"Good morning, little brother," Tom yells in his fake chipper voice. The vice on my head tightens at his words. I haven't been this hungover in a long time.

I sit up and out of instinct toss my pillow on top of Kat's head to hide her. He waves Kat's bra over his head like a lasso. I know what's coming. *Cue the humiliation.*

"It's bad enough you drank my tequila, but did you have to share it with that tramp in bed next to you?" He laughs. "I know you needed it. No one needed to get laid more than you. But why drink my good stuff?" He examines the bra in his hand and a smirk grows on his face. "Are they real? I won't even make you pay for the tequila if they're real." He walks to the side of the bed, grabbing the pillow and tossing it onto the blankets at my feet.

"I've got to see for myself," he says, reaching for the blankets covering Kat's head.

I spring out from under the covers, throwing my body on top of hers, and she groans at the impact. There is no way I am letting him see her tits. "Just let it go. I'll pay for the tequila."

"Nope. You need every dollar I'm paying you this summer to afford that expensive art school of yours. Just let me see her tits. I'm sure she wouldn't mind *me* looking at them. After all, she slept with you, her standards can't be too high."

"They're real, and I mind," barks a muffled voice under me.

"See? She minds."

Tom cocks his head, his brow wrinkled.

"Give me her bra and get the hell out!" What is he waiting for?

Tom's jaw drops in disbelief and he starts laughing hysterically. "Kat? Is that you?"

I turn to stare at him, wishing, like a little kid, that I had laser eyes and he'd start on fire. As I sit up straddling Kat's hips, she pulls the blanket off her face.

"What have you done, baby brother? You were a very naughty boy last night," he scolds me and laughs again. "This was not the girl to use to assert your revenge on Jake. He's not going to take this lightly. Kat, your boyfriend's been looking for you everywhere. He's convinced you've been abducted like Jonathan Williams's woman, but here you are shacking up with my little brother." He stares at the two of us as if he can't believe what he's witnessing. "Was it any good? I try to pass him a bone when I can just so his junk doesn't dry up and fall off. But nerd-boy got you all on his own?"

She glares at Tom with venomous hate and says, "He was the best I've ever had."

I quickly pull my jaw off the floor and compose my expression before turning to see Tom's reaction. I expected her to tell him that we just got drunk and fell asleep, but instead she bolsters me up in Tom's eyes and slams Jake at the same time. *I think I love this girl.* I'm not going to tell Tom I don't take advantage of drunk girls. He'd just mock me for not being able to seal the deal even when the girl is naked in my bed.

"You can leave now," I say, crawling onto my side of the bed.

"You two better hurry up and get dressed before Jake gets here." He steps through the doorway and closes the door with a soft click.

Kat pulls the covers back over her head, and a muted scream vibrates the entire bed. I know just how she feels. I am not ready to deal with Jake Gorboni.

"I'll go talk to my brother. Maybe he hasn't sent Jake a text yet," I say as I slide off the bed. I slip on a pair of shorts and a T-shirt and head out into the suite's living room. This is not how I envisioned the morning with Kat. I wanted to order room service, get rid of our hangovers, and then maybe find our way back into the bed again—only sober this time. I'd like a second chance to have my mouth on her beautiful tits and feel her lips on mine without the influence of alcohol.

Tom's looking through the fridge when I find him. Probably inspecting it to see what I ate. If that's what it's going to be like all summer, I may as well pack up and go home now.

"Don't call Gorboni," I say as he closes the refrigerator and turns to face me.

He rubs his finger along his nose as he considers my words. "No," he says, his brows knitting. "You made the bed. You're going to have to lie in it."

"I didn't make the bed, Gorboni did. Besides, it just happened. I didn't plan it, and I'm not asking for me. I don't care what Gorboni does to me. I'm asking for her. The paparazzi were chasing her. I was just hiding her."

"More like playing hide the sausage. I have to hand it to you. She's a prime piece of ass. Never would have guessed she'd hand the goods over to *you* and you'd be the best she ever had. Savor the moment, little brother. Savor the moment. You won't see another one like it."

As much as I wish his words were just words, I know he's right. Kat is way out of my league. "You can tell Jake you saw her, but give her a chance to get out of here before you do. She doesn't want to see him."

"You know, little brother, you picked a shit time to restart your feud with Gorboni. With the movie Jake and I are doing together this summer and you being my personal security-for-hire, you're going to be spending a ton of time together. He's not going to be happy you fucked his girlfriend."

"Really, Tom?" *As if Gorboni has any right to be mad at me.* I shove my hands into the pockets of my shorts, fighting the need to shake some sense into my brother. "If it's going to be so uncomfortable for you to have us at each other's throats again, don't tell him you saw Kat. It's a nonissue if you keep your mouth shut."

A small laugh bursts from his throat. "You'd like that. Then maybe you'd get another chance with his hot piece. You said you could deal with being around Jake this summer and then you do this?"

I want to tell him I didn't know she was his girlfriend, but I did. Part of me wonders if I would have let it get as far as it did with Kat if she'd been dating anyone other than Gorboni. I can't deny that sending him a sex tape had crossed my mind, at least before I got to know her.

"I can deal with it. I didn't plan for Jake to publicly humiliate his girlfriend. I'll deal with what I need to do this summer. It's not going to be a problem for me unless he makes it a problem."

"And that's what I'm worried about. Once he knows what you did, he's going to go apeshit."

"Don't tell him. Let Kat tell him if she wants. She sounded as if she was breaking up with him anyway. Maybe it won't come up. I won't bring it up."

A breath huffs heavily from his mouth as if I'm stupid trying to protect her. He looks to the black TV screen, not meeting my eyes as he shakes his head.

"Kat will tell him. The only reason she did this with you is to get back at him. She wanted to keep it quiet because if she did something publicly, she'd be the villain in the press. No. She was smart doing it this way. She's going to tell him."

Shit. He's right. She planned this. She wanted to get back at Gorboni privately. I don't think she would have done it if she knew our past, but she definitely was the aggressor last night. And even if we didn't officially sleep together, she can tell Gorboni whatever she wants. "I'm not afraid of Jake. He's the one with everything to lose. I don't have any money."

He stares at me, working through my words. I'm surprised he spotted Katya's motivation before me. I guess I was too involved in the situation to look at it objectively. If I were a superhero, not being able to think clearly when women are involved would be my downfall. He's right. When Jake catches up to Kat, she'll tell him she slept with me to get back at him and then he'll have a problem with me. I'll deal with him.

"You mean he's not going to hit you because you'd sue him for assault."

Ding, ding. I nod. If he's smart, he won't.

"I'll tell Jake she's here without mentioning you. So he doesn't worry about her. He was batshit crazy yesterday. I mean seriously crazy. Don't be pitching a tent for her. She used you. And now you and I are going to have to deal with *his* mood all summer."

My logic must have satisfied him.

"He brought it on himself. Give her a chance to leave on her own. Wait a couple of hours. Please," I plead again.

Tom rolls his eyes and collapses on the sofa, picking up the remote and clicking on the TV. "Clean up your mess, and I'll give you some time."

I tote the shot glasses to the bar sink and begin rinsing them. "I'll call for some more tequila and limes."

"Damn right, you will."

As I make the call to the concierge, I note the clothes from last night strewn across the floor. Kat's fuchsia-colored tank top peeks out from behind one of the chairs. I can picture her stripping it off. God, she's gorgeous. Her beauty bubbles from every pore in her body. It's just there. It fills the room. She's not one of those girls who doesn't know she's gorgeous either. She does. But she doesn't act as if she's better because of it. It's just the way it is. At least she didn't make me feel as if she were better than me last night.

I was stupid to think her intentions were pure. But I don't care. I'd do it again. I'm glad I stopped it though. At least I'll know Gorboni's in the wrong. I find her white shorts. I almost lost it when she slid them off, revealing her tiny pink lace panties with the black bow. I head into the bedroom with our clothes. The shower's running and the bed's empty. I set the clothes on the bed just as Kat shuts off the water. When she walks out of the bathroom, my lower brain is throbbing as bad as my upper hungover one. *Damn it.* She's wearing one of my T-shirts and, I imagine, nothing else.

"You don't mind I borrowed your shirt? I was worried Tom would come in again. Did he call Jake?" She bends over and rubs a towel against her long, dark hair.

"He said he'd wait." I avoid looking at her because all I want is to push her onto the bed and have my way with her.

Tom teases me about not hooking up with random girls. He thinks that because I prefer relationships, I never get sex. But he's wrong. I just think sex for a woman is half in her mind and I don't want a girl if she gets off on one-night stands. But for this girl? I would break my own ethical code. I already have, I guess. I'd love a sober chance with her. "Do you feel okay? We drank a lot last night."

"I don't usually drink that much. I hope I didn't embarrass myself too badly."

"Not at all." I smile, meeting her gorgeous hazel-colored eyes. They are the most striking eyes I've ever seen, a green ring surrounding grayish-amber irises. I don't remember everything she said in our drunken state, but I remember most, and I remember those eyes. I'll never forget them.

They called to me as she stripped off her clothes last night and climbed onto the coffee table in only her lace panties. Her gorgeous eyes beckoned me when she danced on the tabletop and teased that she wasn't a call girl, she was really an exotic dancer. When I couldn't take her pleading gaze any longer, I pulled her into my arms and collapsed on the couch. We made out for a while. She kept asking for more, and we probably did more than we should have. But I knew it wouldn't be right to go any further—even if she was the most beautiful drunk girl I'd ever met. So I carried her to my bed, kissed her one last time before pulling the covers over her, and vowed not to touch her anymore until she was sober. She fell asleep almost immediately, the tequila affecting her petite body more than mine.

"You're a good dancer," I say still envisioning her eyeing me from the tabletop.

"I guess there is a lot I don't remember. I do know that I had a good time with you." She pushes up on her tiptoes and plants a kiss on my lips. A sober kiss.

I wrap my arms around her, pulling her into me. I know she can feel my lower brain's response to her kiss, but there is no hiding it.

"Thanks for letting me stay," she says against my lips.

"My pleasure," I mumble, and we kiss for another ten seconds before there's a knock on the bedroom door.

Katya runs into the bathroom as I answer it. Even with a hangover, she floats as if her feet never touch the floor.

"I've got to meet some people downstairs for an interview. I wanted you to come with me, but I'll let you sort this out," Tom says in a bark, pointing at the bathroom door. He's changed his shirt and spiked his blond hair. "Don't make the situation worse. Jake's going to find out eventually, and the Italian in him enjoys revenge."

I shake my head. Sure, he gets revenge, while I'm supposed to let it go. People like Gorboni never get held responsible for their actions. Their fame gives them a pass every time.

"You've got errands to run for me this afternoon," he adds.

"Okay," I acknowledge. I wish I could spend the day with Kat. But Tom's paying me five-times what I could make at my regular job at the comic book store for the summer. And I've made the commitment to help him; I've got to stick to it. He heads out, and I knock on the bathroom door to let Kat know he's gone.

Micah

Katya didn't act as if last night was a mistake when she kissed me this morning, but, I wish I knew what she was thinking. She smiles as she enters the room, her dark hair bouncing in a high ponytail, and her angelic eyes meet mine. Her silken skin and perfect curves pull impure thoughts into my head. After all we drank last night, how can she look this gorgeous?

"Was Tom mad about the tequila? Was it expensive?"

"No, he was just busting my balls. He doesn't care, as long as it's replaced before this afternoon. He likes to do a couple of shots before big events to loosen up," I say.

"I was supposed to go to the premiere with Jake. Now I just want to go home, but I have to get back to my hotel room to get my stuff. Do you think you could check the halls to see if the paparazzi are still stalking me?"

"Sure. We'll eat, get your stuff, and then I'll drive you home."

"You have food? I'm starved."

"I ordered some sandwiches. They should be here soon." As if on cue, there's a knock on the door, and I open it to a monstrous man blackening the light of the hallway.

"Little Fallston. You got something of mine?" says Gorboni with a deadly serious expression. My head immediately turns to Kat. I can tell she isn't ready to talk to him. She freezes at the sound of his voice as if her stillness makes her invisible.

"I don't have anything of yours," I say, trying to close the door. But he wedges his foot between the door and jamb, preventing it from closing. I block the door from opening any further with my foot.

"I know she's here. Your brother told me." He stretches his thick, muscled neck back and forth, peering through the crack trying to spot her. "Let me in. I just want to talk."

I can't hold this position against Jake Gorboni for long. I lift weights and stay fit, but he has personal trainers at his beck and call who probably pay him for the honor of listing him as a client. The guy's a monster, and no matter how much I want to see him beaten down, I like my teeth too much to volunteer for a fight with him. I look to Kat again, and she slouches in defeat.

"I'll talk to him," she whispers, moving to the door.

I move my foot from blocking the door and open it wide.

"Little Fallston, that's what I like about you. You know when you're outmatched." He smiles, and his expression makes me want to punch his crooked nose. His hand clasps my shoulder, and I brush it off. I'm not conceding. I would have done all I could to keep him out if Kat hadn't agreed to talk. "Run along and let us grown-ups chat. Don't you have some homework to do?" he says as if I'm a little kid. I may be three years younger than him and my brother, but Kat is closer to my age than his.

"Give us a couple of minutes? It won't take long," says Katya, directing him to the couch.

I turn into the bedroom and close the door. I should jump into the shower and give them privacy. But instead, I slide down the back of the door. I need to know if I was just a pawn. I plant my ear to the door and listen for her betrayal. The first words out of her mouth will be telling Jake she slept with me.

"What do you want, Jake? This thing with us is obviously over."

"I was worried about you. Your phone went black. I thought some crazy fan got you."

"Well, you can see I'm fine. You can go now."

"I'm glad you're all right, but we need to talk. Honestly, I'm surprised you went to Fallston's room. You hate Tom. And we have a perfectly good room downstairs."

"Yeah, except for the mob of paparazzi blocking the door."

"The hotel should have better security. That wasn't my fault," says Jake.

"Are you trying to tell me your hands weren't all over that girl's ass and your fingers weren't inside her? I saw the vid."

"Not everything is what it looks like, Katya."

"Let me guess, it wasn't you. You gave your shirt to your double? Or was she auditioning for one of your movies? Oh, no, wait, you never put your dick in her, so it doesn't count?"

"I didn't screw her. I wouldn't do that."

"No, you just told the whole world I wasn't worth anything. I read an article saying I was terrible in bed and if I gave better head, you wouldn't have cheated. You're the one who cheats, and I'm the one who gets blamed."

"I'm being blamed. Ansley says it's affected my approval rating. People are writing shit about me all over. According to Ansley being in a committed relationship makes me more desirable."

"That's your problem. You're not committed to me, or you wouldn't have cheated."

"Kitty Kat, I didn't sleep with her. Come on. I'm still with you."

"What? Me ghosting you was my signal that I don't want to be with a cheater. You're welcome to go find another girl to almost commit to. I'm okay with it."

"Ansley says we need to be seen together. The public wants to know we are still a couple because if they see us together, they'll forget about the video."

"Tell your publicist we're not a couple. You cheated on me. IN PUBLIC. I had to find out from the paparazzi. That guy—Ned. Is that his name? The guy with the red high-tops. He showed me the video. I didn't even know why they were chasing me. My stylist dropped me off, and they descended on me like . . . like you just cheated on me. I got away from them only to find them waiting for me in front of our hotel room. The worst part is, I didn't believe what they were saying until the guy showed me the video. You did this."

"I'm sorry. I didn't plan it. I wasn't thinking. But for the sake of both our careers get past it. You want the paparazzi to leave you alone? This is how we squash it the fastest. Letting this linger is going to hurt both our brands. We need to snuff it out."

I hear her blow out a breath in frustration and I can't believe she's even considering it.

"Give me a minute," she says, and I want to burst through the door and question her sanity. Is she really considering getting back with him?

"Are you texting Megan?"

"Yes. She's one of my best friends. I want her advice, and she's discreet. Would you rather I ask Liam, or Jonathan and Sarah? I'm sure they would be willing to share their thoughts on your cheating."

She's pulling out the big guns. I bet Gorboni doesn't want his friends and their better halves involved. I'll give her advice. Maybe breaking up with Jake would be a boost for her career. People would probably respect her more as an actor if she did it all on her own.

"Stop. I'm not going to kiss you. Not after what you did. Cut it out," she practically yells.

I pop into a standing position and open the door before I realize what I'm doing.

"Is everything all right, Kat?" I ask, knowing it will give away the fact I was listening to her conversation. She doesn't react to that though.

She's almost reached me when she asks, "Do you mind if I use your room to make a call?"

"No. Go ahead," I say, holding the door open for her to slip through and then closing it behind her. She never told Jake about us sleeping together, and I wonder why.

He completely ignores me. Tom must not have said anything either. I walk to the fridge and pull out a bottle of water before turning to him. I twist off the top, not knowing what to say, while Jake fiddles with his phone. When I sit in the chair next to the couch where he's sprawled and guzzle half the water in my bottle, he speaks.

"Tom says you've been bulking up for the security gig. I can tell. We should work out together sometime. I could give you some pointers." Yep. No one told him.

"Okay," I say. He is completely oblivious. Not only to what happened last night but to what he did to me a year ago. How does a guy function so unaware?

"That'd be great," I say. He must not realize how much I despise him. I don't know, but I don't like being all nicey-nice with Gorboni. It makes my balls shrivel and crawl inside me. He's so damn arrogant that it probably never crossed his mind that I hooked up with his girlfriend.

Ex-girlfriend.

He talks about weight lifting for the next few minutes, and my mind starts to wander. How could a girl like Kat date this guy for seven fucking months? They don't have anything in common. It doesn't compute. She's so bubbly and sweet, and he can't think beyond his muscles.

"What do you bench? One fifty? Two hundred?"

"Two twenty-five," I answer. "You?"

He grunts as if he doesn't believe me. "Three thirty. You'll probably never get to where I am, but I bet a good trainer could get you close to three hundred."

Who the hell would want the muscle dystopia he owns? Certainly not me. "I like where I'm at," I answer.

The door opens, and Kat wanders out with her phone in her hand. The corner of her beautiful lips curls up on one side when her eyes meet mine, and I look down because I'm picturing her dancing on the table in front of me.

"Megan says 'fuck you.' She wants to know what's in it for me." She sits on the opposite end of the couch from Jake, and she's so close I can smell her sweet citrus scent.

I like Megan.

"Well, Megan's not in the business. She doesn't understand what's at stake. And Liam does not have as much to lose as you do. I heard he already has a movie contract for next spring. If we break up, you're going to lose all the press attention. Nobody's going to care about you anymore. That includes directors, producers, and studios. You'll never get the movie deal you want."

"I really enjoyed being mobbed yesterday on the sidewalk in front of the hotel—one of the best experiences of *my* life. Not only did I find out that my boyfriend cheated on me, but the paparazzi captured my reaction on film. I'm sure I'll be reminded of it in every interview I have for . . . forever," she says. I'm certain an eye roll accompanied her words, but I couldn't see her face without making it obvious that I'm listening.

I take out my phone, trying to look distracted. This chair is much more comfortable than pressing my ear to the door. Kat's not ignoring me, but in front of Jake, she isn't showing any sign that we were together last night. I'm not sure if it's to protect her or me. It feels as if I'm lying.

"I know how much the producers of your little show love the attention you going out with me brings the show. Why don't you ask them what they think?"

"I don't care what they think. You cheated, and I'm sick of the press."

"The fastest way to defuse this is to go to Tom's premiere with me. I'm sorry. Come on. We can work this out. Let's go down to our suite and talk about it. I'll listen to your point of view, I promise."

Kat looks over to me and catches me watching her. She knows I'm listening. I wonder if it even matters. According to Tom, Kat's going to use our night together as a way to hurt Jake. I was just a pawn. She's probably waiting until I'm not around to tell him. *Thanks, Kat.* At least Jake won't break my face today.

"Okay. We can go back to our room and talk, but that doesn't mean I forgive you," Kat says as she rises off the couch. "As long as paparazzi aren't in the hall snapping shots on our way down."

"Little Fallston, why don't you make sure we get downstairs safely? Come use your security skills to walk us to our room," says Jake.

I read some stuff and watched some YouTube videos; I'm hardly an expert on security. Besides, this is *so* wrong. I shouldn't be involved in his plan to get her back. It goes against everything that is holy. But once she walks out that door, I may never see her again. I can't say no. I stand and walk toward the bedroom.

"Let me grab my key." After I slip my wallet into my back pocket, Kat comes through the door. I realize she's still wearing my T-shirt.

She smiles sweetly at me and says, "I forgot my purse," as she points to it on the bed. As she reaches for it, she adds, "Thank you for taking care of me last night. You're not like your brother at all." She picks up her tank and shirt, shoving them into her purse.

"Compliment, right?"

She nods and turns to the door. I watch her marvelous ass as I follow her out, knowing I will never forget how it looked in the pink lace panties.

"You got everything?" Jake asks, scowling impatiently.

The next time I see him, he may just punch me in the face. But I don't care, I wouldn't take last night back even if it means I end up with a broken jaw.

I walk them down to their suite, no paparazzi in sight. Kat smiles at me over her shoulder, softening my disgust for her leaving with him. I force the corners of my lips up and she politely mouths "thank you" before walking inside with him. She made a choice. I feel stupid and used as the door closes in front of me. I thought we made a connection last night and now she's going back to the cheating douchebag. I walk back to my room certain I will never understand the female species.

When I reach my room, the sandwiches I ordered earlier are just arriving. *Hell.* How long does it take to construct a couple of turkey clubs? It's ridiculous. It doesn't matter. I've lost my appetite.

I leave the food in favor of a long, punishing shower. I'm such an idiot. I need to wash Kat from my brain, just to think clearly. She's never going to be mine.

Chapter 6

Katya

Jake looks at me and smiles as if he just won a battle.

"Just because I'm willing to talk doesn't mean I've agreed to anything," I say, setting my purse down and sitting on the couch. He always gets his way. Not this time. As he plants his body next to mine, I realize I should have sat in the chair. His arm slides onto the back of the couch behind me, driving me forward. I don't want to be anywhere near him. He dominates me with his enormous mass. My mind keeps flashing back to the way Micah protected me from his brother this morning. I wish he were here now.

"Kitty Kat, you have to see the better choice here. I've run the scenarios over with my publicist, and the only rational decision is to go to the premiere together. It's PR 101—face the camera."

"That's not rational. The only option I see with any potential is us breaking up because . . . it's already happened. I'll look like a total flake if I just let this slide. We were exclusive. You talked about it in that interview three weeks ago. No one is going to believe the video is anything other than what it is."

"The press just wants the story that is going to bring the most hits. If you take away the controversy, then they don't have a story, and they stop bugging us. We need to show them Jake and Kat are still J-Kat." His hand grasps my chin, and he turns my head to meet his eyes.

I twist out of his hold and stand. My hands move to my hips, and my stance embodies bitch mode. "I know where those hands have been. You don't get to touch me. You made a big mistake. I was in love with you, and you screwed it up." I'm so pissed at him. I'm so pissed I can't even cry. "You think you can do anything you want and I'm just going to let it go? You're wrong."

"People make mistakes, babe. I'm only a man."

"You were supposed to be a better man, but you're as bad as my father."

"That's not fair, Kat." He huffs out a breath and looks down shaking his head.

"The difference is he cheated and left, while you came back. The pain is the same."

"I made a mistake."

"Was it the first time?"

"She set me up." He looks at me as if I'm irrational. "You know how it is. They're always trying to trip me up."

"So it's just the first time you got caught. I can't trust you, and that's why I can't let it go."

He huffs out another breath as his hand rubs across his furrowed brow. "I'll buy you a car. Come to the premiere with me, and I'll buy you a car. I'm surprised you've survived this long without a car. You know you need one. Whatever you want, I'll buy it. Just come to the premiere and put on a good show."

"I'm not a prostitute. You can't buy me." How ironic that he offers a car. I've never told him about the one my dad bought me for my eighteenth birthday. I always thought he would think I was stupid for not taking it. And he would.

He scratches the side of his brown buzz-cut hair and adds, "Kat, I need this. I've got that big film this summer with Fallston, and I can't afford to have my public approval dip. It will fuck up my contract." His shoulders slump, his big brown eyes pleading with me.

I let out a breath, but it doesn't mean I forgive him.

"What if I got you on the film?" he asks in a flat voice.

I shift my weight where I stand, trying not to show my excitement at his words, but I am sure he spots it. He knows I would kill for a role on one of his films.

"You're on break until September and filming will be done by then. It won't even mess with your little show's contract."

"I'd love to be in that film, but I'm not going to get back together with you." I'm torn as the words spill from my mouth. It's such a big decision and the last time I made a choice out of spite it hurt my brother. I don't know if standing up for my principles is what I should do. And the PR from this could ruin my career if I play it wrong—one wrong move could blackball me. I was hoping to get a movie under my belt before our relationship ran its course. And I could really use the money a movie contract would bring, especially a big one like Jake's. If I got a contract, maybe I could afford to get Cam the treatment he needs to get better.

Jake groans in frustration, pinching the bridge of his crooked nose between his fingers. "If you go to the premiere, I'll get you on the film. There's still a part they haven't filled. We can just act as if we are together. I know you need the money. You could buy yourself a car."

"Why should I trust you?"

"Ansley says, we need to stay together until the end of summer to defuse the video. Even if it's just an act, it has to be longer than just the one premiere night otherwise the fans will know the video is the reason we broke up."

"Your cheating is the reason for our breakup."

"We can have a contract written up. Everything will be spelled out. I'll talk to the director and tell him you're perfect for the role Mia Thompson backed out of. I'll beg if I have to. It's not just a bit role. Your character has almost as many lines as mine."

"Do you really think they'd give me a chance?"

"You'd be perfect for my love interest. He'll see our chemistry right away. I think I can make it happen."

If Jake hadn't cheated on me, I wouldn't hesitate. But working all summer with him now would be really hard. My only solace would be Cam recovering. I'd do anything to make that happen.

"I'll do it if we can agree on the contract."

"I'll talk to my lawyer and the casting director to get the ball rolling. I can't promise you the role, but I've been included in the casting decision for the part and we're running out of time to fill it. I think I can convince them."

If you've been included in the casting decisions, why are you only thinking of me for the role now? It's not worth bringing up, but it irks me.

"Does Ansley have a good cover story?" I sit on the edge of the couch, trying to map the plan in my head.

"She thinks it's best if we just ignore it and don't comment on the video. Because if we try to make it look illegitimate, the press will push even harder to prove its validity."

"I don't see how I can just let it go. That's not me. I need something legitimate to base my acting off of, to put on a good show."

His big brown eyes stare into mine. "It doesn't have to be acting. You could forgive me, and we could move on. My feelings for you haven't changed."

His eyes are what hooked me when we first met. I looked past the crooked nose and the overbuilt muscles into the dark pools of his eyes and felt a connection with him. But now? I don't know if I will ever trust him again. I don't know if I could ever be with him again.

"You should have told me it was an open relationship, instead of exclusive. I wouldn't have felt so committed and wouldn't be upset about you and the redhead. I'm not going to lie, I thought we had more."

"You'd be up for an open relationship? I didn't think that was an option."

"It wasn't. I just mean you're not the only one being propositioned." My mind jumps to Micah's face when he asked if he could kiss me. He was so adorably sexy. The way the fairies inside my stomach flutter when I think of him makes me think sex with Micah was incredible. I wish I remembered. I wonder how much he remembers. We both drank a lot. I don't regret waking up next to him. I don't regret Micah at all.

Two lines form at the bridge of Jake's nose as his lips flatten into a straight line. "Who's been propositioning you, Kat? Was it Fallston?"

For a second I wonder if he knows what happened last night. I blink a couple of times as I sort out his words. He means Tom, not Micah.

"No," I snap. "Just guys in general. Guys at work."

"Does Nordstrom still have a thing for you?" He pulls his body off the sofa and stands, hovering over me, waiting for my answer.

"Liam never had a thing for me. He's marrying Megan, remember? Besides, you don't have a right to be jealous. You are the one who cheated, not me."

"Is that what this is about? You want to get married?"

"Oh my God. You're so full of yourself." I stand up and push past him, walking into the bedroom. *He's such an ass. How could he even think that?* I collapse on the bed, the pounding in my head taking over my thoughts. I can't deal with him anymore.

Micah

As I duck into the limousine behind Tom and his assistant Izzy my gaze meets Kat's gorgeous light-colored eyes. I freeze, my heart skipping a beat.

So stunning.

Her shimmering blue dress clings to her every natural curve. She smiles, a dimple denting her cheek, and somehow it feels as if it's just for me. I'm so dazzled by her that I don't even process who's sitting next to her.

"Hi," I say with a nod like a socially inept middle-schooler. I am such a nerd.

Both Jake and his assistant glance at me as if I'm an infatuated fanboy. I wonder what Jake would say if he knew Kat slept in my bed last night. I'm sure it would wipe that look off his face.

Tom nudges me, breaking my eye contact with her. He leans in and whispers from the corner of his mouth, "Not yours," in a voice so soft I barely hear it. Then he starts sharing filming stories, telling us to watch for a particular scene he thought wasn't going to turn out, but editing made it work.

I'm grateful for the interference. The theater isn't far from the hotel, and when the car stops, I watch like a lost puppy as Kat and Jake step out onto the carpet together. He kisses her lips and then wraps an arm around her waist. Not more than twelve hours ago, she was kissing me and saying she never wanted to see him again.

Tonight is going to be torture.

After the door closes, Tom turns to me with a stern, brotherly face. "You better stop making eyes at Katya. Jake isn't stupid. I didn't tell him what you two did last night, but he's going to figure it out if you don't straighten out. We'll get our own tail tonight. Get a couple of hot bagels under you, and you'll forget all about last night. Let's make it two for each of us. In fact, that's your job tonight—to find some girls at the after-party to bring back to the hotel." He turns to Izzy. "We'll need your help in the morning to clear them out of the room. Micah doesn't have the balls you have to get the girls out quickly and quietly the next morning."

Here we go again. How many times do I have to tell him that fucking nameless girls isn't my thing? Now if Kat were coming home with me, it would be different. On top of it all, why does he have to share my business with Izzy? What if she says something to Jake's assistant?

Ten minutes later, the door to the limo opens again and we climb out onto the carpet-covered sidewalk. It's not the first event I've gone to as Tom's date. Tonight I'm his bodyguard too. I guess I always have been, in a way, but now I'm paid. I know he likes me to hang back unnoticed unless he brings attention to me. I look enough like Tom that people identify me as his brother right away. But sometimes my dark hair throws them off. Tom's is lighter, and right now he has blond tips. He's an inch taller at six feet, and now that I've been bulking up there's not much difference in our build.

Tom walks the carpet and meets up with all his costars. As he does the obligatory photos, I scan the carpet for Katya. I don't see her anywhere. I can't imagine Jake didn't take this opportunity to show the press that the video was irrelevant. Maybe they're inside already. I wonder what he said to change her mind. She seemed smarter than the typical girl who lets Mr. Hollywood walk all over her, but, I could be wrong.

After the movie, we meet up with Jake, Kat, and a couple other friends of Tom's in the lobby before we head back to our hotel for the studio party. Kat's talking to a blonde who seems to be attached to Liam Nordstrom. It must be the girl Kat mentioned this morning, Megan. The girl is showing Kat her ring finger, where a fat blue gem surrounded by diamonds glitters in the low lights. I overhear Jake congratulating Liam Nordstrom or rather consoling him. Liam looks happy despite the jackhole's razzing. Why is it always assumed the guy is being coerced into marriage?

"Did you make a little Nordstrom or something?" asks Jake, groping the girl's stomach.

She slaps his hand, and Liam says, "Not until she's done with her doctorate. I'm still trying to convince her to tie the knot before then, but she's so damn stubborn."

"You're not doing anything for the rest of us dudes when you put a ring on it. Now they all want rings. Kat mentioned it just today." Jake's booming voice blares through the room as he pulls her into his arms.

Is that what he promised her if she got back with him? Marriage?

And she bought it?

I turn around, unable to look at her. She seemed smarter than that. He'll never be faithful, and she knows it. I guess it doesn't matter in Hollywood. Tom's right. I need to have a distraction tonight. I look around the room, but no one stands out.

I glance back at the group, and Liam says, "Really?" With his brows raised and the elephant in the room reflecting in his eyes, he looks directly at Kat. Yet no one mentions the video.

Maybe she lied and like the tabloids said, she *is* sleeping with Liam. Maybe that's what Jake has over her. Now they're even. What-the-hell-ever. I can't deal with these people. It's going to be a long summer. They chatter on, still avoiding Jake's cheating. It's on the tip of everyone's tongue, but no one has the balls to put it out there.

When we get to the after-party, Tom dismisses me to start on my night's mission. I head for the bar. I'm not naturally an extrovert like Tom, but get a couple of drinks in me, and I loosen up. Tom's the doer, diving in and grabbing all he can get. I'm the thinker, the creative. I study the details and figure out how they all fit into the big picture and then determine my path. Last night, I let my imagination get away from me. Kat was never going to be mine. It must have been the alcohol.

There is a delicate balance with my drug of choice. Drink too much alcohol, and you're a falling-down idiot with everyone laughing at you. Don't drink enough and you're the only one at the party not laughing.

"What can I get for you?" asks the bartender as he siphons shots into two lowball glasses.

"A Hennessy and Coke, no ice, and a shot of Grey Goose." I've been to enough of these parties to know the drinks are all ice unless you take away that option. The vodka shot is my primer. The bartender fills my order quickly and I down the shot before turning away from the bar, leaving the glass where I found it. I take about five steps before three girls approach me. It never takes long for them to find me. After all, I'm the gatekeeper to my brother and girls are quick to figure it out.

"You're Tom Fallston's brother, right?" asks the leggy redhead. She reminds me of the redhead in the video with Gorboni. I watched it this afternoon because I was afraid Jake's publicist would find a way to get it taken down and I didn't want to miss it. It was pretty explicit.

"Yeah. I'm Micah."

"Can you introduce us to your brother?" They start introducing themselves. I should tell them not to bother because I won't remember their names anyway.

"Weren't you in that video with Jake Gorboni?" I say to the redhead, and all the girls giggle. They obviously know what I'm talking about.

She smiles, flipping her hair back with her long fingers. Her blush says I flattered her.

"I can't believe his girlfriend forgave him. I mean, that's her, right?" says the perky blonde looking over at Kat and Jake. "Hasn't she seen the video?"

I shrug. "Maybe one of you should tell her. She probably hasn't seen it yet. Otherwise, why would she be with him?" I say. I think it will hurt Jake more than Kat if these girls ask about the video. I take a sip of my whiskey-Coke and say, "You should ask Gorboni why he cheated." I point to the redhead. "He likes feisty redheads. Ones who call out his BS." A smile fills my face. Most of my life I've tried to distance myself from my brother, but I know my smile is the same as his and right now I'm capitalizing on that fact. They'll ask the question I can't—for Tom's movie-star smile.

"You're just messing with us. He'll never talk to us then," one says.

"He does like feisty redheads. We all saw it on the video."

The girls start talking about why they think Kat stayed with Jake. I have no insight to add.

"Maybe she's pregnant," says one and then they all start talking about how all the A-list actors or their significant others are getting knocked up. I almost tell them Kat's not pregnant because I would have noticed last night when I see Kat free herself from Jake's grasp and start to make her way toward the back hall.

"Come find me in a half hour, and I'll introduce you to my brother." I down the rest of my drink and set it on a passing tray as I make my way to intercept Kat. I wait for her outside the ladies' room, and the second she reappears, I clasp my fingers around her arm. She wrenches her arm out of my grasp as she turns to face me. She looks pissed, but the second her eyes meet mine she smiles and places her hand on my bicep.

"Micah." Her whole body relaxes when she says my name.

"Kat, what's going on?"

"I don't know. What's going on?" she says as if we're teens getting ready for a night's adventure. She has to know what I'm talking about.

"With you and Gorboni."

"Oh." Her body slumps as her smile fades. She takes a deep breath, looking down at her feet and shaking her head. "I had the best time with you last night. You're an incredible guy, but my life is really complicated right now, and I don't know how to explain what's happening with Jake. It's messed up. Maybe when I get it all figured out, I'll be able to tell you about it."

What does that mean? She was so open about herself last night. Now she's closed off. I'm just about to ask what has changed since last night when Gorboni lumbers around the corner. Kat's hand immediately drops from my arm as he approaches. He leans in and kisses her on the lips, claiming her right in front of me. He pulls back with a scowl when Kat's enthusiasm doesn't match his.

"What are you doing back here, babe?" he asks. "The party's out there."

"I was using the restroom, and then I ran into Micah," she answers, her hand motioning toward the door she exited.

Jake looks at me for the first time. "Oh yeah, Little Fallston. I hear you have a mission to find some ass for the evening. Tom was just talking about you losing your cherry tonight. You may as well get the summer started with a bang. Or two, right?"

What is he, in high school? My head shakes, and I look at Kat in disbelief. Her eyes are wide, as if she's afraid I'm going to mention last night and set him straight. She hasn't used it as a revenge tool, and neither will I. Even though I really want to put him in his place, I refuse to stoop to his level of assholism. I'm probably just being optimistic. I mean, she is obviously with him, not me, but the look on her face when he kissed her said she doesn't want to be with him.

"I'll catch you later," I say, heading toward the men's room. I'm not going to stick around for more abuse.

Chapter 8

Katya

I thought Micah was different. All his talk about knowing a girl before swapping fluids with her must have been a line. I felt as if we'd gotten to know each other before anything happened between us, but there was no way the girls hanging all over him last night were interested in talking. They made their intentions clear. At least the one on Micah's lap did. When she ran her fingers through his hair, I remembered the soft dark waves between mine. I remember how his kiss warmed my entire body. I wonder if the blonde's kiss felt as good to him as ours.

I don't have the right to be jealous. He thinks I got back together with Jake and I didn't tell him otherwise. It wouldn't have mattered anyway. I can't be with him. I need to stop thinking about him.

"Good morning, sunshine," says Jake, sauntering into the room. "You over it yet?"

"Over what, Jake?" I peel back the sheet covering me as I stand. "That you humiliated me in public? That you told the world I mean nothing to you?" I say, walking into the bathroom and closing the door behind me.

A few minutes later, as the water from the oversized showerhead drenches my face, the door opens.

"Get out, Jake," I say, exasperated. I can't believe he thinks I'm okay with him being in here.

"It's nothing I haven't seen before."

I glare at him but don't bother covering myself.

"I'm sorry. How many times do I have to say it?" Trying to appease me, he turns around until his back faces me. Now he's facing the mirror. It doesn't matter what direction he faces, he still gets a full view. "You don't believe that I'm sorry for what happened?"

"I believe you're sorry. What I don't believe is that if I take you back, it won't happen again."

"It's not going to happen again, Kitty Kat. I didn't think it was that big of a deal. She didn't mean anything to me."

"I want the part on the movie, and I want the contract. Get those worked out and we can talk. Until then, we don't have anything to discuss." I shut off the water, giving up on anything more than a rinse. I grab a towel, trying to ignore Jake's gaze in the mirror. As I towel off my hair and wrap the cloth around my chest I ask, "Do you have a car to take me home or should I call an Uber?"

His thumb and finger pinch the end of his crooked nose as his brow crinkles. I hope he meant what he said about the movie part.

"I'll drive you. I don't think you should take Uber anymore. You know how easy it is to abduct someone from one of those services. I don't understand why you don't buy a car. You make enough to buy one, Kat. It's ridiculous that you don't own a car. This is Los Angeles, for Christ's sake."

"I don't like driving. Besides, I don't have the money. I send everything I can to my mom and brother. I'd rather they keep the house than I have a car."

"If I get you the film role, you have to promise to buy one. Or I'm going to buy one for you."

He thinks he'd be doing me a favor, being sweet, but I know I would just resent him for it. It would be like paying me for letting him cheat. "If I have enough money to pay off my mom's bills and keep my brother getting the treatment he needs, I'll think about buying a car."

I should have expected the cheating. He's been with hundreds of women and never been committed to one before me. Why would I be special? I walk into the bedroom to get dressed, and Jake has enough sense to walk straight through to the suite's living room. After I throw on the cotton dress I planned to wear today, I take the flip-flops out of my suitcase and brush my hair into a high ponytail. Then I toss some makeup on before walking into the other room. Jake always gives me a hard time when I don't wear makeup. I'm sure he would say something if I didn't.

"How long before you're ready to leave?" I ask.

Jake pins me with his big brown eyes. How does he make *me* feel guilty? I'm not the one who cheated. The night with Micah doesn't count. Jake and I had already broken up by that point. I didn't cheat.

"Give me ten minutes." He rises and heads into the bedroom, not meeting my gaze.

He looks sad.

I refuse to feel guilty. He's such a manipulator.

Twenty minutes pass before he emerges with his bags. "I'm sure the paps are still around. I parked in the garage. Do you want to chance it? The public wants to see us together the day after."

"Let's just go," I say. I need to get home.

We make it to the car unnoticed. But as Jake pulls the car out of the parking garage, it's swarmed by paparazzi.

"They better not scratch my paint," he says as he eases the car onto the street. My guilt is gone. He did this. Yes, the paparazzi stalk him, and I'm used to them, but it's never been this bad. The attention usually gives Jake a high. Right now, he's cranky.

Cranky Jake sucks.

By the time we make it to my condo, it looks as if no one is following us. Jake usually walks me in. He thinks my neighborhood is seedy. No drug dealers are hanging out on the sidewalk or anything. Unless you count Pete, the guy who hangs out by the pool. I've heard you can get anything you want from him. My apartment's not in Calabasas or Bel Air, but I can afford it. He parks the car and shuts it off.

"I can make it to my place just fine without your help."

"I always walk you up. If I don't go in at least for a couple of minutes, the press will say we're having problems. We have to make this believable. I'm sure they're in the bushes as we speak. I'll come around and open your door."

He gets out and grabs my bags from the back before opening my door. As he walks me to my condo, I lean into him. I know he's right. They're here. They know where I live. It's easy enough for the paparazzi to guess where we were headed. The fans will want to see that we are really together. Jake will have to come inside for a little bit just to keep the ruse realistic.

Once inside he drops my bags in the bedroom and heads to the kitchen, helping himself to a glass of ice water. Then he takes out his phone and sits on the couch, ignoring me. If I know him at all, he's checking social media.

"If we're going to do this contract thing, we need an NDA. A non-disclosure agreement."

"I know what an NDA is, Jake."

"I don't want anyone knowing we're doing a contract relationship. Not even Megan can know. I want this between you and me only. Otherwise, how can I trust it won't be leaked to the press? We would both be humiliated. It's got to be just us."

"What am I supposed to tell Megan?"

"Tell her you forgave me because the bitch set me up. Tell her it wasn't what it looked like. I don't care what you tell her, but you can't tell her it's just a show."

"She'll never believe me."

"Sell it. You're an actor. Make her believe."

"You'll be celibate all summer, then? Because if another picture or video comes out, the contract is void. And I'm not having sex with you." There is no way he'll last for three months. I just hope he lasts until I get the part and we're too far into filming to replace me.

"I'll make it. Will you?" he asks, a smirk forming on his face. I can tell he's scheming. He's got a plan he's not sharing.

Chapter 9

Katya

Two weeks have passed since the premiere, and it feels like six months. So much happened in such a short time. I rocked the reading. We only did one scene, the one after Jake's character discovers my character has been cheating on him with his best friend. Part of me wondered if Jake had set that up so I would have to put myself in his real-life situation. Not that he cheated on me with Megan, but getting into my character's head did give me a better understanding of how he felt when he came crawling back to me. It couldn't have been easy. My character would have done anything to get him to take her back. She loved him. At the close of the scene, Jake's character leaves me in tears. It was a good scene—very complex, very emotional—and it allowed me to showcase my acting abilities.

When the scene ended, Jake came back in, and as he wiped the tears from my eyes, he whispered in my ear. "I'm sure you'll get it, Kitty Kat. You were amazing." Then he looked me in the eye and leaned in for a kiss. I melted into him, still wrapped in all the emotion of my character.

Now, three days later, I'm sitting in my tiny condo with my agent, Austin Tannen, going over the contract for the movie. They offered me the part. I still can't believe it. I never thought they'd give it to a no-name like me. Sure, Jake with his enormous fan base and Tom with his award-winning acting credibility are both in the movie, and that's enough firepower to bring in top numbers at the box office, but the role I got was slotted for Mia Thompson, and my star power pales next to hers. I look similar to her, and maybe that's why they're giving me a chance. We have roughly the same features—a well-developed chest, dark hair, average height. But while she's a seasoned A-lister with a large fan base, I'm considered fresh meat with an unknown big-screen draw.

"The lawyer looked it over, and he says we're a go. The studio wants it signed and returned today," says Austin, impatient with my hesitation as he fishes out the papers flagged with the "sign here" stickers from the bottom of the pile.

I start reading through it a second time. Contracts are way too confusing. I always feel as if I'm signing over my rights to my first born child. "Jake said to make sure I had a Most Favored Nation clause in my contract, or I could end up in a different hotel than him. I don't see where that is."

"Page nine, second paragraph," he says.

"I guess I missed it the first time." I read through that section and into the next. "What's this part about morality?" I flip to the next page, where it continues. "It seems vague."

"They make it vague on purpose. It basically says you can't do anything that the producers deem immoral during the time of the contract, which stretches from preproduction to two weeks after the film's release. If you do, you will be fined or let go, depending on where the movie is in production."

"Really? Like what? Do I have that in my *Impassioned* contract?"

"Yep." Austin smiles at me. "That's the clause Jake was worried about the video messing up on his contract. It can range from public sex to drunk driving, having an affair, murder or assaulting someone, all the way to using racial slurs. It's pretty much in every contract, and it's never concrete."

"It sounds as if it's a catch-all for problem actors."

"It is. Problems only occur when the actor isn't working out, or the role dictates a specific morality. I can't foresee a problem with this role. Your standard nude pictures or videos wouldn't even turn heads. I mean a video of donkey sex or anything involving children would get attention and, of course, racial slurs. Those are the ones that become problems."

"With good reason," I say.

"Did you see that part in the contract that mentions your relationship with Jake?"

I vaguely remember our relationship being mentioned. "My mind is jelly at this point. I thought I was seeing things."

"It basically says if you two break up and the breakup affects your ability to work together, production will side with the bigger name and your contract will be terminated with no liability on their side. You will be out of the film and Jake will get to keep his job. Even if he's the one causing the problems. You'll get paid scale for your time but that's it. Once filming starts and there's enough in the can, they will overlook most problems between the two of you. But if it's bad enough, they will replace *you,* and you will have to return the advance."

Micah's face pops into my head. I don't know why. Why am I thinking about him?

"I guess we won't break up, then," I say.

Austin clears his throat and scowls at me. Then he pulls out some more sheets from his briefcase and hands them to me. "You need to be honest with me, Katya. I'm on your side. Jake's lawyer sent these over this morning."

"Jake said it was just between us. No one else would be involved."

"Then he should have sent the papers to you, not me. You've fooled everyone so far, but do you think you can keep it up all summer?"

"I hope so," I say, fiddling with my wide silver ring as I bite my lip. I always bite my lip when I'm nervous. It's a total giveaway.

"Well, I'm glad you got something out of the deal, anyway. This movie's going to be your breakout role."

"You said that about *Impassioned.*"

"This is going to make you a household name, baby girl, and get you earning the big bucks."

"That would help," I say.

"I'm a little skeptical about this second contract, Katya. Not the NDA. It's cut and dried. But the wording in the other document looks like a prenuptial agreement. I'm not a lawyer, but it seems off to me. It basically states that if you have relations with anyone outside of your contract relationship, meaning anyone other than him, during the contract agreement, he has the right to terminate the contract. You have the same rights to terminate it. But . . . it's not in your best interest to do so. There is no real stipulation as to the consequences of the contract ending except as long as the contract exists he can't try to get you removed from the movie because of the NDA. If the contract is terminated the NDA still exists, but his commitment to keeping you on the film doesn't. I hope it doesn't get ugly between the two of you."

"Me too." And I thought my mind was jelly after reading the first contract. "I don't see what choice I have." I motion for Austin to hand me his pen, and I sign everything before I have time to change my mind.

Chapter 10

Micah

Tom has this thing about me waiting inside the building for him. He doesn't mind having to walk to the car as long as I'm there waiting when he gets out of his meetings. I think he feels if I'm not at his beck and call, I'm not earning my pay. But I have a cell phone—it's not as if he couldn't get ahold of me.

Four hours ago I watched Katya walk into the large conference room, Jake's arm wrapped around her waist. It's the first time I've seen her since the night of the premiere. I'm mad at her for getting back together with Gorboni. I don't know how else to express how I feel. I'm past the denial stage.

Anger.

The night of the premiere I let how I feel about her affect my actions, and I shouldn't have. Tom's idea of a distraction wasn't satisfying. If anything, it made me feel worse. Jealousy. Pure jealousy pushed me into a situation I regretted in the morning. I embarrassed myself in front of Kat and stooped to Gorboni's level.

Jake got her a lead role on the film opposite him. That's what my brother said. And I'm sure that's why she forgave his cheating. I don't have that kind of influence, and I have to accept that. It's Hollywood at its best. Even after the amazing day we spent together, I'm not even a blip on her radar.

I sit on the floor with my legs stretched halfway across the hallway in the warehouse-turned-office space. Not a chair in sight. It could be worse. I could be stuck in the room with Kat and Gorboni. At least I can draw on my e-tablet while I wait for Tom to emerge from the conference room. The sexy torso rendered on my screen looks an awful lot like the girl who danced for me in her pink lace panties weeks ago.

I started out drawing a kickass heroine like Johanna Redemption. Someone who would kick her cheating boyfriend's ass to the curb when she realized what a douche he was. I imagine the sharp heels of her tall, black boots could do a lot of damage to her overly muscular boyfriend. A plaid school-girl skirt barely covers her curvy, Johanna Redemption style ass. But when it came to her tits, Johanna's seemed too big. All I could envision were Kat's full, round, perfectly sized ones, her nipples pert. I drew from my memory, hoping to preserve the vision forever. And just in case one of the passersby gets too close, I've covered them with a skimpy pink lace bra and an open button-down man's shirt. Not her boyfriend's. I know that sounds childish, but it's my drawing, and I can do with it what I like. I can remove those layers from the drawing later if I want. It doesn't make me a pervert. I'm an artist.

I've just finished my character's long, dark hair and the hint of a dimple on her left cheek when the conference room door opens. It closes right away, and I don't bother looking up to see who it is. I figure it's someone headed for the restroom. People have been coming in and out for the last two hours. They've got to break for lunch soon.

Kat plops down next to me on the floor. I recognize the sweet, citrusy scent of her perfume immediately. Quickly closing the cover on my tablet, I turn to her.

"Are you breaking for lunch? I'm starving. Please say you're breaking for lunch."

"I think they're bringing lunch in at one. I'm done reading for the day, but I have to head over to costume." She bumps shoulders with me, and a smile spreads across her face. She seems happier when *he's* not with her.

"I guess I should have packed a lunch."

"Someone said the Korean barbeque truck out front is good. There was talk of just having Korean barbeque from the truck instead of ordering in," she says, standing up.

"Where's the truck?"

"Come on. I'll show you."

She holds out her hand to help me up, and I stuff my tablet and stylus into my backpack before I reach for her hand. I can't give up the opportunity to touch her. She actually helps pull me up. A dull ache radiates down my legs and back as I rise.

"I think my ass fell asleep."

She drops my hand and slaps me on the butt. "Does that tingle?"

"More than I'd like to admit." I smirk and look away, avoiding her gorgeous eyes. It tingles all the way down my dick.

She laughs. "What were you drawing?"

"Just doodling. Nothing important." I am never showing her that picture.

"Really? I thought it looked great. My butt was a bit too big, but I thought you captured my boobs almost perfectly." She steps in front of me and stops, a smug smile on her face. She cups her tits, pushing them up until they nearly spill out of her low-cut blouse. "But this one is actually bigger than this one. Did you capture that?" She raises one side. "Or is it this one that's bigger?" She raises the other side, looking to me to decide which is bigger.

"They're perfect either way." Does she know she's torturing me?

"Thanks." She smiles, drops her hands, and starts walking.

I rub my hands across my face, trying to wash away the guilt of cartooning her and being caught. I can't believe she saw it. I can't deny it was her—the pink lace bra, the barely there dimples.

"I would have thought you'd be drawing that blonde from the night of the premiere. You seemed into her." She bites her lip and turns to walk in front of me.

"Nope. Not into her," I say, watching her beautiful ass swing as she walks. "I was just trying to forget the girl from the night before. It was hard to let her walk back into her ex's arms."

She turns around, waiting for me to catch up to her. She's no longer chewing her lip, but she doesn't meet my eyes either. "Your drawing looks amazing. You'll have to show it to me later. I've never had anyone draw me before." She completely ignores my comment.

"Maybe you can pose for me sometime?" I don't know where my confidence comes from, but I feel as if we're friends at the very least.

"That would be fun," she says as she follows me out to the front entrance.

When we reach the truck, I expect her to turn and go back into the building, but she doesn't. Instead, she gets in line behind me curbside.

"Hungry?" I ask.

"Well, I'm missing the lunch at the reading, and my fitting is probably going to take me a couple of hours. I need to eat sometime."

We step up to the truck, and I take out my wallet. "What are you having? I'm buying."

No argument, she just smiles at me and places her order. Her order costs less than five dollars, but it still feels good to pay for her meal, almost as if we're on a date. We spend the next fifteen minutes laughing and chatting about the night in my hotel room. She seems relaxed and open as we balance against the building wall with our paper baskets in hand. And the best part is Gorboni isn't mentioned once.

By the time the weekend comes, I realize Kat is toying with me. What I thought was flirting when she weighed her tits in her hands obviously wasn't. She knows I'm attracted to her. But she and Gorboni are hot and heavy. At least that's what he says.

We're sitting near the pool at Jake's house in Calabasas. There are about ten of us around a wooden table on his lanai. It's our last weekend in LA before filming starts. They all have a couple of drinks in them. I didn't realize when I took this job that even on the weekends I would be the designated driver. And here I am, the only one at the table not laughing.

Finally, someone puts Jake on the spot and asks about the video.

"It wasn't what it looked like. The girl set me up, and the camera didn't show the real story," he says.

I watch Kat freeze in place as he continues.

"I just had to explain what really happened and get her a lead role on a blockbuster film, and all's forgiven." He pulls her onto his lap and goes in for a kiss as his hand creeps up her thigh.

"You are such an ass, Jake Gorboni." Kat pulls away. She looks pissed.

"It was easier than buying her a ring. You know how expensive those things are?"

She stands, shaking her head, and then storms into the house.

"She'll cool off. She loves me." He shrugs off her anger as if he didn't just humiliate her all over again. Even if it is true, he shouldn't tell everyone.

I wait a couple of minutes before heading inside to find her. "I've got to use the head," I say. It's not my first time here, but it's been a while. Just over a year, to be exact. It's a big house, but I sure as hell remember where the bathroom is. It's just an excuse anyway.

I find Kat in the bathroom on the first floor. How ironic.

I knock, three quick taps. I know it's her inside. I can hear her crying.

"Katya, may I come in?"

The door opens after a long minute. She doesn't say anything as I step inside, but once the door closes, she whispers my name. Her eyes are glassy with tears, and her mascara is smeared in the corners. I wrap my arms around her, and she practically collapses into me. I hold her wishing I could do something. Say something. I look up, searching for the right words, and that's when it hits me.

This room.

I can't be in this room.

It doesn't matter that I'm here with his girl, all I can focus on is what happened a year ago.

It shreds me just to be in here.

"I don't know what I'm doing, Micah." Kat's voice, though barely audible, pulls me back to her. "I'm trying to do the right thing, but I don't think I'm going to make it." *Trying to do the right thing?*

69

I close my eyes to forget where I am and concentrate on her words.

"Every sentence out of his mouth makes him look like the hero and makes me look like the villain. I'm not the one who cheated."

"Leave him. You don't have to stay with him. He doesn't deserve you."

"It's complicated. I have to stay." Her voice hitches as she sucks in a breath.

I pull her tighter, and I can feel each breath she takes expand against me. "I don't understand what's so complicated. Are you pregnant?"

Her body shudders and I think she's crying until I look at her face, a smile covering it. She's laughing. "You always think the worst of me."

I laugh, too, tucking a rogue strand of hair behind her ear. "Even if you were pregnant, you should just walk away. He's not good dad material. Why can't you leave him? Tell me what's going on."

"I can't because of the movie." The corners of her lips curl down again.

"What can I do to help you?"

"Hold me."

"I can do that." I rest my head against hers and hold her. She relaxes in my arms, and we stay that way for almost ten minutes. Her breathing levels out, and holding her doesn't feel awkward. It just feels real.

A loud rap on the door startles us, and we break apart instantly, as if what we were doing was wrong. I know what it looks like and I drag my hand through my hair, trying to focus on what to say.

"Don't do it, Micah. Not in his house. Not in this bathroom. I don't care what he did to you in the past. You have to let it go," Tom's voice bellows from the other side of the door.

"It's just Tom," I whisper, reality slowly seeping back in.

Kat grabs a tissue and starts dabbing the makeup off her eyes, while I open the door. I glare at my brother for his assumption.

"We were just talking. Your friend's an asshole."

"Yeah, well, he's going to be looking for his girlfriend in about two minutes, and you need to be as far away from her as you can get."

I look at Kat.

"He's right. You don't want to be around when he finds me," she says.

"Do you want me to drive you home?"

"No. Thanks for cheering me up." She pins a fake smile on her face and continues fixing her makeup.

I turn and walk away. I can't help her if she won't tell me what's going on.

Tom and I make it to the kitchen before Jake comes lumbering in.

"Have you seen Kat?"

Tom shakes his head and says, "Nope."

I hide my face in the refrigerator as I grab a water.

"I don't know what her problem is. She's so damn moody lately. Probably just needs a good fucking. We both do." He slides a hand down, cupping his crotch and takes off down the hall toward the bathroom.

"Trouble in paradise?" I ask Tom. Gorboni made it sound as if they were back to normal as a couple and now he admits she's not putting out for him. I don't know what to believe.

"They've never fought like this before. She *is not* happy about that video," says Tom in a hushed tone.

"Ya think?"

Chapter 11

Katya

I call Mom as I head to Jake's bedroom. Jake won't bug me if I'm on the phone. The strong scent of his cologne permeates my skin as I enter. He got big bucks to endorse the fragrance and acts as if it is his own product line. You would think I would be used to it by now. I prefer Micah's subtle cologne to this assault any day. I lay across the bottom of the bed, knowing the pillows are even more perfumed.

"Hi, sweetie. You are not going to believe what your father did now," she says.

I don't want to know. Dad is always doing the wrong thing.

"What did he do?"

"He told your brother that he would be better off in a state-run home and now Cameron refuses to go to school because he thinks I'm not going to pick him up. There's a kid at his school who lives in a home for disabled young adults, and he's afraid he's going to have to live there."

"Let me talk to him, Mom."

"Okay. Hold on just a second." I can tell she's walking to find him in the family room. I picture him sitting on the couch with all his comic books spread out in front of him on the glass coffee table. It makes me sad to think about because he used to have more of a life—friends, a job—but since the accident, he lives an abbreviated life with his comics the focus.

"Hey, Cam," I say when I hear him on the line.

"Kot-tee-yah," he says my name in three long syllables. It's music to my ears. I miss him so much.

"Did you get the comics I sent you?"

"Yep. I don't like Neptune's Surprise. It was not a good surprise. They blew up the entire city. No one lived."

Note to self: don't send any more war comics. The old Cam would have been able to predict that in the next volume the main characters would have found a way to survive just before the explosion.

"Did you like the other ones?"

"Uh-huh, *Kitten Bastet* is my favorite."

"I know it is, buddy. I need to tell you something, okay?"

He's quiet and I know he's listening at least as well as he can. He can't concentrate for long periods of time since the accident.

"You get to live with Mom at the house forever. You never have to go live in a home. Dad is wrong."

"Dad said Mom can't pay for the house after my birthday, and I'm going to have to go live in a home. I can't live with Darren, he ripped a page out of my *Lavender Yang* graphic novel."

Darren must be the kid at school who lives in a care home.

"Cam, you get to stay at the house forever. I got a job in a big film, and I'm going to pay off the house with the money I get. You and Mom will never have to move. Don't worry about what Dad says. He's a big liar."

"Are you going to be Kitten Bastet in the movie? She's *purr*ty."

"Did you just make a joke?" I ask. He's always proud when he makes a joke. It's rare since the accident. He was always a jokester before it. I remember one April Fool's Day when he was twelve, he hollowed out the insides of an Oreo cookie, leaving just an edge of cream filling, and filled the insides with toothpaste before putting it back in the package. Cam laughed and laughed and laughed when I unknowingly bit into it. I couldn't even get mad because I loved to hear him laugh. He doesn't laugh much anymore.

"That was a good one. She's *purr*ty because she's a cat."

"Yep." He hands the phone to Mom. I guess he's done talking to me. His attention span is limited, and he gets irritable when he can't concentrate. I didn't even get to tell him how much I miss him.

"Thanks, Katya. Your talks always make him feel better. He's been grumping around all morning, and now he's smiling."

"I should go, Mom. Jake's entertaining friends and I should get back to them. I just wanted you to know I'm supposed to have some advance money for the movie by now, but there was a delay because I was a last-minute hire. I should be able to transfer some into our joint account by next week."

"Oh, Kat. I don't know how to thank you. I really appreciate your help. The notices just keep piling up. I don't know what I would do without you." With all Cam's appointments, she hasn't been able to work full time since the accident. And she never knows what she's going to get from his moods. Some days she can go into the clinic, others she can't. It doesn't make for a good employment record. So far her manager has been accommodating, but Mom says she's getting more frustrated with her. Mom doesn't know how much longer she can keep her job.

"Just take care of Cam."

"Have fun at your party. I love you."

"Love you too, Mom." I end the call and glance up to see Jake standing in the doorway.

"You look really sexy on my bed. It's been too long."

I'm so not in the mood to have him sweet-talk me, and I'm sure my face says it all.

"You're so patient with your brother. He's lucky he has you." He lies down next to me on the bed, his feet hanging over the side as he turns to me. "You have a beautiful soul, Kitty Kat. Why can't you find it in you to give me another chance?"

This is the Jake I fell in love with—the one who talks to me as if I have value and mean something to him. But times change.

"Did you hear yourself earlier? You basically told everyone I forgave your cheating because you got me a role in your movie," I say, shaking my head.

"It's the truth. Everyone knows it. I just said it out loud. I don't think we'd be lying here right now if I hadn't gotten you on the film. It's how Hollywood works. There's nothing to be ashamed of."

"I did the contract for Cam, not you. My brother can't deal with change. If he and Mom have to move because Mom loses the house, he'll be destroyed. Yes, the movie will help my career, but I need the money to pay off their house. I auditioned for the part. It wasn't handed to me." Even as I try to rationalize the audition process, I know the only reason I got it was because of Jake.

"And I got you the role. You should be a little nicer to me. I want us to be back to the way we were before all this hatred started. We'll be on location together, seeing each other all the time. It just makes sense. We're stuck in this fucked-up contract until the end of summer. Why don't we use each other to take care of our needs? You're torturing me." His hand skims my hip and smooths over the sliver of bare skin on my stomach.

"Thank you for helping me, but it helped you too. And I don't work that way, Jake. You have to earn my trust," I say. "I can't just sleep with someone because it's convenient." And my inner bitch reminds me I want this summer to be really inconvenient for him.

"Come on." He stands up, and I follow him back to the patio.

Back outside, I sit next to Liam and rest my head on his shoulder. Megan smiles at me. There was a time when she was jealous of my relationship with him. But now she understands. She is the only one he wants, and Liam and I are just friends. He's been a good friend to me over the last year. He took me under his wing and taught me how to survive in this cruel Hollywood world. Maybe that's a little dramatic. I had the job on *Impassioned* before I moved here, so compared to most immigrants to this city I had a leg up. But it's still hard to move halfway across the continent to what feels like a foreign country where you know no one and then start a new job. To say LA is different from the Chicago suburb where I grew up is a complete understatement.

And now I consider Megan one of my closest friends. She thinks differently than me. We're opposites. Where she takes time to think about every move she makes and creates backup plans, I'm all in the second it feels right. I know just by the energy given off in a particular situation whether it is right or not. I can tell she has something to say about Jake's cheating and I'm waiting for her sarcastic, yet funny, comment, when I glance up and catch Micah staring at me. I immediately sit up, not knowing why. His blue eyes infiltrate me.

"Are you okay, Kat?" Liam asks. "This crap with the video has to suck."

"It will blow over soon. At least I hope it will," I say, my eyes still locked on Micah's.

I don't know what it is about him that intrigues me so much. He's definitely hot, muscles in all the right places and a panty-melting smile. Yet he's not like Jake. Is it that he's the opposite of Jake? Is it that he drew the sexiest picture I've ever seen and it was of me? Or is it that his bright blue eyes penetrate me from across the room as if he's inside me, and he's the only one to ever command that kind of reaction from me?

"How's your brother doing?" I ask Liam, trying to deflect the conversation from the video. His brother nearly overdosed on heroin last year and has been struggling to reclaim his life. Liam is the one who found him unconscious, and now he's doing everything he can to help his brother stay clean and sober. I look toward Liam, breaking the bond with Micah's eyes.

"He's got a job," says Megan. "In his dad's law firm."

"It's just for the summer. He starts school in the fall, but it's still a struggle," adds Liam.

"He's got a girlfriend too. They're so cute together, and she doesn't put up with any BS," says Megan. "I like her."

I love Megan. Every part of her is genuine. She doesn't try to be anyone but who she is. If we were alone, I would talk to her about what's going on with Jake. If I told Liam, he would definitely say something to Jake, and right now I can't risk him saying the wrong thing to him. School keeps Megan busy, though, and we haven't had a chance to really talk in a couple of months.

"I'm glad he's doing better." I glance back to Micah just as his eyes come back to me. A smile ghosts on his face and I chew the corner of my lip, fighting a return smile. Sex with him must have been so good that my body has this strong of a visceral reaction to him. Next time I'm not going to be drunk.

Oh my God. Where did that come from?

Next time?

I have to make it through the summer, and I'll be free to do what I want.

"Do you have any breaks from filming this summer?" asks Liam, pulling my attention back to our conversation.

"Why?"

"Meg and I are getting hitched. Just a small ceremony at the house. No family, just friends. We'll do a bigger ceremony with family later. She agreed to make it official, and I'm jumping on it."

"He's afraid I'll change my mind. No matter what you say, I'm not afraid of the industrial marriage complex. I just want to finish school." Megan rolls her eyes, but she's smiling.

"We want you there. Nak's officiating."

"Your roommate is a minister?"

"Sort of. He got a certificate online—just for us. He's into it though," says Liam.

I glance at the end of the table where his dark-haired roommate sits with his girlfriend, Leslie. It sounds like something he would do, just for kicks. I laugh at the thought of him being a minister, and then my gaze hits Micah's again. I quickly look at Megan. "When is it?"

"We're just starting to plan. We have to do it before school starts at the end of August. I won't have any time once school starts. Let us know when you're available, and we'll make it work," answers Megan. "It will only be a few people—only our closest friends.

"It won't be fancy—a barbeque probably. It's just something to mark the date," says Liam.

"You realize you're going to have two anniversaries to remember, right?" I ask.

He leans in and *oh so tenderly* kisses Megan's lips. When he pulls back, he says, "Twice as much anniversary sex. How can I lose?" He smiles, tickling the back of her neck with his fingers, before turning back to me. With her, he is nothing like his brooding character on our show. I love watching them. What they have is special. Jake and I never had that.

"I'll text you some dates that work once I have the filming schedule. Don't do it without me," I say.

"The anniversary sex?" Liam asks. "You know I don't do threesomes. But maybe I'd make an exception for you, Kat. It would be great payback for the video."

I hit his abs hard with the back of my fist, and Megan laughs. He's always a flirt.

"I hate you," I say and can't help but laugh too. It feels good to be joking around with friends after all the garbage Jake's put me through. I don't see as much of Liam and Megan when the show is on hiatus, and I miss spending time with them.

Jake and I avoid each other for the most part the rest of the night. It's all I can hope for. My eyes find Micah's often, and each time it happens a smile breaks on my face. But we don't get a chance to talk again. It thrills me that he'll be on location with us while we film. It also scares me to death because Jake still has all the power and I won't be able to kiss Micah again without getting fired.

Liam and Megan don't ask me how I got the role on the film. Jake's right. Everyone assumes he bought my forgiveness and there is nothing I can do about it. I tell them Jake and I are still working things out, and I think they buy it. I feel like such a fraud.

Micah

We've been in Toronto for several days and as we settle into our roles in this new work environment, I recognize working for my brother could be a ballbuster. Over the last couple of weeks, he groomed me to stick close and to be at his beck and call. Even though I have few responsibilities, he wants to know I'm always within shouting distance.

And I finally understand why.

He's not just a dictator. He's a tyrant. A tyrant everyone avoids. Even his PA, Izzy, avoids him during filming. Being his brother, he won't fire me, and I am more apt to laugh in his face at his rage than to quit. As I've become the buffer between him and every other person involved with this film, I realize I'm irreplaceable. He needs me. It gives me leverage.

I don't mind being Tom's mediator. He asks very little of me, pays me a ton, and everyone who uses me as a go-between treats me reasonably, afraid I will make them interact with Tom directly. His bark is worse than his bite. Besides, I know how to work my brother. I've been dealing with him my entire life. Like any other artist, he has certain triggers that set him off—like empty tequila bottles and unexpected, unexplained changes. I try to stay clear of those, and if I can, I just stop listening to him.

Selective hearing. It's a thing.

I'm also teaching Izzy some of my tricks, and she seems to appreciate the help.

Tom and Kat are filming a scene together today. It's a scene where Tom's character convinces Kat's character he's not the villain, and she should join him not only in business but in bed. It's the inciting incident for the plot and a big scene for Tom. A group of us stand just off set next to the clichéd personalized director's chairs for the stars as we wait for the filming to start. Tom hasn't said a word for five minutes, but the tilt of his eyes as they scour Kat's body says he's ready to devour her, both mentally and physically. My stomach twists at the thought of Tom and Kat together. I know it's just for the movie, but I think her being with Tom would gut me even more than her being with her douchebag boyfriend.

I'm not sure why Gorboni is here on set right now. I lean over the call sheets in Izzy's hand to check if Jake is in one of the upcoming scenes and Izzy changes the angle of the pages so I can read them better. I don't see his name.

"Why is Gorboni here?" I whisper, leaning toward Izzy's ear. I'm pretty sure he can't hear me because he's jabbering on about his muscles as he pushes off the floor in a one-handed push-up. Show-off.

Izzy shrugs as she looks over the sheets for herself. "Won't be here on Monday for sure."

"I don't want to be here on Monday. You and I can't be on the closed set, right?" Monday they're filming a bedroom scene between Kat's and Tom's characters and there is no way I want to witness that. "Tom says Kat's going to be topless." He mentioned this just last night.

Izzy flips through her pages and comes up with a list of people approved to be on the closed set. She points to her name and mine. "It's not as if you haven't seen it before. God knows I've seen Tom naked enough to draw diagrams."

"In most jobs that would be considered a hostile work environment," I whisper back with a chuckle.

"It's in my contract. As long as I want the job, I have to put up with kicking girls out of his bedroom, and that equals naked bodies."

I glance over at Kat, Gorboni at her feet doing push-ups. She looks like the sexiest lawyer I have ever seen. Her dark hair pulled up into a knot on the top of her head makes her eyes stand out with a sultry smokiness. Her skirt hits mid-thigh, and with those tall heels, her legs look a mile long. When my eyes meet Kat's, she raises her eyebrows, and one corner of her luscious lips turns up slightly. I can still picture her stripping for me the night we met. I can still taste her on my lips. I glance around hoping no one can read my mind. *Shit.* This is not good for my mental health. No wonder so many Hollywood people have breakdowns.

"Kat, climb on my back. I need more weight to make this worth my time," Gorboni bellows from the floor.

"I'm not climbing on your back. We're about to start." Kat smooths her skirt as if the thought of climbing onto Jake's back wrinkled it.

Gorboni puts his hand out to his PA, and Trey helps pull him into a standing position. "I need a smoothie. Can your loser brother drive Trey to get me a smoothie from that place by the hotel? They're albumin-based, not whey, and if I want to keep looking this good, I need the right ingredients." He directs his question to Tom, not me. *Screw him.*

Tom narrows his eyes at Jake. He hates it when people talk to him before a scene. "Why can't you go? You're not on set today."

"I want to watch Kat's scene. Besides, it'd take an hour if I ordered a car. Can't he be useful and take Trey? He's not doing anything."

"Whatever. Just come right back," Tom says with a huff, meeting my eyes.

"Make it fast, Little Fallston. I'm wasting away here."

Wasting away, my ass. I walk to the car with Trey without responding. I don't want to watch Tom and Kat working up to Monday's scene anyway. That's what today is supposed to be, a workup to Monday's love scene.

"I don't know why he tortures himself," says Trey when we reach the car. "We shouldn't even be on set today. But I don't think Jake trusts your brother or Kat. I wouldn't put it past them to be sleeping together."

"Gorboni's paranoid. That's not my brother's style." Me, on the other hand? I'd like to find a way to convince her to dump his ass. She deserves better than him.

"She was in his suite the morning after the video broke. Why was she there if she wasn't hooking up with him?"

"The paparazzi were in front of her hotel door. She was just trying to escape after your boss's fuckup. Besides, if she was, why not just tell Gorboni? It would be payback, right?" Maybe I should just tell Trey about that night and get my own revenge on Gorboni.

"Not if he gets her kicked off the movie for cheating on him."

"He'd get her kicked off the movie if she cheated? I thought the whole point of getting her on the movie was to make up for *his* cheating. Gorboni owes her."

"Yeah, but Jake still has the power to get her removed from the film. It's right in their movie contract; if they have irreconcilable differences, Kat's the one who will be replaced on the film."

"That's not fair. He can cheat on her all he wants, and she can't retaliate?"

"Them's the perks when you're the star. That's the way the world works."

"She needs to dump his ass."

"Jake's not a bad guy. He's straight up, you know. She knows what's at stake. That's why she shouldn't mess around with your brother."

"Like I said, she's not hooking up with my brother." I throw the car into park in front of the smoothie place. Trey rolls his eyes as he opens his door and jumps out. I don't care if he doesn't believe me. It is not my problem. Kat is not my problem.

I'm working on a couple of drawings for my portfolio for school at the dining table in the suite Tom and I share, trying to distinguish myself by throwing in a few pictures of the filming on location. The lights and cameras throw illumination on the foreground with the focal point on the actors on set. I do most of my work on my tablet digitally, but today my medium of choice is charcoal because I have the rest of the night off. Charcoal makes a mess, and I never work in it unless I have a decent chunk of time. I'm enjoying being able to add dimension with a swipe of my thumb. It's an utterly primal experience.

The knock on the door pulls my attention from my drawing. Tom sits on the couch with his back to the door, his noise-blocking headphones blaring symphony music. He's not moving. I'm sure he didn't even hear the knock.

Not expecting anyone, I flip the bar on the jamb to prevent access to any unwanted guests. Tom's fans slip through hotel security all the time, and I am well aware of the dangers of opening a door. Kat's smile through the crack hits me like a truck.

Damn, she's gorgeous.

I swiftly close the door and unlatch the bar before opening it again. She squeezes through the opening quickly and silently, her ample breasts skimming the door as she slides through. She kisses my cheek in a quick, undefined gesture. Her eyes widen when she sees Tom, and she covers her mouth with her hand as if she didn't expect my brother to be here. I point to my ears, indicating he can't hear because of his headphones, and she places her index finger to her lips in the universal sign to be quiet. I have no idea why she's here but will wait to ask if she doesn't want to disturb Tom. She follows me to my bedroom suite, closing the door behind us with a soft click.

She's practically on top of me. I wait for her to back away, but she doesn't. Her sweet, seductive lips linger inches away from me, and her citrus, floral scent fills my lungs. I'm not going to step away. My body enjoys her too much.

"He doesn't hear anything when he's meditating. It's his way of clearing his head and getting into his role. He practices his lines in his head. He's been doing it for years." She's too close. I can't pretend I haven't noticed any longer. "Why are you here?"

"I felt bad. The way Jake acted yesterday—it was wrong."

"I don't mind. It's part of my job."

"He was rude and what he said was inappropriate." She reaches up, combing her fingers through my hair. "I didn't mean for you to get caught up in any of this."

Her fingers continue curling and uncurling in my hair as she speaks, causing the most impure thoughts to take over my mind. Hollywood people touch a lot. *She doesn't mean anything by it.* But suddenly my lower brain is wide awake, and the only thing that matters is that she's touching me in my bedroom. She searches my eyes, and I wonder if she can see the lust in them.

"It's just for show. This game he's playing with me . . ."

A game? And I'm a pawn. It all makes sense now.

He thinks Kat and I slept together. Or she told him we slept together and now he's trying to show me I mean nothing, and he has her back.

Why is she touching me?

Jake is not the one in my bedroom, running fingers through my hair. He's not the one playing games. She is. She's the one causing my balls to ache from across the room. The one who makes me think she wants me when she clearly has a boyfriend she's not willing to ditch. My eyes move to the arm attached to the pulsating fingers.

"Sorry," she says, untangling her fingers from my hair. "I remember it being really soft and I wanted to know if my memory was all messed up because I was drunk. Your hair's really soft." She smiles that adorable smile, the ghost of a dimple brimming on each cheek. The one, she knows, wipes the mind of any man within a mile radius.

It's her superpower.

Mindwipe.

I can't even remember why I'm supposed to be mad at her. I can't remember anything. All my blood has been sent to my lower brain.

"You should go," I say.

"I want to stay."

She nibbles her lower lip, clinching my decision. I have to taste those lips again. My eyes burn into hers as I turn and back her up against the wall. I cage her in with one hand on either side of her head. As I lean in, she closes her eyes—those beautiful green-brimmed hazel eyes—and I know I made the right decision. I brush my lips against hers, sucking that very lip she nibbled into my mouth and nipping it. She exhales in a whimper and her lips part. I wait to dive in, savoring the gentle twists and turns of her lips under mine.

Both her hands shove into my hair, and she pulls me closer. Not waiting for me to cross the line, her tongue pushes into my mouth, igniting fire, and I slam our bodies to the wall. I wrap her legs around my hips, grinding against her. I can't help myself. She's pliable and wanton. And definitely not drunk. I can think of a million pleasures I want to give her. But I won't be satisfied until I sink balls deep. She's been teasing me for weeks. I want her so much.

I carry her to the bed, setting her on the fluffy white comforter. With her legs still latched behind my back, I hover over her unbuttoning her white blouse. Her face glows with desire. She wants this too.

Just as I reach the last button, there's a rap on the door, the hallway door, not my bedroom door.

You've got to be kidding me.

I slide my hand inside her blouse, ignoring the intruder, and inch my fingers under the lace of her bra. Oh God. I'm salivating at the thought of sucking on her tits again.

Another rap, only louder, breaks into my thoughts.

"Shit!"

They're going to disturb Tom, and then how do I explain Kat in my bedroom?

I pull my hand out and, cupping her breast with a gentle squeeze one last time, I kiss her again.

"I'll get rid of them and be right back. Don't move."

Her legs drop to the bed, and as I step back from her warmth, I almost say fuck it. I scan the room for something big enough to conceal my raging hard-on at the door. My tablet—it's big. Then I rush to stop the next knock.

When I open the door, I just about die. Who else could it be but Katya's boyfriend?

"Have you seen Kat? I saw her walk this way. I thought maybe she stopped to go over those script changes with Tom."

"Nope. I haven't seen her," I lie. "Tom's meditating." I open the door wide enough to prove my point and then start to close it before he gets any ideas about coming in. I should have used the security bar. "I'm working on something."

I lift my tablet just a little, and a smirk crawls onto Jake's face.

"Anime porn. Sorry to interrupt your rub-out." He points to the picture on my tablet—which has mysteriously turned on—and laughs. The drawing is one of Kat. One I haven't finished yet. One without clothes. At least he doesn't recognize her.

After he leaves, I close the door and check to make sure Tom is still meditating. He is. Then I head back to the bedroom determined to complete what we started.

Kat has other ideas though. Her buttoned shirt says it all.

"I thought I could do this." She stands, slipping on her flip-flops and shouldering her bag. "But I can't."

All my momentum is gone, stolen by the jackhole at the door. I empty my lungs with an exaggerated breath. *Unbelievable.* He's always taking from me. He doesn't deserve her. When does the good guy get a break?

"It's okay. I understand." *I do not understand.* What the fuck does she see in him?

"I really like that about you, Micah. You just go with it, and I need that right now." She wraps her arms around my waist, and I hug her back. "I'm going home for my brother's birthday this weekend. I don't want you to think I'm avoiding you. And I don't want it to get weird between us when I get back because I slipped up."

She slipped up? Just like her boyfriend did in the video. That's what he called the video—a slipup.

"Is Tom still meditating?" she asks.

"I think so."

"Do you think I could disturb him to run through the new lines?"

"Why the hell not?" I say, taking a step back. She wants easy-going. I can be flippant. I check on Tom and then lead her to the hallway door. I open and close it, for show, and then walk her toward Tom. I pick up his phone and mute his music, waiting for the explosion. I don't care. It can't be any worse than what happened to me in the bedroom. It's my new flippant attitude. I'm all about not letting anything bother me.

Chapter 13

Katya

I can't believe I just did that. What was I thinking letting it go that far? I almost hooked up with Micah. Again. I need to stay away from him, or I am never going to make it through filming.

Micah turns, leaving me alone with his brother. I've heard the horror stories about Tom and how moody he gets during filming. Even Jake warned me about Tom. Micah buffers his brother for everyone else. Why is he throwing me into the bear's den?

"You're the one who wanted to poke the bear," Micah says as if reading my mind, just before closing his bedroom door.

"What do you need, Kat, a third to make a hat trick?" asks Tom in a low growl. He pulls his headphones off and sets them on the table next to his phone, not even looking at me. He stands up and pours himself a tequila shot. "I'd offer you one, but I've seen how you get when you drink tequila."

I smile, fighting the words that want to burst from my lips. *What an ass.* "I guess I deserve the tequila crack." I tilt my head showing my confusion. "But I don't have a clue what you're implying about a hat trick. Just because I'm from Chicago doesn't mean I follow hockey. Three goals? I don't know what that means."

"Aren't you cute? It's simple . . ." He downs the shot he'd poured and sits back on the couch.

"Enlighten me."

"Jake's balls have been on ice since the video came out. He's been pretty vocal about how frigid you've been. And now I see why Jake's not getting any. You're screwing my brother. I thought maybe you were looking for a third score—a hat trick. Normally I wouldn't be opposed to it. But Jake being my best friend and Micah being my brother, it's a little weird for me, and I'll have to turn you down." He leans back, propping his feet on the coffee table. "If you're using Micah to get closer to me, just stop now. It's not going to work."

"Whoa. You really are as arrogant as everyone says. First of all, I am not sleeping with Micah. We had the one night. I was mad at Jake and I let it get out of control. That doesn't mean we're still hooking up."

"That's funny." He raises his eyebrows and forces a laugh. "Haha. You may want to invest in some black shirts. Micah's high school girlfriend did, and it made all the difference. Your tits and ass look as if the FBI's been dusting them for fingerprints."

I look down at my white blouse, shock spreading through my body, and I start laughing. It's a nervous laugh because the last thing I need is for Jake to find out about Micah. We've barely started filming. With his temper, he'd either force me back into a real relationship with him or get me off the film. I can't believe I didn't notice my blouse. Black smudges smear it all the way down, mapping out every touch of Micah's hands.

"Oh my God. I didn't even notice." I say, still laughing.

"You're not the first girl to get her clothes wrecked by my brother's dirty hands. He may act all nerdy, but he's no virgin. I've made sure of that. Your ass is even worse. Distinct handprints," he deadpans.

Why is he telling me that? I never thought Micah was a virgin. He knows what he's doing with a woman. I never doubted that. He has superpowers. I can still feel his hands on me. Without looking, I know precisely where he marked my ass. "I can't go back to my room like this. Jake will know for sure, and he can't know." I glance down at Tom on the couch. "Micah and I aren't hooking up. I like him and . . . yes, I let it get a little out of hand a few minutes ago, but I stopped. I'm trying to work it out with Jake. We have to make it work. Please don't tell Jake about this."

"Why don't you just have an open relationship like everyone else," he mutters with a scowl and an eye roll as he gets off the couch. He didn't say he wouldn't tell Jake, but he returns with a clean black T-shirt, and that's a good sign. He hands it to me and asks, "What did you want to talk to me about?"

"The line changes we got this morning, can we go over them?" I ask, pulling the clean shirt over my head. It falls to my thighs, covering all the smudges. I'm surprised he's not bitching me out. Everyone always says how horrid he is to work with, but maybe he can be like his brother when he wants to be.

He straightens the crumpled but familiar yellow papers from the coffee table in front of him. He's obviously been looking at the changes. I can see notes scribbled on the top page.

When it comes to acting, Tom is very professional. Very serious. I am used to Jake and his constant parade of jokes. But Tom? He gets down to business right away, and we run through the pages until the word changes flow effortlessly. It doesn't take long, only about thirty minutes. Then we spend another half hour practicing other lines together, and I'm starting to feel less intimidated by his arrogance. He's arrogant for a reason. He's that good. Working alone with him, I've gained a new respect for him that I don't think would have been possible with Jake around. He's not the tyrant everyone claims. He's just serious about his acting.

"Thanks for loaning me the shirt. I'll return it when I get it back from the laundry. Promise," I say as I rise to leave. I want to say goodbye to Micah, and my eyes dart to the closed door of his room.

Tom's brow furrows and his lips purse. "Stay away from my brother, Kat. He and Jake have a past. You teasing him and then flaunting your relationship with Jake isn't going to help him move on. He's a good guy. One of the few. He doesn't need that shit."

"What kind of past?" I ask. This is the first I've heard of it.

He hesitates for a moment and then says, "Just stay away from him. And stop using him to get back at Jake."

Is he serious? I never told Jake about my night with Micah.

"I'm not using him. I . . ." I don't know how to finish the sentence without breaching the NDA. He can't really think that I'm using his brother. I wonder if Micah believes that too. I leave the suite without saying goodbye to Micah, too stunned by Tom's words. What kind of past can Micah and Jake have? Micah doesn't even live in Los Angeles. I rack my brain trying to remember what Micah said about Jake the first day I met him.

He called him a douche. Which is true.

He said I was shallow for dating him.

But for the life of me, I don't remember him telling me about any bad blood between the two of them.

I'm almost to my room when Jake sneaks up on me. He leans in and kisses my neck. I pull back, scanning the hallway. "What are you doing? There's no one here. You can't kiss me when we're not in public."

"Kitty Kat," he says in a groan. "Come on already. How long are you going to punish me?" He backs off.

"Stop calling me that. I tolerated it when we were dating, but I won't now. And you're the one who wanted the contract."

"I didn't want the contract." He leans in and whispers, "I wanted you back." He starts walking backward in front of me as he continues. "And I always get what I want, Kat. We just need to spend more time together to remind you what you're missing. I thought we could go on a date tomorrow night. Anywhere you want to go."

"I can't. I'm leaving after I'm done shooting tomorrow. It's Cameron's birthday, and I promised my mom I would surprise him."

"Kitty Kat, it's our first break from filming," he whines. "We need some time together. You don't need to see your brother. He probably won't even remember you came."

"He'll remember. That's not how his brain works. Besides, we do enough appearances together. The paparazzi get plenty. We hang with the cast all the time."

"We need a quiet romantic date to show how serious we are," he says, switching tactics to business as we reach my door. He must realize he's not going to win back my heart.

"No. They don't know what we do behind closed doors. You act as if we live together. We don't." I tap the keycard against the pad and open the door. "They assume our public life continues when we go home." Of course Jake follows me in.

"Jake, I need to shower and pack. I have an early call time tomorrow." I assume he'll take the hint that I want him to leave. But no, not Jake. He lies on my bed and clicks on the TV, honing in on ESPN. I don't hate sports, I just hate watching a game when I have nothing invested in the team. If it were the Bears, the Bulls, or the Cubbies, I'd be all in. I'd even watch the Packers, but why bother if you know nothing about the team? "Can't you watch this in your room?" I ask.

He looks up from the TV and scans the room. "Your room sucks, Kat. I didn't realize they gave you such a crappy room. This is substandard."

I look around the room. It's a standard suite with a king-sized bed, a sitting area, a fridge, and a microwave. Sure, it's not like Tom or Jake's suites with a full dining area and bar, but I'm not them. Compared to the hotels I stayed in when I was growing up, it's enormous.

"You got the 'Most Favored Nation' in your contract, right? You don't even have a separate bedroom. You should complain." He looks at me as if waiting for me to agree, his brow crinkling. "What are you wearing?"

Just another man's T-shirt to cover his brother's dirty handprints marking every glorious place he touched me. I look down with a shrug. "I have shorts on," I clarify because they aren't visible. "It's just an oversized tee." I grab my change of clothes and open the bathroom door. "I'm taking a shower. Feel free to leave my substandard room without saying goodbye." I close the door behind me, making sure to set the lock before I start the shower.

Chapter 14

Micah

Just my luck. Kat left town to visit her brother, and I'm stuck babysitting her boyfriend, douchebag extraordinaire.

Tom, Jake, some others associated with the film and I are all pigging out at the happy hour buffet downstairs in the hotel bar. It's Friday night, and I think everyone is looking to let loose after the hectic week of filming. Tom and Jake are easily the biggest names, though Pierce Gregory, who plays Tom's boss in the movie, is also here. I don't get geeked out by actors. They usually have more flaws than the average Joe. But if I did, it would be for Pierce Gregory—the quintessential action hero of his time and avid comic book enthusiast. I loved him in *The Houston Chronicles*. Pierce and I are elbows deep in a *Walking Dead* discussion when Jake announces that the party is moving upstairs to his suite.

I'm pissed.

Then Tom interrupts our discussion to inform me that I need to make sure the three girls at the bar in "tight dresses" with "pushed-up tits" find their way to Jake's suite.

"I am far too old for that shit. We'll talk more another time," Pierce says eloquently, or at least it sounds eloquent in his British accent. He claps me on the shoulder before bidding goodbye to the others at the table.

My moment is gone. But I don't have time to moan about it. If I wait too long and the big names disappear, the girls will assume I'm some creeper looking to lure them up to my room. The direct approach is best in these situations.

I smile Tom's smile and ask, "My brother, Tom Fallston . . ." pointing to Tom just to make it clear in case they're stupid, ". . . was wondering if you ladies would join us as we move the party upstairs." Whoa, that sounded sleazy. My new job title: hookup pimp.

Without a single question, squeal, or even chatter among themselves, the girls down their drinks and follow me to the elevator like they expected the invite. Inside the elevator, I get down to business right away.

"There's just one minor business issue we need to iron out before I let you ladies into the party," I say, reaching for my phone. The women look as if they're prepared to drop to their knees and blow me one at a time or all together, right here in the elevator, if it means I will let them into the party. I pull the NDA up on my phone and wait as each one signs a copy with a finger before tapping my keycard to the pad to get us to the right floor. "You'll have to surrender your phones as well. The phones will be in a container by the door, and you can leave at any time, but no pictures will be allowed."

They each hand me their phones without any qualms.

"We're going to Tom Fallston's room?" asks one of the two dark-haired beauties. Her black hair and light-colored eyes remind me of a harsher version of Kat.

"Jake Gorboni's room, but my brother will be there," I say.

"Is Jake Gorboni's girlfriend going to be there?" asks the leggy girl with dark auburn hair. "I didn't see her at the bar."

"Nope. She's out of the picture tonight. Jake's free to party," I say, holding back a smile. *I'm going to hell.* If I weren't positive Kat deserved better than him, I wouldn't bother promoting his dick. Now I'll just let nature take its course.

"Right this way," I say, leading the girls out of the elevator and down the hall.

It doesn't take long for the girls to find Tom and Jake. Tom glances my way and I nod indicating the NDAs were signed. I stay as far away as possible, not wanting to be a part of their mating ritual. Ever since I kissed Kat yesterday, I can't picture myself with another girl—at least until I get her figured out. She fits so perfectly in my arms. So perfectly against me.

But she wants him.

The jackhole who's going to cheat on her again.

I pour myself a rum and Coke and wait.

I wonder if he'll sneak off with one of them—probably the one with auburn hair—and take her in the bathroom. Is that his fetish, bathroom sex?

Why do douchebags always get what they want?

I insert myself into the conversation next to me, trying to forget the past and ignore the present. The discussion is about politics, my least favorite subject in the world, but because of the current political climate, it seems to be in my face constantly. I even find myself cartooning about it. No opposing viewpoints in this group of Hollywood-under-thirty-year-olds—big surprise. Two hours pass in a heated dialogue about all the world's problems and how the current politics makes them worse, not better. At least we're not talking Hollywood. For that I'm thankful.

There are only about twenty people in the suite. Not everyone involved with the film gets to stay in the expensive hotel with the A-listers, and most of the people over thirty didn't follow us upstairs. Everyone knows Tom and Jake didn't invite the group up to sip tea. Music plays from a Bluetooth speaker and laughter spills in waves among the small groups. Drugs tumble onto one of the tables in a share-the-wealth exchange, like kids swapping little clear bags of M&Ms for Skittles. People start pairing off. They always get really handsey at these parties. No pictures. No posts. The unspoken rule insinuated by the phone basket at the front door allows the partiers a chance to unwind.

A tap on my shoulder makes me turn my head to the spare of the three girls I invited up.

"Your brother sent me over," says the harsher version of Kat in a whisper as her fingers clasp my arm. She clings to me as if we're together, or at least there's an expectation we will be. I look up to scowl at my brother and catch his backside heading for the door, the other dark-haired girl digging through the phone basket. Jake and the redhead are gone, just as I knew they would be. I don't see Trey either. I shake my head, wondering if they will be back or if I'm newly elected to stay until the party shuts down.

"I'm Patrice," she says, looking up at me with her fake lashes flapping. *Nope. Doesn't resemble Kat at all.* She's all angular while Kat is soft and beautiful.

"Micah," I say. I smile but then ignore her and join back into the conversation as it morphs into memes, subreddit topics and people I don't know.

When Patrice finally figures out I'm ignoring her, she starts getting more aggressive. She stretches up on her tiptoes as she rubs her thigh against mine and whispers, "Aren't we going to your room?"

An hour later, after I've cleared out Gorboni's suite, I finally settle into my sheets alone. I'd pawned eyelash queen off on some PA. She didn't seem too upset about it. But I'm pretty sure she thinks I'm gay. It doesn't matter because I will never see her again.

My head hits the pillow and just as my eyes close, moaning and grunting from the suite next door, Jake's suite, permeates the quiet of my room.

Damn it.

I'm never going to be able to sleep listening to Jake fucking. Even though I knew Jake brought the girl to his bed, hearing them makes it more real. I should record it and play it for Kat, to show her what a douche Jake is. But I don't want her to get hurt. I saw the night we met just how much Gorboni's cheating hurt her. The thought of her heart breaking ties me in knots. I put on my headphones, cranking up the music, and take out my phone.

I check the comments on one of my sites to bring some normalcy back into my world. With me working for Tom this summer, I've been able to get a couple of pictures posted a week. I started doing a new comic series, and it's gained a decent following. I've picked up a thousand followers just in the last several weeks. Correction: eighteen hundred as of today. Wow. The most recent comment reads, "Hot Damn! This is your best one yet, Mic." I know it's my roommate, Dawson Davis. First, "hot damn" is his catchphrase and second, I write under the penname Notorious. No one knows it's me posting except my friends. Third, his goofy cartooned long horn avatar is staring back at me from next to the comment.

I shoot him a text.

Micah: Thanks for the comment. Looks as if this one is catching.

Dawson: Hot Damn. When did you pick up all the followers?

Micah: Last couple of weeks. Crazy, huh? How's everyone back home?

Dawson: Ran into Mara at Backster's a week ago. She asked about you. Sounded sincere.

Micah: Was she with a guy?

Dawson: Nope. Said she missed you. What kind of weird-ass crap is that after what she did? Sorry, shouldn't have brought it up.

Micah: No worries. Had a long Walking Dead *chat tonight with Pierce Gregory.*

Dawson: You're shitting me.

Micah: No lie. Best conversation ever. Greatest respect. It only ended because my brother and Gorboni invited everyone upstairs for a private party and I had to be the gatekeeper.

Dawson: Dude, you're livin' the life.

Micah: Yep. Livin' the life.

When we sign off, I pull out my tablet and start to doodle. By the time I peel off my headphones, I've encapsulated the evening in a series of panels. I don't know why. I guess I needed to empty it from my brain and toss it away. Drawing it out helps me do that. Maybe it'll be a new series for my site. While Kat's away, the douchemouse will play. And that's how I drew Jake, as a mouse.

Jake and the redhead have to be done by now. I don't hear any moaning. It occurs to me that I haven't heard any moans until tonight. I've heard his TV and music. But tonight is the first sex-fest.

Interesting.

Chapter 15

Katya

The second I walk into my childhood home, I almost turn around and walk back out. Mom is screaming at the top of her lungs into her phone. She waves at me when I come in, but continues her rant.

"You just don't get it, Lance. How can your son get better when I can't even afford to pay for the drugs the doctor ordered? Praying he'll get better isn't working. We need to take action."

I walk down the stairs to the family room where I am sure Cam has set up camp. Sure enough, I find him staring into space, not even acknowledging me until I sit next to him on the worn L-shaped couch.

"Hey, Cam. I flew all the way from Canada to wish you a happy birthday, don't I at least get a hug?"

He still doesn't look up, but he slides his hand into mine like he used to do when we were little and Mom and Dad argued. He was seven and I was ten at the peak of the drama. Whenever they argued, we'd sit on the floor of my closet and I'd hold his hand until he stopped crying or he fell asleep. It seemed like the arguments always happened in the middle of the night. Cam's hand is so much bigger now. It's bigger than mine, and I have to stretch to cover it. It's warm though. It's always warm. He hasn't held my hand since he was a little kid. The last time he must have been ten. I wonder if he's getting memories back or if it's a subconscious act. Either way, I like that my touch brings him comfort.

"Why do they fight?" he asks.

"They shouldn't. Not on your birthday." I squeeze his hand. There are hundreds of reasons they fight. Dad's a narcissist motivated by showing his friends what a great guy he is while simultaneously being the opposite of great. Mom's a struggling single parent who can't move forward in life because her focus on bitterness prevents her from ever finding happiness again. I could go on and on, but I can't say any of the reasons out loud, not to Cam. Not on his birthday. Mom probably called Dad to bitch him out for forgetting Cam's birthday, and instead of making his day better, she made it uncomfortable.

"Which one of these is your favorite?" I ask to distract him, pointing to the comics strewn across the coffee table.

"They always fight about me."

"Do you remember how they used to fight when we were little? How we used to sit in my closet where all my stuffed animals lived? Do you remember that?" His memory has enormous holes. He remembers everything after he got out of the hospital, but he doesn't remember much before his accident, just a few flickers here and there.

"The platypus was blue."

"You remember my stuffed platypus?" I can't believe he remembers. Tears fill my eyes. I don't remember when I got rid of the stuffed animals in my closet, but I know it was before his accident. Maybe all the treatments are working, and I'll get my brother back. I wish Mom would get off the phone so I could ask her if he's been looking at pictures from before the accident. "Do you remember anything else?"

"Dad used to live here. I remember when he left. Now he lives with Amanda." He says it as if it is news to me. He doesn't always get that he's the one who can't remember. His mind doesn't work the way it used to.

"Do you remember the night Dad left?"

He looks down at the floor. "He pushed Mom down, and she cried. She cried and cried."

Woah. I forgot about that. Cam remembered something I forgot. Dad was leaving and Mom demanded answers about where he was going. He wasn't going to Amanda's—he didn't know her then—he was going to Naomi Mansfield's, the other woman he'd knocked up. Mom blocked the door, and he pushed her out of the way. Their fights had never gotten physical before that day, but seeing it must have made an impression on Cam. "Is the night Dad left a new memory?"

He nods.

"Tell me more about what you remember." I need him to remember. "Please, Cam." I would do anything if he would just get his memory back and be normal again. He can't be like this for the rest of his life. He can't.

Just then, Mom pops her head into the room. "Are you ready to go?"

"Did you know Cam remembers the stuffed blue platypus from when we used to hide in my closet when you and Dad fought?" I'm not bringing up the fact that he remembered Dad pushing her down. It would just ruin the day more. I'll tell her later.

Her wide eyes lock on mine, and she opens her mouth to speak but stops. She looks over at Cam and then back at me. "Really?"

"He brought it up without any prompting." I squeeze his hand, and he smiles.

Her face lights with emotion. "Oh, Cam. That's fantastic. What else do you remember?"

"Did you know Dad used to live here?"

Mom smiles and says, "Yeah. I knew that." She turns toward me. "A breakthrough in memory could move him up on the eligibility list for the study. Most of the studies only take freshly injured patients—within the first eighteen hours—but a study in Boston is looking for older injuries with Cam's problems with memory loss, and if he has breakthrough memories, they may take him." Mom's tried to get him into pharmaceutical studies before without success. Most research trials provide free medical care, therapy, and other benefits she struggles to pay for. Even if Cam ended up getting a placebo instead of the experimental drug, the benefits of free health care alone are huge and would lighten Mom's burden, but few considered Cam a viable candidate because up until now he's shown no promise of improving. This could be the break Cam needs to recover.

"Mom, that's great. What are the deadlines for the study?"

"I'm not sure. I'll get it all figured out and let you know. It's a longer study, and I think it's all in-house, meaning we won't be able to afford it. Not with your father calling me on Cam's birthday to ask when I'm going to get the house on the market. You would think he could let Cam enjoy his birthday before uprooting our lives."

"Don't worry, Mom. I'll figure out a way to make the study happen if you get Cam in. And if you get the house appraised, I'll figure out how to get Dad half the value. I promise."

I'm excited Cam may have a second chance. I'll put all the expenses on my credit card and pay it off over ten years if I have to. I want Cam to experience all the joys of life. I want him to be happy, to have a girlfriend, a wife, and children. He should get all his memories back. He deserves all the things I took away from him. I can't live with myself if he doesn't get his life back.

"I'm hungry. Can we go?" Cam stands and straightens the piles of comics on the table as he nibbles his lip. He's just like me when he gets nervous. Lip chewing must be in our genes. I know the drug trial talk is scary for him. He doesn't adapt to change easily, but he once told me he thought participating in a study was his only chance at recovery. I'm so grateful the filming schedule allowed me to be here. I miss spending time with him and Mom.

At the restaurant, I eat my dry salad and take a bite of the rubbery grilled chicken I ordered. Mom thinks I'm starving myself. I'm not. That would just shut down my metabolism. I usually eat more, but I didn't work out today, and next week I'm going to be practically naked on set. If I weren't traveling, I'd be doing a cleanse this weekend. I should be doing a cleanse, not eating at a burger place.

We head home for cake and ice cream, and I try not to eat, but do. *Damn it.*

It's Saturday afternoon when Megan's name flashes across the top of my phone and a sense of foreboding washes over me. It's not that I don't want to talk to her. I do. But she's going to ask about what happened with Jake, and I don't want to tell her. I can't tell her.

> Megan: *Heard you were home for the weekend. I'm in Chicago. I met my brother and his girlfriend, but they had an emergency, and my flight home doesn't leave until tomorrow. Do you have a couple of hours free?*
>
> Kat: *Would you mind coming to my mom's? Not in the mood to go out.*
>
> Megan: *Sounds great.*

Even though this weekend was supposed to be dedicated to Cam and Mom, I need to talk to someone about what's going on with my love life, and Megan's my closest confidant right now. All my friends from high school are away at college, wrapped in their university worlds. They wouldn't understand my problems. Megan will. She's waist deep in the complications of Hollywood. Not only is she engaged to my *Impassioned* costar Liam Nordstrom, whose star power is building, but she's best buds with Sarah Williams, wife of mega–movie star Jonathan Williams. I text her my address, and she's at my door within an hour.

Megan gives the best hugs. She stands several inches taller than me in her heels. She's usually only a couple of inches taller, but not when she's in heels and I'm barefoot. Megan flips her short blonde hair out of her face as her blue eyes meet mine. I've missed her.

"It's so good to see you," I say.

"Thought I might need to get you drunk to extract the information I promised Liam," she says, handing me a bottle of cinnamon-flavored whiskey. It's my favorite, and we've gotten drunk together on it several times over the last year.

"You know all my weaknesses. But I don't know what kind of information you're looking for. I'm not hiding anything."

"Uh-huh," she says as if she doesn't believe me. She always knows when I'm not forthcoming. "Your house is gorgeous, by the way."

"Wait until you see the inside before you make that sort of statement," I say, knowing the outside doesn't reflect the worn and outdated décor on the inside.

I usher her into the living room. "You're going to have to meet my mom and brother before we crack this open." I set the bottle on the coffee table and lead her into the kitchen. Mom stands, resting her elbows on the counter, worrying over a stack of bills, and turns to us as we enter. She sets the papers on the counter and smiles. I planned to sit down with her to go over the bills before Megan texted. Mom's probably mad I made plans, but we'll have most of tomorrow to spend together.

I introduce Megan, and within a minute Cam walks in. I introduce him as well. No matter what Mom says, mentally he is still an eighteen-year-old male and makes an effort to meet my female friends.

"I brought you a present for your birthday," Megan says, pulling a graphic novel from her bag. "I hope it's a good one. I don't know anything about comic books." She hands him the book, and his face lights up.

"I don't have this one. But it's not a comic book," says Cam. He walks to the dining room table and sits down as he studies the book.

"It's a graphic novel," I say to Megan. "And he likes it. Thanks. Social niceties are hit or miss with him since the accident. Sorry. He doesn't always remember to say thank you."

Mom gushes about the fact that Megan brought him a gift and we talk with her for several minutes before making our way back into the living room with lowball glasses filled with ice.

"Don't you think it's time you tell me what is going on with Jake?" she asks the second we sit on the couch.

I glance at Cam, hoping he isn't paying attention to our conversation. "I don't know what you're talking about. Jake and I are trying to work out our problems. He's trying not to cheat, and I'm trying to forgive his inability not to cheat."

She laughs and hands me a glass. "Liam and I are wondering why. Why are you trying to stick it out?"

"Because I need the movie. I need the money the movie gives me to help my mom. She's not bringing in the money she needs. My dad is no longer obligated to support Cam, and Mom can only work a few hours a week with all my brother's therapy. If I don't play nice with Jake, he'll get me kicked off the film. He's told me that much."

"Why does he care? Not to be crass or anything, but he could date anyone."

"The video screwed up his all-American superhero image and the only way to make it go away is for us to be together. If he were Tom or Liam the video would have been accepted by his fans. It would fit right in with his persona, but Jake always plays the good guy, not the villain. That's what he portrays. It's his brand, and that's what the public wants."

"And you're the one paying for his mistake."

"I got the movie deal."

"Are you letting him back in the Kitty Kat playland?"

"I'm trying to forgive him enough to get to that point."

"But?"

"But nothing." As I stare her down, the corner of my lip curls up, betraying me.

"But there's a problem?"

I let out an exhausted breath. She always sees through me. "I met this other guy, and I think I'm falling for him. He's adorable, and he gets my quirky comic book side. But I can't do anything about this crush I have on him because Jake wants us to get back together."

"And Jake always gets what he wants?"

"Right," I admit. "He wouldn't be happy if he found out I slept with Micah."

"What? Tom's brother Micah?"

"Yeah. It just happened the one time. The night I saw the video. But now every time I see him my body goes into dry hump mode. I can't help it." I look around the room to make sure Mom isn't lurking. "He must have been terrific in bed because my body reacts to him like I'm a starving kitten and he's the only milk-filled teat in the world."

"Wow. That's a visual that will need some scrubbing to erase. But wait . . . you don't know if it was good or not?"

"We were doing shots, and I remember wanting to sleep with him. I just don't remember the actual act. We were naked in bed the next morning. Tom found us."

"Tom knows? And he didn't tell Jake?"

"I think it's because Micah's his brother. Blood before buds and all."

"But . . . you're sure you didn't have to fake it with Micah?"

"You were to never speak of that again. I told you about the problem I had with Jake in confidence." I glare at her and down the shot I've been sipping. The burn feels good. I can't believe she brought that up.

"But . . . you didn't have to, right?"

"I didn't. I kissed him again on Thursday, and I almost went off with just his tongue in my mouth. I went to his room to meet with his brother to go over lines, but when I got there Tom was meditating and Micah looked so cute that I forgot why I was there. He has this hold on me I can't explain. Within minutes his tongue was in my mouth and all I could think about was having sex with him. I definitely didn't have to fake it."

"But you didn't have sex with him again?" She tilts her head questioningly, a slight smirk on her face.

"Jake came to the suite door, and when Micah went to answer it, the fog cleared and luckily my brain turned back on."

"Did Jake catch you?"

"No, Micah told him I wasn't there, and he left. I don't know what I'm supposed to do. Micah's on set with us all summer, and I crave him. Then there's Jake, who I have to keep happy or I'll lose my job."

"Micah could be your dirty little secret until you can break it off with Jake. Do you think he would agree to that?" Megan refills both our glasses, then sits back and crosses her long gorgeous legs, drink in hand.

"Doubt it. He prefers monogamy to one-night stands. I can't imagine he would agree to be my side piece."

"Have you asked? Send him a text right now."

"I don't have his number."

"So you're just going to let the opportunity slide with Micah and go back to Jake? Chemistry is important, Kat. You can't ignore it."

"I can't break up with Jake. I need the money. This movie contract won't even be enough. My dad wants Mom to sell the house because legally he gets half the value now that Cam is eighteen. But it would kill Cam to have to move, and he's just starting to get some of his recall back. If he moves all those triggers for memories will be gone. This movie won't even cover the medical bills, let alone the house. I'm just going to have to resign myself to the fact that I won't get any more Micah. This kitten is going to have to starve for the greater good. Jake can help my career, and that's what's going to help my brother."

"That's sad. So Jake can cheat but you can't? You've at the very least told him he needs to prove he's STD free before you let him climb your Kat pole."

I scowl at her analogy. "I will. That will hold him off for a while anyway."

"This movie will lead to more, Kat. Maybe you can get a fragrance or a condom endorsement."

"Yeah." I laugh and turn on my professional spokesperson voice. "When you have a boyfriend like mine, make sure you always protect yourself." I hold up an invisible box of condoms. "Use Cheater's Girl's condoms. Ultra-thick for your protection and ribbed for maximum enjoyment."

Megan laughs so hard she snorts like a pig. And I can't stop the giggles.

"You didn't tell Liam about me faking it with Jake, did you?" I ask when I catch my breath. "It's not like I fake it all the time. It's just he's usually more concerned about himself and I would rather just fake it than . . . I don't know . . . prolong it?"

"I won't ever mention it to Liam or anyone else. I've been in relationships with one-sided chemistry, Kat. There is no comparison to ones with a spark. You need to at least give Micah a chance. Jake cheated. See what good chemistry can do. You deserve that. It's not like you're sleeping with Jake."

"Did you have chemistry with your ex, Chase?"

"Unfortunately, yes. But not as much as I have with Liam. Chemistry was all Chase and I had. Speaking of Chase, guess what I heard about him."

"What?"

"He got arrested. Drug offense. His third."

"What does that mean?"

"It means he's going to prison. I don't really agree with the harsh sentences the government has for drug users, but in Chase's case, I applaud it."

"He did some pretty awful deeds," I agree. "Your ex deserves every minute he gets in prison for what he did to you and Liam and for what he did to your mom. I don't know why you just wrote him off. You should have tried to get him to pay restitution or something."

"What good would that do? It wouldn't bring my mom back. We couldn't prove anything. And we'd still be dealing with him a year later. He's one of those people who is so toxic that it's just better to cut ties." She fills her glass with whiskey, and I hold my glass out for her to fill too. "I always believed Karma would catch up to him. And it did. It didn't hurt that Chase drives a really flashy car—a bright yellow Lamborghini. It's easy to spot. And the cop who found the drugs on him just happens to be a friend of my brothers. Karma is a bitch."

"At least you don't have to worry about him messing with you for a while."

"I think Jake deserves some shade too. He shouldn't have cheated. Maybe Micah is willing to be discreet. You deserve to be satisfied, Kat."

"I am never telling you anything ever again," I say, downing my drink.

"It's funny. You need to laugh about it."

"Okay. It's funny," I admit. "And you're right, I do deserve to be satisfied. But you've seen how close people get on the set of *Impassioned*. It's like a family. It's just as close on a movie set. Everyone knows everyone's business. It would be tough to start anything with him and not have Jake find out."

"I know you have to think about all the financial junk with your brother and I don't want anything I tell you to mess that up. But cheating on you, in public, was disrespectful. Jake's never been great at sticking with one girl. Do you even care what Jake thinks at this point? He's using you to recapture his brand, and you're using him to further your career. It sounds fair. You don't have to let him have your body too."

She's right. The contract is fair. I don't have to get back with him just because it would make his life easier. *What about me? Don't I have a say in my life?* "You're right. It's already balanced and fair. I can do what I want."

"You can."

"So how come you're not?" I give Megan an accusatory look. "Why did you give in on the wedding? I thought you wanted to wait until you finished your doctorate before you got hitched." She said it a hundred times when they first got engaged.

"Liam wanted to get married, and my reasoning was flawed. It isn't marriage I'm against, it's getting pregnant and not finishing school. My parents had a shotgun wedding, and my mom never finished school. I didn't want to repeat her mistake and end up like her. She gave up all her dreams so my dad could have some of his. My parents were never really a good match." She leans closer to me, her voice softening. "Don't say anything to Liam, because I never told him. But, do you remember when I had the flu this spring?"

I nod. "Don't tell me you had a deathbed vision."

"No. But close. My period was late, really late, a couple weeks late and even though I was sure I was pregnant, I was too scared to check. I was sick. I couldn't go to the drugstore and I sure as hell wasn't going to ask Liam to pick up a test. It hurt to swallow, and I'd been fighting Liam all week as he tried to force liquids down my throat. I felt horrible, and I just wanted to curl into a ball and die. Then one morning, Liam crawled into bed next to me with a huge glass of ice water and as he held the water for me to drink, he said, 'Meg, you have to drink all of this because I can't do this life thing without you.' He had tears in his eyes. At that moment I realized I was a selfish bitch. The world didn't revolve around me. I would do anything to prevent Liam from feeling pain. I loved him more than I loved myself. And no matter what life threw at me, I didn't have to do it alone. I drank the entire glass of water. And then the second one he brought me. I got my period the next day. I was so relieved. But I realized it's not that I didn't want to get married or pregnant. It's that I wanted to finish school, and I know I will. I'll find a way because it's important to me. Getting married is important to Liam because his parents never did. I'm not going to fight him on it."

"You're making me cry." I drag my finger under my eye, wiping away the waterworks. "I wish I had what you two have. With anyone."

"Just keep looking. You'll find it. After she met Jonathan, Sarah used to tell me that someday I would find love. I never thought I would have what she and Jon have, and then I met Liam. It'll happen to you too."

Chapter 16

Micah

Physical exercise before sunrise should be against the law unless it's swimming. I've been up for an hour and a half, been to the gym with Tom, showered, trimmed my beard, and am ready to go downstairs to get coffee and the sun isn't even up yet. This is not right.

"Do you need a coffee?" I ask. "I'll grab one if you do. A skinny latte?"

"No. Isabell will bring me one. I don't want her slacking off just because you're here." Tom pulls a shirt over his damp hair and then meets my eyes. "Micah . . . Jake has long-term plans with Kat. Did you get that from the conversation over the weekend?"

"I heard." That's all he talked about yesterday. He kept talking about how he was going to build her career until the two of them were a box office power couple. "He also cheated on her on Friday night. Think that's part of his plan to win her back?"

"We don't know what he and that girl did. They could have been playing cards for all we know."

"Yeah. I heard them playing cards right through our shared wall and she was pretty adamant that he not stop. She must've had a good hand."

"Don't judge Jake. Hollywood is different than home. That's just how it works here. Besides, Kat's doing her share of cheating, too, isn't she?"

"I wouldn't know. What have you heard?" I try to make light of his accusatory tone.

"I didn't have to hear anything. I saw the black smudges your dirty little hands made when she stopped by our suite."

Shit. I shake my head. I saw a couple when I walked her to Tom on the couch that night, but it was too late. I couldn't do anything to change the marks. I didn't think anyone else would know where the smudges came from. Then again, maybe part of me hoped they'd notice. "Did Jake see them?"

"I loaned her a shirt. I'm not going to shade my own brother. But it's got to stop. Kat told me herself, you were a slipup. She's trying to make it work with Jake. You messing around with her is only going to end her career. Jake's not going to put up with it when he finds out. He can get her blackballed."

His words hook my gut. I don't want to hurt her.

"Besides, you're being used. You're just a boy toy to occupy her time, and soon she'll be begging you to be her dirty little secret. Then the next thing you know it will all blow up in your face. Either she will make it permanent with Jake and pretend nothing happened between you two or she'll use you to explode their relationship for even more attention. And then move on to her next mark to build her career. Probably a director or producer. The casting couch is real. Girls like Katya use every asset they have to get ahead," he says as if he hasn't spent his whole life using his good looks to get what he wants.

And he knows firsthand about the casting couch, thanks to his first movie. I remember how the experience made him cynical. An older woman who asked him to undress as part of the audition asked for a callback—a private callback. She told him she could get him the part just before she started kissing him. He talked it up to me as if it was just another acting gig, but I saw the change in him. He was sixteen, and even though he wasn't a virgin, he lost innocence. When he told Mom about it, she said he did the right thing submitting to the woman. It got him the part, and that was all that mattered. It wasn't that big of a deal. That's when he started questioning whether Mom had his best interests at heart. I don't think he would ever do it again—not since he made it big in the *Pure Magic* movie series. But I think the idea that he felt it necessary at the time bothers him more than he lets on. And the fact that Mom was okay with it drove a wedge between them.

"Okay. Thanks for the advice." I tuck my phone into my back pocket and pick up my backpack.

Tom's words bounce through every fold of my gray matter. He's brilliant when it comes to social matters. He understands people—their thoughts, motivations—and it's what makes him such a good actor. I should heed every word he says about Kat because he's an expert and I don't have a clue how to read her. I *should* listen to him.

I should.

Downstairs, I sit at the square wooden table, sipping my coffee and finishing the comic strip panels from Saturday night. I've placed speech bubbles and am starting to fill in the dialogue when Katya pulls out a heavy wooden chair at my table and gracefully glides into it. Even without looking up I know it's her. The sixth sense of her presence is becoming a curse to me. I can feel where she is without using my senses.

"Did you know about this?" she asks with an irritated tone.

I glance up from my tablet, trying not to appear happy to see her. I can't help how she makes me feel, but I don't need to advertise it. She must have found out about Jake's Friday night fuck-fest.

"About what? Jake cheat again?"

"About the hotel taking away my room." She looks up at me, her face drooping in exasperation.

"Nope." I guess I was wrong. Of course she didn't find out about him cheating. "What happened?"

"I came back from the airport late last night and my key didn't work. I couldn't even get up to the floor. I thought it had just been erased, so I went to the front desk, and the person at the counter handed me a new keycard with a new room number. I argued with him for ten minutes because I couldn't understand how my room number could change when I left most of my belongings in my suite. I made him get his manager, and his manager explained it all to me.

"Apparently, Jake told the hotel that I wasn't going to put up with a substandard room. He told them if they didn't have another large suite to give me, I wouldn't need my room at all. When they told him they were completely booked, he convinced them to move all my junk to his suite. They went through all my lingerie, all my personal stuff, and moved everything into Jake's suite. Jake tried to make me feel better by telling me his assistant packed up my belongings. But I don't feel better. I'm so mad. I can't believe they did it without even talking to me. And now my room is booked. They offered to put me up at one of their sister hotels two miles away, but then I would have to figure out how to get to the set. I'd be completely out of the loop. And now I'm stuck living with Jake."

I can't help the disgusted laugh that breaks from my lips. She's just going to let him get away with it. Sounds like he started on his long-term plan already. I want to tell her what else happened over the weekend—Jake having his own sleepover and all—but I don't want her to think I'm making it up to turn her against him. Truthfully, I like spending time with her. Her infectious personality infiltrates every part of me with happiness. I can't have her thinking all I want is to get in her pants or I might not get to see her. And that would be a tragedy.

"It's not funny, Micah."

I love the way my name sounds on her lips. "Well, everyone knows you're sleeping together. What difference does it make, your place or his? Does it matter?"

"Not everything is as it appears," she says, affronted and then quieting her voice continues. "We're not sleeping together. I haven't forgotten the cheating, and I don't want to share a suite with him."

"Well, at least technically, you *are* sleeping together, now."

"The suite is identical to yours. There are two bedrooms and two beds. His personal assistant insists on his own place."

I know the suite has two rooms; I had to clear all the partiers out of it on Saturday night.

She looks down, taking a deep breath. Her face says it all. She doesn't want to talk about her reasons for staying with Jake. I guess I'm just stupid, hoping Tom's words hold no truth. In Hollywood, status is everything. And Jake has name recognition. She's building her career, and he can help her reach her goals. I don't need to club her over the head with it every time I talk to her. The press seems to be doing enough of that. She doesn't need it from me. "Sorry, he's such a dick. You can stay at our place if you want."

Her beautiful hazel eyes sparkle as she reaches for my coffee. She takes a sip and holds it in her hands, coveting it. It's at the perfect drinking temperature. I lift a brow, and she hands it back with a smile, showing her dimples.

"How was your brother's birthday?" I don't want her to leave. I can see on her face she didn't expect me to remember she went home to see her brother. She's surprised. I like surprising her.

"It was terrific seeing him. My dad's been a jerk lately, and my brother is really sensitive right now. He needed his big sister to love on him."

"What did your dad do?"

She spends the next ten minutes explaining how her dad wants her brother to move into a state-run home because he refuses to support him now that he's eighteen. Her brother's disability compensation would cover more if he weren't living as a dependent of a relative.

"It's not that he can't afford it, but he has three other kids with two other women, and he thinks my mom is just after his money."

"Your dad sounds like a douche," I say, handing her my coffee. "I always find if you cut those people out of your life, your world is a happier place." I hope she transfers my words to the other douche in her life.

"Yeah. I'm not going to let him bully my mom anymore. We don't need his money, and he stopped caring about us long ago." She takes a large gulp of my coffee and looks around the shop as if worried someone may spot her with me. We're just talking. It can't seem too scandalous.

"What happened to your brother, Kat? I mean, he just turned eighteen. Why isn't he graduating from school and going to college? What's his disability? I know you told me, but I was drunk and don't remember."

"He had an accident almost two years ago." She sits straighter in her chair.

"We grew up in an, I'd say, upper-middle-class neighborhood where getting a car for your sixteenth birthday was not unheard of. But after the fiasco with me turning down the one my dad gave me a year earlier, Cam knew he'd never get one. Mom couldn't even afford the insurance on a car, so he begged her for a longboard. You know, like a skateboard only longer."

I smile at her explanation.

"It was more respectable for a sixteen-year-old to be seen riding a longboard around the neighborhood than riding his sister's hand-me-down bike, more like a life choice than a necessity. He rode it everywhere. Mom worked an ungodly amount of hours back then. She had two jobs and picked up every shift she could just to make ends meet. She's a nurse and worked in a pediatric clinic." She takes another drink of my coffee. "Oh, God. I should buy you a new coffee. I'm going to buy you another coffee."

"Don't worry about it." I can tell she's stalling.

"Anyway, Cam used his longboard like a car to get around. It didn't seem to bother him. He got good, really fast. One day he came home, said he'd fallen off it and hit his head. He seemed fine. And then within a couple of hours, he was in the hospital with irreversible brain damage. It wasn't his first concussion. He'd had one a few months earlier in a swim meet collision. He was a swimmer too. He was fine before, but this time his brain swelled and he never fully recovered. He's a different person, not the Cam I grew up with. It's like he's stuck at ten years old sometimes. His memory is messed up. He's moody, depressed. He lost all his friends. His emotions are all over the board. He goes to a bunch of different kinds of therapy, and it all costs money. Mom's insurance covered some of the initial expenses, but since Mom cut her hours to care for him, she lost that insurance and had to buy it outright. There's a lot of expenses."

"Why doesn't your dad have to pay support for him?"

"My parents were divorced before the accident. And every time Mom threatens to take Dad back to court to force him to pay his share, he drops his hours at work to make it look like he doesn't make as much as he does. Because of his disability, Cam can stay in high school until he's twenty-one in a transition program to help him be able to live independently, and that's what Mom thinks is best. Dad disagrees. He thinks Mom babies Cam too much, and he wants Cam to move out into an environment with other young adults where he has to be more responsible."

"I'll talk to your dad if you want me to," I say, and I will. "Parent's like me."

She wraps her hand around my arm that's holding the coffee.

"You're so sweet, Micah. And so easy to talk to." She smiles, and her hazel eyes meet mine. "I like you." She looks down as if she's embarrassed by what she said. She's still holding my arm. Her thumb caresses the inside of my wrist, and I stare at her face. She's so gorgeous. So feminine and sweet. I can't look away. I slide my hand off the coffee and grasp her hand. She chews the corner of her lip as if she's nervous.

There's more than a mistake and a slipup between us. The way she's looking at me is not wrong.

Impulsive, yes.

But not wrong.

A text chirps on my phone, and she pulls her hand back.

"I should get some coffee," she says. "Thanks for listening to me rant."

"Anytime." I check my phone. "I've got to get back upstairs. If you need a place to crash, the offer's still open." Yep. I put it out there.

She smiles at my suggestion. "Hey, can I get your cell number? I mean . . . just in case Jake is driving me crazy. I know it's not really possible for us to meet in your room because Tom's there. But maybe we could meet down here if you're not busy."

Shit. I'm going to become her dirty little secret, and there is nothing I can do about it. I'm not going to say no. "Sure. What's your number? I'll send you a text." I'm not letting her have my number without getting hers at the same time. I type it into my contacts as she rattles it off and then I type in a text.

They are definitely the same size. A man can tell just by feel.

It pings on her phone, and she starts laughing as she reads. "With you sending texts like that, I need to be a lot more careful about who sees my phone." She smiles, slowly standing and turning toward the sales counter. "I'll see you around," she says, walking away.

Halfway to the sales counter, she looks back at me over her shoulder, nipping her lip. I have to draw her like this. Even though she's fully clothed and in the middle of a coffee shop, her face is a combination of vulnerable and seductive. It's so sexy and so Kat. I smile, then pack up my tablet. I need to get moving. I can't be in the elevator alone with Kat. I lose control around her and even though it would feel as if we were alone, there are cameras in there. It sounds like Jake has fans working at the hotel. If he can convince them to move Kat's belongings into his room, I'm sure they wouldn't hesitate to show him elevator footage of his girlfriend cheating.

"Hey, man." Trey Maki, Gorboni's PA, pounds his fist on the top of my table before sitting in the chair Kat just left. He looks between Kat and me with a knowing smirk on his face. "I'd tap that. Too bad Jake's claimed her. It's always the innocent-looking ones who are freaky in bed." He glances directly into my eyes, placing his index finger on his chin, and says, "Maybe that's why you caught my eye."

I laugh. Trey flirts with everyone, and I mean everyone. "I'm not innocent, and I'm not gay."

"I'm not either. Labels are so confining, don't you think? I'm really more about just following my heart. How do you know what you like if you limit yourself?"

"Whatever makes you happy, Trey. But you have to count me out. I like to know I can bench press more than my date and your muscles are way too developed for my taste." I turn the rebuke into a compliment. He's a good-looking guy, but a guy.

"Too bad. I think we could have fun."

I stand, shaking my head. "See you later, Trey. Gotta go. Tom's looking for me." Kat walks out in front of me, and I catch up to her at the elevator.

"He didn't ask you why we were talking, did he? Jake gets really possessive sometimes," she asks as we climb into the lift.

"Nope. He asked me out. Well, he tried to anyway." I tap my keycard to the panel on the wall and press the number twelve. She stands next to me, and I can feel the electricity snapping between us. I can't touch her though. Cameras. I was right about being alone with her in the elevator.

"He has good taste," she says, before taking a sip of coffee and leaning against the back of the elevator.

We're silent the rest of the ride. As I fight the need to pull her into my arms, all I can do is imagine how good it would feel to be her dirty little secret.

When I get back to the suite, Tom's ready to go. I turn around, and we head to the car. I wish I could talk to him about Kat. But after what he said this morning, I'm positive he would just remind me that I'm going to get hurt.

Chapter 17

Katya

This is hell. I'm in hell. I meet this sweet, intelligent, incredibly hot guy and I can't act on it. Instead, I'm trapped with a cheater just like my father. I know I need to let it go. Clinging to Jake's infidelity won't help me get through this contract. But I can't even escape to my own suite anymore. He's in my face all the time now. It was bad enough he violated my trust in the video, but then it's as if he did it again by forcing me to stay in his suite. He publicly humiliates me and then punishes me. I read a comment yesterday about how Jake took me back because he felt sorry for me for being fat. I hate trolls. I'm in the best shape of my twenty-two years. I work out more than I ever have before.

I finish my coffee and toss the cup in the trash just as Jake enters the living area.

"I'm going to work out, and you're coming with me. If I know you at all, you haven't done cardio all weekend, Kat. You're going to get fat." Jake holds his hands out, palms up, as if apologizing. He obviously read the comment too. "Come on. Trey will be here any minute, and we're all going to the gym." I hate that he agrees with the troll.

I'm not going to admit I skipped my cardio workout the entire weekend and ate cake on top of that. Instead, I change my clothes and return just as his assistant knocks on the door. Trey Maki is not only Jake's assistant, but he's also his weights partner. He spots Jake on the bench press and encourages him to push harder when needed. Talking weights and form is Jake's favorite conversation subject—only second to sex. Luckily Trey's a mirror image of Jake when it comes to conversation. Trey looks me up and down before his eyes meet Jake's.

Jake cups my right butt cheek. "Feel this, Trey." He squeezes and drops his hand.

Trey grabs my left butt cheek. I smack Trey hard in the gut. What am I, a piece of meat for them to pass around? "Seriously?"

"You're gaining weight, Kat," says Trey brazenly.

"You better put in some extra time today on the treadmill or steps. An extra fifteen minutes wouldn't hurt, and twenty sets of lunges." Jake wraps his gorilla arm around me and tosses me over his shoulder—with my apparently enormous ass sticking straight up in the air as he carries me down the hall.

Screw him. I had a piece of cake. When Jake finally sets me down in front of the elevator, I glare at him and then at Trey. Great, now Jake's discussing my weight with his PA. I narrow my eyes even more at Trey before heading into the elevator.

Once in the elevator, Jake grabs my arm. "You know I don't mind a little extra to hold onto while fucking. It's just the camera that's unforgiving." His hand cups my ass again. "It's nothing a daily sex workout wouldn't fix. I can make sure we work one in."

I brush his hand away and drop behind the two of them in the elevator so they can't watch my butt jiggle. While I pout, they discuss how much weight Trey gained after he tore his ACL two years ago and what it took to get the weight off.

Listening to their chatter echo in the elevator, I realize Jake's right. I should have a daily sex workout. It would help me stay in shape. I wonder if Micah would be up for it.

Ever since we stepped out of the car, Jake's been all hands. Curling around my waist. Sliding down my arms. Caressing my cheeks. Massaging my back. He never touched me this much when we were going out. Now, all of a sudden he feels the need to claim me as his in public.

We're standing on a barricaded street. Today's scenes are set outside, and that always causes delays. We've both been through makeup and stand, waiting for a lighting change to get into place when Jake slides in behind me. His hands glide around me and spread across my stomach. He knows he can't kiss me. He's already been warned about messing up my face by the makeup technician. Instead of kissing me, he dips fingers under my skirt's waistband.

"Please stop," I whisper, trying not to draw attention.

"This makes me happy, Kitty Kat. I got inspired watching you work out this morning. Downward dog. I can't get it out of my head." He pulls me tighter in his arms. "Don't you want me to be happy? You should. I know Phillip wants me happy. Connor wants me happy." He's naming the producers of the film. Unlike me, he's on a first-name basis with them. "The star of the movie gets what he wants. I'm the one who brings in the box office dollars. You're not stupid, Kat. You know I get what I want."

I stiffen in his arms, my heart in my throat. Why is he doing this right before filming? I'm silent for several minutes, unsure how to spin his words.

He bends close to my ear and whispers, "Don't worry. As long as you keep me happy, we don't have a problem."

What motivated him to remind me of his power over me right now? Did Trey say something about seeing me with Micah this morning? Will I have to sleep with him to make him happy? What if he demands it?

I start the slow breathing exercises I use before a scene to clear my head. I can't think about this right now. Filming's going to start in a few minutes, and I have to get in character. I have to remember my lines. Damnit, I forgot my lines. This is going to be a long day of filming and an even longer night.

Two hours pass torturously before the director gives us a much-needed break. I've never messed up my lines more than I have today. I'm really off. I can't focus. I'm on the verge of tears when Jake steps in front of me. His thumbs caress my cheeks, and he looks down at me as he speaks.

"Kat, everyone has off days, but you have to pull it together. Bernie's giving me the eye. He's questioning whether you can handle this role."

"Your threats aren't helping," I blurt out. I don't know why I'm letting him bother me so much. This is my career. I need to make this work.

"I wouldn't push, babe, if I didn't love you so much. Is that a crime?"

"That's why you cheated? Because you love me?"

His hands drop, and he looks around, checking who is within hearing distance. "Are you still mic'd?"

"Sound shut me off right away. I don't think they wanted to listen to me cry."

"Good. Is that what your problem is today? Shit." I watch his Adam's apple bob as he swallows, long and slow. "I can only take so much rejection. I'm a sexual guy, Kat. We need to find a way to make this work. And right now, us, we're not working."

There's something off about his words. His demeanor isn't his normal cocky self. But it doesn't matter. I need to pull on my big girl lace panties and do what I need for my career.

"You're right, Jake. We need to make this work. And I'll do what I need to do to get through filming. But you need to be patient with me in private. I'm trying to forgive you, but you just keep adding to the list." The words flow from my mouth and immediately the weight is lifted from my shoulders. I'm going to do exactly what Megan said. I'm going to push the limits of leading on Jake while I find my sanity elsewhere.

I'm an actor.

A professional imposter.

Now, I'm just doing it full time around Jake.

The rest of filming goes about as smoothly as filming can go and we actually finish early. Early for what was expected, anyway. It's almost midnight by the time we get back to the hotel. Jake kept his hands to himself on the car ride and seemed unusually quiet. He's either as exhausted as I am or he actually heard what I said about needing time. Back in the suite, Jake heads for the TV as I head for the shower. Hopefully, he knows enough to leave me alone tonight.

The liquid steam pours over my body washing the day's dirt off me, helping me think clearer. I have to outsmart Jake. I can't let him control all the strings in this contract. I need something for myself. The shower purges my fear, giving me hope for a better summer. I towel off before searching the drawers someone else filled for something to wear. I really do feel violated by the fact that Jake and his assistant went through my belongings. They had no right to move me out of my room. The green T-shirt catches my eye and I pull it out feeling empowered by it. I tug it on alone with a pair of panties and collapse on the bed.

I snap a selfie. It's not awful, so I post it with the caption, "My pillow calls. Exhausted from filming today." I'm not the best at posting on social media, but I try to keep my posts real. I hate those people who Photoshop the hell out of their pictures, and then you see them in person and you barely recognize them.

I send a text to Micah since it's his shirt I'm wearing.

Kat: Are you up?

Micah: Yep.

Kat: I have a confession to make. I'm lying on my bed in your cat T-shirt.

I send him the picture.

Micah: What? How do you have my shirt?

Kat: I borrowed it. Remember? The morning after our drinking binge. It's super soft. I'll give it back. I just need it for a little while. I had a bad day, and it makes me smile.

Micah: You can keep it if it makes you happy. Heard about your bad day.

Kat: Who told you?

Micah: Your boyfriend is here.

Kat: Don't let him know we're texting.

Micah: Not stupid.

I guess I overreacted. I know he's not stupid. I just can't afford to give

Jake any doubt about my intentions.

> *Kat: Sorry. I know you wouldn't say anything. It's just been a rough day.*
>
> *Micah: Who told you about his Friday night hookup? He thinks it was Trey.*

His Friday night hookup? HE HOOKED UP WITH SOMEONE WHILE I WAS HOME? And then he moves my stuff into his suite. *Screw him.* He says he loves me, but he's still cheating. He must have thought I knew and that's why he was so quiet on the drive home.

> *Micah: Kat?*
>
> *Kat: It wasn't Trey.*
>
> *Micah: I get it. Don't tell me. I don't want to know. I would have told you, but I didn't know how.*
>
> *Kat: It's okay. I should get some sleep. Talk more tomorrow.*
>
> *Micah: K. Good night.*

Unbelievable. I toss my phone onto the bed next to me and cover my face with my hands, not really sure what to think. I'm almost more mad at Micah for not saying anything this morning than I'm mad at Jake for cheating. I mean, how could he not tell me that Jake hooked up with someone on Friday? We exchanged numbers; he could have sent me a text.

My heart's in my throat. And not because of Jake's cheating.

This whole situation is stupid. I don't want Jake. If he cheats, he cheats. He's going to sleep around no matter how I feel about it. And it's stupid to blame Micah for not telling me. How would he word the text? *Hey, Kat. How's filming going? BTW Jake hooked up with some redhead while you were gone.* I assume it was a redhead. Yeah. That wasn't going to happen. I pick up my phone and type out another text.

> *Kat: Next time, you tell me first!*
>
> *Micah: Will do. Promise.*

Micah

Several minutes pass without another word from Kat. I never should have brought up Jake. *Her boyfriend,* I correct in my head. He pretty much ended our conversation, as always.

"Who ya texting? Got some horny chick wanting some Little Fallston?" asks Jake in a belittling tone, as if that couldn't possibly be the case.

"Exactly," I say. "Tom, you mind if I take the car? You're going to bed anyway."

Tom's brow wrinkles. "What was her name again?"

"I don't remember." I laugh as if names aren't important. "I'll let you know after tonight."

"Why don't you invite her up here?" He looks at me as if he knows exactly who I'm texting.

"No way. Then she'd get star-struck and want to sleep with one of you. I'm not stupid."

They both laugh in agreement. Stroking their egos always smooths the way. I type out another text.

Micah: Wanna go for a drive?"
Kat: Yes!
Micah: Meet me in the parking garage in ten?
Kat: I'll be there.

"That girl from Friday with the big lashes?" asks Jake.

"Yep," I lie. "I'm a sucker for big lashes."

"Didn't your brother teach you anything, Little Fallston? You never give a girl access to your phone. Now she's going to be tapping you all the time."

"I don't mind. I can always block her. You know me. I just go with the flow."

"Jake, let's do some shots. You don't want to head back to your room if Kat's still awake. You'll say something you'll regret. It's better to let her cool down." Tom reaches into the fridge and pulls out the chilled tequila.

I'm not sure if Tom believes my lie about the big-lashed girl or if he's stalling Jake to help me meet up with Kat.

"Don't be out all night, Micah. Call might not be until one in the afternoon, but that doesn't mean you can sleep over."

"Got it. Be home before dawn. Thanks for loaning me the car, Dad," I say, grabbing my key fob. Tom and Dad are complete opposites these days, and he hates it when I call him Dad. But when he makes a comment like that, I can't help it.

I head down the stairs to the parking garage. I can't listen to Jake talk about Kat anymore. In his mind, Kat is the problem, not his cheating. He thinks her freezing him out justifies even more cheating. But he doesn't see the other side. I thought actors were supposed to empathize with others and that's how they get into character. Unlike me, I guess Jake's never been destroyed by someone cheating on him.

I pull the car up to the door where I told Kat to meet me, rolling my head across my shoulders as I wait. The garage is eerily quiet. It's just after one in the morning, and you'd think this place was a morgue. Finally, the door opens, and a girl in leggings and a hoodie emerges. I lower the window to show her it's me and she climbs in. She smells heavenly, like spring flowers meet a tropical drink. She slumps down in the seat, as aware of the cameras in the garage as I am. We don't talk until the tires hit the street and then she sits up, pulling her hood off.

"What are we doing, Micah? I can't believe I'm doing this," she says.

I smile at her as we pull up to the first light. "We're getting away from the crazies. There's no reason we have to join them in their loony fantasies."

"I like that," she says. "I was exhausted when I got back to my room, and now I feel like I could stay out all night."

"I was told I can't. They think I'm meeting a girl for a booty call and I have instructions to be home before dawn."

"Are you meeting for a booty call?" she asks, her lips twisting into a smirk.

Her face is so gorgeous. I don't think she has any makeup on and she's easily the most beautiful girl I know.

"I'm not against it. I mean, if I meet the right girl, it's an option."

"So that's how you're playing this?" Her jaw drops open and a look of mischief flashes in her eyes. Then she unzips her hoodie and flashes me my shirt. She's not wearing a bra. The black cat stretched across her tits awaken my lower brain. Not that it was sleeping after her last remark.

"I like my shirt on you." The light turns green and my foot pushes downward, moving us forward to the next light. "Are you hungry? We could grab some food. There's this great little twenty-four-hour café a block over."

"I can't really risk being seen out with another guy. Do you understand?" I can hear the edge in her voice when she says it. She knows it's not what I want to hear.

"Not really," I admit. "I don't get the two of you. I just don't." I pull the car to the curb, putting it in park as I turn to her. "Because every time I see you with him, his hands are all over you and you look uncomfortable and frustrated. And every time you're with me you're relaxed and happy. I don't get why you stay with him. And I don't get what you want from me." I said it. I want to hear her reaction.

"This thing with Jake is complicated."

"Yeah. I've heard."

"I'm sorry, Micah. If I could change what is going on with Jake, I would. And right now, so early in production, he has all the power. I can't upset him too much, or he'll get me fired."

"Would he really do that? It seems as if he just wants you."

"It's not me, or he wouldn't have cheated. It's all about his brand. If we stay together, then he's not a bad guy. People will forget what he did. He's still Mr. All-American."

"So he's not all hands in private?"

She looks to the ceiling of the car as if she doesn't want to answer. "No . . . I don't let him touch me in private." Her gaze meets my eyes. "But you can't let him know you know or he will get me replaced on the film."

"He told Tom you're freezing him out. That's why he felt justified hooking up with another girl this past weekend." She watches me, her chest rising and falling in fast, measured movements, as she nervously twists the fat silver ring wrapped around her right index finger and nibbles her lower lip.

"He said that?"

I don't know how to read her. She could be upset about Jake's cheating, or she could be nervous about what she told me. I smile at her and say, "Don't worry. I won't repeat anything you say. Let's pick up some Cokes and find somewhere more private where we can talk without anyone spotting us."

I pull the car away from the curb and can't help but wonder why I am letting this happen. Nothing good can come of me spending time with her. She'll end up with Jake anyway. Or some director, like Tom said. But I can't help my desire to be around her. She awakens something in me that I can't explain. I haven't felt this way since Mara. And Gorboni took that away from me too.

I find a convenience store a couple of streets up and park on the dark side of the lot, so no one sees her. "What's Katya want?" I ask. I don't know why I word it that way. Maybe because that is the real question. What does she want?

Jake?

Or me?

"Water," she answers, her eyes studying my face.

"Just water?"

She nods as she starts fiddling with her ring again.

"Okay. Just water." I climb out and head into the store. The bright fluorescent glow inside makes me feel like a cockroach when the light switch flips on. I want to scurry back into the dark crevices of the lot. I look around for anything to break the ice with Kat. Girls like chocolate, right? I pick up a chocolate bar because . . . chocolate and sharing are good. Then I grab two waters and pay for it all before heading back to the lot.

She's quiet when I get in, and I hope she's not regretting our outing. I just want to talk. I want to get to know her better. She has this inner light that transcends her gorgeous face and body. But when I hand her the water, she smiles and I can't stop myself. There's this electricity hanging in the air between us, and I want to figure out what I can do about it. If there is anything I can do about it.

I reach over, grasp her chin in my hand, and press my lips to hers. I don't know why. I can't help it. Her soft, plump ones open to me without hesitation and I push inside, unable to stay the corners of my mouth from turning up as I do it. This moment is mine, not his. And I'm going to enjoy it. As my hand slides to the back of her neck to give me better control, a quiet moan hums from her throat and her hands clutch my biceps, pulling me to her. She tastes as delectable as our first kiss, with just a hint of mint and definitely no tequila.

This is real.

I can tell she wants more as much as I do. I wish we could get closer, but the damn center storage between the bucket seats makes it impossible. After a couple of minutes, I pull back, breaking our connection. If I don't stop, I'm likely to recline my seat, pull her on top of me, and take her right here in the rental car in a parking lot of a Stop and Rob. But I can't treat her like Jake treats women and I can't let anyone see us. She unscrews her bottle and takes a sip of water as she stares at me. The electricity between us has grown tenfold, but she doesn't say anything.

I turn to buckle my seatbelt and notice a pickup truck parked next to us, the driver and passenger staring. I don't see any cell phones or cameras raised, but I buckle quickly and throw the car in reverse. I don't want Kat to see them or she may shut down again, thinking the evening too big of a risk. I take off down the road in the opposite direction of the lake, planning to double back, just in case we are followed. The truck pulls out behind us, following our path for three blocks before turning. I guess I'm just paranoid.

At the next light, I glance at Kat as she fiddles with her ring again. I can tell this isn't something she normally does. She looks nervous. The day we met she admitted she never cheats on guys. Her uneasiness tells me she wasn't lying. I don't know why this feels so different from the other day in my room, but it does. It's more premeditated, maybe. And that makes it more tangible.

Chapter 19

Katya

Micah parks the town car in the lot overlooking the beach. I'm not sure what he has planned. Veering onto a path I know is wrong is not something I ever do. Leading Jake on to keep him happy while I fool around with Micah is wrong. And if Micah and I hook up tonight, I can no longer brush it off as a mistake brewed in tequila or a hormone-induced grope session. This is planned.

Condoms.

I'm sure condoms made it into the car. And if he didn't bring any, there are some in my purse. No, there's no mistaken slipup when we're both sober, and my eyes are open wide.

"I'm nervous," I admit.

The beach looks deserted, as it should be at almost two o'clock in the morning on a weekday. But what if someone spots me? What if they get pictures? It could end my career. Micah's beautiful blue eyes find me inside my fear, and he smiles as he tucks a loose strand of hair behind my ear. His thumb caresses my cheek with a tenderness I'm not used to feeling. He's so gentle with me.

"It's just a walk," he says, without looking away. I nod, and he pulls the hood of my sweatshirt up. "Just in case." We open our doors and meet at the front of the car.

His hand covers mine, and I let him lead me down to the shoreline. We walk just out of the water's reach, and I start to relax. If I were walking with Jake, he'd be scheming to throw me in the cold lake by now. He's always putting on a show, and he's not happy unless he's in a constant adrenaline rush. And, stupidly, I'd forgive him because he would convince me he was sorry. But walking with Micah feels natural. I'm not afraid he's going to pull some crazy stunt when I let my guard down. We're just walking, holding hands. And it feels so good. Micah won't hurt me. He has substance, not swagger.

I'm comfortable not talking, but it feels like a waste. I want to know this guy. I want him to know me. I wonder if he would tell me the truth about the bad blood Tom mentioned.

"Can I ask you something?"

He shrugs.

"Your brother said something about you and Jake having bad blood. But he wouldn't explain what he meant by it."

"And you want me to tell you what it is?" he snaps.

"I was hoping you would tell me."

He stops walking and turns to me, dropping my hand. From his body language, I can visually see a wall going up as his back stiffens and his jaw locks. "Why don't you ask your *boyfriend?*" He stresses the word, and I feel the air chill.

It's the first time I've seen him be anything other than easy-going. He shakes his head as if he can't believe that I would bring it up. I guess I shouldn't have. I get it. He's frustrated. He thinks Jake and I are together and he doesn't know what that means for him. "I'm sorry. I just thought if I asked you I'd get the truth. I don't trust anything Jake says lately. I didn't mean to upset you."

"I don't want to talk about it." He blows into his closed fist as if trying to warm his hand. It's chilly by the water but not that cold.

"That's fair. Maybe another time," I say, sliding my hand back into his. I start walking again. Mistake made, not to be repeated. The bad blood must be pretty awful. "The water looks cold."

"Yeah. It does." His hand feels warm, but his voice is still chilly.

"Remember the night we met? Did you really think I was a hooker?"

He laughs somewhere in his chest, but it doesn't break his lips. "I thought you were some girl Tom sent to hook up with me."

"I can't see your brother being a cruise director. And what kind of girl agrees to do that?"

He shrugs again. "Tom's not a bad guy. All my life girls have been all over him. They want to hook up with him. It's nothing he does, just his body, his celebrity status, his designer clothes, and his money. But when girls find out I'm his brother, they look at me as a backup. If they can't sleep with him, they'll settle for me, as if hooking up with me gets them closer to him somehow. I'm always the backup."

"I've never wanted to sleep with your brother."

"But you're dating Gorboni."

"I'm here with you, not him." I give him my best apologetic smile. "I'd rather be with you."

He smiles and brings my hand to his lips. His smile makes my stomach flutter, and his soft kiss spreads warmth through my limbs. Damn. I'm falling for him. I can't afford to fall for him. Does he have any flaws?

"Tell me about your parents," I say. I need to know more about him. What makes him tick?

"Do you want the nitty-gritty version or the juice box version?"

"The darker and more twisted the better," I answer, swinging our linked hands as we walk.

"Let's see." He pauses, changing the grip on my hand and lacing his fingers between mine. "My mom was always the typical dance-mom type with Tom, pushing him to go on auditions and be the perfect adult in a child's body while she basically ignored me. Tom's outgoing, type-A personality fit well with the goals she saw for him. I was the shy kid. I'd rather sit in the audience than be on stage. It was easy for Mom to pay more attention to Tom. She managed his career until he turned nineteen. Then they had a big blow-out and didn't talk for a long time. Now she works as a children's modeling agent. My dad works at a small tech company in Austin, never really around much.

My parents are newly religious, and now that we're grown up they think we should devote our lives to them. You know 'honor thy mother and father' and all that. Tom's the prodigal son who they throw a feast for when he returns. If he ever returns. And, I guess I'm one of the other sons who's always been there working hard and will never be appreciated."

I laugh but choke on it, and I end up coughing. "I'm sorry. My dad is newly religious too. So I get that it's a bit frustrating. For Dad, his new religion has freed him from the guilt of his past. He no longer has to take any responsibility for his neglect as a parent or for cheating on my mom. The past is irrelevant. He reinvented himself."

"That's exactly right," he says, squeezing my hand and smiling. "Mom acts as if she was this perfect mom. She completely forgets about the time she left me at one of Tom's photo shoots and didn't realize I was missing until I called her using a lighting assistant's cell, three hours after she left. I sat there drawing with my crayons hoping she would remember me on her own. But when they started closing down the studio for the day, I realized that wasn't going to happen. She actually got mad at me for not calling sooner. I was six years old, and it wasn't the first time she forgot me on a shoot, just the longest time I waited."

"I can't believe a mom would forget her son." I grunt with disapproval. "Who does that?"

"It happened. I got a cell phone the next day. I was the only six-year-old with a phone at school. My dad was better about giving me attention when he was around, but he worked a lot. Now I'm supposed to drop everything anytime they plan a dinner party. My mom pays more attention to me now that I want them to leave me alone. Mom's always trying to fix me up with some nice religious girl she met at church. I'm not religious. In their eyes, any success is a direct result of something they did. My graduation should be quite the show for their friends, especially if my brother comes. And that's the thing that gets me, that if Tom offered them a minute of his time, they'd drop me like a hot coal. I wouldn't make the cut. My parents don't see the hypocrisy of their lives. I guess that's something you and I have in common."

"And a love of comics," I add.

He nods. "We have that too." He drops my hand and wraps his arm around my waist. "Ever date a nerd before?"

"Hundreds of them."

"Great." He shakes his head and looks out at the dark water.

"No, I just mean that's the kind of guy I dated in high school. I played the violin in orchestra, sang in the choir and I hung around theater people. My best friend played the Cello, and I took advanced placement classes. I wasn't dating the quarterback. I met my first boyfriend on a bus trip to Milwaukee for choir. We dated four months before he told me he was gay." I laugh at the memory. "I'm not very good at reading people."

"I wish I'd known you then." Micah kisses the back of my hand again.

"No, you don't. I didn't get breasts until my senior year. I looked like a boy."

"I don't care what you look like. At least your looks aren't the best part of you."

I raise my eyebrows at his words. "Really?"

"I didn't say your looks weren't a great part of you. I love the way you look. But if a girl's personality sucks, it doesn't matter what she looks like."

I smile at that. Guys always make me feel as if my looks are all I have. Even Jake. Micah's sweet.

We reach a cluster of trees surrounded by grass and Micah stops, leaning against one of the trees and pulling me next to him.

"You wouldn't have even noticed me in high school. I was pretty quiet," I say.

"Your eyes alone would have gotten my attention. They're gorgeous." He looks down at his feet with a smile and then looks up to penetrate me with his eyes.

Wow. The fairies in my stomach beat up my insides.

He slides down the tree trunk, and looking up at me, tilts his head, motioning me to sit next to him. I follow, and he cracks open his bottle of water. He takes a chocolate bar from his jacket pocket and hands me a square.

I glance at his eyes. He really does have the most gorgeous eyes, dark blue in the moonlight. Holding hands as we walk down a beach, talking and sharing chocolate is probably the most romantic date I've ever been on. It feels so much like a date. I pop the chocolate into my mouth and scan the beach as I open my water. We've walked quite a distance from the car, and I only spotted two other people—a couple—headed in the opposite direction. I close my water after taking a long drink, and he tugs me in front of him, wrapping his arms around me. The cool air coming off the water makes me shiver, and he pulls me in closer, my back to his front. I take a calming breath as I rest my head on his shoulder. His light, clean scent relaxes me. I feel as if I have been holding my breath for weeks and can finally unwind. I don't know why but I feel relieved. Being with Micah is easy, effortless.

His breath tickles my neck through my hoodie, sending goosebumps down my arms and legs. Neither of us says anything for a long beat. Instead, we watch the surf wash in, and it feels fabulous not having to talk or put on a show.

"I like spending time with you, Micah."

"Do you though?" I can hear the smile in his voice.

Finally, I said the right thing. "Yes, I do. Tell me more about you. Do you live with your parents? Do you have a condo at school? Do you have a best friend? I know what you're doing for the summer, but what do you do the rest of the year?"

"Well, clown school is super rigorous. There's tightrope walking and makeup class. There was this one time we got to work with a bear, and not just an ordinary bear. This bear could do algebra. Can you believe that? But it ate the professor's cat, so we only got to work with it the one time."

"Oh my God. Stop it, right now."

He laughs and kisses the side of my hoodie, right on top of my ear, and I can feel the burn in my core.

"I want to know more about you, Micah."

"I have a group of good friends. Nobody I would single out as a best friend, but good friends. I live with two of them in an apartment above a comic book shop in Austin. My parents live in the Austin area, too, but out in the West Hills area near Lake Travis. The apartment is closer to downtown. I was born in Nebraska and moved to San Diego when Tom started getting acting jobs. I didn't move to Austin until I was sixteen, when Dad got a new job and Tom fired my mom from being his manager."

"A move across the country in high school. That must have been hard."

"If you haven't noticed, I don't let things bother me. What's the point? Especially if I can't control them."

"That's a real superpower."

"That's not my superpower." His hand nudges under my T-shirt to the bare skin of my stomach. "What happened to your belly-button ring? I really liked it." His finger circles my navel, and he groans when shivers rake through me.

"I had to take it out for filming," I say. I definitely remember what his superpower is. That must be why I can't stop thinking about being with him. He must have . . . I shake that thought from my head and swallow hard.

Screw it.

I twist in his arms, pushing him back against the ground and pinning his shoulders as I pull my face even to his. An inch from his lips I whisper, "Prove it," though I am pretty sure he already has.

One of his hands grasps the nape of my neck as he powers up from below me, melding his lips to mine. Within a blink of an eye, he flips me onto my back, his hard form pressing into me. My body melts into his, my heart racing. Who needs to remove clothes? He could prove his superpower just like this. Pretty quickly too.

His tongue pushes into my mouth, making me clench where I am sure he can feel me squirming. Very quickly. With just a kiss and some pressure. Really? What's wrong with me? I'm never like this. My hands skim under his shirt to feel the strong lines of his muscular back as our bodies sync in movement. One of his hands cups my breast and then his lips trail hot kisses down my neck to meet his hand. His breath burns through my clothes. I want them off. There's not a single person on the beach other than us. Who cares if we get naked? But Micah makes no move to undress us. Instead, his lips find their way back to mine, and his tongue pushes inside again. The glorious torment continues. *When is he going to start stripping?* It better happen soon. I smooth a hand over his narrow hip and tug back his athletic shorts, just in case he is waiting for me to give him the okay.

He pulls back, lifting up to rest on his elbows, his expression completely serious as he stares into my eyes. "Our first time is not going to be in a rushed frenzy in a public park."

What does that mean?

His thumb smooths the wrinkle formed between my brows, and he adds, "I mean, I want you, but . . . I want to take my time with you our first time together. I want to show you my superpower. I can't do that with a quickie on the beach."

I'm pretty sure he could, but I'm confused by the fact that he's forgotten about our first night together. "It wouldn't be our first time together." My fingers trail down his flat stomach and circle his tattoo. The skin is soft, but I can tell without looking where his tattoo is.

"Don't do that," he groans, only it sounds like *more, please.*

"Remember? Tequila shots." I inch my fingers under his shorts. "Your brother finding us naked in your bed the next day. Him wanting to see my breasts. You protecting me. Does any of that ring a bell?"

He peels his body off mine and collapses on the grass next to me. I miss the pressure of him. I miss his warmth.

"You don't remember that night, do you?" he asks.

"I remember most of it. I know I wanted to sleep with you."

He turns on his side, facing me, stroking my cheek as he speaks. "You wanted to sleep with me?"

"Yes. I did."

"We never slept together, Kat. I didn't want to take advantage of you when you were drunk. I'd never do that. I thought you knew."

"I just assumed, I guess. Are you sure?" That can't be right.

He laughs and tugs on a strand of my hair, his brows arched high over his eyes. "If we slept together, you'd remember. I have superpowers."

Oh my God. He's so confident. I don't know what to say. I thought my body wanted him because it knew more than I did. But if that's not true . . . My brow wrinkles again. I'm confused.

He leans in and kisses the corner of my mouth. "I've thought about it a lot actually since our last kiss. I don't want a quickie here or there. I want more."

Never in my entire life have I been shut down by a guy. Is it an insult? I can tell he wants me. He was pressing that proof against me a minute ago. Should I take it as a compliment? I mean, the fact that he wants more than a romp on the beach says something, right?

He actually cares that I orgasm. *That's new.* It's a compliment.

I rest my head down on the grass in disappointment. His fingers comb into my hair, my hoodie no longer a barrier, and I press my head against them. It feels incredible to have him touch me. It doesn't matter where.

"What will you tell Gorboni if he discovers you missing?"

Why is he talking about Jake? "I'll tell him to go screw himself."

"I'd be okay with that. But I know you won't." His hand pauses in my hair.

"I know," I say. "I'm sorry." I have to leave it at that.

"Are you though?"

"Stop it. I am sorry. I wish we could be together."

"What is your cover story, then? We should figure it out before we head back."

I don't want to head back. "I suppose I'll tell him I went for a walk and lost track of time. He'll be asleep, though. He has a nine o'clock call, and likes his sleep. He wouldn't want to have bags under his eyes."

"Text me after he leaves, and I'll come over." A smile blossoms on his face as he leans in to kiss me. This is so natural with him. Nothing's forced. Nothing's fumbled. Every kiss, every caress just feels right.

Micah

The second my head hit my pillow last night, I knew I wouldn't get any sleep. She obviously wanted sex. And we could have gone at it right there on the beach, but my damn mind stopped me. I must have a tiny gland stuck somewhere in my frontal lobe that has ultimate control over the rest of my body.

A morality gland.

Maybe my parents embedded it. They probably gave me Tom's too. I've got two of them. That explains it.

I thought about it all night. What really stopped me? In the end, it comes down to the fact that she's still with Gorboni. Until she can give me a better understanding of what is going on between them, I don't feel having sex will change anything except make me fall harder for her. We'll sleep together and maybe I'll be the best she's ever had and maybe I won't. But will it change what she's doing with Gorboni? I'll just end up hurt in the end. Perhaps it's a self-preservation gland, not a morality gland.

When Kat's text appears. I send her a thumbs up, toss my tablet, some pens, and a sketch pad into my backpack and sling it onto my back. I need something to distract us.

Outside my room, Tom's eating breakfast with Izzy at the table. His assistant always orders enough for all of us, and in the end, I know I'm going to have to give an excuse as to where I'm going. He looks up at me as I approach.

"Where are you headed?" he asks, setting his coffee down. He thinks he owns me.

"Just trying to squeeze in a couple of hours of drawing before filming today. Not sure where I will end up, but this hotel room is crushing my creativity. I need a change." My backpack adds to the believability of my words. I can't pretend to go to the gym because he will just come with me. I snatch an apple off the table and crunch into it, meeting his eyes. The sweet and crisp flavor awakens my mouth like a new start as I ready for his objection. "I have my phone. Promise I won't go far."

Suspicion fills his eyes. He knows Jake's schedule and Kat's. He probably doesn't expect me to do anything so blatant, though, and as he continues to eat, he nods his approval. I grab a cherry yogurt and a water from the fridge and head out into the hallway. I meander to Kat's room wondering who, if anyone, is monitoring the cameras in the passage.

The knock echoes in the hallway and I worry she sent the text by mistake and Jake will open the door. I don't have an excuse. Can't even think of one. Luckily Kat opens it, and I slip inside without onlookers in the hall.

She takes a deep breath, a sign of relief, and brushes a quick kiss on my lips.

I'm still leery. What if I can't control myself? What if Jake comes back?

"He's gone?" I ask, walking farther into the suite. She grabs my hand and pulls me into her room.

"He's gone. But we should keep to my room."

I unshoulder my backpack and toss it onto the bed as she plops down.

She's like a star shining in a dull world. I can't help but follow her. I kick off my sandals and flip to my stomach across the bed. "I thought I would draw you this morning," I say with a smile.

Her eyebrows lift. "How do you want me?"

Naked. On your hands and knees, looking back over your shoulder. "Let's just try it with you lying on your side," I say as I pull the tablet out of my backpack.

She flips onto her side and asks, "Is this what you want? I feel as if I'm at a photo shoot."

"You are," I say, taking a lock of her hair and draping it, just right, over her left shoulder.

"Do you want me to take my clothes off?"

"Always," I say, propping her head in her hand with her elbow on the bed. "But not for this portrait," I add quickly before she starts undressing. I would love to draw her naked, but I can't lose control. I don't know if I would survive being her dirty little secret once I entered her. Not when Gorboni's the other dude. *Shit.* I should have just told her what Jake did to me. Maybe it would wake her up to his evil ways and kick her over the edge enough to leave him. Now if I bring it up, it will look as if I'm whining about the bully kicking sand in my face. I didn't want to talk about it last night, but now that I can think more clearly I realize it was the wrong choice.

I pull the chair out of the corner of the room, moving it closer to the bed. Drawing her was the right decision. I can feel the sparks coming off of her, and those cute little spandex shorts she's wearing would be off by now if I were on the bed next to her. I take the stylus out of my tablet to begin to set up the dimensional parameters of the picture.

"You're going to have to be the one to talk because I can't draw and talk at the same time." I study her form. She's so perfectly proportioned, like a teenager's fantasy. Her hazel eyes meet mine. They look more honey-brown today than greenish-grey. The color really depends on the color of her shirt. Or maybe it's the burgundy bedcover. "Tell me how you got into acting."

"When I was ten my mom put me in a theater class through my school's summer enrichment program. I think it was her way of keeping me out of trouble for the summer. I'd always been the kind of kid who needed an audience. I liked to record myself singing and dancing. I had my own YouTube channel at one time. Anyway, theater clicked with me right away. After that summer, I knew what I wanted to do with the rest of my life."

"I love the way your eyes light up when you talk about acting."

"I thought you couldn't talk." She blushes, and the look she gives me sends electricity right to my cock.

I sketch the lines of her face, hoping to capture her expression as she continues.

"I was in every production I could get into in school, and I even did some community theater. When I graduated from high school, I took some classes at a community college. It was all I could afford. My mom couldn't help me pay for a four-year college, and my dad refused to, claiming since he had put himself through school, I could do the same. My best friend's parents gave me a waitressing job at one of their restaurants, and it allowed me to set my own hours and afford classes. I did that for about a year, and then I got a lead role in a contemporary version of *Pride and Prejudice*. A scout for *CSI* was in the audience on our closing night and asked me to send in a demo tape. I ended up doing a couple of shows, and that role led to my role on *Impassioned*."

"And now everyone knows your name. I remember when Tom had his first super-fan stalking him. Everyone I knew thought it was creepy, but he wore it like a badge of honor."

"Honestly, as long as I don't wear makeup, it's only the paparazzi who recognize me." Her hips shift just a little, and she lifts her leg straight up in a long stretch.

Stay strong. Just keep drawing. And for God's sake, stop imagining her gorgeous leg wrapped over your shoulder. "Try to stay still. It won't be much longer."

"Really? You're so fast. I thought it would take a lot longer." She lowers her leg and positions it back into place.

"It's a sketch. I already have your form figured out. It's just a matter of capturing your expression, the wrinkles of your clothes, and that sexy little freckle under your right ear."

Her head cocks to cover the freckle. "I can't wait to see it. Is it a caricature sketch like the one you drew before?"

"No. It's a portrait. More realistic, but still a sketch. Think Rose and Jack from *Titanic*." I look back down at my tablet, wishing I could capture her spirited soul. I concentrate on her eyes until they are just right because they're a gateway to her mind and incredibly expressive. Then I move down her very kissable neck to her round breasts.

"I didn't know you could do that kind of drawing on a computer," she says after a long pause.

"I can do just about any drawing I want on here. It's all in the software."

"I want to see the other one too. Is it on your tablet?"

"I'll show you, but you have to stay still while I finish. Remember, talking slows me down. Tell me something else."

"Like what?"

I look up again and smile. "Anything. What is one thing you would change if you could go back in time? Something you did or maybe didn't do?"

"Wow. That's a loaded question. I guess I would have stopped my brother from falling off his longboard and hitting his head."

"It has to be something within your control."

"Then I would have taken the car my dad gave me for my birthday. I would have smiled and said thank you, not caring that he only gave it to me so he would feel better. I turned it down because I wanted him to feel bad. I wanted him to realize he couldn't buy my love. I didn't want him to look like the hero. It was childish, revengeful. And in the end, it just hurt me. Me and Cam. If I'd taken the car . . ." She pauses, her eyes turning glassy. "If I'd just taken the damn car, I would have shared it with Cam." The words catch in her throat. "He wouldn't have been on a longboard, and he wouldn't have hit his head. And now he'd be going to college and have a girlfriend, not stuck in some pharmaceutical company's experiment he may or may not get any benefit from. He'd have a normal life." She sniffles. "I was childish. And in the end, it's all my fault."

Tears trail down her face, escaping the dabs her index finger makes. I set the tablet down and sit on the bed next to her. "I'm sorry, Kat." I caress her shoulder.

"It's okay. I'm okay. I shouldn't get all teary-eyed. I guess I've never really said that out loud. I've carried this guilt for so long, and you're the first person I've told." She tries to pin a smile on but fails. "What kills me is I could have saved him. If I'd been more mature and simply smiled and said thank you for the car, Cam would have been driving that day. Or I could have taken him to the hospital right away instead of waiting for my mom to get home. If I'd been mature enough to recognize my dad would never understand that by turning down the car I wanted more from him, not less, I probably would have kept it."

"You were just a kid. We do our best. Growing up is all about learning. Hell . . . most adults don't understand that people only hear what they want. You're only twenty-two. Cut yourself a break." I tuck a loose strand of hair behind her shoulder and pull her in, encapsulating her in my arms. We stay this way for several minutes.

"You always seem to catch me crying," she says against my chest. "I'm sorry. But I feel so comfortable with you, like you won't make fun of me or tell me I'm stupid. You just let me be me. It's effortless with you."

I smile, pulling back to see her eyes. I touch my lips to hers. How could I not after such sweet words? I kiss my way down to her collarbone, her skin soft and sweet-smelling. I want to distract her. I want to make her forget the responsibility she feels. I want her to feel like a twenty-two-year-old without the weight of the world on her shoulders. But the damn gland in my head flicks on and I collapse on the bed next to her, fighting everything I want.

"Why do you do that?" she asks.

"Do what, Kat?"

"You stop. I know you want to keep going, but you stop."

I take a deep breath and blow it out slowly. Should I tell her the truth? "It's wrong."

"It's not wrong. Didn't you hear what I said? Being with you is more right than anything else in my life."

"I don't want to get hurt, Kat. I know if I get too attached to you, I'll get hurt."

"I won't try to hurt you."

"I know. But you will."

"I really like you, Micah. I've never met a guy who understands me the way you do. This whole thing with Jake is just for show. It's not real. It's PR. Give me a chance."

"Realistically, what's going to happen between us? You'll date Jake publicly, and I'll be your dirty little secret?"

"Do you want to be my dirty little secret?" She smiles and winks at me.

"Truthfully . . . no. Maybe if Jake were gay, and weren't trying to sleep with you, I could. But that's not the case. You've dated him for almost a year."

"And he's cheated on me at least twice."

"Probably more," I say.

"Probably more. I don't even like him anymore, but I have to for the film. My film contract says production will side with Jake if we break up during filming. He can get me kicked off the film."

"You don't have a choice but to be nice to him?"

"I don't have a choice."

"Why didn't you lead with that?"

"Because I've learned that sometimes you just need to smile and say thank you. He got me on the film, and if he knew I was fooling around with you, he'd blow up. More on pride than anything. But I want to give us a chance. You and I deserve a chance. We just have to keep it on the down low for now, until filming is done. Then I promise we can be seen out together. But I can't lose this role or no one will hire me again."

"I can be discreet if you promise more." I smile, pick up my tablet, and add a small curve to her lips on the sketch. That's what she said, right? I would be more than a dirty little secret if I waited it out? I shade a couple of lines to add a little depth before I show it to her. "Do you want to see your portrait? It's not done yet, but you can see it now before I finish the shading."

She flips onto her stomach, and I fall in next to her as I hand her the tablet.

"This is sooo good. Why are you working security for your brother? You should be selling portraits for a living."

"Because working for my brother pays actual money. Last summer I worked at a comic book store during the weekdays, and on the weekends I worked in a stand on Sixth Street, drawing caricatures of drunk bar-goers. I worked every day of the week and made about a fourth of what I'm making this summer."

"Artists are so underrated." She shakes her head as she stares at her image. Her smile tells me she likes it. "Someday I'll make enough money to pay you for doing my portrait."

"I'd draw you for free any day." I lean over and bump shoulders with her, kissing her cheek

"Will you show me the caricature you drew of me?" She turns toward me, handing the tablet back, and my eyes fixate on her wet lips. Her delicious mouth calls for attention. I blink to clear my thoughts and then thumb through my tablet to find the proof she requested.

She looks at it and then to me.

"I know. It's Johanna Redemption's butt, not yours. I started out drawing her, but you kept interrupting my thoughts, and I just went with it."

She reaches for the button on my waistband and starts peeling off my shorts. Not the reaction I expected.

Katya

"I need to see her. I don't remember her butt being that big." I tug at Micah's shorts. He quickly kicks them off and peels down his boxers to show me his tattoo. I turn to get a better look. With my face inches from the ink, I trace my finger over the dark lines. He swallows a soft moan. And it's so sexy I fight the urge to pull his boxers off the rest of the way. But I am not making the first move. "Her butt's huge. Do you like big butts?"

He grabs my butt, pulling me up and on top of him. "No. I like your butt. It's just the style of drawing. I'm not really attracted to that in real life."

I lean down and kiss him. "Are you sure?" I kiss him again. "Because I bet the prop department could set me up with some implants."

"No. Not necessary. How much time do we have?"

I reach for my phone on the bed to check the time. Unable to get ahold of it while straddling Micah and not willing to dismount, I drag it across the comforter with my index finger. I don't want to look. I know our time is running out. Micah must know, too, or he wouldn't ask.

"My phone says two minutes to eleven. I have to be in the makeup trailer in an hour and a half. That gives us about thirty minutes." Just as I say the words my phone dings with a reminder about my call time. I know what he's going to say. We don't have enough time, and he's probably right, but I don't want to accept it. "We're never going to get a whole night together, not while filming is going on. The best we can hope for is thirty minutes between scenes. At least until the end of summer, anyway. I know it sucks. But it's better than not seeing each other."

He flips me under him and presses me to the bed. "I guess we should take advantage of every second we have, then." His lips descend on me.

On my lips.

My neck.

My breasts.

My whole body relaxes under his touch, while every cell clenches with anticipation. He slowly slides down my body, undressing me as he gives every inch of me attention. His nimble artist's fingers and tongue bring me quickly to the edge.

"I have a condom in my purse," I breathe out, trying to gain control.

"Not a chance," he lifts his head to speak. "I wanted to do this the first night we met, but I didn't want to take advantage of you."

I don't see how this act could be construed in any way as taking advantage of me. But I don't argue, I let go of all my worries and let Micah take control. I'm wound so tight that I can't make it last and I shudder against his mouth. But he doesn't stop. His fingers slide into me, and within a minute my body's surrendering a second time. That's never happened before. "Sweet baby kittens," I whimper under my breath as I collapse into a puddle on the bed, and it takes several minutes before I can do anything but pant.

When I open my eyes, he smiles and climbs back up to kiss me. My body is like pudding when he wraps his arm around me, all my energy spent. "You're next," I whisper, fighting to keep my eyes open. You always hear about people being exhausted after sex, but I've never experienced it until now.

"Kat, it's time to go. Your car is going to be here in a few minutes."

My neurons start to fire at his words. I've fallen asleep?

"What? We didn't even get . . . you didn't . . ." I look at him. He's fully clothed. "You didn't even get naked."

"That's not what today was about." He smiles. "Believe me, I got just as much pleasure out of what I did to you as you did."

That's a total lie, and I know it. There is no way he enjoyed it as much as I did.

"I'm a giver—what can I say?"

"I've never been with a giver. I didn't even know givers existed in the male species."

"Well, get used to it," he says. "There's more where that came from." He stands up, holding out his hand for me to take. "Right now, you need to catch your car."

I text Micah during my dinner break and ask him to meet me in my trailer. I know it's risky, but I can't stop thinking about him, and I want to show him I can be a giver too. Meeting in my trailer feels a little sleazy but the memory of his beard tickling my skin is like chocolate cake soaked in rum, and I'm going to take risks for chocolate cake soaked in rum. It's worth it.

"I don't think anyone saw me," he says as he locks the trailer door and pulls me into his arms. The drapes are closed, and no one should disturb us for the next hour.

"We have to be quiet, or the rumors will fly. Anna Hyde shares the other half of the trailer, and I heard her earlier through our shared wall. She's one of the biggest gossips on set."

"I can be quiet," he whispers as his lips move against my neck. He unties the robe I'm wearing, and then his hands smooth across the skin of my bare abdomen. "Do you greet everyone in a robe and panties?"

"Only the ones I can't stop thinking about." I slip my fingers under the hem of his shirt and tug it over his head. "I have a costume change, and wardrobe hasn't sent over the new one yet." I run my hands up his hard pecs, and his gorgeous blue eyes devour me.

"Lucky me," he says. He slides my robe over my shoulders, pinning my arms at my sides with the sleeves as he sucks on my collarbone. His beard tickles deep in my core.

I don't know if it's pheromones or what, but I can't control myself with him. He's so damn sexy and sweet and adorable. I just want to run my hands and tongue over every inch of him.

He lifts me and sets me on the small wood-grained tabletop, my robe still hanging off my shoulders. His lips find mine again as his hands cup my breasts. My whole body tingles under his touch. I reach for his belt and start unbuckling, half expecting him to stop me, but he doesn't. He pulls back from our kiss and watches me as I strip him down to his plaid boxers. They look so sexy on him, as if he's a lumberjack who just came in from chopping wood. I run my finger over the lines of his tattoo as my hand slides under the fabric covering him. A well-endowed lumberjack.

A knock on the trailer door freezes my hand on him.

He smiles and breaks out laughing. I kiss him to keep him quiet. I'm not answering it.

"Kat, are you there? I have your wardrobe for the next scene," says my assistant, Sherri, as she knocks again.

Micah points his thumb toward the bathroom as he pulls up his shorts and buckles his belt. I nod, and he walks to the bathroom. I wait for him to close the door before I fasten the belt on my robe and let Sherri inside.

"Thanks, Sherri." I take the dress and a bag from her. "Was there anything else?" I ask, because she's not leaving.

She looks around the trailer as if she expected to see someone.

"I thought I saw Micah come in here."

"Micah?"

"Yeah. Tom Fallston's brother."

"He's not here. Maybe he's talking to Pierce next door. I hear they're both big *Walking Dead* fans." Micah told me about the talk he had with Pierce when I was home visiting Cam.

"I could have sworn it was your door."

"Nope." Hopefully she doesn't notice his shirt on the chair behind her. "Good luck in your search. I'll let him know you're looking for him if I run into him."

"No. Don't. It's personal."

I open the door to ensure she understands I want her to leave. "Thanks for bringing those over."

"No problem," she says, glancing around again, her eyes catching on Micah's shirt. She moves toward the door. "Are you sure you haven't seen Micah?"

"Not today."

She looks as if she believes me as she steps out the door.

I lock the door behind her and feel the tension loosen in my muscles. Jake told me not to trust her. She has no loyalty to me. Production employs her, not me. They hired her since I didn't have my own assistant, and she's decent. She knows how the set works better than I do. But PAs are notorious for leaking information, and I hope with all hope she doesn't mention seeing Micah come into my trailer to Jake's assistant. I'm probably just paranoid. It could be my shirt or Jake's. She couldn't know for sure unless she picked it up.

I knock on the bathroom door. "The coast is clear. Get out here."

The door opens, and Micah steps out.

"Why were you laughing? Do you have something going on with Sherri? Something personal, perhaps?" I ask half jokingly, half worried he may be seeing her.

"No. You're the only girl I'm fooling around with," he says, wrapping an arm around me.

"Good, because you're the only one I'm fooling around with." I push on his shoulders, and he falls back on the red-cushioned couch. I lean over him and make quick work of his belt again. I'm going to show him I can be a giver too.

"I'm not sure I have time to fool around. Tom already sent a text," he says with a smirk. Sweet baby kittens, he's sexy leaning back with his elbows on my couch. His dark beard is just long enough to be a beard, and his blue eyes shine with playful mischief I can't wait to satisfy.

"Tom can wait," I say, taking his phone from him and placing it on the couch out of his reach. Then I set a pillow on it just in case his brother texts again.

Micah

Bang, bang. Bang, bang.

The hammering on the suite door booms all the way through to my bed, vibrating the very sheets I'm wrapped in. Kat's sweet floral and tropical scent lingers on them from this afternoon. We snuck off while Tom worked out with his trainer and Jake met with his agent.

After Tom returned, I disappeared to my room to recollect my thoughts on Kat. She's incredible. I could talk to her for hours and never get bored. I could have sex with her for days, years, and never get bored. She pushes me to a new level in everything—not just sex—, but my drawing and the way I think about the world. She and I are like puzzle pieces that snap together perfectly, without effort. I can't wait until we don't have to sneak around anymore.

I should get up to answer the door, but I'm positive it's not room service pounding.

"Open the Goddamn door, Fallston. YOU BETTER FUCKING OPEN THIS DOOR." It's Jake's voice, and if I had to guess, he's found out that I'm sleeping with Kat. I thought we'd been careful over the last couple of weeks, but someone could have seen us together.

I'm not answering the door. Let him assault me in public if he wants, but I'm not inviting him in to smash my face in private. The more cameras, the better. I pull a pillow over my head and wait for the banging to stop. It eventually does, not because he's given up, but because my brother, in his ultimate wisdom, has decided to open the door. I rise out of bed, listening intently to their conversation as I slip on a pair of athletic shorts. I don't want to be in my boxers when the paramedics come.

"I trusted you, Fallston. And you piss in my face."

"What are you talking about?"

"Someone on the hotel staff told me she saw you kissing Kat outside your room. Was it just for your scene? Swear to God, if you are sleeping with her I'm going to rip your nuts off."

Oops. My bad.

"Seriously? Think for a second. She doesn't even like me. I'm not sleeping with Kat. Listen to yourself, Jake," says Tom in his calm, deflecting voice. "What the hell is wrong with you? You're listening to rumors from the hotel staff? What's really going on?"

My brother is good at talking people off the ledge. In a crisis, he thinks clearly and makes decisions quickly. Hoping he cares enough about me not to point Gorboni in my direction, I sit back on the bed and pull a shirt on, cautiously waiting. Kat and I have been a little careless lately and making out in the hotel hallway was not the best idea. But it sure felt good at the time. She brings out this side of me that's reckless. I've never been a risk taker, and she brings that out in me. It's getting harder and harder to keep my feelings for her under wraps. I know Tom can tell I've fallen for her, even if we avoid the subject. I guess Jake's just discounted me again. In his mind, it couldn't possibly be me sleeping with Kat. I don't even register as competition for him.

"Fuckin-A, Tom. I was ready to put some serious hurt on you. Somethin' must be wrong with me. You're right. Kat hates you. She's not going to run to you when she could have me. It's just she had this T-shirt in her stuff when we moved her in, and it makes me wonder. It was Alexander McQueen, and I know it sells for around five hundred because I looked at them, but they don't come in my size. Here's the thing, Kat would never pay that much for a cotton shirt. And it was a guy's shirt. I figured it had to be yours. Who else on set would own a McQueen shirt? And then there's the fact that she showed up in your hotel room the day the video came out."

"She was just looking for a place to hide from the paps, and the shirt *is* mine. She was over, we were running lines, and she spilled her water all over her shirt. She didn't want to walk through the hall for everyone to see, so I loaned her a T-shirt. Are you sure she's cheating? She seems into you whenever I see her."

"That was your shirt?" Jake huffs.

"Yeah. But I'm not sleeping with her. I'm not gonna creep around with your girlfriend."

The door to my room is cracked open a couple of inches. I left it open, hoping to get some air moving in my stagnant room. But now I'm stuck, silenced by the fact that I don't want either of them to think of me as the guy in the hall, and yet I want to know what Jake is thinking.

"Let's brainstorm this together," says Tom, and I can hear them moving deeper into the suite. I quietly get up and walk closer to the door, not willing to miss a word.

"I don't get what's going on with her," Jake says. "She's so damn different from the other girls I've dated. She's my longest relationship so it can't be all bad, right? We've talked a little about marriage. Thought living together during filming would bring us closer. Sure, she says she hasn't forgiven me, but when I'm inside her, she doesn't complain. I think she's just trying to get a bigger commitment from me."

What the fuck? I storm through the door before I realize what I'm doing. They both turn and look up, startled by my sudden appearance. I freeze, scratching the back of my neck as I try to come up with a reason why I came out of my room at that precise moment. "Thirsty," I say and head to the fridge.

"Izzy mentioned some rumor going around set, but I hadn't heard it from you. So you're sleeping together again?" asks Tom. I know he's asking for my benefit and it pisses me off that he feels the need to rub it in.

"Of course we're sleeping together. It'd be weird if we weren't. She's my girlfriend, and we live together."

"Right. It'd be weird if you weren't," says Tom slowly. "Just wanted to make sure that's what you meant."

"What part about being inside her didn't you get? You know how to fuck a woman, right?" He cocks his head, studying Tom. "Are you just messin' with me or is something going on here? Why are you acting like this?"

"It's just . . . last I heard, she was freezing you out. If you're sleeping with her, she's not sleeping with someone else. She obviously still wants to be with you. I think you're letting the script get to you. Her character cheats on you in the film, and you're transferring it to real life. It happens to the best of us. Don't let the project wreck your relationship. I'd never sleep with your girlfriend. Just because the character I play does it, doesn't mean that I will. I'm not a villain in real life."

"Shit. You're right again." He repositions himself on the couch. "I feel like something is going on. And I don't want to lose her. Sex is just sex with other girls. She's worth more to me. She's never been one of those girls who wanted something from me, you know? It was part of my attraction to her. That and her supple ass and perfect tits. Maybe I should take the next step with her."

"Marriage?" Tom clarifies. "You don't want to marry. You marry her and no matter how good the prenup, she gets your money when it ends."

"But that's it. I think she might be it for me. She stuck with me this far. She wants a commitment. I'm sure of it."

"You think she'll be okay with you cheating when you're married?" I say because he's obviously delusional. I crack open the water bottle I got from the fridge as I turn to face him.

"What the fuck is your problem, Little Fallston? I'm not going to cheat on my wife. That's another level of commitment."

"Are you serious? What's going to change? You cheat on her now. What will be different?"

"I'm in love with her. You've probably never been in love," he says, as if I'm too young to understand.

"I've been in love before." I'm ready to unload on him. He apparently doesn't even remember.

"Let it go, Micah." Tom's voice booms above my building rage. "Why don't you go get us some food? I don't care what it is. Just go."

My mouth drops open in disbelief. *How is this my fault?*

"I just don't get what makes him think he can stay faithful. He obviously doesn't respect her enough to be monogamous. He doesn't even think *she'll* be monogamous. I mean, two minutes ago, he was accusing her of cheating, and now they're getting married?"

Jake's brow crinkles in confusion. And then a sneer of enlightenment takes over his face. "Is this about that girl from a year ago? She was asking to be fucked. Begging. She obviously didn't feel any strong ties to you to ask for it the way she was right in front of you. You can't put that on me."

"Fuck you, Gorboni!" I get up and walk out before I reveal the real reason I'm pissed. No matter what Tom thinks, I *have* gotten over Mara. She chose the bragging rights of screwing a movie star over me. I may not understand the logic, but everyone makes choices in life, and she wasn't the person I thought she was. I can't change what she did. I can only control how I respond to her actions and try to avoid girls like her in the future. I'm standing in front of Kat's door before I realize what I'm doing.

I knock and when she answers she sticks her head out to check the hallway for voyeurs. I didn't even look before knocking. She opens the door wider, and I walk in. She starts walking toward her bedroom, but I don't follow.

"Are you sleeping with Gorboni?" I'm not going to waste any more time with her if she's pulling a Mara on me.

"Why would you ask that?"

"He says you are. He says you don't complain about his cheating when he's inside you. Tell me the truth. Are you sleeping with him?"

"No. Is that why you're here? To accuse me of cheating on you?" She steps close enough for me to be warmed by her heat. It radiates, like her beauty, off her.

I don't know what we mean to each other. We never talk about us. Do I even have the right to ask? But I have to know.

"Yep. That's what I'm asking. Because if you are sleeping with him, I don't want to be with you."

Her soft hands slide against my jaw, and she tilts my head until my eyes meet hers. "I'm not sleeping with Jake. He's lying. We haven't been together since before the video came out."

I close my eyes. I want to believe Gorboni's a liar. He's got to be.

"What am I to you, Kat? I have to know. I can't keep doing what I'm doing with you without knowing what I mean to you."

She slides her hands from my jaw into my hair at the back of my head and stares at me. I close my eyes, trying to mask the pain I feel. I shouldn't have to ask. I need more from her. More commitment. More truth. This whole thing with her is fucked up. Why do I do this to myself? When I open my eyes her gorgeous hazel ones pierce me with her willingness to make it right with me. They tell me she wants to give me everything I need, but she can't. I knew this day would come and I was dreading it.

She reaches up on her tiptoes and presses her lips to mine as she slips off her panties from under her dress. "I promise we will be together when filming is over."

Her promise ignites hope in me. Hope that I'm not just a side piece to her. Hope that what I feel for her is real. Our lips mesh hungrily into one. Time passes, and we break apart only when I pull her dress over her head. She tugs my T-shirt off before we join again. She smells exotic, as if she showered in a tropical drink fusion. I love the way she smells. And looks. All soft and curvy.

It hasn't escaped my notice that Gorboni could walk in at any moment, and she doesn't seem to care. She arches off the wall, pressing against me, and I smooth my hand up her thigh to where she begs to be touched. A moan breaks from her throat, but I need more. It's not just sex with her. It never has been.

"Micah, I've always used a condom. Even though I'm on the pill," she starts to say, but when I push her bra cup down and take her nipple in my mouth her words falter. Shivers rake over her skin, and I pull back to look her in the eyes and let her finish.

"I . . . I've never trusted a man enough to go without. I trust you, Micah. I want this with you, no one else."

Trust is the one thing she will never have with Gorboni. I'm harder than I have ever been in my life. I straighten, pinning her with my eyes. "Are you sure?"

She nods, and I hesitate a second, maybe two, before my shorts are on the floor and I tug her legs up around my hips. I press her to the wall, balancing her in the right position. I've never done this before with no condom. I've heard it's like the difference between swimming in a tux and swimming naked. I love that she trusts me enough to do this. I kiss her one more time before gripping her ass and taking my time to sink into her.

I lift one of her legs higher in a desperate need to be closer. I move slow, drawing out her moans as I savor her. Worship her. Love her.

"This is what you wanted, right?" I ask.

Her glazed-over eyes try to focus on mine as she answers. "I thought maybe the bed. But this is good." She barely gets the words out.

God, I love Kat's sex face—her lips turned up in a slight smile, her eyes unfocused.

"Not bedroom sex," I say. "I want you to look at this wall while you're eating breakfast and think about how you had the best orgasm of your life with me bareback inside you."

"Oh, God . . . I want that too." Her fingers hungrily claw into my back, pulling me even deeper.

"I want you to remember how it felt when I hit the spot in you that makes your toes curl. Because I can tell by the way your insides quiver that I'm hitting it."

"Oh, God."

"I want you to fall for me as hard as I'm falling for you."

I can feel the orgasm as it explodes her body around me.

She chants my name into my shoulder until her words turn garbled and incoherent. Her whole body trembles.

It's so intense, I lose it too.

When our breaths start to slow, and her body turns limp and pliable, she rests her head against the wall and says, "Micah," with a very satiated smile.

"I think you liked that," I say with a wink. I'm pretty sure I could go again right now.

"My toes actually curled. This is the best wall ever," she says, biting her lip and patting the wall. "I don't know how you did that."

"Here, I'll show you." I start moving again. I can't help myself. She wraps her arms around my neck, and within a blink of an eye, she's squirming again. I don't want to do it standing, though. I don't have enough energy. I pull off the wall and with one hand lean down to snatch up our clothes the best I can, piling them between us as I carry her to the bed. I drop them on the floor before closing and locking the door.

"I think I got everything," I say, and she giggles as if she doesn't care.

I lay her on the bed, burying myself deep. I can't get enough of this girl.

Micah

I brush a strand of hair out of her eyes as she snuggles into my side exhausted but thoroughly satisfied. "We have a future, then?" I ask because I want to hear it again. "After filming ends, we'll have . . . what . . . a week? My classes start on August twenty-third. Then what?"

"Then we'll see each other when we can. I'll come to Austin, and you can come to Los Angeles every chance we get. We'll make it work." Her hand rests on my chest as she stretches up to kiss my cheek.

I want more, but we're not even dating officially yet. "I can't wait until we can go out in public together."

"Me too. Can I ask you something personal?"

"Always."

"Where did you learn to do that?" she asks, her hand smoothing over my chest.

"What?"

"Um . . ." Her fingers tap rhythmically against my skin as if she doesn't know how to put her thoughts into words. "Specifically, that twist and snap thing at the end. Oh my God. It blew my mind."

A deep, guttural laugh escapes me. She doesn't want the truth.

"I mean, how does a twenty-one-year-old know how to do that? And don't say porn. They don't do that in porn. Porn is always about the man. Where did you learn it?"

She's not giving up.

"I learned some of it from Tom."

"Bull!"

"Swear to God." I weave my fingers with hers. "He didn't want me to be the comic book nerd who never found the crystal palace. He used to give me so much crap about the comic books. I was thirteen when he drew the first diagram for me. And every time he discovered something that worked on a woman, he'd tell me about it in great detail. I collected a notebook full by the time I got to try them myself. At first, it was a disaster. I almost threw the guide out, convinced it was all lies. No stamina."

She giggles. I love her giggle.

"But then I got a steady girlfriend, and I asked a lot of questions during sex. By the time I met Mara, I'd fixed the stamina problem and began to test out Tom's lessons. And I'd learned a bunch of stuff on my own. Mara was always very verbal during sex. Not afraid to tell me what she wanted, —that girl."

"She was your first love?"

"No. My first love was Mia Thompson. I met her when I was eighteen. She exudes sex—so hot. She was dating Jonathan Williams at the time but, you know, I figured I could win her over." I expect her to laugh at the idea of me competing with mega movie star Jonathan Williams over a girl, but she doesn't. "Mara came after Mia broke my heart."

"You lied. You said you'd only been in love once."

"I guess technically Mia was just a crush. I never even kissed her."

"People say I look like her. Is that why you're attracted to me? Because of a crush on Mia Thompson?"

"Who said I'm attracted to you?"

Her hands pull from mine and her fingers dance down my abdomen, calling my lower brain to attention again. "This guy, here, seems attracted to me."

Yeah, she went there.

"He betrays me every time—such a narc. I guess I'm a little attracted to you." I pull her closer into my side.

"I could tell," she says, her voice softening and her eyelids growing heavy. "Are you sure you have to go back to school? Can't you just stay in Los Angeles?"

"Yep. I need to go back to school." I could easily go again, but Kat looks exhausted. Her eyes flutter shut for longer and longer periods as I watch. It's almost comical. I want to tell her I love her. I want to talk for hours about the future, but I should let her rest. She has to be up in a matter of hours.

The suite door opens, and within a minute Gorboni's trying to open Kat's bedroom door. *What the hell?* Does he come into her room at night?

"Kitty Kat, I found the present you left me." He starts pounding. "Come on, babe. Why'd ya leave your panties out here if you're going to lock the door?" He tries the knob again and knocks some more. "Kat. Come on, open the door. I didn't know you wanted it tonight or I never would have left."

Part of me wants to answer the door. I won't, but I want to. He still thinks he is going to get her back. It's pathetic, really. If I didn't know what a douchebag he was, I'd feel sorry for him. When he finally gives up and I hear his bedroom door slam, I debate whether I should stay the night or head back to my room before morning.

My phone vibrates from somewhere on the floor. I know it's Tom and I don't want to get up. When the buzzing starts back up a second time, I crawl out from under Kat's arm to find the back pocket of my shorts and my phone. It's him, just as I thought. I silence it and type out a quick text.

On my way to the suite.

He doesn't reply, but he doesn't call again either. I read through the texts. For a while, he actually believed I would bring food back. The last text he sent was a warning about Gorboni heading back to his room.

I reluctantly pull on my clothes, taking one last look at the beautiful woman on the bed. I don't want to leave, but I know it's for the best. I can't be here in the morning. Actually, I could. It would solve some of the problems. But what if she picked him over me? I'm not ready to give her up.

Not wanting to wake her, I lean over her, touching my lips lightly to her temple. She smells so good. "I love you, Kat," I whisper, knowing she won't hear. It's cowardly to profess my feelings when she can't hear them, but I need her to say the words first.

I straighten and make my way to the door without looking back. I quietly crack it open and listen. No sound. I feel like a kid sneaking out of a girl's room when her parents are sleeping in the next room. Jake's bedroom door is on the opposite side of the suite and is closed, but that doesn't mean he's not sitting on the couch or making a sandwich. I ninja out of the suite, spying around corners as I make my way. Once in the hallway, I breathe a sigh of relief, but still keep my head down in case someone is watching the cameras. I walk the long way around to my room just in case and check that the hall is clear before opening the door.

The second I walk in the door Tom says, "I'm covered in your dirt," his brown eyes digging into me. "What were you thinking?" His nose crinkles as he sniffs near my shoulder. "You smell like her. And sex." As he backs away from me, his chin bucks up, challenging me to deny his words.

I tuck my keycard back in my wallet and ask, "What do you want me to say? I think I'm in love with her."

He growls.

Why did I have to be honest with him? I should have just kept my mouth shut.

"Shut the fuck up." His hands clench and unclench at his sides as if he's working two stress balls into oblivion. "What you do affects me, little brother." He walks farther into the suite and death-grips the back of the couch. "This is not one of your comic books where the nerd gets the girl. I don't know how else to say this, but she's not going to pick you. You're not a superhero. She's going to pick Jake. She already has."

"What am I, a pity fuck? What's the point in screwing me when she has all she wants with him? Why would she risk what she has with him to be with me? I mean something to her. We have a relationship. She's going to break it off with him. She just has to wait until filming's done."

"I knew this was going to happen. You were supposed to take the one night you got and walk away. You can't fall in love with her. I am not talking you off the ledge this time." He shakes his head in disgust. "I'm filming. I don't have time for your fanboy crushes. You're supposed to be helping me, not the other way around."

"Give me a break, Tom. I'm not a sixteen-year-old honor student, fantasizing about Mia Thompson. She isn't my first girlfriend."

"No. She isn't your girlfriend at all. She's Jake's. Break it off while you still have some dignity."

"She's going to leave him. I'm not breaking it off with her."

He stares at me for a long minute and then walks into his room. He thinks he's right, but I know he's wrong.

She trusts me.

Not Jake. Me.

Chapter 24

Katya

Micah left sometime this morning while I was in the deepest, most blissful sleep I've ever had, and I still can't put what we did into words. I've completely fallen for him. He leaves a smile on my face and fairies dancing in my stomach.

"You are one sadistic, teasing bitch," Jake says as he closes his bedroom door and walks toward me at the dining table in the suite.

I give him a death glare. Who starts a conversation like that? All I'm trying to do is replenish my energy stores after last night. I open the bottle of green smoothie and take a significant draw.

"You leave me a trail of breadcrumbs and then lock your door? That's cruel, Kat, even for you."

He pulls the panties I wore last night from his pocket and drops them on the table next to my coffee. *Damn.* I close my eyes to disguise the panic filling my stomach.

"Why would you do that?"

He thinks I left them for him to find. He doesn't know Micah was here. A small amount of relief washes over me as I open my eyes and conjure a bitchy glare.

"I had a momentary lapse in judgment. But then I realized you cheated on me and have yet to show me a clean bill of health. I'm not sleeping with you until you can prove you're not a walking public toilet."

"What am I supposed to do, run to a local STD clinic?"

"I don't know, but I'm sure you can figure it out. Show me your clean bill of health and next time my door won't be locked." I hope filming ends before he finds an inconspicuous place to get tested or a doctor who will come to the hotel.

He picks up his phone and dictates a text. "Trey, find a discreet place I can get tested. Kat wants a clean bill of health ASAP." He pushes a button and turns to me. "I'll give you what you want because I respect you. I can humble myself if that's what you need. But the ice queen thing's got to stop. I'm tired of it."

I narrow my eyes at him. "Am I wrong or are we working off a contract? Nowhere in that contract does it say I have to have sex with you. If I do, it's purely at my discretion. Maybe you should be trying to convince me without threats. I don't respond to them. If you weren't such an ass to me all the time, I'd be nicer to you." I pick up my smoothie, my coffee, and my phone before walking into my room and closing the door. I type out a text to Micah.

Kat: Had a good time last night. We'll have to have a repeat.

Micah: What are you doing tonight?

Kat: IDK. Jake found my panties and thought I was giving him the green light. We need to be more careful.

Micah: He accused Tom yesterday of hooking up with you. What would he say if he knew it was me?

Kat: You sound like you want him to find out.

Micah: I can wait until the movie ends.

Kat: Good. Mom's calling. Talk later.

I answer the call as I sit up on the bed.

"Hey, Mom, are you settling into the apartment?"

"We've been here almost a month, honey. We are about as settled as we're going to get."

"I can't believe it's been a month. It seems like you just got there."

"You've been busy filming. Do you want to talk to your brother?"

"Of course."

She hands the phone to Cam.

"Hey, Kat. Did you finish filming?"

"No. Not yet. Four more weeks."

"I can't wait to see you. I feel so good, and I'm getting tons of memories back. Like the time I put toothpaste in that Oreo cookie, and you ate it." He laughs in a deep timbre that melts my heart. I haven't heard the sound in so long. "You know what else? I met this girl. She's part of the study too. She has this huge scar across the side of her head, but her hair covers it. She's cute even with the scar. I asked her out for coffee. We're not supposed to drink coffee, but we had smoothies, and I think I'm going to ask her out again."

He sounds excited, and I can't help the tears gathering in my eyes.

"I want you to meet her. I told her you were my sister and she wants to meet you. When are you coming?"

"I'll be there the day after filming wraps."

"We'll get burgers and fries, and you'll eat because you're done filming."

"I can't wait, Cam."

"I'll let you talk to Mom. I'm supposed to do some exercise before we go to the center."

"See you soon, Cam."

Mom comes on the line, laughing.

"Isn't it amazing? He's doing so well. The problem with the slurred speech is clearing up, and every day he tells me about another memory he's retrieved. I can't wait for you to see him. He looks good."

"That's the best news, Mom. I can't wait to see him. I have to get to set. We'll talk soon. Love you."

"Love you too."

I end the call on a huge high. I can't believe Cam's talking about a girl. He hasn't had an interest in anything but comic books in so long. He must be getting the correct medication for him to be making improvements so quickly. Cam's going to get his life back.

When I reach the set, I don't think the day can get any better until I spot

Micah at craft services. His smile brings back all the deep emotions I felt last night. I can't wait for filming to be done. I smile back, biting my lip.

"Having a good morning?" he asks with a shoulder nudge.

"So far. I talked to my mom and Cam. The drugs Cam's taking are working miracles. He sounded great. He's even asked a girl out."

"That's great news. I'm glad he's finally making some progress. I can't wait to meet him."

"I was going to head to Boston for a few days after filming is done." I look around to make sure no one can hear me and then whisper, "Do you want to come with me?"

"Yeah." He picks up three almond-and-caramel bars. "I'll follow you anywhere, Miss Avery."

I know it's a line from a movie, but I can't place it. "Let's plan on it. Talk later."

He arches a brow and nods with a suppressed smile. His hair is messier than usual this morning. Sex hair. Amazing-sex hair. I fight not to run my fingers through it. I love his hair. The old me would have declared my love to him in words last night instead of gestures, but the new me is waiting for him to say it first. Four more weeks and we can be together.

Sherri catches me as I round the corner.

"Did Deana from wardrobe find you?"

"No. What did she need?"

"Something about a missing belt. I'm sure she'll get it figured out."

I shrug.

"You *do* know Micah after all."

I look at her with my best innocent, doe-eyed expression. "He's Tom's little brother and Tom is Jake's best friend. Of course I know him."

"I'm not accusing you of sleeping with him. You'd tell me if you were, right?"

I glare at her while I shake my head. Hopefully, it's enough to convince her I'm not.

"He's so cute and sweet. Do you know if he has a girlfriend?"

Seriously?

"I'm pretty sure he does. I met her once at a barbeque." *Take that.* "They're pretty serious, I think. All I remember is she's gorgeous."

"Too bad. All the PAs are asking. Izzy didn't think he had a girlfriend. You would think she would know."

Hope I didn't shoot myself in the foot with my comment. "They may have broken up," I add to cover myself. "I just remember her because she was so pretty."

"So . . . there's still hope." A smile grows on her face. "He's not gay, right? Izzy said he's not, but Trey is always talking him up. I don't want to try to hook up with him if my chances are zero."

"He mentioned her just this week," I say, my voice showing my frustration.

"Whatever. I guess I'll ask him myself, just to make sure. Maybe he's not as serious about her as you think. You know how 'laxed people get on location. Serious relationships always turn open on set."

Damnit.

Micah and I are exclusive. Him asking me not to be with Jake if I'm with him, that's what last night was all about. It means we're exclusive, doesn't it? He won't sleep with Sherri even if she throws herself at him. I take a deep breath and relax. I know he won't.

Chapter 25

Micah

Tom's had me running around doing pointless garbage all morning, his way of punishing me for being stupid, I guess. I got him coffee. I've been to craft services twice. I'm just returning from a drugstore with the eye drops he asked for when I realize this is BS. I need five minutes for myself. I've spent most of the summer taking orders from him without questions. He bosses me around, and I just do what he says. I figure part of my job this summer is to keep Tom calm and arguing with him about crap that doesn't matter in the end doesn't keep him calm. I'm an easy going guy, but his complete lack of respect for my feelings about Kat is wearing on me. I'm not imagining what Kat and I have. I can't be.

I know he needs his eye drops, but I have needs too. Five minutes. Maybe ten. I deserve a break. Time for me. I'm sure Tom's still in makeup anyway. He needed a haircut, and they were going to have to lighten the tips to match what he had before the cut. He won't even notice I'm missing.

Looking for some quiet away from the chaos of filming, I punch in the code to unlock Tom's trailer door and take the three steps up. With one of my favorite songs blasting in my wireless earbuds, I don't notice the man and woman in the trailer. But when I look up, I see Jake's mouth moving as he stands behind . . . *Shit*. I swallow hard. She's bent over the back of the chair, and his pants are on the floor. I click off my music. Obviously, they didn't expect me.

"Tom gave me the code. Said I could use it. You got some sick voyeuring fascination?" asks Jake as he continues to fuck her from behind. He doesn't even stop.

"Nope. Didn't know you'd be here." I turn around and walk out. I'm shaking. I can't help it. For a second I thought it was Kat. The dark hair blanketing her face threw me. I walk a half block before taking out my phone.

> *Micah: Don't trust your assistant Sherri. I just walked in on Jake*
> *fucking her in Tom's trailer. Thought you should know.*
> *Kat: ???*
> *Micah: Just what I said. Sorry to text it. But you made me promise*
> *I would tell you first.*
> *Kat: Not your fault. Jake's an ass! And she's a little bitch. Guess*
> *I'll be getting a new assistant. Gotta go. Text you when*
> *I'm done.*

I head to the hair and makeup trailer to meet Tom, and he's still getting styled in the chair where I left him. The stylist uses a laminated photo of him to achieve consistency. I understand why actors become narcissistic, what with everyone telling them how good they look and kissing their butts all the time.

"I stopped by your trailer on my way over here. Do you think Kat will mind Jake giving her assistant a workout in your trailer?"

Tom's eyes meet mine. They say *shut the hell up*, and I do. I've said enough to get the staff talking. I don't need to say any more. Tom takes out his phone and texts me.

> *Tom: Did you tell her?*
> *Micah: Yep.*
> *Tom: It won't make a difference. She's not going to leave him. If she*
> *were, she would have already done it.*

He sets his phone on his lap as if he's said everything needed. The stylist sprays his hair and starts running her fingers through his mop to manipulate it just right.

"Good as new," says Tom. He looks back and forth between the mirror and the photo and smiles. "Am I done?"

The green-haired stylist holds up a finger and snips a rogue hair before stepping back. "You're free to go."

Tom dismounts his chair, and I follow him out of the trailer.

"Micah, stop meddling in Jake's love life."

"I walked in on him screwing another woman. You can't expect me to not tell her. Even if we were just friends, I'd have to tell her."

He cocks his head and raises his brow.

"And what was she doing last night? Jake's my best friend. Should I tell him what she was doing?"

I shrug. "Sure. That'd solve my problems. We wouldn't have to hide it anymore."

"You don't see the whole picture. She's not going to pick you. You need to find a way to come to terms with that end result."

"It was her assistant. Kat needed to know she couldn't trust her."

He holds up a hand to stop me from talking as he turns to me.

"You're going to wreck her career. Does that mean anything to you? You say you care about her, but you kiss her in the hotel hallway where anyone could snap a picture. What if it got out she's sleeping around? It doesn't matter what Jake does, Kat's the one who will lose everything if she gets caught. I told Jake he could use my trailer because we still have filming to do, and I didn't want Kat to catch him. You heard how it affected her when she found out last time. Even the best actors screw up when their personal lives are a mess. But if she muddles her lines again, all anyone is going to remember is that she's flaky, not dependable. This film's important. Jake's sex life doesn't matter. What do you think happens to Kat when he dumps her because she's sleeping with you? He's Mr. All-American, and if she cheats, he'll find another woman the next day. Kat's the one who loses. She needs Jake. That's why she hasn't dumped him even with his cheating."

I let out the breath I'm holding as Tom's words sink in. She's the one who loses. She's the one who suffers for being with me.

"Did you get my eye drops?"

"Yeah." I pull the box from my pocket, open it, and hand him the bottle.

Am I pressuring Kat into making the biggest mistake of her life? Kat and I need to find some time alone to talk, really talk.

Chapter 26

Katya

His fingers grasp my hip with a squeeze, curling me into his side, and as his lips touch the top of my head in a kiss, a string of flashes goes off. I instinctively turn, hiding my face in his dinner jacket.

"I can't believe they found us," I say, my words muffled. I shouldn't be surprised the paparazzi show up wherever filming occurs.

"Why are you hiding, Kitty Kat? They're just keeping us relevant."

Jake's always liked the paparazzi more than I have. He feeds off their attention, craves it like an addict. I get the high. It's great to be wanted, to be liked. But living in his shadow has drawbacks he rarely acknowledges, like the hate that can accompany a lousy shot. I pin a smile on and face the cameras. The more time I spend with Micah, the harder these shows become.

"I didn't expect them tonight."

"I mentioned where we were going to a clerk at the hotel. It's not brain surgery," he says under his breath. He leans down and takes my chin in his hands, pulling my lips to his. He's never gentle anymore. It's all about the show, as if he owns me. I wonder how much longer I can do this with him.

He keeps pressing the issue of my rogue panties. Then on top of it, he cheats on me with my assistant. If he does end up with a clean bill of health, how do I know he will stay clean? Ultimately, that could be my excuse for the breakup. I need to bring up the cheating, I know that much. But not until after this meeting. This meeting could be useful for both our careers and I don't want Jake sabotaging me tonight. The power couple we're meeting are industry icons. They've produced some of the biggest films in Hollywood history. I know they're here to meet with Jake and I'm just arm-candy for the evening, but having face-to-face exposure with them could impact the rest of my career. If they know who I am, it could help me secure movies, big movies.

After Jake's gotten his fill of the paparazzi, we're rushed through the restaurant door and seated at a high-top table with the Mendez's. Jake introduces me to Paul Mendez and his wife, Gena, and I do my best to play the doting girlfriend.

After several minutes of butt kissing—Jake's butt not mine—Gena targets me with her dark, scrutinizing gaze and asks, "So, Katya, what was really going on this spring with that video of Jake and the other girl?"

I'm stunned. I can't believe this woman went for the jugular right out of the gate. Even after months of searching for a feasible answer to this question, I still don't have one. I pick my jaw up off the floor as I turn to Jake.

"What you have to understand, Gena, is that all relationships have ups and downs. Kat and I weren't in a good place. Neither of us were happy. Everyone always acts as if living the Hollywood dream is easy. I'm not complaining, but it's not easy. You saw what we had to walk through just to get in the restaurant." His hand rubs across my back in a soothing motion as he continues. "I'm not proud of what that video showed. But it has done one good thing. It's brought Kat and me closer together. We're in a good place now, happier than we've ever been."

She smiles as if she's heard her share of excuses. She looks to her husband and then back to me with a slight eye roll. Her innocent-looking hubby probably cheats. "Katya, I'd like to hear it in your words. I saw the clip of when the paparazzi revealed that wretched video to you. It was the first time you'd seen it. You were taken aback."

What? Does this woman work for TMZ? Is she recording this? My hand moves lovingly to Jake's thigh, and as I sink my nails into his muscle to show him how unhappy I am to be in this situation, I glance at him with an adoring expression. "Well, . . . of course it wasn't a good time for us. But as Jacob said . . ." He hates it when anyone uses his full name. "We're in a better spot now. In fact, we've taken the relationship to the next level and have moved in together." Okay, yes, I'm stretching the truth. But, seriously, who asks such personal questions at a meet-and-greet dinner? Besides, the fact that Jake and I are cohabitating on location is already out in the press.

Jake kisses my temple, and his eyes twinkle with approval. "How can I not love this woman?" Jake asks.

I sink my nails into his leg again with a smile. His hand covers mine on his leg, essentially retracting my claws.

"We'll let you in on a little secret if you promise not to tell the press . . . promise?" asks Jake. He entwines his fingers with mine, probably to prevent further damage to his leg. Jake is great at building hype. He knows all the strings to pull and when to pull them. It comes naturally to him.

"Of course. Your secret is safe with us," says Gena, turning to her husband with a delicious smile. She loves the idea of knowing our secrets. She's eating it up. Insider information is a hot commodity in Hollywood, and Jake's a huge name. Even after the video, everyone loves him.

"Should I tell them, Kat?" Jake asks.

"If you think you can trust them," I play along, not knowing what he plans to tell them. But I don't care. He can say whatever he wants. It's all part of the dance.

"Kat and I are engaged." Jake moves our joined hands onto my lap. I guess he doesn't want to take any chances with my claws. "We don't have the ring yet, but it's in the works. We're just waiting for the right moment."

The news doesn't even faze me. This is an acting gig. I don't care what he tells these people. With a soft nod and a smile, I add credibility to Jake's words.

I think that sold it.

I relax into Jake's side, touching shoulders with him, and he lifts our joined hands to his lips, kissing my ring finger. What a show-off. I know the paparazzi are outside the windows with their giant telescoping lenses capturing every

PDA, but unless they read lips they don't know what we're talking about, and this news will never hit Micah's ears.

"When is the wedding?" asks Gena.

I look to Jake, he squeezes my hand, and I answer. "Next summer maybe. We haven't even officially gotten engaged. A lot of planning goes into a wedding. Especially when you're marrying a guy like Jake. He likes a big show." It's easy to lie when it's fiction.

"We would love to be included in your plans," says Gena without apology, her brown eyes sparkling with anticipation.

"We'll keep that in mind. I want to hear more about this movie." Jake easily ups the ante, inferring they will be invited to the wedding if he gets the role he wants.

"I like a man who can stay focused on goals. Honestly, we were a bit worried about your ability to stay true to ideals. But we can see that real life wasn't as bad as the press made it out to be," says Gena.

Oh my God. They are so wrong. Can't they see this is just make-believe? I'm losing any respect I had for them. After the inquisition, the conversation settles back to more appropriate *getting to know if you're right for the role* dialogue. I try to stay engaged in the discussion, but my mind keeps drifting to Micah.

His silky dark hair.

His amazing toe-curling kisses.

The warmth that spreads through my body when he smiles.

Jake leans into me and whispers, "Try to keep up, Katya. These people are important."

I look up at him with my adoring face, smile, and then try to join back into the conversation. I nod and smile at Gena, having no idea what I've agreed to.

"Then you would be interested?" asks Paul. "It's a role of a lifetime, with the best-selling book and all. It's going to be huge. Jake suggested we consider you."

Jake actually suggested me for a role? "I guess I would have to look at the script and the contract," I say, completely confused. Did they just offer me a movie?

"The fans will go crazy for another movie with the two of you together," adds Gena.

"Especially if the wedding occurs near the release. We'll work up a contract, get you a script, and you can let us know what you think."

They talk about the film a bit more. It's a time travel movie similar to *Outlander* but with the hero and heroine of the present day returning to World War II. My recent roles have been contemporary, and the historical aspect intrigues me.

By the end of the evening, the excitement of possibly gaining another movie role from my association with Jake thrills me. Jake and I talk, I mean really chat when we get back to the hotel. We haven't talked like this since before the video. We talk about my brother and the strides he's making in the study. We talk about his grandmother and how her health is starting to fail. He's planning a trip this fall to visit her in Italy. I don't bitch at him for his mistakes, and he doesn't treat me as if I'm an object.

When he leans in and touches his lips to mine, I don't pull away. We kiss in the suite where no one can see us, and it feels good, like old times. It feels good until my gaze catches the wall by the door—the best-orgasm-of-my-life wall or at least the first-best-orgasm-of-my-life. What am I doing? I push on his shoulders, and he tightens his grip on me.

"Stop, Jake. I can't do this."

"Kat, you can. You were ready to sleep with me a week ago. Why not now?" His lips cover mine again, and I close my mouth to him. He pulls back. "How long are you going to punish me? I could have any girl I want. You're lucky I picked you."

"I know," I say, because he could, and dating him has definitely opened opportunities, I wouldn't have without him. "I just need a little more time before we go any further. And I want to see a clean bill of health on you first."

"My patience is thin. This weekend we're going to make up properly."

"Not without a clean bill of health from you. Besides, I'm not going to be around this weekend. I promised Megan and Liam I would show up for their wedding ceremony. They scheduled it around my schedule. I can't let them down."

"They invited you and not me? What the fuck? Is Jonathan Williams going?"

"Most likely. Megan said the date I was available worked for him."

"I've known Liam for years. He probably thought I was too busy. I'm going with you. Your plus one."

"You better ask Liam if it's okay."

"Piff." He pulls his phone from his pocket and starts typing on it. I hear it ping, and he says, "Fallston didn't get invited either. We're both going to crash. Liam won't care."

This was supposed to be my weekend to get away from Jake, away from Micah. I was supposed to have time to sort through the mess I made and figure out what I'm going to do after filming's done.

"Is he bringing his brother?" What did I just ask? *Damnit.* Maybe Jake won't notice. All I need is for them both to be at the wedding. Micah will spend the whole weekend pissed at me for letting Jake touch me, and Jake will spend the weekend pissed at me for not letting him touch me.

"I don't know. Probably. Tom won't have time to hire a babysitter, not with filming going on."

"Cut it out, Jake. Micah's only six months younger than me. You calling him a baby makes me a baby too."

"But you're my baby, baby," he says. "And we're getting married."

"Ha ha." His joke isn't funny.

Chapter 27

Micah

My eyes keep slipping to their intertwined hands because I can't figure out why she feels the need to put on a show for me. Granted, it's subtle. She's not making out with him, but it still irritates me. I don't need this. I get up to walk to the back of the plane, and Kat's eyes meet mine for the first time. I look down at her lap, where Gorboni's hand sits, and without glancing at her eyes again, head for a seat out of eye shot of her.

I don't know what's going on with Kat. Ever since she went to dinner with Gorboni, she's been acting weird. We haven't had any time to be alone and the two times we had a texting conversation of any substance she talked about Liam's upcoming wedding and possibly getting another movie role. We haven't talked about us. Or the future. I don't know what's going to happen in two weeks when filming ends. Do I need to book a flight to Boston with her? Is she going to book it for me? She asked me to go with her to visit her mother once filming ended the last time we were together, but she hasn't mentioned it since.

Now, I'm sitting on the private jet Gorboni rented, wondering why I'm here. This is fucking torture. I barely know Liam Nordstrom. There is no need for me to go to his wedding. Tom claims he wants me there for security, but I suspect the real reason is that he wants me to see firsthand how well Gorboni and Kat are getting along.

I walk past Tom, who's wearing his noise-eliminating headphones, and Gorboni's assistant who, just yesterday, asked me if I would be interested in "a private workout session" with him. I park my butt next to Tom's assistant, Izzy. At least I can have a conversation with her without being propositioned.

Izzy is nice enough. Maybe a bit too take-charge for me, but nice enough. She looks up from her tablet when I sit.

"Hey," I say.

She lifts her dark-framed designer glasses and perches them on top of her head. Her golden hair is pulled back in a high bun on her head, and she reminds me of a dirty librarian comic I once drew.

"Tired of the show?" she asks.

I nod, wondering if she's just as grossed out by the constant display of PDAs as I am. "It gets to be a bit much after a while."

"Trey says Jake's been hitting hard to make up for his cheating—taking her out to dinner, buying her gifts. He's even convinced her to do another movie with him. Looks like they're working out their problems, anyway."

I humph out a breath as if she kicked me in the stomach. I lean forward, looking down so she can't see my face. He got her into another movie with him. *Shit.* Is she ever going to be free?

"You're a bit smitten with Kat, I can tell." She smiles, and I have to wonder if all this pretending is worth the effort. It doesn't seem to matter anyway. "Hey, was Trey serious when he asked if I would be interested in a threesome with you and him?" she continues. "I can't, and just so you know, it's no reflection on you. But I have a boyfriend, and my mamma would kill me if I ever did something like that. Besides I'm pretty sure he just wants your ass in his bed, not mine. He talks about your ass every time you walk by. It's a nice ass but . . ."

"Thanks, I think? Truthfully, he hasn't offered up the threesome yet. I don't know how to make him understand that just because his sexual preference is fluid doesn't mean mine is. Any ideas?"

"Tell him you have a girlfriend. Or we could pretend to be dating. That would piss him off."

"I think there's enough playacting going on," I say. "Thanks for offering though."

She looks at me with a sympathetic smile.

"Are you going to the wedding?" I ask.

"I got invited when Tom told Liam he was crashing. I used to work for Liam's housemate, Nak. Nak's girlfriend Leslie and I are good friends. We met at UCLA. Anyway, I want to go to the wedding, but my boyfriend has issues going anywhere he can't wear flip-flops. Are you going?"

"Tom thinks I need to be wherever he is. I *am* his bodyguard. You should come without your boyfriend. Otherwise, I'll be stuck talking to Trey while I watch Kat and Jake make out."

"Trey's not going. I hear Jonathan Williams is going. Maybe Mia Thompson will be there too."

"Damn. My brother has a big mouth." I shake my head in disgust. "Is nothing off limits?" I can't believe Tom told her about my crush on Mia Thompson.

"Don't worry. Nothing he says goes beyond me. Micah, you seem like a really nice guy."

"Haven't you heard that nice guys finish last?" I run a hand through my hair. How many girls have told me I'm a nice guy?

"Every guy I've ever dated has been an asshole. I always pick good-looking guys with no future who I think I can change. I don't know why I do it, but I do. My current boyfriend keeps hinting that we should move in together and I know if I say yes he'll quit his job and max out my credit card. It's happened before."

I laugh, but she's serious.

"And I'll let him because I can't tell him no. Yet he won't even go to the wedding with me. My point is, if Kat cared about you, she'd put you first. Stop trying to change her. The only person you can change is yourself. Yes, I know I need to listen to my own advice."

"Thanks. And if I cared for her, I'd stop seeing her. Nothing's easy." I kiss her cheek. I need Kat to give a little. Me always being second to Jake burns like nothing else. But I don't want to give her up either. "You are so organized, how is it you're such a hot mess in your personal life?"

"Just lucky, I guess. I've always been that way. Thank you for all your help with Tom. You were so right about him only listening to ideas he thinks come from his head. My daddy is the same way. I mastered puppeteering him when I was six. Tom and I get along great now."

"Anything I can do to help. Maybe you should ask for a raise."

She clasps her fingers around my forearm and smiles. "How did you turn out the polar opposite of your brother?"

Kat brushes by, her hand lingering on my shoulder as she passes. "Hi, Izzy. Micah." She stops and turns with her hand on the cushioned back of my seat. "Are you two enjoying the flight?"

My heart pumps harder with just the touch of her soft hand and my name on her lips.

"We are," says Izzy. "Who knew Tom's little brother was such a gem?" She squeezes my arm but doesn't remove her hand.

"Oh, Micah's quite the charmer." Kat looks to Izzy's hand on my forearm and back to me as if me sitting next to Izzy is the same as her holding hands with Gorboni. Not even close.

"Can I talk to you for a second, Micah?" Kat asks.

Izzy lets go of my arm as I stand.

"What's up?" I ask, trying to sound confused by her singling me out.

"I was hoping you could help me out . . ."

We walk to the back, where we are out of earshot of everyone. "Can you come over to my condo before heading to Liam's?"

"Why?" I ask.

She looks down, and the corner of her lips curl up. When she looks up again her eyes smirk. Is it possible for her eyes to smirk?

"I assume Gorboni won't be there."

"Just come over when I text you, please. I don't think I can make it through the weekend with Jake without getting my fix of you first."

I smile at the thought of her being addicted to me. "I'll be there," I say, sliding my hand to her ass and pulling her against me. "I can't wait for filming to be done."

Her brow wrinkles and her smile fades.

"What's wrong now?"

"When do your classes start?"

"I have one week after we get back to LA before I head to Austin." I've told her this before. My answer isn't going to change.

"I wish we had more time."

"Me too," I say. What I want to say is that she's wasting all our time with Gorboni, but I stay silent about her ex.

"I better get back," she says as she slips out of my grasp. "I'll see you soon."

I nod, and as she walks away, I draw in a deep cleansing breath. This is stupid. Why do I do this to myself? Why can't I find an ordinary girl who doesn't have to pretend to be in a relationship with her ex? Someone who's never slept with Gorboni. If I weren't completely in love with Kat, I'd look for a girl who hates celebrities. I just have to trust she'll hold true to her promise.

Micah

I spent three uninterrupted hours with Kat this afternoon, and it proved to be the best three hours of my life. We took full advantage of our time together, and I showed her, once again, my superpower is not a myth. That's why as I sit across from her in the lounge pit on Liam Nordstrom's deck and Gorboni snuggles her in his gorilla arms, I don't feel the need to pull a gun from my side holster and shoot him in the middle of the forehead. Okay, I've thought about it. I've contemplated how I could get away with it. And in reality, his life has been spared by the fact that I don't have a gun and my good-looking derriere would not be a positive attribute for prison life.

Kat lifts her hand, flashing me the cat sketched on the inside of her wrist as she fiddles with her earring. Our eyes connect, and she winks. Yes, I drew the picture of Kitten Bastet on her wrist, marking her as mine. And maybe in her blissed-out state, she didn't know what I was doing. But she didn't wash it off. Instead, she's showing it off, and that makes me a little less bitter about the arm wrapped around her.

"Oh my God. Did you get a tattoo?" asks Megan, reaching for Kat's hand.

She's sitting next to Kat. I don't understand how she even saw it from her angle.

"It's a cat . . . how fitting. Is it permanent?" Megan rubs her finger over my drawing.

I almost laugh until I see the confounded look on Kat's face. "Is that one of those Kitten Bastet fake tattoos they sold at Comic Fest?" I ask.

"Micah, how did you know that?" Kat plays along.

"They were all over social media. I think Mia Thompson even had one." I add the last part to push Tom into changing the subject. I'll take the blow, and Kat won't have to explain my drawing.

"Mia Thompson? Hell . . . I don't understand that girl. She pulled out of our movie without warning. That kid of hers has to be a year old. What's the problem? I've seen her. She lost the baby weight." Jake takes a sip of his mixed drink and asks, "Jon, are you sure it's not your kid? You did a DNA test for it, right?

Jonathan Williams laughs. His wife stiffens in her seat with his kid on her lap. I'd be pissed. Guess he's a better man than I am. "Jake, not every guy cheats. Sarah and I were engaged, and I hadn't been with Mia for a year. No DNA test required."

"Am I the only one who hasn't slept with Mia Thompson? How about you, Tom?" Gorboni looks at my brother.

Yeah, I remember the reason I stopped crushing on her now. "Too bad she backed out of the movie," I say. "It totally screwed up your chance with her, Gorboni."

Gorboni completely ignores me. I should be used to it by now—especially with the names sitting on this deck. I'm not even human to these people, always overlooked, just like when I was growing up. My parents and everyone in our life circled around Tom. The only place I have an identity is at school, where people don't know or care that my brother is a famous celebrity. Part of me wishes Tom had changed his last name when he became an actor. At least then no one would make the connection between him and me.

"You're Tom's brother, right?" asks Jonathan Williams' wife. "Hi. I'm Sarah and this," she flips the baby around to face me, "is Nya Jane."

The baby's big blue eyes flutter open, and she stares at me as if I am an entirely new species she's never seen before. It must be my beard. She has her dad's blue eyes, that much is obvious. Her hair is dark like her mother's but sticks straight out like a Play-Doh Barber Shop doll. "Oh, my, she is adorable. May I hold her?" I can't resist. "My roommate has a kid who stays with us every other weekend. After a year I've learned a few tricks. She looks like an angel compared to Leo."

"She *is* a perfect baby. She takes after her dad." Sarah holds Nya up, and I gently take her, balancing her on my knee.

"How old is she?"

"Four months."

I bounce her gently. "You're going to be a heartbreaker, aren't you?" I coo to the baby and her face lights in a smile.

"Don't let Jon hear you say that. He's already super protective. Poor Nya won't be able to date until she's thirty."

"I'd be the same way if she were mine." I glance at Kat. I can imagine having babies with her. I don't know why that pops into my head. We don't even have a defined relationship. I guess I'm falling harder for her than I thought.

"Are you kidding me? Who is this stranger holding my niece? If anyone should be holding her, it's her Aunt Jessica. Hand over the baby." A girl with reddish-brown hair grabs my shoulder.

"Is she really your aunt, Nya? She doesn't look anything like you," I say.

"Jessica is my brother's wife, and we've been friends since middle school," says Sarah. "Just hand her over. She'll keep bugging you until you give her up. Jessica thinks that because she was there at Nya's birth and she's her godmother she takes priority over everyone else."

I smile and hand the baby over.

"I'm Micah Fallston," I say. "Not a stranger."

Jessica kisses Nya on the top of her head and then sits next to me. "Nice to meet you, Micah. This little darling is my favorite person in the world and I hardly ever see her. I live in Minnesota, and my niece lives here. I have to take advantage of every second I have with her."

"You saw her a few weeks ago when Jon and I came home to visit," says Sarah.

"And look how much she's changed since then," adds Jessica.

I listen to the women talk babies and childbirth for several minutes as I watch Nya. Babies, I can relate to . . . women not so much. I'm not the most sociable person unless I've been drinking and I am stone-cold sober. Technically I'm working security for Tom right now. In reality, he didn't want me drinking and mouthing off to Gorboni tonight. I look around the deck and spot one of Jonathan Williams's security people. I've met him before. Maybe I should be sitting off to the side like he is. Then I see he's talking to Nick Reyes, —the lead singer in the band *EXpireD*. And Nick's arm is draped over the shoulder of mega pop star Ashley Taylor. *Holy criminy.* I can't believe the names who are here. The tabloids could dedicate an entire magazine to pictures from this little gathering, and it's the day before the wedding, not the actual event.

"Is Nick Reyes dating Ashley Taylor?" I ask no one in particular.

"Uh huh," admits Sarah. "I think with all the weddings going on in our group of friends he's finally decided to get serious with someone."

She says it as if the two are just regular people, and that's when it hits me. Unlike Jake and Tom, these people don't think of each other as famous.

Weird concept.

A soft hand touches my shoulder, and I know her smell. She and Megan stand cooing over the baby, and she's standing right behind me. I close my eyes and lean my head discreetly to caress her where she touches me. I wish so badly that I didn't have to hide what I feel for her. I think my movement's too subtle for anyone but her to notice until I open my eyes and find Gorboni glaring at me. His eyes squint as if he can see her thumb smoothing up and down the back of my neck. I'm not sure what to do. Kat would probably want me to tell her. If I do that she'll pull away and then he'll get even more suspicious. Filming is almost complete. Maybe it's time he figures out she and I are together. She could still pick him, but it's a risk that I need to take.

Katya

"Gorboni's watching us," announces Micah. "Next thing you know he'll be putting a collar on you and telling you who you can and can't talk to."

I don't look up as I give Micah's shoulder a brotherly squeeze and pull my hand away. After the afternoon we spent together, I didn't even realize I was touching him.

Megan gives me a sideways glance. I'm sure she's wondering what's going on. Someday I'll tell her, but not in front of all these people.

"Are all Liam's buddies from school here for the wedding? Wasn't there something about a bet where the last single man standing gets a boatload of money, and if they miss even one wedding they forfeit their winnings?" I ask Megan. Liam mentioned it when Jonathan and Sarah got married.

"They're not all here. A couple are eliminated from the pot because they're already married—like Jonathan and Chris Hanson. Nick Reyes is here, and that only leaves Hayden Nappo. But since the wedding was such short notice, we decided to make the ceremony with our families the one that counts for the bet. It wouldn't be fair otherwise. Nick came because he wanted Ashley to meet his friends."

"It blows me away that Liam grew up with all these talented people. Was there something in the water? It would have been so amazing to know them all before they became famous," I say, glancing up to check if Jake is still watching me. I'm not sure what he saw, but I'm confident I can sweet-talk my way out of it. His expression says he's not happy as his eyes burrow into me. I flash a flirtatious smile, hoping to defuse his mood. I knew this weekend was going to end in disaster.

The truth is, if it weren't for the other movie offer I would tell Jake today there is no chance of us being together again. Filming is almost done. Even if he makes the last two weeks ugly, the studio is not going to replace me. I know it's not fair to lead him on. But now that there is another film to think about, I'm torn by the opportunity. I got the screenplay yesterday. And the second I picked it up, I couldn't put it down—a thriller. I need to be in this film. It calls to me like no other project ever has.

I'm an awful person to even contemplate not confessing to Jake after I promised Micah we would be together. I don't know what to do. I have this great career opportunity on the one hand and this great guy on the other. Mom always says if you wait long enough to make a decision, it will be made for you. I'm not usually a procrastinator, but I think I'm going to sit on this one at least until filming is done.

I doubt Micah will be up for waiting for me, with his issues with girls using him as a backup. That's the biggest problem: I want to be with Micah. I really want to make a go with Micah. I'll have to talk to Jake. Maybe he and I can end it amicably.

"Kat, you're coming to brunch tomorrow morning?" asks Megan. Her tone says I've missed part of the conversation while I zoned out. "It's a tradition for all the girls to eat brunch together before the wedding. I should say we're making it a tradition. We did it at Sarah's and Jessica's weddings."

Crap. My hand is in Micah's hair again. I look up, and Jake cocks his head, raising an eyebrow at me. *Double crap.* "I'd love to come," I say, extricating my hand from Micah's hair. I'm going to have to deal with this. Why didn't Micah say anything this time? He had to have known Jake was watching me run my fingers through his hair. I glance at Tom, and he's glaring at his brother. Is there something going on that I don't know about?

"Jessica makes the best mimosas. It's just going to be Jessica, Sarah, me, Leslie, Izzy, and you. Ashley already has plans for the morning. Izzy couldn't make it tonight, but she's coming tomorrow," says Megan. "I have to run and grab something from the kitchen. Would you help me, Kat?"

"Sure," I say with a shrug and follow her into the house. We walk right past the kitchen where a woman wearing a chef's uniform works to plate a tray of cheesecake. When we get to the bedroom, Megan stops and turns to me.

"What's going on with this little love triangle out there?" she asks, closing the door behind us. "I take it you and Micah see each other behind Jake's back. And don't get me wrong, I'm the one who told you to go for it, so I'm not judging. But Jake seems a little pissed."

"I was hoping no one noticed." I collapse on the bed, flipping onto my side to face her.

"Well . . . in all honesty, you probably shouldn't be fingering Micah's hair if you don't want Jake to find out."

"He's got really soft hair. Yet it has all this body. You should touch it. It's amazing." I smile, trying to shrug off her suspicion. Her brow furrows. "And I'm kind of falling for him, but I'm officially with Jake. We've got another movie to film together. I don't know what to do."

"Liam told me, a month ago, you'd fall for Micah. He thought you would make a good match, —you both liking comics and all. You and Jake weren't supposed to last this long."

It's strange to hear her admit Micah and I would be a good couple. I've thought a lot about what it would be like to be officially with Micah. I know it would be great. I'm sick of hiding my feelings for him. Being a couple openly would be so good.

"Well . . . I don't know what I'm doing."

"You'd have to break it off with Jake to know for sure if you and Micah work for real."

I slouch back on the bed. She's right.

"You and Jake are still hot and heavy, then? And, again, I'm not judging. I just want to have it straight, so I understand fully."

"Um . . . uh . . . no. We haven't since the video came out. But he's pressuring me, and I kissed him a few days ago." My head crashes to the bed. I can't even admit it to myself, and now I'm telling Megan. I look up in complete regret. "We'd had a long talk, just like old times. I feel guilty, as if I've cheated on Micah. And I have. I was avoiding Micah because I didn't know how to react. Should I tell him about the kiss? Should I not? We were supposed to be exclusive. Then there's this other movie Jake and I are doing. And how is that going to go if I break it off with him to go out with Micah? Jake's not going to do another movie with me."

"You're hooking up with Micah?"

"Four times today."

She laughs and clears her throat. "I don't know what to say, Kat."

"If I get the second movie, I'll have one more notch in my career bedpost. It'll increase my longevity, and I'll make enough money to pay off most of my mom's debts."

"Have you talked to Jake and told him how you feel?

"No." A nervous laugh gurgles in my throat. "I don't think that would go over well. There's still unexplained bad blood between them, and Jake . . . I don't know how he would react. He used to be all joking and fun, but now he seems serious. Something has changed with him."

"But he knows you're just with him because of the movie, or you'd be sleeping with him?"

"I guess." I don't have the nerve to tell her any differently. "But he also doesn't know that I'm sleeping with Micah. Or at least he didn't suspect it before today."

She stands and offers me a hand. "Okay. We'll talk about it tomorrow morning. Right now, the boys out there are wondering where you are, and we probably shouldn't add to their suspicion."

I reluctantly crawl off the bed and follow her to the door. I know it's my decision, but I was hoping that Megan would give me some advice.

When I get back outside, I know where I have to go, and I sidle up next to him, slipping my hand into his. I have to try to fix this, even if it is just for now.

Chapter 30

Katya

"Kat and I had dinner with Paul and Gena Mendez this week. They have the rights to that MJ Logan book. You know the one that's been blowing up the best-seller lists for the last year. Kat's going to play Elizabeth. I suggested her for the part. I know I shouldn't talk about it until the contracts are signed, but it's a done deal. They want it bad. We're doing another movie together," Jake announces to the group, pulling me closer, his voice showing no indication he's threatened by Micah.

Maybe he hasn't figured it out. My eyes meet Micah's. Jake's announcement isn't completely new. Izzy let it slip that the movie deal I had told him about was with Jake. Micah didn't like it, but he seemed to understand.

I fiddle with the ring on my index finger, thinking about the time I spent with Micah today. It was perfect. More than I could have imagined it would be. I watch him talking with Sarah and Megan's friend Jessica, and I can't help but think about what it would be like if the tables were turned. I wouldn't be as gracious as he if I were his dirty little secret.

When the night comes to a close, Micah offers to drive me home, and I want to ask him to give me time to talk to Jake, but Jake cuts him off.

"She's coming home with me, Little Fallston," he says, wrapping an arm around me. "Get your own girlfriend. This one's mine."

Micah narrows his eyes at Jake, and I can tell what he's thinking. He so badly wants to put Jake in his place and tell him he was the one who made me purr four times this afternoon, he's the one I love. But I beg him with my eyes not to say anything, and I watch the look in his eyes turn from anger to disappointment. Anger I can deal with, but disappointment stabs a hole in my heart.

When we get in the car, Jake asks, "Does that comic book freak really think you're going to choose him over me? What an idiot."

I stay silent, not knowing what Jake knows or what he thinks he knows.

"Seriously, Kat. Why the hell would you sleep with that nerd?"

Okay. He knows. Do I deny it? Or do I tell him the truth? He turns toward me without turning on the car, waiting for an answer. I watch as Micah climbs into the car behind us in the driveway. Our eyes connect for a second, and he looks away. He's mad at me too. As the car behind us pulls out and takes off down the road, I realize there's no denying it.

"You cheated on me in public. Do you not remember that?"

"So this was revenge? You wanted to get back at me by creeping around with a nerd?"

"Cut it out, Jake."

"When did it start, Kat? Tell me when it started." He stares at me, his entire body frozen, waiting.

"We were together the night the video came out."

"Yeah. Right. It wasn't a revenge thing at all," he says, his voice dripping sarcasm.

"He was sweet to me, and you were such an ass."

"Kat, have you been sleeping with him the whole time we've been filming?"

"Not the whole time," I admit. "I didn't plan it." Those were the words he used to explain the video. "Not unlike the video."

He squints at me in disagreement and starts the car. We ride back to his house with hip-hop blaring so loud I can't think. He knows I hate mind-curdling loud music, especially hip-hop, and that's why he plays it.

"You could have just dropped me off at my condo," I say as he shuts off the car. It's my first chance to speak and be heard.

"Kat, if I dropped you off at your place, I'd call up some girl to fuck, and that's not going to help our relationship. You're staying here tonight. We need to talk." He gets out and walks into the house.

Our relationship? I wonder what that means. I follow him inside and sit at the breakfast bar. We do need to talk. Twirling my stool around, I watch him pour two glasses of red wine, a Malbec—not my favorite. He hands me a glass, and I take a sip. Yuck. Dry and flat. He probably opened the bottle before we left for filming. I guzzle the drink anyway to summon courage.

"I need to be back out in Malibu by ten tomorrow."

"Not a problem," he says, walking into the living room. "I've got six cars."

I rinse out my glass and refill it with ice and a couple of shots of fire whiskey. It's what I was drinking earlier, and it tastes better to me. I sit on the opposite end of the black leather sofa, moving the stack of pillows to get comfortable. The scent of Jake's cologne wafts from the pillow's fabric. The whole house smells like Jake. I never used to mind the odor, but now?

"So . . ." I say, trying to start the conversation. He was pissed in the car, but he seems more relaxed now. I don't know what's changed. Maybe he's just had time to sort through his feelings.

"I don't want you sleeping with him anymore. You having a tryst with him is way worse than what I did on the video."

"Are you trying to tell me that you haven't been hooking up with other girls the whole time we've been together?" I can't believe he thinks I'm so stupid.

"All right. You caught me. I hooked up with Rachael Marrerro on my last film. But we had barely started dating when it happened, and it was all over social media. I figured you were down with it. It's not like we were exclusive at that point." He looks down at his drink and then meets my eyes again.

"You didn't hook up with my assistant Sherri in Tom's trailer or some bar girl when I was home for my brother's birthday?"

"Sherri? Why would I hook up with her? Is that why you fired her?"

"You didn't?" *I can't believe he denies it.*

"I'm a sexual guy, Kat. You've locked me out for months. What am I supposed to do?"

"Be patient and try to win my trust back."

"While you're off fucking another guy. Those girls were just sex. Like jerking off. They didn't mean anything. I didn't care about them. I love you, Kat." His lips narrow, and he sits forward as if agitated. "Did the nerd tell you? You know, he's got this vendetta against me. He's been rubbing in this thing between the two of you for weeks."

"What?" My voice shrieks with surprise.

"I've known for a couple of weeks. Your little lover's been taking every chance he can to brag about the vile things he's been doing to *my* girlfriend. I heard all about the time in your trailer. Until today, I thought he was just making it up. But then I saw your hands in his hair, and I realized he wasn't lying. Didn't you see the smile on his face? It was his victory smile. He could tell I finally believed him. Tom saw it."

"I don't believe you. He would never talk about us." I shake my head, but that would explain Tom's expression. And how else would Jake know about Micah and me hooking up in my trailer?

"Believe it, Kat. Let me guess, this whole thing was his idea? You being with him was way worse than me with a couple of faceless girls."

"Why would Micah have a vendetta against you? What did you do to him?"

"Oh, poor Micah. I'm always the bad guy. He's just a helpless little nerd-boy."

It's the first time he's used Micah's real name.

"What is the bad blood between you two?" I ask in a muted tone, trying to sound less judgmental.

"I think I may have hooked up with his girlfriend. He made a big stink about me fucking some girl a year ago. Caused a scene at *my* party and I'm at fault? I didn't force the girl. She was very willing. I remember that much."

My heart sinks. Jake slept with Micah's girlfriend? The one Micah was in love with. The only girl he's ever been in love with. Unlike me, Micah doesn't fall easily. He's only been in love once. I can't believe Micah refused to tell me. I would have understood the animosity he has for Jake.

Unless he was trying to keep it from me.

I remember Tom saying something about not taking revenge with this girl. Is that what Micah was doing? Was he using me? Did he make me fall for him just to get revenge on Jake? That's worse than anything Jake's done. At least Jake's problem was poor impulse control, not vengeance.

"Oh," I say before taking a sip of my drink. I can't seem to clear my head. "That must have been heartbreaking that she cheated on him."

"I didn't know she was with him, and the next thing I know he's blowing up at her and me in front of everyone. He could have handled it better, been more discrete. Ruined my party and the girl left crying. He proved to be an ass that night. He must have known how easily you fall for the underdog. I can't believe you let him manipulate you like that. There are so many sick people in the world. You've got to stop being so trusting, Kitty Kat."

I was worried about hurting Micah, but Micah could be just using me. He knew from the beginning that I was Jake's girlfriend. Was I part of his plan to get revenge on Jake? I never would have trusted him if I'd known Jake was the one who slept with Mara. Now what am I supposed to do?

"Come 'ere," Jake moves closer to me, wrapping an arm around me. "You're young. Chalk it up to a learning experience. I'll get you all trained up. You'll be as cynical and untrusting as I am in no time."

Great. I'll be just like my mother.

My phone chimes with a video call. It's Mom, and I swipe to answer. She always calls at this time. It shouldn't surprise me. Dark bags droop under her amber eyes, and she looks exhausted.

"Mom, what's wrong? You look like you haven't slept in days."

"Oh, honey. I don't know how to tell you this." Her eyes fill with tears, and she shakes her head. Her jaw quivers as she swallows. She can't seem to speak.

"You're scaring me, Mom. Is Cam okay? Where's Cam? I want to talk to

Cam." The words pour out of my mouth at hyperspeed.

She looks far off in the distance behind her phone, still shaking her head. When she meets my gaze, she wipes her thumb under her eye, shedding the tears hanging from her lashes.

"Talk to me, Mom. What happened to Cam?" I try to calm my voice to coax her into explaining as I prepare for the worst news of my life. It has to be really bad, or she'd say something.

"Cam . . ." She pushes her hair out of her face and looks directly into the phone. "Your brother," she starts again, "started having seizures a couple of days ago. Grand mal. Like the ones he had after the accident. Last night they started coming one after another. I couldn't do anything."

I know what comes next after "I couldn't do anything." Tears pour from my eyes.

Cam. My stomach starts to heave, and I swallow hard.

"The doctors didn't have a choice. Don't be upset. But they had to induce a coma. They had to, to get the seizures to stop."

I thought he was dead. "Is he going to be okay?"

She shakes her head again. "I . . . I don't know. He's hanging in there. He's still unconscious. They think he may have had a brain bleed. They're running all kinds of tests." Tears run down Mom's face. There's more. I can tell.

"What else? What aren't you telling me?"

"They kicked him out of the study after the first seizure. Said he no longer qualified to be in it. And none of this would have happened if I hadn't pushed so hard for him to be in the study. The drug hurt him. And with him out of the study, all the hospital bills are out of pocket. The insurance won't cover out-of-network hospitalization. I can't afford to get him treatment." She bursts into tears.

"I'll figure it out. I'll fly out on the next flight. We'll get him through this, Mom."

"Don't. I know you have Megan's wedding this weekend. The doctors won't be able to tell us anything until they take him out of the coma. And they won't do that until Monday afternoon. You'll just be sitting around until then. Stay for the wedding, honey. Will you be able to take time off filming?"

"I don't know. I'll have to make some calls."

"Don't worry about being here. I'm getting through, and honestly, Cam is going to do what he needs to do whether you are here or on set. He won't know the difference in his state."

"How can I go back to set when Cam's in the hospital? I'll see what I can get off. It's late, and I better make the calls as soon as I can. I'll let you know when I can get there."

I end the call, and then the tears start. I can't stop them.

"I'm sorry, Kat." Jake sits next to me and wraps a big bear arm around me, pulling me close.

I don't know what to say. What can I say? I snuggle against his chest, absorbing any comfort he gives. I wish Micah were here.

"Tell me what's going on."

He heard the conversation. He knows all I know.

"My brother is back to square one. He's back in a coma. The hospital bills are racking up again just as I thought I was catching up on the debt from the accident. My mom's insurance plan sucks, and everything is out of pocket because it only covers hospitalization in Illinois, not Boston. It was all we could afford, and the study was supposed to cover any medical expenses in Boston, but he got kicked out of the study when he started having seizures. I have two weeks of filming left, and how am I going to act when I don't know what's going to happen to my brother? On top of it all, my boyfriend broke my heart, three months ago, when he cheated on me, and now, my career is going to plummet into the toilet because he's going to get me blackballed in Hollywood for doing the same thing as he did."

Jake purses his lips and watches me as if I'm about to combust. I could. I feel as if I'm going to. He makes a grunting sound deep in his throat as he shakes his head slowly. I have no idea what it means. He and I are not in sync lately.

"Please, just take me home? I have a ton of phone calls to make."

He shakes his head even more, and I take out my phone to bring up a car service app. He takes the phone from my hands. It slips away easily. I have no fight left in me.

"Let's just start over. A clean slate, Kitty Kat. You deserve a better life. You shouldn't have to be burdened by your mom and brother. You spend way too much energy worrying about them." He takes out his phone and types out an email. "I just asked my accountant to transfer a couple hundred thousand into your account. I'll have to talk to him on Monday to finalize it, and I will. Will that be enough to ease the burden?"

"No, Jake. I can't accept it. It's too much. I want to do this on my own."

"Kat, nobody does it on their own in Hollywood. Everybody who makes it gets a leg up from someone. They're paying me thirteen million for the film we're working on, and that's just on the front end. What are you making?"

They're paying him thirteen million plus? Is he joking? I'm in at least as many scenes as him, and they're only paying me a hundred and twenty thousand. My agent told me it was a great contract.

"Yeah. That's what I thought. Just take the money. You deserve it."

I can't help but wonder if this is one of those moments I should just smile and say thank you. The money obviously means less to him than me. It feels so wrong, but maybe he's right. I've worked just as hard as he has on this film and I'm getting paid a fraction of what he's making.

"Why are you treating me so nicely?"

"I love you. Everyone makes mistakes." He turns, and I think he's going to kiss me, but he doesn't. "I can get over you sleeping with the nerd. He was kind to you and sucked you in. You fall fast, everyone knows it. He lied to you to get back at me. I bet he told you all kinds of stories about me cheating. You can't let some lying fuck bent on revenge steal away our future."

"Our future?"

"Hollywood is about the image. It doesn't matter what celebrities do behind closed doors. My fans want to feel good about me. The public just wants a good show, and I know we could be a great show, Kat, if you'd just let us. Don't get me wrong. If I do this for you, I want a commitment from you in return."

"What kind of commitment?"

"Marriage. You're going to have to marry me if you want my help, my money. I'll pay for whatever treatment your brother needs. We're meant to be together, Kat. Hollywood needs us together. After the publicity starts for our film, there'll be no stopping us. We'll have the other film starting in February, and you and I as a couple will be completely solid. We'll be a force to be reckoned with."

"A contract marriage?"

"No. A real marriage, Kat. Sex, and babies, if you want, and no nerds allowed." He laughs, but it sounds calculated. "It doesn't have to be forever, just long enough for us, as a couple, to make our mark."

I stare at the wall in disbelief.

"Are you okay, Kat?"

I nod, not meeting his eyes. I'm completely lost. I have so many mixed feelings about my dad, about Jake, and about Cameron. If I agree to this, it could do so much for Cam. Jake's money could help my brother recover. And if my career takes off, I'll make my own money. I look to Jake, and a smile grows on his face.

"Good. Because I have two more things I'm giving you. Kitty Kat, you sure you're okay with this?"

I nod again, and he stands.

"I'm buying you a car. I should have a long time ago. It's what boyfriends do. And you need one."

I take a deep cleansing breath before smiling and saying, "Thank you." I'm not sure I made the right decision, but it's the opposite of the one I made all those years ago. I can't expect a different outcome unless I make a change.

He gets up and walks into his master bedroom. When he comes out, he's smiling from ear to ear. "My Nonna sent this before filming started. I was waiting for the right moment to give it to you."

"I've never even met your grandmother. Why would she send me anything?"

He sits next to me and opens the blue velvet pouch in his hand. "If we do break up I want it back. You understand, of course, it being Nonna's ring and all. It will all be in the prenup." He pulls out a silver-toned ring with three large rubies embedded across the front of the ring. It's beautiful.

"You know how much I love Nonna. This ring brings all the love I have for her and gives it to you. That's how much I believe in you."

I can't breathe. It's as if I've left my body. He takes my left hand and slips the ring onto my ring finger.

"We can get it sized. Nonna's a bit meatier than you." He smiles.

I'm not really here. He kisses me, but it's not me he's kissing. It's like I'm playing a scene from the movie and I've forgotten all my lines.

Micah

What does Kat want from me? She should have just told Jake it was over. It was hanging in the air; everyone knew. Jake acts as if he owns her, as if she loves him. But I know better. There is no way she could have made love to me this afternoon the way she did and still love him. So why didn't she just tell him?

Tom pours an amber liquid into two lowball glasses filled with ice and hands me one. He cocks his head toward the saddle-colored couch, and I sit on one end while he takes the other.

"You all right?"

I nod, my thoughts stuck somewhere in my stomach. "Why the fuck didn't she tell Gorboni to fuck off?"

"You know my opinion on the whole thing. You're just a toy to fill her time while she punishes Jake. You're not going to win in this game of hers."

"Did I mention we have bareback sex? I'm the only one she's ever done it with. We're exclusive. We talked about it. She trusts me. She doesn't trust Gorboni."

"Would you trust Gorboni?"

"No. He keeps cheating on her. The guy couldn't be faithful if he were alone in a room with no doors or windows."

Tom laughs. He rubs his tongue across his teeth under his lip. "She went home with him." His eyes meet mine. "Not everything is about fidelity. Not in Hollywood." He leans back and takes a sip of his whiskey. "Perception is more important. Your brand. Your next film. Your reputation. They're all more important than being faithful. She obviously is getting what she wants out of the relationship. If she weren't, she wouldn't put up with his crap."

"She said she was going to end it with him. She said we'd be together after filming."

His phone pings and he reads the message before looking up. "Did you get it in writing?"

I scowl at him and down the rest of my whiskey. "You'll see."

"I hope so, bro, because I don't want it to mess you up like Mara did."

"Why do you always act as if the thing with Mara was my fault? She's the one who cheated on me."

"It is your fault, man. You never put yourself first in a relationship. Girls sense when you value them more than you. When you believe you're not as good as them, they start to believe it too. She probably thought you'd take her back even if she got caught. What did she have to lose?"

"Well, it didn't work out the way she thought, did it? Cheating's a deal breaker. That's not going to fly with me. Why would she think that?"

"Because you let her. Does Kat know cheating is a deal breaker? Because to me, it looks like she's cheating on Jake and you're the side piece."

"It's not what it looks like."

"Has she told you she loves you?"

"No. But I know she does."

He takes a deep breath and looks down at the floor, shaking his head.

"What's that look for?"

"Well . . . The one thing I know about Kat is when she falls, she falls fast. She's not stingy with the L-word. I think she told Jake on their third date."

"She told Jake on their third date?" She admitted she falls in love fast. Why hasn't she told me she loves me? It is love, isn't it? I hate that I'm questioning her because of my brother.

"Ever think she might not feel the way you think she does? Women are all liars. And actors are the worst of the worst. They're professionals." He holds out the whiskey bottle and refills my glass. "She can't hurt you unless you let her. Adjust your attitude and see your relationship for what it is: a fling. And you'll leave yourself an out." He leans back, stretching his arms above his head as if he's got all the answers. "You're lucky. Most guys wouldn't get a chance with a girl like her."

Here we go again.

"She's hot. And an amazing kisser."

"Fuck you." I knew he couldn't keep quiet about the love scene he and Kat shot together. I'd blocked it out of my head, but he seems intent on rubbing it in my face.

"What?" He sits forward again. "I can't mention it to Jake. You saw how violent he gets. He was ready to punch me in the face because of a rumor."

"You don't think I'll punch you?"

"No. You aren't hyped up on 'roids." He smiles and takes a sip from his glass. "I can't lie. My character was totally into her. Hell, I was into her. After shooting the scene where she was topless, I couldn't help myself. Those tits of hers . . . insane. You're lucky."

I shake my head in disgust.

"When the movie comes out men all over the world will be envisioning Kat as they pleasure themselves. If you can't handle me thinking about her, how are you going to handle that? You stay with her, and you'll have to get over it. Her tits, her ass, her supple, kissable lips . . . those are her income."

"I know." I need to find a way to stop questioning what I mean to her. "It will be easier when our relationship is out in the open."

"No, it won't. Every time you turn around some dick will be flirting with her. You'll have to be incredibly secure in your relationship with her, or you'll drive a wedge between the two of you."

"Like what happened when you dated Mia Thompson?"

"Yeah. Exactly like that. I was convinced she was sleeping with Jonathan Williams. But she wasn't, and now that I know Jon better I understand it was just their past, nothing more than flirting. It messed up our relationship, and that's on me. You need to have your eyes open going in. And before you feel too confident, you need to remember Kat went home with Jake tonight. She didn't come home with you."

I stare at the large, brightly colored, abstract painting hanging on the wall behind Tom's head. My thoughts have come full circle. Why did she go home with him? It would have been the perfect opportunity to tell Gorboni it was over. What am I missing? Maybe I don't know the whole story.

"One more thing to be aware of . . ." Tom taps his phone against the leather couch, showing me a blank screen. "Jake sent me a text a little bit ago telling me he locked it down with Kat. I'd assume he meant they hooked up. You may have to accept Kat's been lying to you. Something's going on with them. You need to get your head into place and figure out what she means to you. Are you the kind of guy who is willing to be a woman's side piece?"

What will I do if this isn't real, if she doesn't feel the same as I do? I don't know. I just don't know.

Chapter 32

Katya

I stare at the loose-fitting ring on my hand, and even after a night's sleep, I haven't figured out my feelings about it. Jake was exceptionally relaxed about the whole "getting married" notion. He agreed to take on all of Cameron's bills, and all I have to do is marry him. He promised it wouldn't have to be right away and not forever, but I'm still in a daze. I've kept my hand hidden from the ladies at brunch, holding my mimosa with my right hand and keeping my left on my lap as we chat.

"I thought you were going to bring Nya. Is Jonathan babysitting or did you give in and hire a nanny?" asks Jessica.

"Jon is not babysitting. He's her father. It's called parenting. And he's better at it than I am. It's natural for him, and I have to work at it. Besides, she needs her daddy-time, and I need my friends-time," says Sarah before downing her mimosa and handing the glass to Jessica to refill. "It's going to be a pump-and-dump day, ladies."

Is she talking about breast milk?

"Kat, what's up with you this morning? You've barely said a word. Did you and Jake have a fight about a certain man with super soft hair?" asks Megan.

"Not exactly. I don't want to ruin your big day with my troubles."

"Signing these papers today isn't going to change anything between Liam and me. This is just a practice run anyway. The real wedding isn't for another year. That's the one I'll be nervous about. My dad and brothers will be at that one. Spill. What's going on?"

"My mom called last night. My brother Cam started having seizures again, and they kicked him out of the research study he was in. The seizures were so severe the doctors put him into a medically induced coma until they can figure out what's going on with him. I might fly out to Boston tomorrow. My production manager hasn't gotten back to me to let me know if it's possible or not."

"Is he going to be okay?" asks Sarah.

"Only time will tell. I hope his recovery won't be like starting over. He was doing really well in the study, and now he's back in a coma."

"Wow. I'm sorry, Kat," says Megan. "Is there anything we can do?"

"No." I pin a smile on my face, and I hold up my left hand to show them the ring before I start crying about Cam. "I've got Jake. We're getting married."

Megan laughs as if I'm kidding, while some of the others congratulate me.

"You've got to be kidding. You should have said no. You might be the first girl to ever turn down Jake 'Gorgeous Body' Gorboni, but you can still say no." Leslie, Nak's girlfriend, potently meets my eyes, her long blonde hair perfectly wrangled onto the top of her head. She works for Jonathan Williams. I think she's his cousin or something. She and Izzy are good friends, and she's known Jake for a long time. I've never gotten the impression she cared much for him.

"Does he know about you and Mr. Four-times-yesterday-afternoon?" asks Megan.

Jessica, Leslie, and Sarah look at me wide-eyed as I groan.

"Do I really have to talk about this now?"

"It's my day, and yes, you do," says Megan.

"Jake knows. He's known for weeks, apparently. Micah's been bragging about us to get back at Jake for sleeping with his girlfriend last year. Jake thinks he's been using me this whole time." The room sobers with my words. I don't mean to villainize Micah, but I don't even know what's real and fake right now.

A couple of them moan as if the party where it happened is still fresh in their minds. "So you all knew about the bad blood between them?" I ask.

Sarah and Leslie nod.

"I was there," says Leslie. "It was pretty bad. Micah was yelling at the top of his lungs at Jake. Swinging at him. Jake pushed him across the room. They almost got in a fistfight, but Tom stood between them—basically, holding his brother back—and then Micah started in on the girl, calling her a whore. He didn't let up. It was pretty brutal. She was crying by the time her ride got there."

I guess Jake wasn't lying about that. Micah's always been so laid-back, I can't even imagine him going off on someone.

"Did you see what happened before that?"

"Nak said Jake flirted with the girl all night right in front of Micah. When they both disappeared, he went looking for them. He heard them in the bathroom and caught them red-handed when they came out. Jake was still buckling his belt, and the girl's dress was inside out. It was obvious what they'd been doing."

"I can't imagine Micah getting that upset about anything. He's always so calm and easy going."

"My first impression of him was that night." Leslie purses her lips and meets my eyes as if she's not sure about her words. "I didn't walk away feeling good about him. He was kind of a dick."

The conversation stops for several seconds, and everyone focuses on the food on their plates. Maybe I don't know Micah as well as I thought. Maybe he's as good an actor as his brother.

"You and Micah?" asks Tom's assistant Izzy. She's been staring at me as if I've grown another head. Maybe Micah was stepping out on me with her, and this is all a new revelation.

"Yeah," I say. I may as well admit it. It's already been said out loud. "But it's over. I don't have a claim on him anymore." I can't quite say the words *he's all yours* because it hurts too much. Everyone starts eating again and several minutes pass in silence.

"You're marrying Jake, but you sound as if you'd rather be marrying Micah. Seriously? Four times yesterday?" Sarah breaks the silence. "Did Jake win because he upped the ante?"

"It's complicated," I say, wishing we could talk about anything other than me.

"See if I understand this right. As the world knows, I don't care for Mia Thompson. No matter how much reassurance Jon gives me about his ex, I will never trust her. She thinks she has some unearthly claim on my husband and I admit if we were placed in a room alone together we would probably gouge each other's eyes out. Micah and Jake probably feel as if they are competing for you and with all their history neither wants to lose. All's fair in love and war, right?"

"I don't know about that." Jessica stands and starts pouring orange juice into the empty mimosa decanter. "Guys are weak. My experience has always been the second there's any resistance their walls go up, and they act as if they don't care. They don't want a girl if it means they have to work for it."

Sarah sets her fork down and stares Jessica down. "You don't think my brother would cut off his right leg to keep you in his life?"

"Sure, he would now. We're soul mates. But how long had I been flirting with him before he asked me out? He didn't want to have to work at a long-distance relationship during college, and he definitely didn't want to deal with what would happen if he broke up with his sister's best friend. Guys want everything to come easy. Which one of the guys is putting in the effort? I mean, I've met Jake before. He hooked up with a friend of ours when we were visiting Sarah a long time ago."

Megan and Sarah throw dirty looks Jessica's way as if what she just said was taboo and I'm not sure what she said wrong, but she blows them off.

"Jake does what he wants. He doesn't seem like the type of guy to commit so maybe him proposing is more effort than Micah's putting up with being a side piece. Micah was the one who was getting sex and Jake is the one who actually committed." Jessica pours alcohol into the orange juice and meets my eyes.

"I don't like either of them. Find a new guy," says Leslie before downing her drink.

"Don't hold anything back." Megan shoots Leslie a look to tell her she's not helping.

"I like Jake. I don't really know Micah. But he seemed nice enough yesterday. He was really good with Nya," Sarah holds her glass out for Jessica to refill. "And you couldn't seem to keep your hands off of him. That's got to give him merit points. Jake did cheat. It really just comes down to who you trust."

"Like you said, Jake cheated on me—over and over—he admitted it. Micah told me about them, and maybe it was revenge fueling him, but it doesn't matter. I'm marrying Jake."

Megan looks at me with narrowed eyes. "Why?"

"Because it's what I need to do."

"What's he have on you?" asks Megan to me with a glance at Leslie.

"No one's blackmailing me. I just realized how much Jake means to me. We worked out our problems, that's all. We've both agreed, it doesn't have to be forever. But for now, it's the right thing to do."

Jessica refills my glass, and I take a large gulp of mimosa, barely tasting the citrusy goodness as the bubbles rush down my throat.

"Do you love him?" asks Jessica. "Because if you don't love him, you shouldn't get married. It sounds as if he's giving himself an out, not committing to forever."

"Just tell us what's going on, Kat. No one here is going to leak anything to the press. We've all been vetted. We're not leakers," says Megan. "It will feel good to get it off that sizable chest of yours."

"Marrying Jake is what I need right now." I take a bite of cantaloupe, and when I look up again, everyone is staring at me. "I love him," I lie.

"Okay then," says Leslie. "To new beginnings." She holds up her drink, and we all follow, clinking our glasses.

"To new beginnings," I echo. *Whatever that means.*

I'm just going to forget everything I know and move forward. At least that's what I told myself during brunch. Now I'm standing on the deck of Liam's house in Malibu. Tall bamboo plants line the outside of the deck, keeping the ceremony private. I'm in a silky mid-thigh halter dress next to Jake, who's dressed in beach formal. Big band music starts and Megan and Liam begin swing dancing down the center of the small crowd. They are amazing together. When they reach the front, where Nak stands looking very official in all black with a white collar, Liam dips Megan, kissing her before Nak even starts. They look so happy.

Liam's in linen pants, a button-down, and flip-flops. I've never seen him more relaxed. Megan is wearing a form-fitting lace crop top with a silky white A-line skirt. She's gorgeous. I have to wonder if I will be as happy as them when I get married.

I take my first glance at Micah since he and Tom arrived. I've been avoiding him. I don't know how to tell him. He's not looking at me. Instead, he watches Megan and Liam. He looks so innocent. I hate to hurt him. I need to talk to him today before Jake makes a show of the engagement.

I told Jake I would wear the ring if he didn't say anything today about us getting engaged. I gave the excuse that it would infringe on Liam and Megan's day, but I know part of it was because I wanted to talk to Micah first. He needs to understand why.

I listen as Megan recites her vows. She told us this morning that they wrote them together. Words about love and trust and forever. Words I doubt will ring true at my wedding. Maybe after I get my career in order, I will be able to find something real.

"From the moment you told me you weren't one of the mindless plastic chicks I was used to and you could think for yourself, I knew you were special," says Liam, taking Megan's hand and staring into her eyes. "Then after we danced together that first time, I was hooked. I thought of no one but you. I'm the luckiest man alive because, now, I get to keep you forever. You're my best friend, and I love you, Megan." He slides the ring onto her hand and everyone claps. Nak announces them husband and wife. It's not a traditional wedding, but it's perfect for them.

Tears stream down my face. I can't help it. They're so good together. I dab my fingers under my eyes, trying to stop the damage to my makeup and as I look around to see if I'm the only one crying, I spot Micah watching me. I straighten, tucking my hands at my sides, where they'd been most of the ceremony. His gaze follows the ring. He's seen it. Did Izzy tell him? I pull my skirt around my hand, hiding it, but the damage is done, and I just made it worse. I can see it on his face.

I have to look away. What I felt with him was real, and it hurts me to see him so disappointed in me.

Megan and Liam are kissing again. I close my eyes because they won't stop watering and I don't fully understand why. I'm happy for them.

"Stop crying. Your makeup looks like crap," says Jake in my ear.

"I know. I can't help it," I say. "I'm always like this at weddings," I lie. This is the first time I've ever cried at a wedding. A sob creeps from my throat, and Jessica hands me a tissue. She's crying too. I watch as her husband wraps his arm around her and when she leans into him, he kisses the top of her head. They're happy too. Watching them makes me sob even more.

As the music starts again and Megan and Liam dance back down the aisle hand in hand, Liam grabs my hand, pulling me into the dance with them. Jessica grabs my other hand, linking into the chain with her husband on her other side. All the guests join the line, half on Liam's side and half on Megan's. Jake's at the end on Megan's team—the last to join in. Liam kisses my cheek and squeezes my hand before he and Megan duck into the center of the ring. We all circle around them as they perform a fantastic show. If Megan hadn't told us at brunch that they would be freestyling the dance, I would have thought that it was professionally choreographed. Amazing. I'm pretty sure I am the only one off throughout the song.

After the dance, champagne flutes are passed, and Jonathan makes the first toast. "As most of you know Liam, and I have been friends a long time. I was ten when my parents moved in three blocks from Liam. We drove to school together almost every day for eight years. It's been six years since we graduated and in all the time I've known him we've leaned heavily on one another for advice. On this most important day, I have the best advice for you, Liam. It may sound canned, and truthfully it's a line from a rom-com I was once in. Up until I met Sarah I laughed at it. But now I live it. Are you ready?" He smiles at Sarah, and she grins back. "When you find someone who stops you mid-stride and makes you change direction, take their hand and never let go. Megan stopped you, and you've changed direction. The rest is up to you. To Megan and Liam, may you never let go." He holds up his glass, and we all follow.

Never let go.

Is that what I am doing, letting go of Micah?

I twist the awkward ring on my finger. Suddenly it feels as if the weight of the world rests on my hand. I tuck my hands into the folds of my dress and look over at him. He looks super sexy in his suit jacket. His hair is coiffed perfectly, and I just want to run my fingers through it and mess it up.

What am I doing?

I have to stop obsessing over him. He's not mine, and I'm not his.

Jake grabs my left hand and lifts it into the air.

Damn it.

I told him not to say anything.

"Nordstrom, I'm following your lead, man. You and Jon have shown me what's important. Kat and I have been talking about getting married for a while, and I finally locked it down." He leans down and kisses me on the lips as everyone congratulates us. I feel as if I'm having another out-of-body experience. It's not me he's kissing.

I watch as Micah heads into the house, and I wait a couple minutes before excusing myself. I can feel Jake's eyes on me, and I'm sure he knows where I'm going, but I have to talk to Micah. Jake reaches for my hand and stops me mid-stride.

"Don't, Kat," he says, shaking his head. "Just let him go."

"I will. But I have to talk to him face to face. Please, just let me talk to him one last time."

I stand outside the first-floor bathroom waiting for him to come out. When the door opens, his blue eyes pierce me like no one else's can. I think about the way we made love yesterday. Being this close takes my breath away. What we have together is so far beyond anything I've ever experienced, I never recognized its impact on me. I'm actually in love with Micah. In love for the first time. Real love.

"What about us, Kat? What about us?" Micah whispers, leaning into my ear as he comes out of the bathroom, his normal ease gone.

Stepping in front of him, I block his path. "I need to talk to you. Can I call—"

"Why do we need to talk?" he interrupts. "You're wearing his ring. I think that says it all."

"No. I need to explain."

"No need. It's been fun. A good time while it lasted." He pushes past me and walks back out onto the deck.

He won't even listen to me. I type out a text to him and wait until I'm on the deck before pushing send. I need to see his reaction when he reads it.

Please let me explain. PLEASE.

I watch for several minutes, but he never checks his phone. As I amble back to the lounge area on the deck, staring at my phone and trying to figure out the right words to text, large gorilla arms pluck me off the floor.

"There you are." Jake pulls me onto the lounge with him and then picks up his drink.

Why won't Micah look at me?

Three hours pass in a haze. And then we leave. I congratulate Liam and Megan with kisses on their cheeks and walk with Jake to the car. I never get to talk to Micah.

Chapter 33

Katya

Production rearranged the schedule so that I was able to take two days off of filming to visit Cam. I should be grateful, but I almost regret coming. Cam looks awful in his unconscious state. Mom says the dark bruises under his eyes appeared all of a sudden, days before he admitted he was having seizures. She thinks he fell down during a seizure but didn't tell her about it because he knew it would mean he would be dropped from the study. The click of the mechanical breathing machine sooths my nerves. At least I know he's still breathing. Lights blink on monitors around the small room, and a nurse sits at a computer just outside the door typing.

"It makes me sad thinking he was so desperate to get better that he would put his life in danger." I massage Mom's tense shoulders as I stand behind her at Cam's bedside.

"I know. I couldn't do anything by the time I found out. By then, the seizures were coming so frequently that nothing could be done."

A tall, balding man wearing a lab coat walks into the room, touching the nurse's shoulder as he enters. He holds out his hand and introduces himself to me in a thick Bostonian accent as Dr. Bakke. He and Mom seem familiar with each other, and he greets her as well. He stands on the edge of Cam's bed, lifting Cam's hand and examining his fingernails. Then he looks around at the monitors before turning back to us.

"Cameron is struggling. Homeostatic mechanisms are often lost after head trauma. And this bleed *is* an additional trauma. Traumatic brain injuries don't just stack like adding one plus one equals two. In TBIs, one plus one could equal ten. Cameron's cerebral perfusion pressure is not where we would like to see it. It is a tricky balance with brain injury, keeping his brain oxygenated just enough to keep the intracranial pressure low without starving the brain cells. So far it has been a struggle with your son, especially with the unpredictability of the seizures. The good news is his EEG is reading right where it should be, his brain is still functioning, and we've gained control over the seizures. But the neuro-ICU team feels Cameron will benefit from being sedated until we can get his stats stabilized, essentially giving him more time to heal before we wake him up."

"Oh." Mom stares at the doctor, her eyes filling with tears. Being a nurse, Mom probably understood way more of what the doctor said than I did. From her reaction, it must be bad.

"The longer the brain has to heal in a reduced-stress state, the better. Since the drug he was given during the study has a negligible track record and we can't pinpoint a reason for the bleed in the first place, we need to be cautious. If another bleed occurs, it could pose another set of problems. I haven't ruled out surgery yet. But for now, this is our best course of action. We will just have to wait it out. Do you have any questions?"

Mom shakes her head, and the doctor smiles at me as he turns to go.

"Did you understand any of that?" I ask Mom.

"Most," she says, wiping under her eyes with the back of her thumb. "They're going to keep Cam unconscious until his blood and intracranial pressures normalize. They need to keep his blood oxygenated enough to keep his cells alive, but if his oxygen level is too high, it can cause the pressure in his head to increase. It's a balance. We will just have to wait to see what happens. At least you're here. That makes all the difference."

I place my hand in hers, and we sit in silence and wait. We wait for a miracle. We watch as the nurse adds another bag of liquids to the mechanical pump attached to Cam's arm and then steps out of the room. Cam looks so much like pictures of Dad when he was young, it forces me to ask, "Have you told Dad yet?"

"I haven't told your father. I was hoping Cam would wake up and I wouldn't have to tell him, Cam could."

"I could call him if you like. Dad needs to know."

"That would be great, Katya. He and I will just argue if I call him."

I wipe a rogue strand of hair off of Cam's forehead and take a deep breath, psyching myself up for the call. When I squeeze Mom's hand and she places her other hand on top of mine, her fingers trace the stones of my new ring.

"Is this new?"

I nod. "Jake gave it to me."

"Katya, Jake asked you to marry him, and you didn't call me?"

"You were busy with Cam."

She gives me a look that says I should have called anyway.

"He proposed on Friday."

"The day I called you about the seizures. I'm sorry, honey. I didn't mean to ruin your day."

"You didn't know. Besides, you had to tell me about Cam. He's way more important than this." I hold up my hand and Mom takes it to examine the ring closer. "No matter what happens, Mom, I'm in this with you and Cam."

"Tell me how he did it. How did Jake propose?"

"It's kind of personal." I can't tell her we were arguing about me sleeping with another man right before she called with the news about Cam, and Jake offered to pay Cam's hospital bills if I agreed to marry him. That wouldn't go over well with Mom.

"What, were you naked or something?"

"No. We weren't naked. It was intimate, but we had our clothes on."

"You know everyone is going to ask. You'll have to come up with something better. The press has to get their pound of flesh."

She's right. Someone needs to make up a fabulous engagement story.

"Jake's publicist will come up with the official version. It's his Nonna's ring, his grandmother's. I guess he's been planning to ask me because she sent it all the way from Italy at the beginning of summer."

"We have a wedding to plan."

I shake my head. "Not until Cam is better and can come to the wedding. Can you imagine how mad he'd be if I got married without him?"

"You're right," she says with a smile and a wink. "He'd be pretty upset."

"You know it." I sit in the empty chair and scoot it up next to Mom. We both look at Cam. I know, like me, Mom would change places with him in a minute, just to free him from his injury.

"This engagement's good news in this pile of garbage we're buried in. At least we have something to look forward to when all of this is done."

"Why don't you go back to the apartment and get some rest, Mom," I suggest. You look as if you haven't slept in a week. I'll stay with Cam."

"Thanks for the compliment." She still has some fight in her.

"Do you want honesty? Or sugarcoating?"

"At this moment in time, I could use some sugarcoating. A giant bowl of sugar. But you're right." She kisses Cam on the forehead and me on my cheek before heading for the door. "I'll have my phone on me. Call if there's any change."

I move to the more comfortable of the two chairs and recline back into the tight space of the room. I love my brother more than anything, and I would sell my body to keep him safe. In a way, I am. The whole situation is surreal. I never envisioned marrying Jake. But how could I say no, when my brother sits in this hospital room surrounded by hundreds of thousands of dollars' worth of equipment? I'd never be able to afford the treatment he needs without Jake.

What I regret is hurting Micah. I love him and probably always will. I wish I didn't have to take the path I am. I look at the ring on my finger as tears fill my eyes. I'm so emotional lately. *What is wrong with me?* I close my eyes, trying to fight off the sobs pushing to the surface. If I tell Micah the truth—that I love him and I'm only marrying Jake to help my brother—will he try to get me to change my mind? It's probably better to let him think I was just using him to get Jake to marry me. Will my actions turn him into a bitter man? What if I don't have any impact on his life at all?

I take out my phone, and, somehow, stop myself from hitting up Micah's phone. I make the call to Dad instead.

"Dad, I have bad news about Cam."

"What is it? I have a meeting in ten minutes."

"He had another brain bleed, started having seizures again, and is in the hospital in Boston."

"What is he doing in Boston?"

Did Mom not tell him Cam started the study? Have I talked to Dad since Cam moved to Boston? I don't think I have.

"He was in that drug study." I won't elaborate in case he just forgot.

"Your mother knew I didn't want him in that experiment, and she went ahead and did it anyway."

"Dad, you had to know about it. Cam's been in it for most of the summer. Haven't you talked to your son in three months?" My sugar and ride to reality shut him down.

"Let me talk to Cam."

"He's in a medically induced coma to help his brain heal; you can't talk to him. You can talk to me. I'm with him."

"Like I said, I need to get to a meeting. Text me the details about the hospital, and I'll call them later."

"Mom has power of attorney and Cam's eighteen. You may have to talk to her to get you added to the list of people who the hospital is allowed to talk to about his condition."

I'm sure Mom hasn't added him yet. She wants him to depend on her kindness. I hate parenting my parents.

"That's ridiculous. I'm his father. How much is this hospitalization going to cost?" He doesn't ask about Cam's condition, but wants to know how much it's going to cost him? Classic!

"It's not going to cost you anything. Mom and I have it covered, Dad. By the way, I wanted to let you know before the press finds out, Jake and I are getting married, probably in Italy. We're just at the planning stage, so don't tell anyone, but make sure your passports are up to date. It won't happen until Cam's out of the hospital."

"That's great, Katya. Keep me updated on everything. I've gotta go."

He ends the call, and I shake my head in frustration. Did he hear anything I said or does he just not care? It's always a crapshoot talking to Dad.

I listen to the click of Cam's breathing machine as I imagine my life differently. If I were free to live my life, I would be with Micah, not Jake.

"Cam, did you hear? Jake and I are getting married." I smile, imagining we're in a real conversation. "Jake's a great guy—a little crazy, sure—but he's good to me. Except for the cheating . . . but I'll figure that out."

The old Cam would argue with me and ask why I wanted to marry my father.

"I don't love him anymore. Maybe I'll learn to love him again someday. I'm in love with his best friend's little brother. You'd like Micah. He loves comics, and he's an amazing artist." I look down at the faded cat drawing on my wrist. "He drew Kitten Bastet. See?" I hold up my wrist to show him even though his eyes are closed. I wonder if he can hear a word I say. "Someday his drawings will make him famous like his brother, Tom. He's that good. I'm pretty sure he hates me for accepting Jake's ring, and I can't blame him. But it's for the best. I just wish he would let me explain why I'm marrying Jake."

I replay yesterday in my head. I should have talked to Micah when he first arrived. I felt as if the second he and Tom appeared, Jake stuck to my side like glue. I should have just done it. But I don't know if it would have mattered. He'd never accept me marrying Jake and all that comes with it.

"You need to get better, Cam. You need to be able to fly to Italy. Jake's grandmother has big plans for the wedding." I wonder if Jake's Catholic. I bet his grandmother expects us to marry until death do we part. Jake's problem, not mine. "Jake's grandmother raised him. The wedding is more important to her. All I care is that you get better." It's not the wedding I want. Why would I want to celebrate it?

I look up to find the nurse typing on the computer by the door. I wonder what she heard. My voice was soft enough, she probably didn't hear a word I said over the noise of the machines in the room. I need an attitude adjustment. I can't regret helping my brother. I don't have any regrets there.

My phone pings with a text. In my mind, it's Micah's reply to one of my twenty or so texts, but it's not.

Megan: How's your brother?

Kat: Healing. He looks awful. How's married life?

Megan: Satisfying. Liam is super into it. Keeps calling me his wifey.
He's so weird. Why are you really marrying Jake?

Kat: He asked me, and I said yes. Chalk it up to my impulsive
personality. It's right for now. It's what I need to do.

Megan: Okay. It just seems sudden after he literally caught you with
your hand in Micah's hair.

I don't know what to say to that. I watch Cam's chest rise and fall, rise and fall. My brother is worth more than a guy. I don't even know if Micah and I would be good together in the real world. We may never have panned out.

Kat: I never meant to hurt Micah, but I know I would regret not
marrying Jake.

Megan: Hope he satisfies you in the end.

Kat: I hate you.

Megan: I know. But it was funny. Talk soon.

We end our conversation, and I laugh at her comment about Jake satisfying me.

I spend the next day and a half with Mom at Cam's bedside talking about Cam's future, medical bills, weddings, and my future plans with Jake, while internally I map out the words I will tell Micah when I corner him on set. I don't know why, but I can't let it go. I can't let him go. I have to try to smooth things out with Micah if only to ease my conscience.

By the time I make it back to set, I have a good idea what to say to Micah. He has to listen. I'm not going to give him a choice. As soon as Tom arrives alone on set, I know something is wrong. I feel panicked. Why do I feel panicked? I scour the background for Micah. He's always near his brother. Instead, I find Izzy. I need to talk to him. I need to tell him about Cam. I need to explain the ring on my finger.

When I finish filming, I rush back to the hotel. "Answer your damn phone, Micah," I mutter under my breath as I rush to the elevator.

I didn't get a chance to talk to Tom before he headed off set. He seemed to be avoiding me too. Something is definitely wrong. I go straight to Tom and Micah's suite. I don't care who sees me.

"Is Micah here?" The words pour from my mouth the second the door opens.

"He's not," says Izzy. She steps back, allowing me inside.

"Where is he?" I walk to his room, opening the door, hoping to catch him avoiding me. It's better than the alternative. But the place is empty—all his clothes, all his drawing supplies, all his electronics are gone. I frantically check the bathroom—empty.

Tom walks into the room behind me. "He left. He headed back to Austin early. Said something about his roommates needing him." He walks out into the central part of the suite and Izzy hands him a paper without a word.

"He left you this," he says, handing me a single piece of paper. I take it and skim through the writing on it. It's an NDA—a printout of the standard one I know he had on his phone for Tom's hookups. My name is where he normally puts Tom's, and he's signed it. "He didn't want you to worry about him telling your story to the press, I guess."

I never asked him to sign one. I would never ask him to sign one. I'm stunned. He's gone for good. He wouldn't have left this if he planned to let me explain. I can't believe he's gone. He's not going to let me explain. I don't know what to say to his brother. I guess there's nothing left to say. I turn to leave.

"He left this too." Tom hands me a flat rectangular paper bag.

I pull out the contents—a comic book encased in a plastic sleeve. *Wow.* It's

Kitten Bastet issue twenty-six. The only copy I'm missing. He remembered. The note is short.

> *To complete your collection. (It came through the shop I*
> *worked at last summer, and the owner snagged it for me.)*
> *–Micah*

That's all he said? That's it? I look to Tom wanting more of an explanation.

He shakes his head. "I told you to stay away from my brother. He's an idealist, Kat. He doesn't get our world."

"He gets it more than you realize," I say. "He just doesn't agree with it."

I head back to my suite, wondering if I just messed up the best relationship I'll ever have.

Jake looks up when I enter. "Who drowned your kittens?" he asks with a chuckle. I'm not in the mood to deal with his sense of humor, and I walk to my room without responding, collapsing on my bed.

"Are you bummed because your nerd left?" Jake stands in the doorway, stretching his arms as he grasps the doorjamb above his head.

What an ass. I roll my eyes. He loves this. He feels vindicated, as if his cheating wasn't as bad as mine.

"What do you expect? He would stay your side piece after we get married? Guys don't think that way. They want to know they're the only cat using the litterbox."

"You're really gross, Jake. I just didn't think he would leave without talking to me first."

The bed dips and his arm wraps around me. His voice softens, and he says, "Your personal life is part of your career. At this point in your life, there's no separation. He's never going to fit into your career plans."

I know what he's saying is reality. I need to focus on my career, on my upcoming marriage. But it wasn't supposed to be this way. Micah was supposed to know the truth. He was supposed to know I love him. I never got to tell him I love him. Tears edge into my eyes. I fight them as long as I can, but they leak anyway.

"We're getting married, Kat. What do you think would happen if he started talking to the press?"

"He signed an NDA."

"Look at you. You're learning. I knew you weren't a total idiot."

Great. I'm not a total idiot, only because Micah's a giver.

Chapter 34

Micah

The ceiling fan in my room thumps unbalanced with every rotation. *Fump-fa-falala. Fump-fa-falala. Fump-fa-falala* it whispers above my head. I'm sure the noise isn't new—just never noticed it before. The sound wedges farther into my psyche like a nail pounding deeper into my skull, reminding me to get up and get my shit together.

My roommates made plans for us to play footgolf at a new course near Zilker Park, their idea of getting me back on the horse without resorting to the bars or clubs. They wanted to hit some live music venues on Sixth Street last night, but I'm still not ready for that kind of social experiment. Nothing good will come of me getting drunk. Footgolf is the compromise.

My soccer ball is flat—par for the course of my life—and I have no idea where the pump is. I can't play footgolf without a soccer ball. Wish I could find a pump to refill the air in my lungs. Ever since Liam's wedding, it's been hard to breathe. The fact that she could look me in the face and not deny her plans to marry Gorboni ripped my heart out. The fact that she wore his ring? Shit. I don't know how anyone could make a decision like that after what we shared.

She must not have a heart.

Soulless.

That's what I've told myself for the last few days. I don't have any other explanation. But in my heart—the one no longer in my chest—I know that's wrong. She has a beautiful soul. It brightens all who come in contact with her. But the drive to be a star must be so strong that she can't leave him. And he's offering her it all.

My parents are always saying "Go to the light. Let it draw you in." But me chasing after a light I will never get, that's not living. I don't want to go toward the light anymore. I need to live. I need to live a real life, not some made-up one that will never come true.

The worst part isn't that she's the second woman I've loved who left me for Jake Gorboni. It's that I knew she would. All the while I was falling for her, I knew she was going to leave me for him. I may have told Tom otherwise, tried to convince myself by convincing him. But I knew. I did this to myself, and that's the part that sucks the most. I can't blame her. It's all on me.

Fump-fa-falala. Fump-fa-falala. Fump-fa-falala.

Maybe Tom's right.

Maybe men should just fuck nameless, faceless women. Sex is just a physical need, like food and water. There's no need to get attached to women. It only makes life unbearable when you get involved. I'm twenty-one years old. I'm not looking to have children; I'm just feeding my dick, or rather, exercising it. No need to have attachments when all I need is a workout.

"Mic, you ready to go?" asks Dawson, walking into our shared bedroom. He takes one look at my soccer ball, digs a small hand pump from his desk drawer, and tosses it on my bed.

"Just about." I start filling the ball. When it's firm, I pull the needle out and stand, handing the pump back to Dawson. The thing I like about my roommate is he doesn't ask questions. He knows I'll talk when I want to talk and not before.

"We gonna do this?" he asks, stashing the pump back in his desk and heading for the door.

He ducks through the doorway in the only way a six-foot-four guy can, and I follow with my soccer ball. We meet up with the rest of the guys and all pile into Fitzpatrick's SUV. My phone goes off three times in the car, and I don't even look at it. I know it's her. Unless she's calling to tell me she broke it off with the douchebag I'm not going to give her my ear.

"Dude, what's with your phone?" asks Campbell.

"Creditors," I say because they'll all understand that.

"I call BS on that one," says Dawson, running his hand through his reddish-blond locks. "I heard what your brother paid you. You don't have any debt. I think it's a girl. That's why you're all discombobulated. Creditors wouldn't get his goat and fleece it. It's a girl."

"Yeah, not going to talk about it." I shake my head. They all know what happened with Mara. I'm not sharing this story.

"Did Dawson tell you we ran into Mara at Backster's?" asks Fitzpatrick.

"Yep."

"It's not her hitting up your phone? She said she might. Did Dawson mention that?"

"Nope and nope. Like I said I'm not really in the mood to talk about it." I'm not going to talk to Mara either. She shouldn't waste her time. All I see in my future is nameless, faceless women. Could be this whole experience was the all-knowing, whatever it is, working its magic to get me where I need to be as a man. To get me to grow up.

"I didn't tell him 'cause I knew it'd mess with his head, dumbass," says Dawson, punching Fitzpatrick's shoulder.

"I'm fine." It's bad enough that I believe I'm a pathetic, ball-less loser, I don't need my friends believing it too. Even though I'm the one who broke it off with Mara, she cheated first. I left Kat, but she chose Gorboni first. Loser. "Let's go to Backsters after golf. I need to get laid." I think I just shocked them. Fitzpatrick's eyes meet mine in the rearview mirror.

"What the hell happened to you? You're not looking for Mara, are you?" asks Dawson, turning to me with genuine concern in his dark eyes.

"No. Just rethinking life."

I tried to jump back on the horse a month ago, and despite all my efforts to pretend emotionless sex does it for me, it doesn't. And the worst part is I don't feel any closer to getting over Kat. Along with my class schedule and my commitment to my new YouTube channel, I find less and less time to berate my summer stupidity, but I still can't forget her. Even though I've regained my interest in drawing—an improvement from a month ago—I probably just need to get a girlfriend. At least I'm drawing again. And I'm actually making money off my comics thanks to the follower who suggested I start a YouTube channel. I should thank Kat too. She was the inspiration for the new comic series. It's a cat and dog story set in Hollywood. And even though the main character isn't based off her, it kind of is. That's probably the reason I can't let her go. I am constantly making up new storylines for the comics, and since she's the main character, she's always on my mind. I wouldn't have made the new strip without her pushing me to go outside of my comfort zone. The strip's a little risqué, and the lead character is female, not my usual style or genre.

I figured I could write from a Hollywood insider's view since I lived it this summer. It's all fiction, but everything I write is inspired by personal experience. So far I've remained anonymous, but that changes next week when an interview I did gets posted. I learned a lot working for my brother. Using all your assets to get discovered isn't something to be ashamed of. I waited this long because I didn't want to be embarrassed if the comic failed. But when you're writing about Hollywood, having a brother who's a famous movie star adds to your credibility. So in the interview, I admit that I'm Tom's brother. It came off as if I reluctantly confessed it, which I thought would resonate with my followers better than bragging about it. Tom gave his stamp of approval on the interview, and all is a go. I didn't say too much, anyway, just that I had worked for him this summer and was inspired to start a comic about Hollywood.

Tom's busy this week with Gorboni and Kat, shooting promos for the movie from this summer. I'm glad to not be a part of his daily life. Once in a while, I'll get a text or call from Izzy. She's got to be vying for the best assistant award. I think she's crazy sometimes. The crap she shares about Tom makes me blush. Now that he's done with filming, he sounds much more relaxed. I wish I knew that side of him better.

Kat, on the other hand, is not only doing promos, she's deep into production of her cable show. It started a week ago—about the same time that her engagement announcement came out. Even though I was expecting it, it felt like a punch in the face. The internet has been clogged with stories about her and Gorboni, and I'd like to say I've avoided the entertainment news, but I've probably seen every article. Guess it gives me fodder for the comic. She looks happy, and I hope she is.

Chapter 35

Katya

Jake and I sit at the large mahogany table in a windowed conference room at the lawyer's office, discussing the last few changes in the prenup. He wants it finalized before our trip to Italy next month. I keep telling him we are not getting married until Cam gets out of the hospital. But I overheard him talking to his grandmother about a church ceremony in the small village where she lives. He hasn't mentioned it to me. Cam's lack of progress frustrates everyone, but I won't get married until Cam can come.

If I'm honest, I feel trapped, cornered into marriage by Jake and my debt. It's like I didn't really have a choice. It all happened so fast. Once he slipped the ring on my finger, everything changed. All my options dissolved. My voice disappeared. I know I shouldn't look at it like that. Jake agreed to pay Cam's bills, but I don't think he realizes how much it costs to be in intensive care for three months. I can only hope the three movie deals in the works for me pan out. I'm a sought-after commodity now, and Jake keeps touting my greatness, making me more relevant.

I'm marrying Jake "Gorgeous-body" Gorboni, and I am finally worth hiring. It's great. Every girl's dream. But as a child, as I watched my parent's marriage explode, I vowed never to marry a man like my father, a cheater. When I married, it would be forever. And for love. But here I am with an almost hundred-page exit plan. The contract spells out every possible escape from a marriage that hasn't even started.

Line after line discusses what happens if Jake cheats, if I cheat, if we both cheat. The contract doesn't give me much confidence in our ability to be faithful to each other. The prenup is like one of those the audience-decides-the-ending TV shows—when one door closes, another one opens. If Jake gets caught getting a blow job in his trailer, I get this much money to stay married. If I choose to end the marriage because of it, then I get less money. If I cheat, I don't get any money. If we both decide to dissolve the union within the first six months, then we leave with the assets we each came in with. Which means I go with nothing except a bump in my career and Cam's bills paid. Five years together equals this much, ten that much. If we have kids an entirely new scale kicks in. I can't imagine having kids with Jake when I can't even trust him enough to go without a condom. I swear he cheated on me when I went to visit Cam last. But if somehow we do have kids, I have to return to my original weight within three months of the birth and if I don't Jake can divorce me with zero spousal support, only child support.

I figure we won't have kids before we split anyway.

I nod when the lead lawyer asks if I agree with a fifteen-million-dollar settlement after five years. Jake is actually very generous. But I find it funny no provisions have been made in the contract for my career taking off. I'm a nonentity. If Jake's career takes a dive and mine takes off, he still has to pay me. I guess he doesn't have as much confidence in me as he says. Or maybe he just has a lot more money than I realize. Money wasn't my motivation for dating him, but circumstances change, and Jake is the one who made the marriage a stipulation of helping pay Cam's bills. It was all his idea.

"You'd think they could push this along a little faster for a thousand dollars an hour." Jake leans into me as he swings his arm around the back of my chair. "We should have signed them before we came in."

"If we are all in agreement, then all that's left is the signatures." The lawyer in the four-thousand-dollar suit hands Jake and me each a packet and a pen.

My phone buzzes in my purse and Jake gives me a look, daring me to answer it while he's paying a thousand dollars an hour. I smile and continue to sign and initial while it goes off a second time.

When it goes off the third time, Jake shakes his head and says, "Unbelievable."

I reach into my purse and silence it without looking at it.

By the time we make it to the car thirty minutes later, my phone vibrates again in my purse. It's Mom. I should have answered it earlier. Cam had a rough weekend, and I'm catching a flight to Boston in three hours. I hope she's calling to let me know he's doing better. After this grueling afternoon, I could use some good news.

"Mom?"

"Thank God I got ahold of you." Her voice quivers with frustration.

"What's wrong?"

"Cam . . . he . . . he had another bleed. At least they think it was a bleed."

"What do you mean? He's in the hospital. How can he have another bleed? Aren't they monitoring him?"

"Kat, Cam didn't make it."

What? The hair on the back of my neck stands on end. "He's dead?"

"The doctors think his blood vessels were weakened and one blew out. It was too much for him. His heart stopped, and he didn't survive."

My whole body trembles as her words sink in. I can't believe it. Tears flood my eyes, and I can't breathe. Cam died? That can't be right. He's only eighteen. Eighteen-year-olds don't die.

"That can't be right, Mom. That can't be right."

"He is. I'm sorry. I know how much you loved your brother. I was going to wait until you got here to tell you, but I didn't want you to show up and have the hospital staff tell you. They already moved him out of his room. It happened a couple of hours ago. I tried calling you." She sucks in a breath and is crying too.

"Oh, Mom. What are we going to do without Cam?" Sobs rake through my body. It can't be true. I shake my head. I don't get it. "Are you okay?"

"I will be, honey, once you get here. We'll get through this, you and me.

We'll get through this."

When I end the call, Jake presses his lips together in a straight line as he examines my face. I don't know what to tell him. I can't do anything but sob.

I feel as if someone drilled a hole in my skull, pushed an immersion soup-blender inside and liquefied my brain. I've stopped bawling by the time we make it back to the house, but Jake still hasn't said much about my brother dying. I packed my bag before leaving for the lawyer's office this morning, and all I have left to do before I leave for the airport is get ahold of my emotions.

"The car should be here soon." Jake places his hands on my shoulders and examines my face. "I'd go with you, Kitty Kat, but I'm no good with death and funerals. Ever since my parents died, I can't deal with them. And it'd become a media circus if I was there. You're better off without me."

I let out an exasperated breath and check my purse for my passport. His parents died in a boating accident when he was six. I doubt he remembers much about his parents' funeral.

"It's just that it would help me to have you there."

"Kat, it's different when you have time to process death. I never had that luxury. But Cam's been failing for three months. You had to expect this. I did. Finally, there's an end to the torture he's been putting you through. And a funeral costs less than another month of hospital bills. You're better off that it didn't drag on any longer. It was never going to end well."

I swallow hard to fight the retching building in my stomach. I've thought about what would happen if Cam died, but I never really thought it would actually happen. I always thought he would get better. At the time, the idea of his death was unthinkable. I still can't accept it. I wish Jake could see beyond himself and come with me. I don't want to go through this alone.

"I need you to come with me."

"When you get back we'll start working on the wedding. Nothing is stopping us now." He kisses my forehead almost gleefully. The car pulls up, and I get in. I don't know how to process Jake's reaction. I can't even process mine.

Chapter 36

Katya

By the time we get Cam's body released to the crematorium and drive back to Chicago, I'm numb. I'm sure Mom is too. She took on the burden of all the decision-making. She looks ten years older than the last time I saw her, just weeks ago. Cam's death has taken its toll on her. Dark bags droop under her amber eyes, and gray lightly peppers the brown hair around her temples. She's taken the brunt of the blame for Cam's death, from Dad and other family members as well. She wanted him in the study and the study is what probably killed him. But we won't know for sure until the final autopsy report comes back. If Dad had just paid his share of the medical bills the drug trial may not have looked so beneficial and Cam may never have been put in it. In the end, I financed the study. No one knows that but Mom. Cam wouldn't have been able to do the study if I hadn't helped Mom out financially. Maybe I'm more responsible than she is for Cam's death. He'd be home looking at comics if not for my meddling.

The dusty, stale air of a house not lived in for five months fills my lungs as we enter the kitchen from the garage and mudroom. The house seems empty and eerily quiet. Not that Cam took up ample space or chattered endlessly, but without Cam, the house has no meaning for me, no purpose. I fought hard to save it from foreclosure and what for? It didn't save Cam.

A stack of mail sits on the island, compliments of one of our neighbors, probably Mrs. Johnson. Mom forwarded the post to the apartment in Boston but switched it back a few days ago, trying to avoid missing bills.

I reach for a tall glass and fill it with ice and water from the dispenser on the front of the fridge before handing it to Mom and filling a second for me. I feel parched all the time, as if I can't get enough water into my body. A byproduct of crying, I guess.

I take out my phone and shoot a text to Jake to let him know we made it home safely. Ever since Cam died, he's been distant, avoiding me. I wish he would talk to me. He knows better than anyone how devastating losing someone you love can be. And I sure could use his help to get me through this. I turn and face Mom. "I can't help but think that if I hadn't helped finance the study, this never would have happened."

"You can't think that way, Kat." Mom stands and wraps her arm around me. "Cam wanted to get better. He would have done anything to get better. He hated being less than himself. That's what he said. Those are his words, not mine. And he did get better. He was happy for the first time in a long time. He would have asked your father if you hadn't helped."

"And Dad wouldn't have helped and he wouldn't have died."

"We don't know that. He may have still had a bleed. They don't know what caused it. He wouldn't have been happy though. You helped him be happy for the last two months of his life. He wouldn't have been happy here in the house with no friends, no hope."

I wipe my eyes. He sounded happy when I talked to him. Happier than he had since the accident.

"I suppose we should make some picture boards or a montage video. Most of my pictures of Cam are on the computer in the den. We should go through them, find the best ones. Why don't you take a look while I make a call to the church about the memorial? It could be therapeutic," she says.

"Okay." I tuck my phone in my back pocket and head into the den. It's the down times that are the worst. I need to keep moving, stay focused on a task or I'll just end up in a ball at the bottom of my closet.

I copy pictures one by one to a new folder I labeled "Cam's video." I have about thirty so far when I pause on one typical of my brother. He's standing by my bed, where three headless Barbies lay. His hands are out as if I'm falsely accusing him, but in the picture, I can spot blonde doll hair sticking out of his cargo pant pocket. I remember him acting so innocent and me calling him a serial killer when Mom snapped the picture. I may have been too old to play with Barbies, but I didn't want anyone killing them. It was the first time I called anyone a serial killer. Now I say it all the time. Cam and I laughed about him killing my dolls the last time I talked to him on the phone. *Cue the waterworks.*

"Thank you for taking care of the photos. It's still too soon. I don't think I could deal with looking at them." Mom enters, a stack of mail in her hands.

"Did you get rid of my Barbies?"

"No. I think I saw the case in your closet, top shelf. I haven't thrown anything away. Take them with you. Take anything you want. I think I'm going to sell the house. I won't have much room in a smaller place."

I nod in understanding. She needs a fresh start. There are too many memories here. "You should move out to LA, Mom. I'd love having you around."

"I can't." She forces a smile onto her solemn face. "My home's here. My friends are all here, and I'm pretty sure I can get back my job at the clinic. I talked to my clinic manager before we left Boston. Betty is retiring, and I can take her position if I want it. I need to keep busy."

"I get it," I say, clicking on the serial killer picture to copy it to the video folder.

Mom sets a pile of invoices on the desk shelf above the screen. "We'll go through those later," she says. "But for now, I went through the cards if you want to look at them. I don't recognize some of the names. They could be fans."

There are about twenty-five envelopes, mostly neighbors and friends of Mom. I read through them. I figure it will make me feel better if I know others care about my brother. Most of my friends have sent me texts or condolences on social media. I posted a picture of Cam and me from his eighteenth birthday, telling the world how sad his loss made me. The response was overwhelming and is one of the only things keeping me going. Snail mail is just another form. I open a card from a girl I knew from the community theater group I was in. She was always lovely. I should reconnect with her and see what she's doing now. I separate her envelope from the pile. The next card doesn't have a return address. I slide it out of the envelope and read the front.

How do you get over a loss when it leaves every cell in your body broken?

What a strange card. I flip it over wondering if Hallmark has a new imprint, but there is no manufacturer on the back. I open the card with the strangest feeling tickling my stomach.

Kat, I'm sorry about Cam. I know how much you loved him. —Micah

"Sweet baby kittens!" My hand covers my mouth as shock spreads through me. He drew a small cat head at the bottom of the card. The same one he sketched on my wrist. Kitten Bastet. I bet he made the card. A comic-type illustration of a grumpy cat scowling fills the front with his words.

I read through it again. *How do you get over a loss when it leaves every cell of your body broken?* Damn him for knowing exactly how I feel. I read it three more times. Is he talking about us? Is he talking about me or how I left him? I hold the card up to the backlight of the computer screen. The picture on the front is hand drawn. It's an original Fallston. I bring it to my nose and sniff it. It smells like him—baby powder, fresh springtime, and ink. I close my eyes and bring the card to my chest, savoring it as I contemplate all the possible reasons he sent me the note. He must still think about me. I think about him constantly. I look up, and Mom is staring at me.

"I thought maybe that one was a stalker, but you must know him."

"Yeah. I know him." I leave it at that, shoving the card back in the envelope and placing it in my personal pile.

"Well, he managed to put a smile on your face. Who is he?"

"A guy I worked with last summer. A really good guy. If I weren't marrying Jake, I'd marry him."

She laughs as if I'm joking. "He seems a little intense. Good thing Jake asked you first." She pats me on the shoulder as she turns to leave. "I need to make some calls. Your father's wife keeps calling."

"Her name is Amanda, Mom."

"I know." She rolls her eyes and walks out of the room.

I take out my phone and type out a text to Micah.

Kat: Thank you for the card. You always know just what to say.

I don't expect him to answer. I'm sure he blocked my number months ago. He hasn't responded to any of my texts since the day of Liam's wedding.

Micah: You're welcome. How are you doing?

He actually answered. I can't believe he hasn't blocked me. Did he read all my texts and ignore me? I thumb through the last couple. I sent them over two months ago.

Kat: About as good as anyone with every cell of her body broken.
Micah: I've been there. It will get better. It just takes time. I've got
to go to class.
Kat: Can we talk again? I miss you.

I stare at my phone, willing it to ping with an incoming text. It doesn't.

What am I doing? What the hell am I doing? I'm only going to hurt him again. I pull the stack of bills off the shelf above the computer. Three thousand dollars for an MRI. How many did Cam have? Six? Seven? I shake my head in disgust for even thinking I could see Micah again. I wipe the tears from my eyes and start clicking on pictures again.

Chapter 37

Micah

I walk into the kitchen and turn off my phone before handing it to Dawson. "Keep this from me for the next couple of days? I can't be trusted with it."

"Hot damn. The plot thickens. Who is she? That little Baptist virgin you met at dinner with your parents on Sunday? Is she getting you all hot and bothered with no follow-through?"

"No. It's not her." Virginia was her actual name. It fit her. I will never be interested in someone my mother finds for me. The girl had never seen a graphic novel. She asked me if superpowers were considered magic, insinuating magic was evil, and if they were magic I shouldn't read comic books. There is a huge line between fact and fiction, and I don't think she could distinguish between them. I sit next to Dawson in one of the eclectically mismatched wooden chairs at the farmhouse-style kitchen table. The white painted table is too long for the narrow kitchen, but we make it work. I like it because I can lay out an entire book's worth of panels without having to stack them.

"The phone is locked so don't even think about hacking into it. I . . . I just need to distance myself from the temptation of calling someone."

"Tell me her name, and I'll delete her from your contacts."

"I can't do that." I run my hand through my hair and take a calming breath. I shouldn't have sent the card. But I know how much she loved her brother, and she has to be hurting. I did what I could, and now I have to walk away.

"Hide it somewhere I won't come across it, but don't forget where it is, or I will shave off that scraggly-ass beard you're trying to grow. It's just for a couple of days."

His hand goes to his chin, and he pulls the longest of the red hairs into a cone. "You wouldn't dare."

"I would." I make scissors with my fingers. "Chop. Chop," I say, and his jaw drops in disbelief. "I need this. Please, just do it."

"Fine." Dawson walks out toward our shared room with my phone in his hand.

"And don't put it in your underwear drawer next to your weed. That's the first place I'll look." Dawson is a great friend, but he's really predictable.

"Why is Dawson hiding your phone in his underwear drawer?" Fitzpatrick sits down across from me at the table.

"I told you we'd turn 'em." Ron Campbell squeezes Fitzpatrick's shoulder as he passes him on his way to the fridge. Campbell doesn't pay rent or officially live here, but he's here every day at dinnertime. He and Fitz have been together two years and rarely miss eating dinner together.

"You caught us, man." I laugh. "I have a thing for Dawson's underwear. You should see him in his pocket briefs."

Campbell's dad thinks gayness is a lifestyle choice, so Campbell always jokes about Dawson and me choosing to change teams. It's Campbell's way of coping with his father's stupidity.

I shake my head. "I just need to distance myself from my contact list for a couple of days. I can live without my phone."

"You know you can access your contacts from your computer or tablet, right?"

I nod, staring at Fitzpatrick. He's a tech genius but can be so dense sometimes. Why would he remind me of that when I just told him I didn't want access to my contacts?

"Not helpful, man," says Dawson, entering the kitchen empty-handed.

My phone's in our room somewhere. *Shit.* I hate that I want to go find it. I need to get out of here, away from my phone, away from my tablet, and away from my thoughts about Katya. "Let's go to Backster's. The first round's on me."

"Dinner too?" asks Campbell. Cheap bastard. He's always looking for a free meal.

"Sure. One entrée each and no dessert." I have to set limits, or the guys would eat a week's worth of food. I pat my back pocket for my wallet. Got it. "I'm getting drunk. Someone else needs to drive, and don't let me do anything stupid."

A commercial for arthritis medication bursts like a bomb in my head, the narrator shouting side effects and death warnings in my ear. It doesn't feel right. I attempt to crack open my crusty eyes, but can't. The room is too bright. Why is Dawson's laptop so loud? My head hurts. I should not have drunk that much last night. Big mistake. "ESPN weekly stats report," the announcer yells. Okay, I slept on the couch. ESPN only plays on the TV, right? Did Dawson pick up a girl? It's not his usual thing since he became a dad, but it's feasible. I rub my hands across my face and open my eyes again. Yep. I'm on the couch. I push my body upright into a sitting position to see who's messing with the TV. My whole body hurts.

"Morning, sunshine." Dawson smiles, but it doesn't match his expression. He's pissed about something. I should be the one who's mad. I'm the one on the couch.

"What's up?" I ask, closing my eyes and hoping my head doesn't explode.

"You tell me. Did you find your cat?"

I look up at him, trying to figure out why he's so mad at me. "I don't have a cat. Fitz is allergic to them."

"Well, you were looking for your cat at four in the morning. I was sleeping on the couch, and you woke me up. You kept talking about your missing cat. You wanted me to help find it, and then when I got up to use the bathroom, you took my spot on the couch. I ended up sleeping on my bed, ten feet away from the naked girl in yours."

"I brought a girl home last night?" I press my palm against the base of my skull, trying to ease the throb.

Dawson shakes his head and grunts out a laugh from deep in his throat. "You didn't bring a girl home last night; you brought Mara home. She's naked in your bed." A fake sugary smile grows on his face as he watches my reaction.

I rake my fingers through my hair and squeeze the top of my head. *How could I let that happen?* I don't remember coming home. I squint, trying to recall the night. I remember seeing Mara. She looked good.

"Please tell me she's naked because I spilled my drink on her and her dress needed to dry."

"Nope. You gals are back together. That's what you said, anyway. You forgave her and wanted her back. You kept saying it."

"But I was too drunk, right? Tell me I was too drunk."

"Nope. You slept with her. No one in the apartment got any sleep until you were done. Seems like Mara revels in voicing her opinion. And then you lost your cat. The night was full of adventures. And I didn't get any sleep. I have daddy duty in two hours, and I didn't get any sleep."

"Sorry." Shit. "I can help you with Leo if you want."

"You will."

I huff out a breath, piecing together the night in my head. I remember Mara pulling a chair up next to me and sitting. "Why didn't you stop me?"

"Oh, there was no stopping you. Believe me, I tried. I even offered to drop her off at her place, but you wouldn't have it. You said Mara could help you with your missing cat."

I sit forward with my knees on my elbows. Why did Kat have to say she missed me? That's where the missing cat came from. I'm so screwed. I'm sure I was looking for my phone.

"I should talk to Mara."

"Good luck, man. She seems fired up 'bout gettin' you back."

That makes one of us. But maybe Mara is the only way I'll get over Kat. Perhaps she's the only one who can distract me. I need to keep an open mind about this reunion. I head into the room as I go over in my mind what I'm going to say.

Katya

My phone pings with a text and I head to the restroom to check it. I don't need someone posting a picture of me texting at my brother's memorial service.

Jake: How's it going? Are you almost done?

Kat: The service is about to start. I'll be here for a couple more
hours. I wish you were here.

Jake: You know I'd be there if I could. Tom's coming over, and we're
going to watch the basketball highlights. Hurry home.

Kat: See you soon.

I leave the bathroom and walk out into the main room. Cam's video plays on a large screen near the front wall. It turned out well, but I can't watch it anymore. I end up bawling every time I catch a glimpse of it. The funeral home is packed with people, and I've done more than my share of greeting acquaintances and strangers. Mom is talking to some of her old coworkers, and I don't want to interrupt her chance to catch up with them, so I join my stepsisters in the farthest corner from the entrance.

Ponca and Demeter, my father's children with his current wife, are seated on a couch, and I sit between them. Ponca is thirteen with long, straight brown hair, and she's a little bitch who I usually avoid. But her younger sister, Demeter, is still sweet. She's ten with short, dark hair, and her personality reminds me of me. They are both too young to watch my cable show and up until recently didn't really recognize me as a celebrity. But since the engagement announcement, they treat me as if I'm royalty.

Demeter's eyes are glassy with tears, and I hand her the box of tissues from the table in front of me as I wrap my arm around her. My stepsisters didn't know Cam well, but they did see him once in a while at family gatherings. My father seemed to shelter them from Cam after his brain injury, as if Cam was dangerous and might hurt them. I wish they had a chance to get to know him better.

The room quiets, and I look up to see what has grabbed everyone's attention. Across the room by the entrance door stand Megan, Liam, Nak, Leslie, Izzy, and Tom—my gang from LA. Oh my God. I can't believe they came. I rise and walk the length of the room to greet them.

"We missed you. You've been gone so long, we figured we needed to find you and bring you home." Megan wraps her arms around me in a huge bear hug.

"Is this party for us?" asks Liam, joining the hug and kissing my cheek.

"Just for you," I joke. "I can't believe you came." Tears fill my eyes. I guess funerals show you who your real friends are.

I hug each one of them, even Tom, as they offer their condolences.

"I'm glad you all came. Thank you." I still can't believe it.

"Where's the big guy? Did he step out for a flask hit in the alley? He's got to be looking for someone to drink with after three days," says Tom, looking around the large room.

"Jake?" What is he talking about . . . three days? "Jake doesn't do funerals. He can't deal with death."

"Is he at the hotel?"

"He's not coming. He's not even in town." The words catch in my throat. "Did I mention how happy it makes me to see you all?"

"You're kidding me," says Megan. "Your fiancé isn't here?"

"No. He couldn't do it. His parents' deaths still mess with him. He couldn't stomach coming. What did you mean 'after three days'? Did he say he was coming?"

Tom's brown eyes dart between mine and Izzy's. He wasn't supposed to tell me about Jake. I bet Jake will be pissed.

"He said he was hopping on a flight three days ago. I figured he was coming here to be with you. I figured he'd need a break by the time we got here. But I could be mistaken." Tom's eyes meet Liam's and Liam's lips flatten into a straight line.

"He didn't tell me he was going on a trip. Did he say where he was going?"

"He probably didn't want to bother you," says Izzy, and it is obvious she is trying to cover for Tom's slipup.

"Or he didn't want me to know."

"How's Micah doing?" I ask Tom, emboldened by the fact that my fiancé is probably cheating on me while I mourn my brother.

"Great." Tom shrugs noncommittally as if me asking isn't weird. "He's got half a million followers on his YouTube channel, graduates from his fancy art school in a few months, got back together with his ex-girlfriend, and someone approached me the other day interested in talking to him about a Netflix series. Seems like he's doing fine." He looks at Liam and then to Nak. Is he keeping something from me? "Did Nordstrom tell you he just signed a contract for a Netflix movie?"

"You did?" I turn to Liam. I hope he's not leaving our show. "Congratulations. That's awesome. Why didn't you tell me? You're not leaving the show, are you?"

"You were busy. Filming starts in May, after I'm done with the movie I'm doing in January. It won't conflict with *Impassioned*." He smiles and winks at me.

"I'm so happy for you. But you're so busy, I'm never going to see you." I take his hand and squeeze it. "Can we all go out after this? I've spent the last three weeks with my family. I could use a night away from them." My brother died. My fiancé is lying to me. And Micah got back together with Mara. "I'm going to need a drink."

"Katya, introduce us to your friends." My father stands in front of us with his arm around his gorgeous bleach-blonde trophy wife, his daughters at his heels.

"Everyone, this is my father, Lance, his wife, Amanda, and their daughters, Ponca and Demeter. This is Liam Nordstrom and his wife, Megan." Oops. I probably wasn't supposed to call her his wife. "I work with Liam on *Impassioned*." I moved my hand down the line. "This is Daniel Nackerson, or Nak, as we call him and his girlfriend, Leslie Daily. Nak is Liam's housemate."

"But Liam's married. How does that work when you're married?" asks Amanda in a judgmental tone, completely baffled. She can't understand anything outside her bubble's norm. She assumes they're all sleeping together.

"They just share a house." I turn to face away from her and roll my eyes, not wanting to deal with her on any level. "Lastly, this is Tom Fallston and his assistant, Izzy Mulligan."

"We know who you are," says Ponca. "You played Demetri in the *Pure Magic* series. I read all the books and saw every movie. Can we get our picture with you?"

Tom looks at me to see if it's all right. It seems inappropriate at a funeral, but I smile, and he bends down to get on the same level with them as Izzy snaps a picture with Ponca's phone.

"Let's get another with all of us," says Dad, handing his phone to Izzy.

Super inappropriate, Dad. It's one thing for my stepsisters to pose for pictures at Cam's memorial service but another for a forty-seven-year-old grown man to do the same. But that's just who he is. It's all about him. We gather for the picture, and I don't smile. I'm not giving him that. He probably wants to show it off to his church friends. I doubt he'll tell them where it was taken.

Dad pockets his phone and asks, "Where's Jake?"

He just now notices my fiancé is absent? He's spent the last two days with me.

"Probably Aspen or Aruba with some redhead," I mutter under my breath, and I notice the corner of Liam's lip turns up. He must have heard me. No one else did.

My mom's brother gets on the mic asking for everyone to take a seat for prayer, and I am grateful because Dad can't ask me any more questions.

Last night, my LA friends and I ended up in a small pub near the hotel where everyone was staying, and I got pretty buzzed. I spent the night on the couch in Liam and Megan's hotel room. They're really good to me. They even dropped me off at the house this morning on their way to the airport.

I pull out my phone, a little scared to see what I posted last night in my uninhibited state of drunkenness.

"Okay. Okay. It's not that bad."

"What's not so bad?"

I look up to see Mom hovering over my shoulder as she stares at the pictures on my phone. I instinctively bring my phone to my chest to block her view.

"I follow you on Instagram. I already saw your posts. 'I love my friends. They flew all the way to Chicago to help me say goodbye to my little brother.' 'Best friends ever.' 'Missing my brother.' Did I miss any of them? There were only three, right?"

"Only three." I hold up the picture of everyone at the bar and stare at it as I feel my insides twist. These people flew halfway across the country to support me when my fiancé was a no-show. If I were with Micah, he would have been there for me. I'm sure Jake will bawl me out for posting them, say I intentionally made him look bad.

"I'm with the girl who posted the comment, 'Where's Jake?' Why couldn't Jake make it when all your friends made time to come?"

I rub my eyes with the butt of my hand. "I don't know, Mom. I thought it was because he couldn't handle his parents' death, but then I found out he flew out somewhere, and he lied to me about it. He said he was at home."

"Is he cheating on you?"

"Probably."

"If he's already cheating, why would you marry him?"

"I don't really have a choice. We're getting married whether he cheats on me or not."

"You're twenty-two years old. Your life is full of choices. The papers aren't signed."

I laugh. How can she be so naïve? "The prenup is signed."

"But if he's cheating on you already, do you really want to marry him?"

"How would it look if I pulled out of the engagement now? The press would crucify me."

"It would look as if you are confident enough not to let a man take advantage of you." She sits next to me on the couch and takes my hand. "Don't repeat what I am going to tell you."

"Of course, Mom. You know you can trust me." I nod.

"Your father cheated on me when I was pregnant with Cam. It was the first time I knew for sure he was cheating. My best friend Marlene saw him cozying up to a blonde at a restaurant. Marlene was seated in the booth behind them, and she heard their whole conversation. When she told me, I cried and made her swear she wouldn't tell another soul. I never confronted your father then because I was too afraid of what losing him would mean. I was pregnant and had a toddler in diapers, and I didn't want to have to raise them on my own. I convinced myself it was a fluke and it wouldn't happen again."

At least I'm not that stupid.

"Of course, it did. There were business trips that weren't really business trips and nights when he never came home. He had great excuses. I don't think he knew I knew about the affairs. Honestly, I didn't want him to know I knew. I found out about two other affairs before Naomi got pregnant. I think your father would have stayed if I let him, but I had a preteen daughter who I didn't want to learn from my example. It's one thing to have an affair that can't be substantiated and another to have a baby. You can't deny it when a baby is involved. How was I supposed to explain to my daughter that I was okay with her father's cheating? And then, his current wife was pregnant before our divorce went through. She didn't know about Naomi's baby. I don't know when she found out. Maybe she still doesn't know."

"Why did you put up with it so long?"

"I was in denial. When we met in college, we were on equal footing. Your father was handsome, and I fell fast. His career took off, and mine got delayed by kids. It's hard to focus solely on your career when you're raising a family. And I'm not blaming you and Cam for me not making the big bucks. My job was never going to pay the big bucks like your father's. We built his career together. I traded a job with career potential for a job with flexible hours so he could stay late at the office and build his legacy. I thought we were a team."

"So you ignored his cheating because life was easier together than apart?"

"That and I didn't want everyone to know I was a failure. I couldn't keep my husband from straying. I put on ten pounds with each kid and I owned all the responsibility, all the guilt of his cheating. I don't want you to make my mistakes. Jake's the one responsible for cheating, not you."

"Mom, I know what I'm getting into with Jake. And I know it's not going to last forever. I'm marrying Jake because he agreed to pay Cam's bills if I married him. And he's marrying me to keep his all-American brand. It's a trade-off. We're both benefitting from it. And I'm not having his children."

Mom collapses against the back of the couch and won't look at me. She points her chin up and swallows hard as she shakes her head. The large vein in her neck throbs as I wait for her to tell me what she's thinking. I've never seen her this mad. With all she admitted, I thought she would understand.

"Say something."

"I'm not taking any more of your money. Don't marry him on my account. I've always liked Jake, but that was before he cheated on you. I am not going to be responsible for another failed marriage."

"Let me do this, Mom. It's not a failed marriage if you both know there's an end. I'm getting a career boost too. We're both benefitting."

"I'm still not taking your money. Your benefit is shrinking. Is it still worth it?"

"Marriage doesn't matter that much in Hollywood."

"Just so you know, your father's wife . . ." She laughs. She never calls Amanda by her name. "She let it slip that your father had a life insurance policy out on Cam. Two hundred and fifty thousand dollars. And since Cam was eighteen, the bill collectors will go after his estate. Life insurance money is considered part of Cam's estate. All I have to do is point them in your father's direction. He'll have to part with every penny. Serves him right."

I don't know why this makes me smile, but it does. Dad will finally have to pay his share. It will all be from the insurance policy, but still, I bet he had plans for the money.

"I hate that Dad having to pay makes me happy." I miss Cam. *Cue the tears.* "I just want Cam back."

"I know, honey. Me too." Mom wraps her arms around me, and we rock in each other's arms until the tears stop flowing.

"You need to confront Jake. Talk it out. Don't let him think you're oblivious to what he's doing." She brushes the hair out of my eyes and smiles encouragingly. "I'm going to sell the house, and I'm going to buy something more manageable. Then I'm going to pay you back for everything you've given me. Don't let money dictate love. If you love Jake, work it out with him. But if I were you, I'd go find that really nice guy. The one you said you'd marry if you weren't marrying Jake."

I smile at that thought until I remember he's back together with Mara. "It's too late, Mom. Someone else snatched him up. The good ones don't stay on the market for long."

"Then find someone else, someone who will love and respect you."

I wish it were that easy.

Chapter 39

Micah

"But I don't understand why I can't go." Mara stares, her dark brown eyes burrowing into me as if I canceled Christmas, not Thanksgiving.

Do I tell her the real reason? I don't think she's ready for reality. "It's a family-only dinner. You're not family."

The dark wooden table wobbles as she reaches across to touch my arm. It feels insincere, as if she's trying to manipulate me. I grab my cup and sit back on my metal stool, out of her reach, as I contemplate her motivation. Why does she want to go so badly?

"I always used to go to your family dinners. It's tradition. I've only missed one Thanksgiving in three years." The words rattle from her mouth as if she's reading bullet points off an outline.

"Mom wants it to be just family." I don't tell her Mom doesn't know I'm dating anyone. When I told Tom I got back with Mara, he spent an hour bitching me out. "I'll go to your family's meal on Sunday."

"It's not the same. I just don't understand why I can't go." She huffs as she crosses her arms, producing a hint of cleavage that normally doesn't exist. "Besides, Tom's going to be there. I haven't seen him in forever."

It's Tom she wants to see. "My family's not really on Team Mara anymore. You should be happy you don't have to go. *I* don't want to go."

"If you can get past it, why can't they?" Her eyes flick from her cleavage to my face, her lips pursing, as she realizes what I didn't say. "You didn't tell your family we got back together, did you?"

I avoid her eyes, but then admit, "Tom knows."

"But your parents don't." She sits forward, cocking her head as if I've committed a crime, and the table rocks again. Good thing I haven't set my coffee back down.

"Nope."

"I don't understand what the big deal is. Why can't you just bring me?"

"It's the first time Tom's been to Thanksgiving dinner at my parents in four years. We want an intimate dinner with the four of us. What's there to understand?"

"You've changed." She turns her body and starts digging through her backpack on the bench next to her. "The old Micah would never exclude me from a family dinner."

"Well, I'm adulting now, and need to consider all parties' desires, not just yours."

She looks up and rolls her eyes. "Whatever." Her straight brown hair curtains her face as she goes back to digging in her backpack.

"I have to meet my professor. I'll catch you later." I shoulder my portfolio bag as I stand.

"We're not done talking about this."

The old me would have kissed her just to make sure we were still good after our discussion. I'm glad I'm not the old me anymore. Tom was right. Girls don't respect nice guys. They walk all over them. I'm putting myself first for once. I'm sure Mom wouldn't mind if I brought a date, but I want to be able to talk to my brother at Thanksgiving without Mara hanging on his every word. The only woman I ever dated who didn't drool over Tom was Kat. And we never officially dated.

Tom actually showed up at Mom and Dad's for Thanksgiving dinner. I wasn't sure he would make it. He and our parents don't see eye to eye, and part of me believed he'd cancel at the last minute. It's uncomfortable as hell, the four of us sitting at the overly decorated table. Nothing is spared when Tom comes to dinner. The fine china, the crystal water goblets, the lit candles, the linen napkins folded into turkeys all say the prodigal son has returned, so I sit quietly watching as Mom takes every opportunity to extract information from her golden boy.

"What projects do you have coming up, Tom?" Mom forks a bite of cranberry fluff, her eyes glued on my brother.

"I have a few things lined up. Jonathan Williams and I are in talks about a production collaboration. It's a psychological thriller his wife wrote. More my genre than his, and that's why he pulled me in. It's a compelling script. I think we could make it shine."

"Is it like *Gone Girl*? Because that was a work of art."

"It's fresh. Written for the screen. I don't think there are any comps out there for it." Tom takes a drink of his water and glances at me. He's as uncomfortable as I am.

"I saw that you're back together with Mia Thompson, and Jonathan's okay with that?"

"Mom, they dated for a couple years but Jon's married to someone else. Mia is free to date whomever she wants. Besides, we're not dating. It was just one charity event. Did Micah tell you he was back with Mara?" A smirk twists on the corner of Tom's lips as he smoothly redirects Mom. *I hate him.*

"You're back together with Mara? That's fabulous, dear. You should have brought her. She is such a sweet girl. Her parents are members of our church. Amazing family. I never understood why you broke up with her."

"Micah never told you why he broke up with her?"

"Don't," I mouth, but it's too late, I can see it in his eyes.

"Mara fucked another guy in the bathroom at a party. Such a sweet girl." Tom likes to shock them, especially Mom. I can't really blame him for jumping on the opportunity, but now bringing Mara to Sunday dinner may be a problem. I should be more upset, but I'm not.

"Language, Thomas," Dad says in his best Captain America voice.

"How else should I say it?" Tom cocks his head looking at Dad. "She copulated with another guy while her boyfriend listened outside the door? Screwed? Bumped uglies? No, fuck is the best description. She fucked him. I don't know why Micah would ever take her back. Why'd you take her back, Micah?"

I swallow the urge to tell him taking her back was the only way I could get over Kat marrying Gorboni. And maybe it's some weird punishment for allowing myself to fall for Kat in the first place, but it's how I'm able to cope.

The room falls silent. I suppose Tom expected me to respond, but I can't, not in front of Mom and Dad. He must really hate that I took Mara back to turn them against her. We all return to eating. Five minutes pass. Ten. I feel the climate change as we eat. If it were a comic book, it would be a blank panel. A reset. Mom's keying up for more questions.

"I see Jake's getting married. Is she a nice girl?" *Fuck!* Mom passes me the rolls, and I take one before setting the basket in front of Tom. He avoids bread, and the yeasty aroma of the white highly processed rolls should torture him.

"Yeah. She's great. She was in the movie we filmed this summer. She's a sweetheart."

"I saw you flew to Chicago for her brother's funeral. Are you sweet on her or are you just friends?"

"We're friends. A bunch of us went. I thought Jake was going to be there, but he had other plans." Tom picks up the basket of rolls and passes it to Dad without taking one.

"Why wasn't Gorboni there?" I ask. I'd seen a post of Kat's.

"He was in the Caymans, I think." Tom's eyes meet mine. "I don't think she was too happy about it."

"Bet not," I say. Tom's expression says, *I'm sure Gorboni was cheating on Kat, and she knows it.*

"Well. It was gracious of you to go, especially if Jake wasn't there. Your father and I must have taught you something."

Tom and I both smile at her crediting herself for his good deed. I wish I could ask for more details. The fact that Tom's sharing Gorboni's cheating with me tells me something's changed between the two of them. They may be friends, but Tom doesn't agree with the way he's treating Kat.

We're seconds away from Mom touting church news. The air is ripe for a lecture, and I am sure it will swing at Mara's ungodly behavior. I can tell by the way Mom glances at Dad. *Time to change subjects.*

"I met with my advisor on Monday. He showed my portfolio to a connection he has at University College London, and the guy wants to interview me for their world-renowned master's program." I don't tell them the guy is a Jerwood-prize winner known worldwide for his contemporary drawings. He teaches at the university and has ultimate decision-making on who gets into the program. If I give them too much information, they'll pressure me into going, and I'm not sure that's what I want. "I don't know if I'm interested, but it's an honor to be noticed."

"That's great, dear." Mom doesn't look up from her plate as she speaks. "Your drawings are exceptional, you *should* get your masters."

"You wouldn't do that right away?" asks Tom. "I have another proposition for you. Netflix wants you. I have a meeting set up for your winter break. You interested? They want to make a series out of your YouTube channel."

"Are you serious? Hell yeah, I'm interested."

"They contacted me because of the interview you did. They couldn't find contact information for you online, but they knew you were my brother. Thought you might want it."

"I love you, man." I reach an arm around Tom's shoulder and squeeze. "That's the best news I've had in months. Years. A series trumps London easily."

"A series?" Mom's entire face perks, her brows, her cheeks, her nose. "For your comics?" Doubt fills her words.

"Yeah. For my comics."

"They said something about full animation and voice actors." Tom smiles because he knows this is my dream.

"Will you come with me to the meeting?"

"Of course I'll come with you. I'll just have to rearrange my schedule. What day did you say it was, Tom?"

"I think, he meant me, Mom." Tom stifles a laugh, and I know what he's thinking. Mom's trying to insert herself into managing my career.

She looks at me as if Tom is way off base.

"He's right, Mom. I meant him. They approached him, and he knows Hollywood."

"I knew she'd want to sink her claws into you, so I talked to Davin. He said he'd represent you if you want."

His agent? This is insane.

"My claws, Thomas, really? Why would you say such a thing?"

"I'm not trying to rekindle our problems, Mom. I'm just doing my job as a big brother and giving him a leg up the best way I can. Sorry if that offends you. That wasn't my intent."

Family dinners always end up in this place when Tom comes. I look over to Dad, and he raises a brow before looking to Mom.

"Darla, let Tom help him. You were just complaining about how many clients you have. You work way too many hours already. Micah will survive without you."

I like my dad.

"Is it too early for pie?" I ask.

Chapter 40

Katya

I walk into the house and find Jake lying on his overstuffed red leather couch, the TV blaring. He sits up and clicks off the TV when I enter the living room. Even though neither of us has mentioned his whereabouts during my absence, he stopped texting his lies yesterday. I'm sure Tom gave him a heads-up and he's spent the last twenty-four hours working up a new lie.

"Are you ready to get serious about planning the wedding?"

He completely ignores the obvious. No *I can explain*, or *Tom was mistaken, I never left.*

"Not really, Jake. My brother just died."

"He died three weeks ago. It's time to move on. I thought we could move up our trip to Italy. Nonna wants us to meet with the priest as soon as we can." He's looking at his phone and not me.

A quick laugh slips from my gut, a knee-jerk reaction to the absurdity of his words. I turn to stare at him, his face somber and unwavering. How easy would it be to ignore his cheating and continue in the direction I was going? All I would have to do is marry him. The Mendez movie would fall into place, and once that was in the can, we could split. My career would be set in motion—two films, a successful cable show. It would be a good start, anyway, and I wouldn't have to pay back the money Jake's given me.

I think about Mom, and all the years she overlooked Dad's cheating.

Could I ignore Jake's affairs? Could I look the other way? Or would they eat up my insides, turn me bitter like Mom? Would the paparazzi show me another video of Jake with some redhead? What about Micah? Sweet, adorable, sexy Micah. If I marry Jake, he'll disappear. He'll never forgive me. I'll never get another chance with him. His smile, his laugh, they'll never be mine again. He's better than Jake. He wouldn't cheat. Micah is a better man.

"What were you thinking posting this picture?" Jake holds up his phone with my Instagram photos from the night of my brother's memorial on it, but when I reach for his phone, he pulls it back.

Is he scolding me for showing the world his true colors? "I wanted to thank my friends for making an effort to show me they care."

"It made me look bad, Kat." A text pings on his phone and a smile unrelated to our conversation creeps onto his face.

"I can't help that it made you look bad. Why didn't you come to Cam's memorial?"

He laughs. Is he even listening to me?

"Let me see your phone, Jake," I say to start the conversation.

His eyes narrow and he shakes his head. "Why?" He stashes his phone in the back pocket of his athletic pants.

"Just unlock your phone and hand it to me." He's stalling. He knows where I'm headed with this.

"I'm not giving you my phone." Jake places his hand over his back pocket as if guarding his most prized possession.

"You will if you want to get married."

"You have real trust issues, Kitty Kat. If we're going to get married, you need to trust me."

"You make it hard, Jake. Give me your phone." I hold my hand out, palm up, waiting.

"I'm not giving you my phone. This is ridiculous. Do I ever ask you for your phone?"

"Where were you?" I soften my voice. "Where were you when I needed you? Am I going to be ambushed by another video of you cheating during the past three weeks?" I collapse against the back of the couch, my head pushing into the fluffy cushion.

Jake's nostrils flare and his Adam's apple twitches. He doesn't want to answer because he can't deny what I know. He stares at me in silence for a minute.

"Kat, I have a problem."

Obviously. I sit forward again and cock my head to show I'm listening.

"I'm a sex addict. I can't help what I do."

At least he doesn't deny the cheating. "Who was it? Who were you with while I was mourning my brother?" The words don't seem to sink in no matter how many times I say them. And he doesn't see how much he hurt me.

"If you'd been around it never would have happened. You can't leave me like that."

"So what you're saying is every time we're separated you're going to cheat on me? Every time one of us is filming I should expect you're cheating?" My voice raises ten decibels with each word.

"I can get treatment. There's treatment for sex addiction. I can make it through treatment if you are there to support me."

"Like you were when my brother died?"

"That's different. You know what happened to my parents."

"Yeah. They died in a boating accident when you were six. Get over it. You expect me to move on after three weeks when you can't after eighteen years. You are such a hypocrite. I needed you, Jake. I needed you to help me get through the last three weeks, and you didn't even try. You didn't even care. Instead, you take some redhead on vacation because you can't last three weeks without sex."

"I have a problem, Kat. I admit it."

"I want to be with a guy who respects me and my family enough to push through difficult times and be a man."

"I am a man. If you'd told me you wanted me there, I would have been there." He shakes his head as if not going to Chicago was my fault.

"I did ask you to come," I practically yell with narrowed eyes. "I think you had the sexcursion already planned."

"I don't remember you asking me. Are you going to help me through treatment or not?"

"You know what happened to my parents, right? My dad cheated on my mom over and over. I can't be with a cheater. It's like you having to live at a funeral home. You couldn't do it. It's not good for me mentally to be with you, and I have to take care of myself first." I pull the ruby ring off my finger and hand it to him. I take a deep breath, trying to calm myself. "I know you'll find someone, Jake. I'm sorry I can't be your someone."

"Come on, Kat." He stares at me as he holds up the ring in the palm of his hand. "I'm not a cheater. This isn't what you want."

"You're the definition of a cheater. Google the word. I'm sure your picture will pop up. I know you'll find the right girl someday, someone who can heal you. You can have any girl you want; find someone good." I stand and smile encouragingly at him. "I don't want us to end on bad terms. I care about you. I just can't deal with your addiction. I'm going to pay back the money you gave me for Cam's bills. I don't have it right now, but I'll get it to you. Bye, Jake."

His fingers curl over the top of the ring in his palm as he turns and punches the couch cushion with a hard smack. Then he leans back without a rebuttal, crossing his arms in front of his chest. I can feel his eyes on me as I walk toward the bedroom to gather my belongings. I don't know if I am doing the right thing, but at least it feels like the right thing for me.

Chapter 41

Katya

When I handed the ring back to Jake five days ago, I knew this day of reckoning would come—the consequence of both our broken promises. I got the call to meet with Gena Mendez about the movie Jake and I are supposed to start filming in February and was told to meet Gena for a casual lunch to discuss the film—no Paul or Jake, —just the girls. Neither Jake nor I have officially posted about the breakup and there has only been one paparazzi picture with me not wearing my ring. I don't know how Gena found out, unless Jake told her, but I'm sure she will want the scoop on the engagement, and I'm not sure what I can legally tell her and what I can't. I doubt I will be able to salvage the movie contract once she finds out we're not getting married, and it's probably for the best. Working with Jake on another movie might kill me.

I arrive at the posh eatery on time and am seated in the middle of the ample space just inside the open lanai doors.

"Ms. Mendez is running late, but she would like you to get started with a bottle of her favorite wine," says the hostess. She waves her hand, and a man appears with a bottle of wine. He starts pouring the wine into my goblet, and then stands with a smug grin presenting the bottle for my inspection. I thought I was supposed to approve before he poured. But it's not as if I would refuse Gena Menendez's favorite wine, and he knows that. I don't know enough about wine years and brands to be impressed. I smile and pick up the glass. He sets the bottle near the linen-covered table's edge.

"Please let me know if I can get you anything before she arrives," the college-age male server says before backing away and standing in the corner, waiting. He must be our server and no one else's because when I look at him, he suddenly animates and returns to the table.

"Did you need anything, Ms. Avery?"

"No, thank you." I feel stupid and don't look at him again.

When Gena arrives, the server returns to pull out her chair and pour her wine.

"It's so good to see you, Katya." Gena smiles as she kisses my cheek. She settles into her chair and picks up her wine. "Do you like the wine?"

"Yes. Thank you." I nod. "It's lovely.

"Let's order. Do you know what you want?"

I open my menu and pick the first salad on the page. After our server leaves Gena's face turns serious.

"You're probably wondering why I asked you to lunch today."

I nod again. She isn't someone who beats around the bush. She grasps my left hand in both of hers and takes a deep breath.

"I thought we should share some girl time to talk about what's going on with you and Jake Gorboni. You're not wearing his ring anymore." She moves her hands to her lap and straightens her napkin.

"I don't know what I can tell you."

"The truth would be a good place to start."

"We're not getting married. We planned to but I . . ." I don't know what to say. She's going to tell me she's canceling my contract and she's already found my replacement. "I can't marry him."

"What happened? Did Jake cheat on you again?"

I look down at the napkin on my lap. How can I tell her without telling her?

"You can tell me. It's just us girls."

I reach for my wine and take a sip, trying to gather wine-courage. I feel as if she has a hidden microphone and anything I say will come back to haunt me.

"Are you the one who cheated?" she asks with an open posture and narrowed brows.

I shake my head, and I look up to meet her eyes. "I understand if you want to find someone to replace me in the movie. I don't think Jake and I will be able to work together on this project with all our baggage."

"Let me tell you a little about myself." She sips her wine and pulls on a sugary smile. "When I met my husband, Paul, I was a nineteen-year-old struggling actress, and he was a twenty-nine-year-old boy who never worked a day in his life. He lived off a trust fund his grandfather gave him. He'd never known what it was like to avoid the landlord because he didn't have money to pay the rent, or to go out with his friends to a bar but not drink because he only had enough money to pay the cover charge. I knew these things well, and I was determined to make my mark in Hollywood. I fell quickly for Paul's charm and money. But I was smart enough to know his attention span for women was limited. If I were going to keep his attention, I'd have to convince him he wanted more out of life. Paul was a great guy, generous and smart, but he lacked ambition and knew nothing about business. I convinced him to start a production company to showcase my acting, and we built the business together using my instincts and his money. I realized quickly that I preferred producing to acting, and once I took over the day-to-day production, the business grew. I am the brains and ambition that made our company what it is today. Paul may act as if he rules the company, but he doesn't make a decision without my okay. We're a team."

The server delivers our meals, and I smile at Gena, wondering if she's trying to mend Jake's and my relationship. Is that why she asked me here? To convince me to get back together with Jake? Did Jake persuade her to talk to me, hoping to win me back? I take a bite of my salad, waiting for her to continue.

"Paul and I work best when we are together."

I have to tell her a reconciliation is not possible. She can't expect me to marry Jake just because she asks. "Getting back together with Jake would destroy me. I can't do it."

"I was going to say," she pauses, "Paul has a weakness for twenty-year-old actresses. I put an end to his indiscretions when I find out about them, and he cowers back to our bedroom. He seemed fascinated with you."

"I would never. That's not something I would do." I need to squash her doubts right away.

"That's not where this is headed. Just hear me out. I know my husband will never leave me. He loves his life too much. A divorce would split up our assets, and he can't run the business without me. Most of his self-worth comes from our company. Without it, I doubt the twenty-year-olds would even notice Paul."

She stabs her fork into a water chestnut slice on the edge of her plate and holds it up as she speaks.

"I'm not asking you to get back together with Jake Gorboni. And I'm not warning you to stay away from my husband. Maybe I am warning you about Paul, but that's not why I told you what I did." She brings her fork to her mouth and chews the vegetable for almost a minute before meeting my eyes again.

"I see myself in you, Katya. Your brains, your idealism, and your desire for Jake to be a better man all remind me of me. I look back at my life and wonder if I made the right choice with Paul. I love him, and I know he loves me, but I'm tired of policing him. If I had known he would continue to cheat, I might have made a different choice. Do you want to be in our movie, Katya?"

"I do. I love the script. I love the book, but I don't think I can work with Jake. He's hurt me too many times."

Her lips straighten into a line, and she stares at me several seconds before speaking. "Katya, I think you embody my vision for Elizabeth. If we replace Jake, would that make it easier for you to honor our contract?"

"You'd do that?" Warm excitement waves through my body. I can't believe they are willing to replace Jake and keep me.

She nods. "My instincts have never failed me before. This feels right with you as Elizabeth. I always envisioned Harold's character a little less bulky than Jake. Paul was the one pushing for Mr. Gorboni, but I make the final decisions."

I smile and say, "Thank you." Jake will quickly find another project to fill the hole in his schedule. The loss of this movie won't affect him at all.

Chapter 42

Katya

I stare up at the door to the second-floor apartment, wondering if this could really be the right place. The address on the front of the building matches and the owner of the comic book store on the bottom floor assured me there was an apartment back here amongst the trash bins, but the rusted iron stairs say no one lives here. The steps look way too narrow to actually be usable. Not in my heels anyway. I'll have to walk on my tiptoes the entire way up to keep the heels of my boots from catching on the holes in the rungs.

I look ridiculous. I shouldn't have worn this tiny plaid skirt with these thigh-high boots. And my sweater is way too tight. I just wanted to make an impression, a way to get my foot in the door. It's a grand gesture, me coming here dressed as I am. But I don't know what else to do to get him to talk to me. No one will blame him if he refuses to see me.

What if some serial killer lives here? I'd never get back down these stairs to save myself. I'd have to take off my boot and impale him with my spiked heel.

I shove the fake vampire teeth into my mouth and grab the railing, pulling myself onto the first step. I hope he's home. One step at a time, I tell myself. *Don't look back. And definitely don't look down.* When I reach the top and step onto the roof, the rancid smell of rubber mixed with melting plastic and sour milk fills my senses. I hope it's not an omen. I walk across the white, rubber-lined roof to the door outlined in colorful twinkle lights and knock before I lose my nerve.

The worn wooden door opens almost immediately, but it's not Micah answering it. The guy stands hunched in the doorway, ducking to see my face as he rubs his red goatee.

"Hot damn. Aren't you a saucy little turn of events? What brings ya here, sugar?" the guy says with an amazingly smooth southern drawl.

"Is Micah home?" I say, garbled, —my mouth full of plastic vampire teeth.

"Course . . . Mic!" he calls, turning halfway. "You're the hot vampire chick. I shoulda recognized ya." He steps back and motions for me to come inside. "Mic, Johanna Redemption's here," he calls into the tiny apartment.

I feel stupid, and I must be blushing because he smiles at me as if I'm pathetic.

"You've seen the tattoo? Tell me you've seen the tattoo," he asks, and I blush even more with a nod.

"Dawson, I swear your drawl is getting thicker. Are you eating my peanut butter again? I thought you said, Jo . . ." He rounds the corner and freezes when he sees me.

God, he looks good, his dark beard trimmed short and meticulously groomed. The coiffured hair on the top of his head calls to me. I wonder if it's still soft. His hard pecs push against his tight T-shirt, and my fingers tingle with the need to touch him. I hope I'm not drooling.

"Johanna Redemption. Yer welcome." The tall guy bows slightly to me and turns, walking into what looks like a kitchen and laundry room combined.

Micah's blue eyes penetrate me. He definitely didn't expect me. I wish I knew what he's thinking.

"Hi." I smile before spitting the fake vampire teeth into my hand, then step forward and kiss his cheek, the rough scratch of his beard tickling my lips. He smells just like I remembered—fresh like baby powder and peppermint. "I'm glad this is your apartment and not a serial killer's." I stuff the teeth into my leather bag. "I guess I was the serial killer the first night we met," I add, trying to get a conversation started.

When he motions for me to sit on the couch and still doesn't utter a word to me, my stomach starts doing flips, but not in a good way. *This is a mistake. I waited too long. I shouldn't have come here.* He sits in the large, worn, burgundy-colored recliner, obviously to avoid getting close to me.

"Why are you here, Katya Avery?" He leans forward, scrutinizing my costume. *My full name is not good.*

I planned out the words I would use the whole way here. I've thought about them for the last three months. Why am I having such a hard time getting them out?

"Umm . . ." I need to be eye level with him. I sit on the couch and smooth the fabric of my short skirt across my thighs. "I needed to talk to you, and you wouldn't answer your phone."

"Talk, then," he says, looking past me, his tone not showing a drop of the easy going guy I knew.

"I'm sorry. I'm so sorry I let it happen, Micah. I made a mistake. It hurt you. I never meant to hurt you."

"Okay. Great. Now that you've got that off your chest you can go home to your fiancé. Thanks for coming." He stands, looks toward the door and then back to me. "Hope you and Gorboni have a kick-ass life together. Well . . . at least until he cheats on you. Oops. Guess that's not a deal breaker."

I watch his face steel and his eyes narrow as tears prick my eyes. He doesn't want me here. I've hurt him too much.

"I shouldn't have come. I'm sorry." I stand and make my way toward the door. "I just wanted you to know I never stopped loving you." My hand grasps the knob with a twist and pulls open the door. I never should have assumed he loved me too.

Chapter 43

Katya

"Kat." Micah rakes his hands up and down across his face. "Wait." His expression softens as he cocks his head and looks at me as if he truly sees me for the first time since I arrived.

"Why would you tell me that when you're marrying him?" His eyes dart to my left hand.

I hold it up to show him. "I broke it off a week ago. I can't marry him." I thought he understood.

I watch the rise and fall of his chest as he processes my words. I hope my truth still matters.

"You are the only person who ever made sense in my life. I make a lot of decisions on the spur of the moment, and I don't think them through. It's my fatal flaw."

His eyes meet mine again. "What does that mean, Kat?" Cynicism pours out of him.

Did I do this to him? Did I make him this way? I just told him I love him. What is there to understand?

"It means she picks you, idiot," his roommate calls from the kitchen. "She loves you."

"Stay out of this, Dawson. Is that what it means?" He cocks his head again as if he doesn't believe me.

"I love you, Micah. I screwed up, and I should have told you how much you mean to me. At the time, I thought I was doing what I needed to do to help Cam and my mom. Cam had all these medical bills and Mom wasn't able to work. Then the night before Liam's wedding, Cam got sick again, and the bills started pouring in, tenfold. Jake agreed to help me pay if I married him—and only if I married him. I thought I was doing the right thing. What I didn't realize was I needed to do what was right for me, not everyone around me. I didn't realize until Cam died that I need to take care of myself first. Like putting oxygen on in an airplane. You have to put it on yourself before you can help anyone else. You're my oxygen, Micah. You have been since I met you. I'm no good to anyone unless I have you. I never should have put you second in my life. You deserve better."

Sapphire-colored eyes pierce my soul as he stands to face me, his hand grasping his chin. I wish I knew what he was thinking. He's completely unreadable.

"I'm sorry about your brother."

I nod. "Me too." I'm overwhelmed with emotion. Cam really would have liked him. I push my emotions down hard. I won't cry. "He would have liked you."

"Yeah, I'm a likable person."

"And a giver."

The corners of his lips turn up. He knows the reference. The hope of a reconciliation burns inside me as I study his face. It's the first smile to break on his face since I arrived, and I'm going to push until I get a full-blown grin.

"I always liked that you were a giver."

He laughs. God, I missed his laugh.

"A giver is more rare than you might think. You may actually be the only one. A unicorn, really."

The bashful look he gives me reminds me just how genuine he really is. His embarrassed eyes and reddened cheeks make me want to jump into his arms and kiss him.

"How did you know where to find me?" he asks.

"The *Kitten Bastet* comic book you bought me had the store's address on the plastic sleeve. You gave me the best gift anyone's ever given me, and then you disappeared. I never thanked you properly."

"Do you want to go for a walk? My roommates don't need a front-row seat to this."

Dawson pokes his head into the room with a huge smile. "Don't leave on my account. I won't tell Fitzpatrick." He scrunches his nose and looks at me. "He's the real gossip in the apartment. I won't tell him about the vampire girl, promise."

Micah rolls his eyes. "You don't need to tell him. He's in there with you." He turns to me. "Fitzpatrick is our other roommate."

Another guy, dressed in athletic shorts and a university sweatshirt steps into the living room. He's big like a lacrosse player with dark hair and cherubic lips. He's not as tall as Dawson but a good couple of inches taller than Micah.

"Haven't we waited long enough? Inquiring minds want to know," he says. "She's dressed like Johanna, and she's not one of your fangirls. Just give us a little snippet." He holds out his fingers about an inch apart.

"No."

Micah places a hand on my lower back and directs me toward the door. His touch feels incredible, but his answer doesn't sound reassuring. If he was happy to see me, wouldn't he want everyone to know? When Tom told me Micah got back together with Mara, I thought for a minute that he said it to hurt me, but now I'm afraid he *is* back together with his ex. I'm too late.

Once outside, his hand drops. I don't know what I expected. Him to pull me into his arms and kiss me? I can see now, that's not going to happen. I walk across the roof to the rusty stairs with my heart in my stomach. I just want him back. I struggle down the rickety stairs to the sidewalk as he follows. Even if he doesn't want me back, I made the right decision leaving Jake. I couldn't live with Jake's cheating. It would have destroyed me.

When he reaches the ground, I pull out my huge sunglasses from my bag. I don't want him to see my eyes. They always give away exactly what I'm feeling.

Micah's shoulders hunch, as if he thinks I'm still trying to keep him a secret. I'm not.

"Tom said you got back together with Mara. I'm not trying to break up what you have with her, but when you sent that text, I knew you still cared, and I had to tell you I never stopped loving you."

"What do you want from me?"

I deserve that.

"I want to date you in public. More than that, I want to be the person you talk to when you have a crappy day and just need to vent. I want to be the first person you text when you sign a contract for your cartoon series. I want to wake up next to you every morning." I pause, hoping what I'm about to say doesn't scare him. "I want to be the mother of your children, and the only mother of your children. I want to plaster pictures of us kissing all over my Instagram. I'd do it right now if you let me."

"I thought you didn't like grand gestures."

"I don't. But I'd do anything to have you in my life. I'll even put the vampire teeth back in. They make me drool when I talk, and they smell funny, like I'm chewing on a slap bracelet, but I'll do it."

He laughs and finally looks at me. "I've missed you, Kat. I can't deny that."

"But?" I say it because it sounds as if there's a *but* coming.

"I did get back together with Mara," he pauses as his eyes meet mine, "but I broke it off with her. We want different things. She wants a guy she can brag about to her friends, someone she can focus her self-worth around, but I don't want to be the focus of someone else's goals. I want someone who will strive to be their best self, not someone who takes credit for my accomplishments. When I told her Netflix was looking at my comics for a series, she made it sound as if she set it up. I don't need another mother in my life."

I smile. I can't help it. He's not with her. I take a deep breath, finally relaxing. "Does that mean I can post a picture of us kissing?"

"No." His brow wrinkles.

Is that all he can say today?

"Why not?

"People will hate me. I'm not going to be the reason J-Kat broke up."

"You are the reason J-Kat broke up. Your smile—I know you think you have Tom's smile, but it's all yours—your gorgeous blue eyes, your tender, giving personality, all stopped me and made me change direction."

He tilts his head and stares me down, his eyes checking mine to make sure I'm telling the truth. He remembers Jonathan's toast.

"That's why I can't let you go." I beg him with my eyes.

"I don't want people to blame me. I have a public image to uphold. It's better if they think Gorboni cheated, not you."

"Jake didn't come to my brother's funeral. Isn't that reason enough? I posted pictures documenting my friends who came. Your brother was there, but not Jake. Tom doesn't even like me, and he flew all the way to Chicago with everyone out of respect for my brother. But Jake couldn't. People were commenting about Jake's absence. I don't think anyone will accuse you of breaking us up."

"Tom said Jake was cheating on you during your brother's funeral."

"I know. And that just adds to the reasons why I ended it." I hold up my phone and ask, "Can I post a picture?"

Chapter 44

Micah

I stop on the side of the road and turn to her. I can't deny I want her back. I thought I could resist, but I'm weak when it comes to Kat. I never would have reacted the way I did if her text telling me she missed me hadn't clipped my soul. Part of me doesn't want to accept any of her excuses after what she did to me. Wearing a man's ring when you are clearly in love with another man is the worst kind of betrayal. And what kind of woman is that cruel? But the need to save her brother is pure and unselfish. How can I deny my desire to be with her when she unselfishly gives all she has to others? The grand gesture of coming here gives her points as well.

"I don't know, Kat." I look up to the sky to clear my head. Not a cloud in the sky. "I don't know if I can do this with you. You hurt me."

"Will you go on a date with me? Just one date?"

She pulls off her sunglasses, and her eyes dive into my soul. I can't fight her.

"I don't date just anyone," I say. I'm serious. I'm not going to let her walk all over me. If she wants to date me, she's going to have to jump through some hoops. I reach out and stroke my fingers down her cheek. Her skin feels soft and warm, and she looks incredible. I swallow hard. *Mindwipe.* I shake my head and let the air out of my lungs. "I have some stipulations if you want to date me."

"Tell me. I'll do them."

I look at the ground, trying to clear my head. Damn those boots she's wearing. I blow out a breath. "First, always tell the truth. The whole truth. I don't want to be with you if you're not going to be honest with me."

She nods, and says, "Always."

"Second, if something important happens in your life, you tell me first. I don't want to find out about it on the internet. If we are dating, we know each other's secrets."

"No secrets. Got it." She stares at me with hunger in her eyes.

"Katya, I'm serious. I won't date you if you can't—"

Her fingers cover my lips to stop me from talking. "I will always tell you first, Micah. What else?"

"I'm the only one who gets to see you naked between scenes. What you do in front of the camera, I'll learn to deal with, but off camera, you're mine and only mine."

"I like that," she says, stepping closer. I feel the heat of her body and smell her sweet tropical-drink scent.

I comb my fingers into her hair, exposing her gorgeous neck. I want to kiss it but stop myself.

"If you ever fall out of love with me, you will tell me the second you suspect."

She starts to slowly shake her head.

"You will. Because I'm going to need as much time as possible to get over you."

"No. I'm not going to."

"You waited until today to tell me you love me. You owe me this."

"No. I never told you I love you because it didn't seem like the right words. I didn't know what to label what I felt. It was more than anything I'd ever felt for a guy, and I thought I was in love lots of times. You've always been more than just some guy I'm in love with. I'm in *more than love* with you, and I'm never going to fall out of *more than love* with you. It's just not going to happen. But I will agree to whatever it takes, with all my soul, if it means I get you back."

I lean down, pressing my lips to hers. She tastes as sweet as I remember. Her lips part and I push inside. *God, I've missed her.* She stretches on her toes to deepen the kiss and I wrap her legs around me, lifting her. With her arms around my neck and my hands on her ass, we devour each other. There is only one thing that could be better than this, and I'm not doing it on the side of the street.

When I pull back to look at her, she's smiling.

"Lastly," I say, "you have to wear this Johanna Redemption costume every Friday."

"Hmm." She brushes the hair out of my eyes, shaking her head. "You'll get sick of it if I wear it every week."

"Fine, once a month, then. But you're wearing it to Comic Fest next year when we go."

"I wanted to dress up as Katrina, your character from your comic, at Comic Fest. I have this strange connection with her." Her eyes sparkle. She's seen my channel and knows the character is based off her.

I like the Johanna Redemption costume, but the thought of her dressed as a character I invented is way hotter. I kiss her again before she can say any more. I don't think I can control my actions if she keeps talking.

Chapter 45

Micah

"Take it to your room," Tom barks as he passes Kat and me on the couch, a stack of papers in his hands. It's been two weeks since Kat and I started dating, really dating. I'm staying at Tom's for my winter break and Kat's been here since I arrived three days ago. We have all our clothes on, so I don't know why he's complaining. I raise my eyebrows to proposition Kat. I wouldn't mind taking her to bed.

"I was just about to do that," I say, and Tom smiles.

Kat's straddling my lap, her hands in my hair. What is this obsession she has with my hair? I can't complain because her fingers on my scalp feel amazing.

"Did you ask her yet?" Tom asks as he studies the papers in his hands.

"Don't ruin it. I was just about to ask her."

"Ask me what?" Kat's hands freeze. She pulls them out of my hair and presses them against my chest as she looks at me.

"My brother's so pushy. 'Don't have sex on my couch.' 'Get your girlfriend to sign a contract.'" I make a duckbill with my hand and move it as if it's talking. "'Blah, blah, blah.' He's always telling me what to do."

"You want me to sign an NDA?" Kat cocks her head and looks at me, the sparkle in her eyes draining to disappointment. "I never asked you to sign the one you signed." Her brows furrow as if she's confused.

"I didn't want you to worry about me spilling all your secrets."

"I'll sign one if you want me to." Her eyes look wary, as if I'm telling her we won't last.

"Do you think I need one?" I tease, trying to bring her back to reality. "Netflix wants you to voice Katrina for my series. I may have mentioned that I have an in with you, and they thought you'd be perfect for the part. Would you consider it?"

"Are you serious? Hella-yes! Katrina's a kick-ass warrior actress. I'd love to voice her. She's everything I strive to be." She smiles and climbs off my lap. "I'm going to be a comic book character." She wiggles with excitement, a dance that just makes me want to take her to bed more.

I don't have the heart to tell her she already is a comic book character.

Kat stands and smiles at Tom. "Let's celebrate your new series. Tom, do you have any tequila?"

Tom laughs. "Yeah, I might be able to find some." He sets his papers on the table next to the sticks in a vase he calls art and walks toward the butler's pantry.

A couple of minutes later Izzy walks in with a tray of shooter glasses, lime wedges, and salt.

"Tom's bringing out some samples from a couple of distilleries. He wants his own label. Everyone in Hollywood is doing it. If he can't find a tequila he likes, he may open his own distillery. So just give your honest opinion, and don't mock him. It's not a game to him." She lines up twelve glasses in four sets on the table in front of us before Tom walks into the room, carrying four bottles of tequila. Izzy's oddly protective of Tom lately, and it makes me wonder if more is going on between the two of them than an employee-and-boss relationship.

"No swinging my bra around like a lasso this time, Tom," says Kat. I love her sense of humor. She doesn't get embarrassed. The more I get to know her the more I love her.

Tom laughs. "Then don't take it off in the middle of my living room." He uncorks a bottle of tequila. "Did you tell her I'm voicing her love interest in your series?"

She laughs. "You are not."

"Yes, I am." Tom smiles as he pours the clear liquid.

"I'm sleeping with the writer-slash-illustrator. I bet I can get him to kill off your character."

"I bet you *could* convince him to kill off his only brother." Tom laughs again. He holds out his hand toward Kat. "Truce?"

She meets his hand and smiles. "Truce."

"For the record, I like you better with my brother. You seem happier." He finishes filling the glasses with tequila. "Micah's a better man. Hang onto him."

"I will," says Kat before kissing my cheek.

"Time to celebrate. No one deserves a cartoon series more than my talented brother. You're an amazing artist, Micah. It's about time the world knows." Tom corks the first bottle and starts pouring the second.

It's the first time he's told me I'm talented. It feels weird but gratifying. I never would have gotten the series without him. He set up the meeting and coached me on what to say. Then his agent swooped in and negotiated the hell out of the deal, allowing me to keep much of my creative control. It happened much quicker than I expected. I thought we'd be settling the contract for weeks. Tom said they wanted to snatch me up before anyone else discovered me. Now that the deal is signed, I have a ton of work to do. Full animation is different than stop panels, and I hope I can pull it off. I start working with a team from the studio in February to begin animating. I'm staying with Tom until he gets sick of me. I'll take the spring semester off and finish my degree in the fall. If the show takes off and gets a second season, I'll adjust my plans to accommodate.

"Taste each one first, and tell me which you prefer. I've narrowed it down to these four for my label, but I'm not completely sold on them." Tom corks the last tequila bottle before picking up the first shot in the lineup and sipping it.

We all sip them and give our opinions. One tastes fruity, like cherry or almond. But every single one tastes like Kat to me. Tequila equals Kat in my mind. She smiles at me, and I wonder if tequila reminds her of me. She raises her eyebrows. She looks edible. I want to devour every inch of her.

"Can I get a shot to post to celebrate your series?" Kat asks, holding up her phone.

"Yeah. Let's do it," says Tom, wrapping one arm around me and one around Izzy.

Kat holds out her phone and leans in to kiss me. My mouth automatically finds her lips, and she takes the shot. She captures about thirty shots before holding up one for my approval.

"Can I post it?" She cocks her head and pleads with her eyes.

She picked one of us kissing with Tom and Izzy looking on. She's been bugging me since we got back together to let her post a kissing picture. I don't know why I've put up a fight until now. But signing the contract for the series makes me less worried about what others think, and the news of her and Gorboni's engagement ending is already out there. Maybe it's the rumor that she's dating my brother that pushes me over the edge today, freeing me to accept the consequences of a public announcement. At least no one will think she's hooking up with Tom anymore.

"Does Gorboni know we're together?" I ask, handing her phone back to her and picking up a shot.

"I don't know. I think he probably assumed I would go back to you. He knew how much you meant to me. But I haven't talked to him."

"He knows," says Tom, and then sips one of the shots, swishing it around in his mouth before swallowing. "He wants me to kick you out. I told him I wouldn't. He doesn't understand how Kat could leave him. I don't think he'll ever see his role in the breakup."

"He'll get it someday." Kat taps out a message to go with the picture. She sets her phone on the table and smiles. And just like that, she outed our relationship to the world.

"You see it, though, right?" I ask Tom.

"Yeah, I see it. He went to the Caymans with another girl while Kat was dealing with her brother's death. He should have been with her and not screwing around. I've had girlfriends, and I'm not a heartless asshole."

Maybe we've both evolved this last year. Him from heartless ass to a human being and me from an idiot who didn't respect himself to a superhero with real superpowers. I smile as I drag my thumb across the soft crevices of Kat's neck, sending quivers through her body. I lean down toward Kat's ear.

"Want to test out my superpowers?"

She nods as a dimpled smile takes over her face. Then she slams her last shot and picks up her phone.

"We're taking it to my room. Thanks for the tequila."

"Really?" asks Izzy. "We haven't finished with the taste test."

"We need to get our costumes figured out for Comic Fest," I lie.

Tom glances at Izzy, and then they both turn to us. They know we're lying.

"All right. Truth? We need to leave before the clothes start coming off. It's a common courtesy thing. Tequila messes with our heads. We're just trying to be polite," says Kat.

Tom rolls his eyes but smiles. He never expected me to end up with Kat, and maybe I didn't either. But like Kat said about putting your own oxygen on first, I needed to find my way before I could actually be with someone I deserved. And Kat and I are meant to be together. It just took a while to figure it out.

"You know me with tequila," says Kat as she reaches for my hand and starts walking toward my bedroom. She frees me to do what I want, be the person I want to be. My lips touch hers as she backs out of the room. I love this woman and can't get enough of her.

Chapter 46

Katya

I t's been four months since Micah and I became Instagram official. Since then I've posted at least thirty pics of us together, and it feels incredible sharing our life with my friends and fans. When I was with Jake, I was always worried about some online troll hijacking my happiness. Sometimes it was Jake who stole my joy by telling me I shouldn't have posted whatever it was that I had posted. Micah doesn't criticize. I can be myself around him, always, and that's one of the many things I love about him. With Micah, I have a partner in everything I do who accepts me as I am, not a man to lead me around and guide me to what he thinks is best.

Another unusual trait of Micah's is that he doesn't cheat on me. I've been away filming in the UK for eight weeks and we haven't seen each other the entire time except on video chats, and still, I am confident he wasn't sleeping around. Weird. I trust him with all my heart and soul, and he trusts me.

I slept most of the almost thirteen-hour flight back to Los Angeles, so I am wide awake as my ride pulls onto the brick turn-around of Tom's drive. Micah's staying at Tom's indefinitely. Tom's house is ginormous, bigger than Jake's mansion. The egos on those two—why anyone would want to live in a house this big is beyond me. Micah will probably live with his brother for a while, which means I will be spending most of my time at Tom's house as well. At least Tom and I are getting along better now that he realizes I'm not using his brother.

The car stops, and a tap on my window steals my attention to the here and now. There he is, his gorgeous ocean-blue eyes staring into me. His dark hair looks a little longer on top, but his beard is perfectly trimmed. I crack open the door, and as he steps back, I drop my purse to the brick and jump into his arms. One hand immediately finds his soft hair, and the other drags across the scruff on his chin as he grabs my bootie. He smells amazing—sunshine and baby powder. Our lips lock, and the wonderful warmth I always feel with him spreads through my body. I know we should stop, because the driver is waiting, but I missed him, and I don't want to stop.

Micah pulls back and sets me on the ground, his adorable smile beaming. "I missed you," he says as he takes my bags from the driver. We head inside, and the second the door closes, my hands dive into his hair and my lips are on his, again. I can't keep my hands off him. I've thought of nothing but him since filming ended three days ago, and now I get to be with him until my next project starts in June.

"Are you hungry?" he asks. The smirk on his face says he has plans for our evening.

"Starved. What do you have in mind?"

"Early dinner by the pool. Maybe some skinny-dipping? Tom's in NYC until Friday. Tonight, let's just relax. Sound good?"

"Sounds perfect." I bite my lip and smile. I just want to catch up with him. We talked all the time while I was away, but it's not the same as being face to face.

"Did you call your mom yet?"

"I'll call her right now to get it out of the way, so she doesn't call me later."

Micah caresses my cheek and sensually wipes his thumb across my bottom lip before walking toward the kitchen.

This phone call is going to be quick.

"Mom. My flight got in, and I'm home. Well, I'm at Micah's."

"I'm glad you're home safe. Your filming went well?

"Yes. It was amazing, and I'm so lucky to be a part of the film. I can't wait for you to see it." A wave of sadness washes over me as I realize Cam will never get to see it. It's not Mom's fault, but every time I talk to her, I think of Cam and his senseless death. His autopsy proved inconclusive as to the cause of the weakening of Cam's blood vessels in his brain. The drugs could have caused the thinning of his artery walls, or they could have been that way since he was born. I walk into the kitchen to find Micah. When my eyes meet his, he stops what he's doing and places the food in his hand on the cutting board. He knows me so well. His arms wrap around me as he touches his forehead to mine. I close my eyes and take a deep breath, letting his touch calm me as I listen to Mom. One of his hands entwines with my free hand, and he squeezes. Sweet baby kittens, I love him.

"I thought I could come out for a visit. What do you think?"

"Of course. I'd love you to visit," I say. Mom hasn't been out to Hollywood ever. She was always too busy caring for Cam. It would be great to show her my life.

"Did you see the deposit in our joint account from the sale of the house? What's there is yours. I figure you can pay Jake back the money I owe him. Your father didn't get half because he stopped contributing to the mortgage years ago. My lawyer dealt with your father's settlement, and the rest is yours. You helped me more than I should have asked of a child."

"Mom, we're family, and we take care of each other. I'll send Jake his share this week. Whatever is left you can have. I got paid from the movie a couple of days ago. I don't need it." She needs the money worse than I do. I have three more movies lined up, my cable series, and I start voicing Micah's animated series next week. "Why don't you bring your guy with you when you come to visit? I'd love to meet him." She met a guy named Max in her loss support group. He'd lost his wife and son in a car accident a year ago, and he helped Mom through the worst parts of the last several months. They bonded over their losses. I'm just happy she's finding a way out of her grief. Micah kisses my forehead. He's worked his magic calming me, and he squeezes my hand again before letting go and returning to making sandwiches.

"I have to admit, honey, Max is younger than me."

"How much younger?" She never mentioned his age before. *Please don't let him be my age.*

"Eight years. He just had his fortieth birthday. But he's an old soul. He's much more mature than your father was at forty, or is now."

Hmm. At least he's not in his twenties. "Once you hit thirty, eight years is nothing, Mom. You deserve to be happy." I'd love to hear more about Mom's love life, but I talked to her two days ago and Micah is ten feet from me, looking exceptionally sexy with his athletic shirt stretched across his abs and his sweats hanging low on his hips.

"I have to go, Mom. Micah has lunch waiting for me. Send me pictures of Max. I want to make sure he's not too old for *you*. Love you."

We end the call in a rush as I wrap my arms around my man. He slices cucumbers and red peppers for our sandwiches, and it takes all my willpower not to peel his clothes off while he has a knife in his hand.

"Don't get any ideas. We're eating all this and then we're going swimming."

"Didn't your mother ever warn you about eating before you go swimming?"

"She did, but I don't plan to be swimming laps."

At least we're on the same page.

Somehow we make our way to the table on the lanai with our food and down half of it without ripping each other's clothes off. Micah's quieter than usual, which means he's nervous, and it's making me nervous. I wish I could read his mind. I take my last bite of mango, set my fork on my plate, and narrow my eyes at him.

"What's going on? Why are you so nervous?"

He looks up, startled by me calling him out. His eyes meet mine, and he smiles. "I'm not," he says, shaking his head. "I was just thinking about all the comments you made when you were trying to convince me to date you. Remember? Waking up next to me every morning and being the only father of your children, those comments?"

"Of course I remember them. I meant them. Why?"

"Your condo's lease is up next month. What would you think about us getting a place together? Your place is too small. My drafting table would take up your entire living room. But if we got a place together, we could wake up next to each other every morning. Tom says you can stay here until we find a house."

He looks apprehensive as if I'm going to say no. I smile as I climb onto his lap, straddling him. "Can we get a dog? Kids are a long-term plan, like ten years from now."

"You read my mind." His lips press against mine while his arms wrap around my body, pulling me closer.

Warmth radiates to my core as his fingers inch under my blouse and smooth across my lower back. I've missed his touch. I didn't know what love was before Micah. All my other relationships were never real love. Love means putting the other's desires before your own. Love means standing up for what you believe while knowing the one you love will support you because he loves you. Love means mutual respect. I love Micah with all my heart, and I don't doubt I always will.

I pull back to strip his shirt off of him, and my eye catches new ink near his tattoo of Johanna Redemption. I slide his shirt over his head and stand up so I can get a better look.

"You got more ink while I was gone."

"Did I?" he asks, not admitting it and not quite denying either.

"Take off your pants. I want to see."

"You are such a romantic, Katya Avery." Micah laughs as he takes a step back.

"Show me."

He grips the edge of his sweats and flashes me a corner of the new tattoo. A pink bra that looks suspiciously like the one I wore the first night we met pops from his hip. He takes another step back.

"It's Katrina. I used to fantasize about Johanna when I was young. She fostered my love for comics, but she's flat, just a black-and-white sketch, because she was never real." His eyes meet mine. "Katrina, on the other hand, she's real. I know her thoughts, her words, her voice. She got full color. I'm going to be fantasizing about Katrina for the rest of my life. I love her. She taught me not just about love but about respect. And I respect the hell out of Katrina."

Damn. He can read my mind.

As he kicks off his sweats, he yells over his shoulder. "If you want to see my ink you have to join me in the pool." He dives into the water, and I quickly strip, no longer worried about seeing his ink. I'll see it. We have the rest of our lives.

Schussler's Books

Check out the rest of the books in Schussler's celebrity/college student series, Between the Raindrops.

Between the Raindrops

Hollywood heartthrob Jonathan Williams can have any woman he wants as long as he is willing to be used for his celebrity status. But when he falls for a girl he anonymously connected with online, he finally sees hope for a normal relationship. That is, until Johnathan reveals his true identity to her on stage at a rock concert and the press begins to pursue her relentlessly. Now he has to decide whether to protect her from his tabloid-ridden life by ending their relationship or selfishly drag her into his world.

Between the Lies (Jonathan and Sarah's story continues)

Now that Jonathan and Sarah are engaged, the media is even more determined to pull them apart. It doesn't help that a stalker is sending threatening notes, someone close to them is selling their intimate secrets to the tabloids, or that Jonathan's gorgeous ex-girlfriend would do anything to get him back. When Jonathan starts keeping secrets from Sarah, she has to decide whether to live with the lies or walk away from him forever.

Between Friends (A stand-alone novel of the Between the Raindrops series)

Megan Billings refuses to repeat the mistakes of her past. She wants to leave her toxic relationship with her high school ex behind, but their sizzling connection keeps pulling her back in. After four years, she still hasn't found anyone else to take her breath away. That is, until her smoldering kiss with Hollywood bad-boy Liam Nordstrom. And even though the heartthrob tells her they can never be more than friends, she can't stop thinking about the kiss. When Megan discovers her ex kept secrets from her about the night her mother disappeared, she turns to the one man who she can trust, her friend Liam.

Between Scenes (A stand-alone novel of the Between the Raindrop series)

When paparazzi catch her movie-star boyfriend Jake Gorboni cheating on her, Katya Avery realizes breaking up with him isn't an option. He holds the strings to her first movie deal, and without him, she will never make enough money to get her brother the treatment he needs. If she could forgive Jake's cheating, all her problems would disappear. But she never counted on falling for the sexy cartoonist Micah Fallston and if she can't keep her feelings for him under control, she will lose everything.

Acknowledgments

Thank you to my amazing readers who gobble up every book I put out. You are the reason I write and my inspiration. Thank you to my critique partners Crystal and MJ—you are probably so sick of this book that you will never see this acknowledgment, but I still appreciate all your help. Thank you to all my beta readers, especially Cathy and Gloria, for helping morph this book into what it is today. I love your insights. You are the triple-fudge syrup on this book sundae. Thank you to Women of Words, RWA, and Midwest Fiction Writers. You provide encouragement and resources and without you, I'd disappear in the cracks. Thank you to Anne at Inkstand Editorial. I appreciate your patience and diligence. You are amazing at what you do.